Cyril Cook was born in Easton, Hampshire, but at the age of five was brought to live on a farm in Mottingham, Kent. Educated at Eltham College, he matriculated in 1939, joined The Rifle Brigade in 1940, and was commissioned and transferred to The Parachute Regiment in 1943. He saw considerable service in the 6th Airborne Division in Europe and the Far East where for a period he commanded, at the age of 22, a company of some 220 men of the Malay Regiment.

His working life was spent mainly as the proprietor of an engineering business which he founded, until he retired to start the really serious business of writing the six volumes of The Chandlers.

By the same author

THE CHANDLERS

VOLUME ONE – THE YOUNG CHANDLERS
Published in 2005 (Vanguard Press)
ISBN 1 84386 199 2

THE CHANDLERS

Volume 2

The Chandlers At War

Cyril Cook

THE CHANDLERS

Volume 2

The Chandlers At War

To Ray and Margaret with very best wishes,
Cyril.

Vanguard Press

VANGUARD PAPERBACK

© Copyright 2006
Cyril Cook

The right of Cyril Cook to be identified as author of this work has been asserted by him in accordance with the Copyright, Designs and Patents Act 1988

All Rights Reserved

No reproduction, copy or transmission of this publication may be made without written permission.
No paragraph of this publication may be reproduced, copied or transmitted save with the written permission of the publisher, or in accordance with the provisions of the Copyright Act 1956 (as amended).

Any person who does any unauthorised act in relation to this publication may be liable to criminal prosecution and civil claims for damage.

A CIP catalogue record for this title is available from the British Library

ISBN-13: 978 1 84386 292 5
ISBN-10: 1 84386 292 1

*Vanguard Press is an imprint of
Pegasus Elliot MacKenzie Publishers Ltd.*
www.pegasuspublishers.com

First Published in 2006

**Vanguard Press
Sheraton House Castle Park
Cambridge England**

Printed & Bound in Great Britain

Dedication

This Volume is dedicated to my father

JOHN COOK.

As a regular soldier in the Hampshire Regiment, he fought on the North West Frontier and in Afghanistan in the days of the Raj, followed by active service in the Boer War in South Africa at the turn of the 19th century. Upon leaving the army he became profoundly deaf, an affliction which never, in all his long life, reduced in any way his sense of fun, despite hearing aids being unknown in his day.

He was of the old school, working to bring up a large family without state handouts, above all, being very proud of his six soldier sons in World War Two.

Main characters from Volume 1 - The Young Chandlers

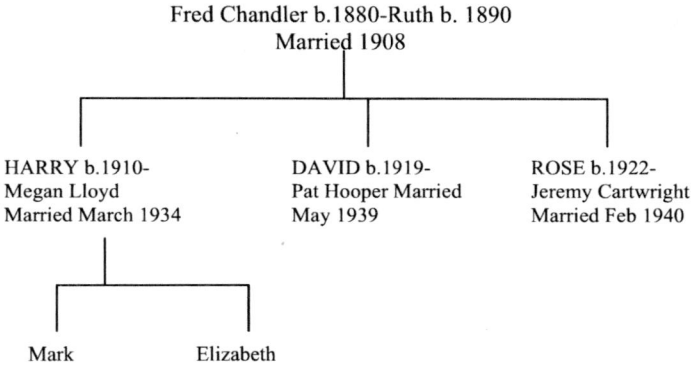

Fred Chandler b.1880-Ruth b. 1890
Married 1908

HARRY b.1910-	DAVID b.1919-	ROSE b.1922-
Megan Lloyd	Pat Hooper Married	Jeremy Cartwright
Married March 1934	May 1939	Married Feb 1940

Mark   Elizabeth

Twins b. Dec 1937

OTHER FAMILIES

JACK HOOPER   Divorced Pat's mother. Married Moira Evans, Megan's aunt March 1935. Have son John b. Aug 1937

TREFOR LLOYD   and Elizabeth. Megan's parents.

BUFFY CARTWRIGHT   and Rita. Jeremy's parents

KARL REISNER   Refugee from Nazi Germany. Father of ANNI now married to Ernie Bolton, David's friend.

DR KONRAD VON HASSELLBEK and wife. Parents of Dieter, David's great pre-war friend now in German Army. Also daughter Inge, ardent Nazi, married to Himmler's nephew.

Chapter One

It was Tuesday 21st May 1940.
   In Europe the 'phoney war' had ended.
   Ruth Chandler sat by the Aga in her kitchen at Chandlers Lodge slowly drinking a cup of tea, having seen her husband Fred and daughter Rose off to work. She had a premonition that all was not well with her three 'boys', Harry and David, her sons, and Jeremy her son-in-law only recently married to Rose, her youngest. Harry was a sergeant in the Royal Army Service Corps and was in France, having been in the first of the British Expeditionary Force contingents back in September 1939 when war was declared. Like Harry, David and Jeremy were territorials who, when war broke out, were immediately called to the colours but they were in the City Rifles, a crack infantry regiment, who had been stationed in Essex up until now, and had, therefore, been able to get home fairly regularly.
   So why, she asked herself, do I have this feeling that all is not well? The news from France, it was true, was terribly depressing. The Germans were advancing on all fronts and sweeping all before them. They were very worried about Harry, but why this feeling about David and Jeremy? Rose had received her usual Friday night telephone call from Jeremy, so she assumed Pat, David's wife had received a similar call at The Bungalow, which had been their home since they married in the May of 1939.
   As she sat finishing her tea, she mused that David and Jeremy obviously hadn't heard the results of their applications for commissions yet, otherwise they would have telephoned last night. Little did she know that last night the two brothers-in-law were sitting on a troop deck in the bowels of a ship steaming to France, having been given eight hours to get out of their billets and alongside at Harwich Docks with all their vehicles.

   There was a lot of tension on the troop deck that night, as the ship slipped down the east coast. There was suppressed excitement from those who saw going to war as a big adventure and couldn't wait to get there. There was the continual chatter from those who were all keyed up inside and found talking about anything and everything a way to allay their fears, others were silent and introspective. These latter would be the ones who probably would be either solid, reliable soldiers under fire, or conversely little use at all. Finally, there were the jokers. As

David said to Jeremy, "You never know whether they're trying to bolster their own spirits or everybody else's."

"Probably a bit of each," said Jeremy.

"Corporal," said Rifleman Beasley, addressing David, "You've been abroad. What does a knocking shop look like?"

Rifleman Piercey chipped in, "I don't know why he wants to know – he still thinks it is to pee with."

There was loud laughter at this old army joke, much louder than it would normally have warranted, indicating again the tension to which they were all subject.

At seven o' clock on the morning of the 21st May, at the time Ruth and Fred had got up to start their day, the trooper met two others at Dover, and with an escort of three destroyers moved south of east across the Channel. As they got under way again Mr Austen, their platoon commander came down on to the troop deck with Sergeant Harris, the platoon sergeant.

"Right, gather round," bellowed the sergeant.

"It's now pretty obvious to you," said the lieutenant, "that we're going to France. I now have more specific orders. We are going to Calais with two other Rifle battalions and tanks from the Royal Tank Regiment. When we get there, the plan is to strike south towards Amiens in order to prevent the Germans reaching Boulogne and Dieppe. We shall get more detailed orders when we land. That is all for now."

The general buzz of conversation resumed, some of the men asking David and Jeremy where Amiens was, where Boulogne and Dieppe were in relation to Amiens and so on. Most of them had a rough idea where Calais was. 'Right opposite Dover' being the general opinion. Most of them had heard Amiens mentioned by their fathers and uncles over the years from their time in the Great War, those that is whose fathers and uncles had come back from that carnage.

Suddenly the conversation was interrupted by the furious cacophony of anti-aircraft guns being fired from one of the nearby destroyer escorts. With its multiple pom-poms and bofors guns firing hundreds of rounds a minute, it was like bedlam inside the steel troop deck. As suddenly as it started the firing stopped. "Obviously a Jerry plane came to welcome us to France," said David cheerily, but inside, his stomach had turned over at the thought of being locked in this steel coffin if they were bombed.

It was exactly at that moment that Ruth was sitting in front of the

Aga, and as she sat thinking of the past years and how fortunate she and Fred had been to have their three children grow up into such fine young people and to be married to such delightful partners, for the twins now two and a half years old born to Harry and Megan, for the new baby Rose was carrying, and the prosperity and social standing they all now enjoyed, she wondered if the pendulum was about to swing the other way.

The fact that the boys had not telephoned was ominous. Except for the time when they were on stand-by to go on the expeditionary force to Norway, their part in which being subsequently aborted, they had always telephoned to their respective wives and families every Sunday evening. "Oh God," she said to herself, "where are they now?" and with this thought in her mind she knelt down with her elbows on the chair and said, "Dear Lord, take care of our boys and keep them safe. Amen."

She hadn't noticed that in the doorway behind her one of the two Canadian officers who were billeted at Chandlers Lodge had appeared. He withdrew quietly and waited a short while before re-appearing in the kitchen, saying as he came through the door

"Any news of the lads?"

"None at all Alec, I'm getting a bit concerned." Alec Fraser and Jim Napier, both majors in the Canadian infantry battalion stationed at the local camp, had been the guests of Ruth and Fred for five months now and were part of the family. "Neither have we heard from Harry for over a week. I know things are chaotic over there, but it is worrying."

"Well, no news is good news in these situations," said Alec. "Just imagine, when soldiers went off to the Peninsular War and places like that, their families didn't have a word from them until they turned up on the doorstep again five years later! Anyway, they'll write as soon as they can – it shouldn't be too long before you hear – you see if I'm not right."

On board the ship Sergeant Harris appeared again on the troop deck. "One each," he bellowed, "fill them in and they'll go back to England today when this ship goes back. They're to go to your next of kin."

They each in turn took one of the khaki coloured cards headed 'Field Service Card.' On one side was the space for the address and on the other there was a series of messages.

"I am well."
"I am wounded."
"I will write soon."

And so on.

"Now listen," continued the sergeant, "you cross out what doesn't apply and just sign your name. Don't put your unit. Don't add other messages or the censor will hold on to them. Any questions?" There were none. David and Jeremy quickly dealt with their cards and then helped the three men in the platoon who couldn't read or write to fill their cards in with the address and deletions. When they had done this, David noticed Rifleman Barclay standing with the card in his hand without having written anything on it. "What's the matter Barclay?" said David. Barclay had been a notorious deserter; in fact he had nearly cost David his stripes on one occasion when he escaped from the guard house where David was guard commander. When he was recaptured David had had a straight talk with him and had persuaded him to give the army a try, not to keep running away, and so far he was proving to be a better soldier than might have been expected.

"What's the matter Barclay?"

"I've got no next of kin Corporal."

"No mother, father, sisters?"

"I was brought up in an orphanage. I don't have nobody."

The thought that, if anything were to happen to Barclay no one would know and no one would care, hit David like a sledgehammer.

"Send it to my mother," said David. "I'll write and explain it all when we get the chance."

He had no idea why he had so impulsively said this, but it had a very strange effect on Barclay. His face went quite pale.

"Do you mean it Corporal?"

"Yes, of course I do. She'll then be thinking of you until you can write to her yourself."

"I can't write proper, Corporal."

"Then Corporal Cartwright or I will help you as we do with some of the others."

There was a pause.

"You're a bloody good bloke Corporal. I shan't forget it."

David mused afterwards to himself. He had done nothing really, and yet it was obviously everything to Rifleman Barclay to have just one person, even if he didn't know her, who would be thinking about him and be concerned about him. David was not to know that Barclay had had no one in his whole life who had thought tuppence of him since he was found abandoned, a newborn baby on the steps of the Royal Free Hospital, twenty odd years ago. He had lived in one orphanage after another, one or two good enough to be sad about leaving, the majority unpleasant and one or two downright evil places for a young boy to be brought up in. At fifteen he was on the streets, just about able to write his name, having to live by his wits. The fact that he had survived thus far without having got into serious trouble, apart from his army desertions, was more by luck than judgement. Now he would have someone who might be saying to herself, 'I wonder how Kenny is getting on?' and it mattered. It mattered a lot, not that he would have admitted it to anyone, except perhaps the corporal if the subject ever arose.

Again, Sergeant Harris appeared to collect the cards. "Stand by for disembarkation in thirty minutes," he called. "NCOs – check no one leaves anything behind."

They felt the engines slow down and then stop, followed by a few bumps and noises they were unable to identify, as the ship was tied-up to the dockside. This was followed by noises they had no difficulty in recognising, even if they had only heard them on newsreels before. First the loud, ever increasing noise of the Jericho sirens on the wheel supports of a Stuka hurtling earthwards towards them, followed immediately by a furious bombardment by anti-aircraft guns of all sizes, and finally five explosions of the bombs landing, which shook the ship from bow to stern.

"Jesus, that was close," said Rifleman Piercey. "I'll be bloody glad when we're out of here." There wasn't one man on the troop deck who didn't join him in that fervent desire, but in fact, they had to wait another half hour and through two more dive bomb attacks before the command came.

"A Company on deck now – move!" They filed up the steel stairway and came blinking out into the morning sunshine. They had little time to take in their surroundings before they were hustled down the gangway on to the dockside and told to fall in, in platoon order.

"Where are our vehicles sergeant," said David, it was obvious nothing was being unloaded.

"Bloody frogs have all scarpered so there's no one to work the cranes," said Sergeant Harris. "Anyway there's been a change of plan – you won't need them – you'll hear about it in a minute."

Major Grant, A Company commander, was talking to the platoon officers a little way away. They all looked very grim faced at what he was telling them, each consulting a map they had just been given. After a minute or two they all folded their maps, took a pace back, saluted and hurried over to their respective platoons.

"Right, listen carefully," Mr Austen told Two platoon. "The attempt to stop the Germans getting to Boulogne has been put off. Our job now is to fortify Calais and prevent them from taking the town and thus prevent any advance on Dunkirk. Dunkirk must be held as a supply port for the British troops in north west France. We are to proceed to the south east corner of the town here and dig in. Any questions?"

David answered "Sir," he said, "half our ammunition is still on our trucks."

"Yes I know," said Lieutenant Austen "but HQ Company are going to rescue all they can before the ship goes back. Right now get ready, One platoon are moving off, we've to leave a hundred yards between platoons."

As they moved off three more Stukas appeared but confined their activities away from the dockside, to ships entering and leaving the harbour. David's platoon led by Mr Austen with David and Jeremy at the rear and Sergeant Harris on the left flank had covered some four hundred yards when, through the noise of the anti aircraft fire, they heard the sharp crack of a rifle shot and a loud cry from Mr Austen as he slumped to the ground and lay motionless. David instinctively looked up at a large warehouse they were passing and saw a fleeting shadow move from one of the openings on its face, normally used to pull goods in off the hoist operated from the top of the building.

"He's on the sixth floor sergeant," bellowed David, and Sergeant Harris who was nearest the entry to the building shouted, "You two come with me," pointing to Piercey and Barclay. They raced up the stairway, the noise of their boots masked by the increasing fury of the anti aircraft guns, until they burst through a pair of swing doors on the sixth landing, rifles at the ready. Across the warehouse floor a figure in dark civilian clothes was again kneeling in a firing position aiming at the next target, but hearing the doors crash open he swung round, immediately saw he was outnumbered, threw his rifle down and stood in front of the opening with his hands high in the air. The three walked towards him, Sergeant Harris in the centre, their rifles aimed at the snipers middle. Three paces from him, Sergeant Harris swung his rifle round in a big arc and before the fifth columnist realised what was happening the heavy butt hit him in the chest making him stagger back, trip over the sill of the opening and fall screaming to his death on the cobbles fifty feet below, landing ten yards from the body of the man he had killed only minutes before. Sergeant Harris turned. "A bullet was too good for a bastard like that," he said and doubled off back to the stairway followed by two young soldiers who were very rapidly beginning to realise what war was all about.

As they joined the platoon, Major Grant and Company Sergeant

Major Ward arrived at the double.

"Mr Austen's dead sir," said the sergeant "but we got the bastard who did it" – pointing to the other body.

"Right, said the major, "You take over the platoon Sergeant Harris. Take Mr Austen's map case, service watch, compass and revolver and carry on to your platoon position – I'll come and see you as soon as I can."

"Sir!" replied the sergeant and turned to the platoon. "Divide into two files and keep close into the buildings – move!!" and with that final command bellowed at them the men rapidly sorted themselves out and moved off at a brisk pace away from the dock area on to the Rue de Verdun, crossing the crossroads where the famous Route NI runs south west parallel to the coast to Boulogne and then on south to Abbeville and Paris. B and C Companies were to defend this approach whilst A Company was to move on for another kilometre to defend the approach from inland on either side of a large canal. They were all very thin on the ground to say the least observed the major to his second in command, Captain Priddy.

They swiftly reached their company position at a point where there was a footbridge over the canal. Major Grant took two platoons over the bridge along with his company headquarters leaving Sergeant Harris to take up positions around some small houses where they had a good view down a minor road leading to Guines and Ardres. Digging in was a slow process with the small entrenching tools with which they had been issued, so David detailed two of his section to scour the outhouses of the nearby cottages for spades. They were immediately successful and returned with arms full of shovels, spades and pick-axes, groaning under their weight, and very soon having dug their slit trenches, they set to on filling sandbags to fortify the cottages behind. It seemed to David almost sacrilegious to be clumping around in someone's living room and bedrooms. The living room of the cottage behind his slit trenches faced down the road they were to cover so they pushed the heavy mahogany dining table under the window, knocked out the glass and stacked sandbags to make a good emplacement for his Bren Gun, which would be able to fire freely over the heads of the men in front in the slit trenches when the time came.

During the course of all this work they were visited constantly by Sergeant Harris chivvying them on, and then by Major Grant who expressed himself well satisfied with the platoon's dispositions.

"Put two men out forward during the night," he said to the

sergeant, "we don't want anyone creeping up on us."

The air attack had lulled during the afternoon, but at seven o'clock three flights of Stukas came over, followed by a wave of medium bombers with a fighter escort and for half an hour the platoon sat in the bottom of their slit trenches whilst the war from the air and in the air raged, about which they could do nothing. In the middle of all this mayhem, David looked down the road back towards Calais town and to his astonishment saw a company HQ truck trundling along totally ignoring the Stukas, the masses of shrapnel falling from the exploding anti-aircraft shells and the debris in the roads. The truck drew up close to David and a slightly built rifleman wearing glasses but no steel helmet climbed down and called to David, "Are you A Company?" David's reply was drowned by a 250 kilo bomb screaming down and exploding about two hundred yards away, followed by a succession of brickbats and other debris falling around them. David picked himself up from the bottom of his slit trench and looked up to see this diminutive figure smiling myopically at him. "Exciting isn't it?" he was saying.

"Not what I would call it," said David, "but yes this is A Company."

"Oh good, I've got a hot meal for you."

"Do you mean to tell me that you drove through all that lot just to give us a hot meal?" said David incredulously.

"Well you see corporal, it's my job." There was no answer to that. David put his arm round the little man's shoulders and said, "One day I'll buy you the biggest pint you've ever had," which was a bit daft he thought afterwards, a pint is a pint, no more, no less. He couldn't know the little man's days were numbered anyway.

The planes, having now done their worst and disappeared, David's section unloaded the dixies and hay boxes and he sent a runner to the other platoons to 'come and get it.' They needed no second invitation. It was the first hot meal they'd had for over twenty four hours so they dished it out, piled the containers back on the truck and the little man made his return to the battalion cook house, set in the kitchen of the King George V hotel, totally unaware of the fact that a hundred men thought he was a bloody hero.

The night passed quietly. There was some sporadic firing to the north east, which David thought was probably along the road to Gravelines, but most of the night when he was able to sleep; he slept soundly until wakened for stand to just before dawn. During the day of Wednesday the 22nd of May there was considerable sniping activity in the town from fifth columnists who had crept out of the woodwork during the night. They were dealt with swiftly and ruthlessly. The air attacks were again heavy in the morning and again in the early evening but were still not fearsome enough to stop the little man with his evening delivery.

"What's your name?" David asked him.

The little man seemed a little reluctant to reply, but at last said "Schultz, Corporal," and then added, "my father was a prisoner of war from the German Navy in the Great War and decided to stay on in England because he likes it so much. I'm English."

"Well, I'm blessed," said David, "what's your first name?"

Again, a pause and then "Cedric, corporal."

David suddenly had the thought that Cedric had not been blessed with a good physique, good looks, nor above all, a particularly ringing name, but he had been blessed with a lion's heart. "We are going to call you 'Cedric the Brave' from now on," said David, the men around loudly agreeing. It was the first time in his life that Cedric had ever received the plaudits of his peers, he felt happier than he thought it was possible to be, he was now a man among men.

During that evening they heard the first distinct rumble of guns. They seemed to come from both the south towards Boulogne and the south east towards St Omer. 'It won't be long now by the sounds of things' thought David, experiencing a turning over in his stomach at the thought, and wondering how he would react in a real battle. On manoeuvres it had been all good fun, you knew you were not going to end up dead and that you would have a bed to sleep in, in a night or two if not tonight. Now was the real thing – he hoped he would be the soldier he would like to be and what his father and brother Harry would want him to be. His father had fought in South Africa and in the trenches in the Great War so he knew a bit about it. He never spoke much about it, and now David was wishing that he'd asked him more. He had faced what David was facing many times both out on the kopjes and the veldt in South Africa and in the Mons retreat and after that the trenches of Flanders. It seemed to David that all the family had taken his father for granted whereas, in fact, he was an extraordinary man among perhaps hundreds of thousands of extraordinary men, but no less extraordinary himself for all that. His thoughts were interrupted by a voice at his elbow.

"Dreaming or something?" It was Jeremy, his dearest friend and brother-in-law.

"I was just thinking that we've always taken our fathers for granted and yet when you think they've faced what we've got to face now time and again and never made a song and dance out of it. It must make them pretty special."

"You're right of course," said Jeremy. "I wonder if we'll be the same when our children say, "What did you do in the war Daddy?" What he didn't know was that it had been confirmed only a few days before that his first child was, in fact, on the way.

After stand-to that night, and the forward picquet posted, David went to sleep leaving his lance corporal in charge for three hours when he would relieve him for the rest of the night until morning stand to. It was an uneventful night except that the sound of the guns was much nearer which meant that our artillery was falling back fast. The dawn of 23rd May was greeted as usual by the sound of the Stukas diving in out of the blue and the furious response of the anti-aircraft guns both on land and at sea. As dawn broke, Two platoon had been visited by the commanding officer, Lieutenant Colonel Scott-Calder and it so happened he was right alongside David's slit trench as the first bombs fell. Together they both ended up, the colonel and the corporal with their legs all tangled up in the bottom of the trench and laughing uproariously. "Well David," said the colonel ('David?' thought the corporal – 'what have I done to deserve this?') "Who would have thought we'd end up in the bottom of a trench together a few years ago eh?"

Mr Scott-Calder had been David's House Master at Cantelbury where he and Jeremy had first met and become chums. The colonel had been in the regiment in the Great War where he had won the Military Cross. He was second in command of the battalion, but with the C.O. away when they were rushed to France, he had been promoted from major to command the battalion. So far he had seen every platoon every day and was immensely popular, even among the defaulters.

"How far away are they Sir?" said David.

"We can't be sure, but their forward recce units can't be far away. Both Arras and Amiens have been captured and they're attacking Boulogne now. We're holding them at Lille and there is a 50 kilometre salient around Dunkirk out to Lille." He paused for a minute, "but all of that may be history by now for all I know."

The bombing having stopped, they climbed out of the trench and the C.O. strode off. At mid morning they heard a different sound, way over to their right where B and C Companies were facing towards Boulogne. It was a whistling noise ending in a solid 'crump.' "That's a heavy gun," said Sergeant Harris, "although it's a long way away."

They had little time to ponder this when the momentary calm was shattered by a salvo of shells landing very close to the left of their position where a French unit was dug in. "Stand-to," yelled Sergeant Harris and to David, "This is it I think, old son, best of luck," and disappeared back to his platoon headquarters.

The shells came in more and more frequently as the day wore on and gradually the buildings around them started to suffer. There was still, however, no sight or sound of armour or infantry, which was just as well as they had only one two pounder anti-tank gun in their company position. If there were to be a mass armoured attack it would be a walk over. The only weapon the Rifles had was a .5 inch anti-tank rifle which, if it didn't break your shoulder when you fired it, was so useless when it was fired that it would hardly penetrate a paper bag let alone a tank. Despite the shelling, promptly at seven o'clock 'Cedric the Brave' appeared, smiling benignly as usual, waited patiently whilst the food was dished out, and then went on his way rejoicing, dodging the shell holes as he went.

There was little sleep to be had that night because of the incessant shelling. The first casualties were across the bridge in Three platoon, three men were caught in the open when changing the outlying picquet but then a heavy barrage came down for nearly half an hour and gradually all the platoons began to sustain casualties. Because the battalion was so spread out it became very difficult for stretcher bearers to collect the wounded and take them to the battalion medical centre at Battalion HQ near the post office in towards the town centre. In fact two stretcher bearers and the wounded man they were carrying were all killed as they approached the HQ. It was decided therefore that medical orderlies would treat the wounded as best they could until ambulances could transfer them direct to a ship lying in the harbour, though how much longer ships would be berthed there was anyone's guess.

All day long on Friday 24th May there was no let up in the shelling. Whereas it had been coming from the south east, it was now coming from the direction of the Boulogne road, which indicated even if the Germans had not captured Boulogne they had by-passed it and were pressing on towards Calais on the N.I. By 4pm sustained rifle and light machine gun fire broke out on the Boulogne road. B and C Companies were being attacked, and although their positions could not be seen from David's position because of the buildings in between, they seemed to be holding on. At 4.30 pm a loud shout from the forward picquet called out "Tank coming", and in a short while, during which the two men on the picquet covered the hundred yards back to the platoon position in well under ten seconds, the tank came into view up the by-road David's section was covering. It was about eight hundred yards away, moving slowly and apparently on its own. When it reached about three hundred yards from their position, it hulled down off the road with its gun and turret high enough to fire.

"Piercey," said David. Piercey was the crack shot of the company, he could put a hole through a half crown at a hundred yards. "He may be going to take a look out of the turret. You've got 400 yards. A pound says you can't get him."

"You all heard that," said Piercey, and to David, "You're on." He snuggled up to the sandbags.

Gradually they saw the lid to the cupola lifted but still no one appeared. Then they could just distinguish a pair of hands holding field glasses appear at the opening. Piercey took careful aim having first given the butt of his Lee Enfield a gentle kiss. A face and just the top of a pair of shoulders emerged and as it did so, Piercey squeezed his trigger and the onlookers saw a pair of field glasses float up into the air and the head and shoulders slide back into the tank.

"That, I reckon, is a quid you owe me," said Piercey.

"Hey up, he's moving," called one of the section.

The tank was climbing up the bank and moving fast towards them. From their left they heard the loud bark of their two pounder but the first short missed. A second shot was fired which hit the side of the tank a glancing blow but did nothing to stop it. However it did cause it to be more cautious in that it slewed off the road down into a field and reappeared at the end of a little row of single storey roadside cottages found so commonly in Northern France. In trying to get back on to the road, it had apparently broken off a concrete post at the side of the road, the stump of which had very neatly caused its left hand track to come off. And there it sat, its machine gun and turret gun pointing straight at A Company and too low down for the two pounder to hit it. In seconds the machine gun opened up, raking the buildings but as everyone was flat on the floor, little harm was done. It was a different story when the turret gun opened up and started blasting the positions. It soon became apparent that a very considerable casualty list would be building up if nothing was done to stop it.

David swiftly appraised the situation. "Brenner, pop down the cellar, get three grenades and bring my P.T. shoes up out of my big pack." Without a question Brenner did as he was told and David started to take off his gaiters and boots.

When Brenner returned he said, "There's only rifle grenades."

"That's alright – I'll use those," David replied.

The problem presented by there only being rifle grenades was the fuse time. It was David's plan to climb up on to the low sloping roof of the cottages and then run along to the far end, jump down on to the tank, lift the lid from the outside which would be quite possible, drop the grenade in and then 'hop it quick.' Whereas an ordinary grenade has only a four second fuse, the rifle grenade had a seven second fuse which meant that if he released the firing pin and dropped it in, there would conceivably be time for someone inside to pick it up and throw it out again. He would, therefore, have to release the firing pin, hold the live grenade in his hand for 3-4 seconds and then drop it in. That prospect he didn't look forward to at all.

Without further delay he crawled out of the back of the house and through some bombed buildings, ran quickly across the road without being spotted by the gunners in the tank, and reaching the row of cottages, climbed up on to a water butt and then on to the roof. As he was doing this the C.O. having crawled through hundreds of yards of rubble, appeared in Sergeant Harris's platoon HQ, or what was left of it.

"What's going on?" he said.

"A tank is stuck about two hundred yards down the road Sir, and blasting us."

The colonel slowly raised his head above the sandbags.

"Who's that on the roof over there?" he exclaimed. "By God, it looks like Chandler, what the hell's he up to?"

"I reckon he's going to leave a calling card Sir," said Sergeant Harris. At that moment, there was another shot from the tank followed immediately by cries from men hit just on their left. "That's Cartwright's section isn't it?" said the colonel, but Sergeant Harris was already away crawling through the debris to Jeremy's strong point. It was an awful sight that met him as he burst into the sandbagged room. The Bren gun team was a mangled mess in among a pile of sandbags, the base of which obviously having taken the full blast of the shell. Jeremy had been blasted against the wall and had a huge wound across his neck and shoulders. He was quite dead. The sergeant bellowed to the men in the slit trenches in front, "Any casualties out there?"

"Two with head wounds sergeant."

"Right, Lance Corporal Rogers, take over the section, but don't move until I come back." He did his crab like crawl back to the C.O.

"Jeremy Cartwright's dead Sir," said the sergeant.

"Oh my God – his poor wife!" replied the colonel, and then

"Chandlers' just priming the grenade by the look of things."

David had reached the end of the roof overlooking the tank. He jumped the eight feet or so down to the ground; climbed up on to the back of the tank, pulled out the safety pin, let the handle fly off, counted three, yanked open the lid to the turret and dropped the grenade in. Like a hare he was off the tank and into the back garden of the first cottage up on the roof and was half way back before there was an explosion followed by an even bigger explosion and a sheet of flame into the air as the tank's petrol blew up. What he didn't see was that the driver had turned his head at just the second David opened the hatch, immediately realised what was happening and in the seconds before the explosion, opened his own access door and threw himself out on to the road. Having picked himself up, he ran straight towards Two platoon positions and at the same moment as the grenade went off, Rifleman Piercey, having given the butt of his rifle another little kiss, shot him neatly between the eyes.

"Two out of two," said Piercey, "not bad for an amateur."

David ran back across the road and into his section position, straight into the arms of his colonel. David was grinning widely with the excitement of what he had been doing. "That'll teach them to fart in Church, eh Sir?" he said. There was no answering smile on Scott Calder's face, and David immediately sensed something was very wrong, as the colonel had kept his hands on David's shoulders.

"David, Jeremy has been killed," he said.

"Oh no, oh God no, he can't be – not Jeremy, oh my God, what will Rose do?" He immediately, despite the violent sickness in the pit of his stomach, regained control. "Where is he?" he asked.

"Come on son, I'll take you," said Sergeant Harris.

"I'm getting back to Battalion HQ David," said the colonel, "I'm sick inside about Jeremy, but we've got to fight on. That was a very brave thing you did out there, I shall recommend you for a decoration."

"Thank you Sir," said David and saluted as the colonel left, but not really having taken in a single word he had said. He just couldn't register that Jeremy, who had constantly been at his side for the last ten years, would never ever again joke with him, pull his leg or be his staunch comrade. And Rose, poor Rose – what would happen to her?

"Come on son, let's get it over with." The sergeant led David into the other emplacement where a medical orderly had laid the three bodies out in blankets ready for burial.

"Padré's coming at seven o'clock," said the medical orderly, "there's been another four in Three Platoon this afternoon so you'd better get digging."

David felt a senseless rage coming over him at the totally heartless tone of the medical orderly talking as if they were discussing the disposal of a run-over dog. He was just about to choke the daylights out of him when Sergeant Harris grabbed his elbow and said, "Right now, come on corporal, we've got work to do. I'll see to the burial party." In fact, one of the men with head wounds died shortly afterwards and in another furious burst of shelling, two more in the platoon were killed by a direct hit on their slit trench. The platoon was down to twenty-six men

At seven o'clock, the Padré arrived. Platoon HQ had dug the grave in the soft earth of one of the gardens and the six men were laid side by side in it. The Padré having said a few hurried words, they were speedily covered, six makeshift crosses with their names on pushed into the soil and a steel helmet hung on each. In B and C Company they were doing the same. A veritable forest of crosses was appearing around the fair city of Calais. David turned to see 'Cedric the Brave' beside him.

"I hear your mate got it Corporal," said Cedric, his eyes brimming with tears. "I'm ever so sorry. Like you, he was a lovely fellow – you will take care won't you?" and with that he was off to his truck with David staring after him. It was only as he was mounting the running board David called – "and you too Cedric." The truck drove away. It had gone less than a hundred yards when a shell screamed over causing David to fall flat on his face and when he looked up all that remained of Cedric's truck was a mangled mess of steelwork lodged at an angle against the wall of one of the houses. There was no point in running to see if Cedric was alright or not.

All the evening the shells came in. They stood-to as usual, and again the forward picquets were put out. Tonight it was the turn of Riflemen Beasley and Barclay. They had no field telephone by which they could keep in touch with the platoon, the most they would do was to give a warning if anything strange was going on. This they did by the simple expedient of pulling a length of signal cable David had scrounged, which was attached to a piece of wood hung from the ceiling in David's Bren gun position. If the wood swung, it hit the side wall with a clonk, and that meant something was up. So far it hadn't been used. Let's hope it stays that way thought David as he settled down for his three hours sleep. Tomorrow would be Saturday 25th. They had been here four days. It seemed like a lifetime.

Chapter Two

Ruth went about her work as usual on the 21st, hoping that Alec's reassurances about hearing soon would indeed come true. David's wife Pat called in on her way from the bungalow to the dress shop she owned in Sandbury. They consoled each other that no news was good news but secretly neither of them believed it. The midday and afternoon posts produced nothing, there was no late evening post now because of the blackout, so unless the telephone rang they would hear nothing, at least until the morning. Fred came home early from the factory he and Jack Hooper owned, which was flat out on war work building special vehicles and other contracts for the three services. Sometimes he was there until ten o'clock at night to see the night shift on, but this evening he left it to Ernie Bolton, David's old boyhood pal, now a tower of strength in helping to run the production side for Fred. Ernie had had rheumatic fever when he was a boy and had been confined to a wheelchair. After several years of physiotherapy and devoted help from his wife Anni, he had regained the use of his legs, but would never be fit for service in the forces. 'Their loss is our gain' Fred had said.

On Wednesday 22nd, still no news. Rose had looked so starry-eyed a few days before when it had been confirmed she was carrying Jeremy's baby, but now the strain was beginning to show a little Ruth thought, although Rose herself made no obvious signs of worry.

On Thursday 23rd, the Field Service Cards arrived, one for Rose, one for Pat, at the Bungalow and one for Ruth from someone she'd never heard of. Pat had rushed over to join them at breakfast having phoned her father at the Hollies, not far from Chandlers Lodge. It was funny about Chandlers Lodge. When Fred and Ruth first bought the property back in 1933 it already had that name which they put down as a good omen, and which, up until now, it had more than proved to be.

"Well, at least we know where they are," said Fred and as he spoke the kitchen door opened and in strode the huge figure of Jack Hooper, himself an ex artillery man from the Great War.

He studied Pat's card and said, "Don't believe in telling you much do they?" Ruth said that at least it was a comfort to hear from them and continued,

"But I've got a card here from a Kenny Barclay and I've never even heard of him. I wonder how he got to send it to me?"

"I bet I can answer that," said Jim Napier one of the Canadian majors living with the Chandlers. "I remember that name. That was the deserter chap that nearly lost David his stripes when he escaped from the guardroom at Christmas. I bet he's got no next of kin, so David said he could send it to you and you'd think about him. How otherwise would he get your address?"

Ruth studied the card again. "How sad it is. To think, if that is the case, how lonely he must feel."

"That's probably why David did it," said Jim.

"I'll write to him as soon as we know where to write to," said Ruth.

"You're an old softy," said Fred, "and you get worse as you get older," but he gave her shoulders a squeeze as he walked past her saying "well, I've got a factory to run – cheerio everybody."

At that moment the telephone rang which Rose answered. "It's Megan," she called to the others. Ruth watched Rose's face intently in an attempt to judge whether it was good or bad news and as Rose was smiling into the mouthpiece she relaxed into her chair again. Rose having rejoined them said, "Megan heard from Harry this morning. The letter is several days old and has two lines blacked out by the censors which has never happened before, but he's fit and well and cheerful as ever, to quote Megan," and with that small crumb of comfort, they all went about their work.

Dinner was to be early that evening as Fred had to be out on LDV duty. The Local Defence Volunteers had been formed a few days before to patrol the countryside with the object of preventing the parachuting into Britain of what had become known as Fifth Columnists, such operations having caused chaos in Holland and France in particular. They were also to guard sensitive installations such as telephone exchanges, water pumping stations and so on. Hitler had already made his views known on this organisation, they were not in uniform (all they had was an armband), they were armed, they were therefore agents' provocateurs and therefore they would be shot. As Fred had said, "Yes, but you've got to get here first old lad."

Before dinner Ruth had at last been able to contact Jeremy's parents, Buffy and Rita Cartwright, to tell them Rose had some news for them. Rose told them of the Field Service card and the rest of the conversation was small talk between Rita and Rose about the baby, Rita saying she'd already started knitting and would Rose allow her and Buffy to buy the pram. When Rose said that would be lovely she replied

"Well thank goodness for that – we saw a beautiful one in Bournemouth today and we just went in and bought it! Although the salesman looked at us somewhat quizzically I must say!"

As Ernie was at the factory that evening, Anni called round to give them all news of her father from whom she had received a letter. Being a German national, Karl had been interned earlier in the month when the invasion scare had started, and was now in a camp, which, in fact, was a whole street of small hotels all surrounded by barbed wire fences in a seaside town in North Wales. His letter was very cheerful, he shared a room with a pleasant fellow from Hanover of about his own age. He was beginning to take a serious interest in chess and learning how to play bridge. The food was 'reasonable' which Ruth interpreted as being poor, knowing the kind interpretation Karl would put on anything to do with his adopted country which had taken him and his daughter in their hour of need.

Anni was blooming. She too was expecting and as Fred had said, "What with the pair of them, we're going to have an expensive time come February."

Later that evening as he arrived home from his LDV patrol, Jack Hooper received a telephone call from Pat. "Dad – are you doing anything? I've got something I want to talk to you about." With her father saying he was quite free – Moira was on duty that night at the War Office, she said she would cycle over straight away. Moira, Jack's wife, was a very senior civil servant in the War Department and often had to be away for two or three days sometimes visiting other parts of the country or on duty in Whitehall. At the present time she was engaged in a most highly secret project with Sir Henry Tizzard, the Chief Government Scientific Officer and a small select body of others, in the design and production of what was to become known as 'the Atom Bomb.' The responsibility of the knowledge of the eventual power of this weapon, the fact that they were racing against time in case the Russians or Germans were developing it and, above all, the fact that she could not share her dreadful secret with anyone, not even her Jack, was an enormous burden to her, which after the first few days from being appointed to the project, she shouldered bravely so that her relationship with her family would not suffer.

Pat arrived in a few minutes to the welcoming words, "If its money you want – how much?" She laughed, and kissed him. She loved this big burly father of hers. Her mother had left them when she was six years old. He had brought her up alone until he met Moira at Harry's wedding, Pat being sixteen when he and Moira married.

"No, it's about property," she said, and on being told to fire away continued, "the freehold of the two shops and flats over, next to 'Country Style', are coming up for sale. Both of the shops and all but one of the flats are let and producing income. I'm told that in today's market the prices will be very low."

"Oh, so we've got a property dealer in the family now have we? And where, may I ask, did all this information surface from – I've heard nothing about it in the town."

"Well, that's one of the advantages of being such a beautiful woman as I, you will agree, surely am!"

"I'll agree, and compliment you on your incredible modesty."

"Well, a young land agent named Ivor Lewis from Maidstone came into the shop and asked me if he could 'speak to the proprietor love.' I replied 'I was the proprietor love' which knocked all the wind out of his sails. 'Well' he continued, 'I wondered if I could look over your premises,' and when I asked him why he said he would have to tell me in complete confidence. I told him to carry on, he could rely on me completely, keeping, I may add, my fingers crossed on both hands behind my back. Anyway he said that the next two buildings were, he believed, identical to ours, which I agreed was the case. He said the freehold was going to be put on the market but he didn't want to go to the existing tenants and cause them unnecessary concern, particularly as the owners wished to dispose of the properties as a whole and not in bits and pieces."

"The latter probably being the more important consideration," observed Jack.

"Anyway, to cut a long story short, I showed him over the shop and upstairs. He took me to lunch at the Angel, passing the raised eyebrows of John Tarrant who pointedly asked whether I'd heard from David lately, and worked my charm on him to find out what sort of price he'd be looking for. He reckoned the two shops and the four flats would go for just under five thousand pounds. I told him I knew someone who might be interested. Could he hold any advertising of the property for two or three days and then I'd invite him to lunch to discuss it. He jumped at it like a shot."

It was now getting on for nine thirty.

"I'll ring Fred," said Jack. "I'll tell John your lunching there was all in the line of duty when I see him next – mustn't have your name sullied in the great metropolis of Sandbury!" (John was the manager and co-owner of the Angel and a good friend of Jack and Fred).

Fred answered the phone and when he heard Jack's voice he said "They've invaded!!" Jack laughed, but the main reaction was at Fred's end. Ruth, Rose, Anni and the two majors were all sitting around the big deal table in the kitchen and could clearly hear Fred. Ruth often said 'we have a perfectly good sitting room and yet we always seem to gravitate to the kitchen'.

"They've invaded" they heard, and then Fred said no more until they heard him say, "Right, see you in ten minutes."

He came back into the room and met the combined stare of five strained faces, and with Ruth saying, "Where have they invaded?"

"Invaded? What do you mean invaded? Nobody's invaded," said Fred.

"We distinctly heard you say they'd invaded," said Ruth.

"Oh, I was just larking about with Jack," replied Fred.

"Well, all I can say is if you lark about like that again Fred Chandler, I'll hit you over the head with my soup saucepan – you frightened the life out of us."

"Oh, sorry everyone," said Fred sheepishly, "didn't mean to put the wind up you. Anyway Pat and Jack are on the way round, they've got a bit of business to talk to me about."

"What, at this time of night?" said Ruth.

"Well, apparently it's just come up and Jack won't be available for the next couple of days."

As they were talking, Jack and Pat arrived.

"Get another couple of glasses Rose love will you?" said Fred, "while I get another quart of Whitbread's out of the cupboard." Fred's cupboard under the stairs was renowned for its seemingly inexhaustible supply of Whitbread Light Ale, which by now the Canadians also positively relished.

"Well if you want to talk business you'd better go into the sitting room," said Ruth, "have you had supper yet?" to Jack and Pat, "if not, I'm doing sandwiches and pickles for us."

"Just the job, Ruth, I'm starving and I know old hungry here won't say no," said Jack nodding at Pat.

Having got themselves seated, Jack quickly ran through all that Pat had told him. "If we could buy these two places we then have a really sizeable holding right in the middle of town. In addition, they've all got a biggish piece of land with outhouses at the rear. I know it's long term but after the war one of the big multiples will give a small fortune to have a site like that right in the centre of a place like Sandbury, particularly if the district grows as rapidly after the war as it did in the thirties."

"You're assuming we'll win?" said Fred with a wry grin.

"Of course we will," said Jack, "well, at least we've got to assume we will haven't we?"

"I was just pulling your leg," replied Fred, "although I ought to stop saying things like that. I have already been threatened with grievous bodily harm by my wife this evening because of my playful ways."

"I always understood she liked your playful ways," Jack said, catching from the corner of his eye Ruth entering with the tray of sandwiches. "She's always boasting about them in fact," – and then, "oh, hello Ruth, just talking about you!"

"Pat," said Ruth, "how on earth did you put up with him all those years?"

"Well, I suppose there are worse," Pat replied, "mind you, I can't think of one at the moment."

Pat and Jack loved coming to the Chandler's. There was always gay banter going on, particularly in the times when Harry and David were at home. The Canadians had soon entered into it, Ernie Bolton added to it when he came with Anni, it was such a happy, easy going house. Little did they know that in a few hours all would change, all would be different, it would never ever be quite the same again.

Ruth left them with their sandwiches and pickles and a mug of cocoa for Pat.

"Well," said Jack, "shall we get our minister extraordinary to make an offer to our Mr Lewis, and if so, how much?"

"Let's give Reg Church a quick ring now. He never goes to bed early. Perhaps he can give us a lead. I take it we'll buy it through Sandbury Properties?" Reg Church was their accountant and Sandbury Properties was their company which owned the factory, Pat's shop and several other sites and parcels of land in and around Sandbury.

Reg was quick in his response. "Excellent site, particularly since you've got the trump card with the freehold of Country Styles. It's nothing near so valuable without that, so I'd offer them four thousand and be prepared to go up to four and a half. Make sure you tell them the cheque could be with their solicitors on a subject to survey basis within twenty-four hours. If the owners are needing the money that would be a good inducement."

"Thanks Reg, you can have the rest of the day off now," said Jack, and putting the receiver down passed on his message to the others.

"Think you can manage it?" Jack said to his daughter. "I mean without one of us with you?"

"Why not? Mrs Draper has taught me how to haggle with the gown travellers and they're as tough a breed as any. I know this is an enormous sum of money compared to the amounts I deal in but the principles remain the same. You tell me any upper limit and I won't go beyond it."

"For everything you make below four and a half thousand, we'll go fifty-fifty - how about that Jack?" said Fred.

"So, if I get it for four-two I make myself a hundred and fifty pounds?" queried Pat.

"Exactly so," said her father.

"I'm in the wrong business," she said, "you're on."

They rejoined the others and soon all broke up to go to their respective homes or beds. That night Ruth added to her prayers, one for her new boy Kenny, and all their comrades in danger in France. It was a long time before she, at last, got to sleep.

The next morning Pat telephoned Mr Lewis and arranged to see him for lunch on the following Monday 27th May. Having made the appointment, she telephoned Fred to give him the news and then her father, who was at his office in the city. She found him in a terrible rage, which was most unusual. She could count the times she had known her father really angry on the fingers of one hand.

"Calm down, Daddy, you'll have a stroke," she said, "what's the matter for goodness sake."

"Despite the fact they arrested Mosley and his henchmen on the 23rd, we've just heard the results of the Middleton by-election" he replied " and do you know there was a FASCIST (he almost bellowed the word) candidate and that four hundred and eighteen people voted for him. I ask you, in the middle of a war against fascists and four hundred and eighteen idiots vote for fascism. They ought to shoot the bloody lot and I'd volunteer to be in the firing squad."

There was very little Pat could do to soothe him, but eventually he calmed down and went on. "We talk of fifth columnists and collaborators in other countries like Holland and France. If we've got four hundred and eighteen fascists in a place like Middleton how many have we got in London? I find it absolutely unbelievable – just shows we need the LDV that's all I can say. Anyway, enough of all that, how did you get on with your admirer?"

"Lunch on Monday," said Pat, "although I don't suppose he'll be in a position to say yea or nay to the offer until he's consulted his principals. I'm rather looking forward to my first venture into big business."

"Well, good luck to you – I'll see you on Sunday, take care."

On the Saturday and Sunday, the whole family, including Anni and Ernie had planned to 'Dig for Victory.' The government was exhorting everyone to dig up their flowerbeds, and lawns as well, in order to plant vegetables. On Saturday afternoon and on Sunday after church parade, the two majors helped to turn Chandlers Lodge into a miniature market garden. Fred flatly refused to allow them to dig up the main front lawn which swept around in a big curve to the side of the house, but the back lawn was sacrificed and by four o'clock on Sunday it was all ready for planting.

"We'll do that next weekend," said Fred. "It's a bit late for some things but we'll plan out what we can sow for the best results. It's no good having a glut of things you can't keep, so we'll do it in stages so that we can harvest manageable amounts."

They all trooped into the big kitchen. "It's thirsty work this gardening," said Fred, making immediate tracks to the cupboard under the stairs and returning with a wooden crate containing four quarts of Whitbread's, into which the four men made rapid inroads. In the meantime, Ruth was pouring tea for the girls, having already given Megan's twins large glasses of lemonade made, of course, from lemonade powder, lemons being a thing of the past.

"You'll never get the dirt off those two," she said to Megan. The three year olds had each been given a little box to put weeds in and then empty them on a big heap to be burnt, but they had succeeded in covering themselves every time they upended their boxes.

"I'll bath them here before I take them home," said Megan, "I brought spare clothes with me when we came yesterday – I guessed they'd probably end up like this."

As they sat talking, there was a rat-a-tat-tat on the front door, "Who's that on a Sunday afternoon," said Ruth and got up to go to the door.

"I'll go," said Alec, "I'm Duty Field Officer today, it may be for me." A few seconds later he looked round the door into the kitchen and said, "Mrs Chandler, could you spare a minute?"

"Which one?" Megan said with a smile.

Fred noticed there was no answering smile on Alec's face when he just replied, "Senior." Ruth got up and walked into the hall and as she turned the corner she saw the peak-capped telegraph boy framed in the doorway, and Alex standing with a telegram in his hand.

37

"It's addressed to Mrs Cartwright," said Alex in a low voice.

"Oh my God," said Ruth, "not Jeremy," and her hand shook as she took the buff envelope. "Can you ask Rose if she'll come in the sitting room," she continued.

Alec trying to be as casual as possible went back into the kitchen and said, "Can you have a word with your mother. She's in the sitting room." Rose got up and walked to the sitting room, followed by Alec, whilst the others carried on with their conversation, not overly curious about the events in the hall or by the caller who had precipitated them.

"Rose dear, I think we may have bad news," she said, holding the telegram for Rose to see.

"Please open it Mummy," she said clutching Alec's arm.

Ruth opened it. It bore the stark message "The War Office regrets to announce the death of your husband, Corporal J. Cartwright who was killed in action on 24th May." She slowly handed it to Rose saying, "Jeremy has been killed in action."

Rose's face froze into a mask of pain and disbelief. Ruth moved towards her but she was sinking to the floor until Alec held her, picked her up and carried her to the sofa.

"I'll get Fred and Megan," said Alec, "you sit with her."

They looked up expectantly as Alec came back in. From the grim look on his face Fred could tell that something was very much awry. "What's happening?" he said, somewhat harshly.

"Rose has just had a telegram from the War Office to say Jeremy has been killed," Alec replied. "Will you and Megan please go into the sitting room."

Fred and Megan moved as one and hurried away. Anni was silently crying, with Ernie doing all he could to comfort her. Jim Napier and Alec sat grim faced looking into their glasses, and the twins sat very quiet knowing that something was very terribly wrong.

Rose came round, and started to shake violently. Megan held her close and said, "Hang on, Rose, you must hang on."

She quietened and then said, "Someone must tell my mother and father-in-law."

"I'll do that love," said Fred and went back to the hall to book the call. Being Sunday it was only two or three minutes when the cheerful booming voice of Buffy Cartwright came on the line.

"Cartwright here."

"Buffy, it's Fred."

"Oh hello Fred, how are you all? We were only talking about Rose this afternoon, how are you all keeping?"

"I've some pretty desperate news Buffy. Rose has just had a

telegram to say that Jeremy has been killed in action in France."

There was a sickening silence for a long time at the other end until an entirely different voice, but coming from the same person, answered with, "Have you got any details?"

"No, just the bald announcement," said Fred. There was another pause. "As soon as Rose is able she'll telephone you, and Ruth will ring Rita this evening. By God, Buffy, I thought when 1918 was over we'd seen the last of all this. I wish I could get my hands on that bastard Hitler."

"I agree old son. I'll ring off now. Rita will be back from her walk any minute. God knows how I'm going to tell her. Come to that, I can't sink it in myself. I don't know what I'll do when it does hit me. Cheerio now, give our love to Rose and Ruth," and he hung up.

Fred went back into the sitting room and found Rose sitting up. He sat beside her and put his arms around her. He said nothing but she could feel the strength of his protection of her and his love for her and she was comforted. "Poor, poor David," she said, "poor David." They knew what she meant. The two lads had been inseparable for ten years.

"I think I would like to lie down," she said and stood up rather unsteadily. Ruth put her arm round one side and Megan the other. "My legs feel like jelly," she said.

After she had slipped under the eiderdown and Ruth had pulled the curtains across to shut out the bright sun, Ruth said to Megan, "Do you think we should call the doctor?"

"I don't think so," said Megan, "but if you like I could stay here tonight and keep an eye on her and go to work tomorrow evening from here. I'm not on until 6 o'clock, I'm on nights all next week and Nanny is looking after the twins." Nanny was employed by Jack and Moira to look after their John, who was the same age as the twins. She loved looking after them and felt she was helping the war effort at the same time by releasing Megan who was a sister at the Sandbury Hospital, now receiving casualties from France.

"I would be so grateful if you could stay," said Ruth. "I'll go down to the others now and then bring us up some tea."

She returned to the kitchen and sat down at the table with them. "She's quieter now," she said. "Would anyone like some tea?" The men elected to stay sipping their beer, but Anni said tearfully that she would like some.

"We've now got to phone Jack and Moira and get them to tell Pat," said Fred, "and we must phone Elizabeth and Trefor in Carmarthen, and then Doctor Carew." Doctor Carew was the boys' old headmaster.

"Could you do that dear while I go back up to Rose and Megan," said Ruth, and having laid a tray with a pot of tea, milk and sugar containers made her way back upstairs.

Anni said, "Ernie and I will go now Auntie Ruth, I really am so heartbroken for Rose."

"And so am I," said Ernie, "give her our love won't you?"

"I will. Goodnight my dears."

Fred phoned Jack, who was horrified at the news and within twenty minutes he and Moira arrived having collected Pat on the way. As Jack said, "I know there's nothing we can do, but we're all family so I thought our place was here."

Doctor Carew was very upset. He was just going to the evening chapel service at Cantelbury College and said they would pray for Rose and the family that evening. Jeremy was their first old boy killed in the army, following the loss only two weeks ago of two Royal Navy officers serving on the same ship in a North Atlantic convoy. "I do hope it will not be as it was in our time Mister Chandler, when people had columns and columns of names to look through to see if relatives and friends were included. That was horrific."

"I shouldn't think it will be quite like that," said Fred, "whatever happens, this is going to be a mobile war, and casualties shouldn't be on the same scale as the old set piece trench warfare."

"I agree, on the other hand we haven't experienced any aerial attack yet. That could give a whole new dimension to our sufferings."

His words were truly prophetic.

Chapter Three

The morning David's ship had steamed into Calais docks, his brother Harry was less than half a mile away making what was to be his last trip from Bergue to Calais to collect ammunition. As had happened in the past, the ship discharging this was at a berth at some distance from the other docks, and as the troop ship moved slowly past their berth, he caught a flash of green from the stripes of one or two NCOs waiting on deck to be the first to land. His captain was with him. "Can I borrow your binoculars Sir?" asked Harry, and on being given them could plainly see they were the Rifles on that ship now moving away from him across to a dock on the far side of the harbour.

"That's the Rifles Sir," said Harry, "I'm wondering if my brother is with them. I should think he's bound to be."

"Well, I can't let you go round and have a look," said the captain, "we're all ready to move off, and the sooner I get these loads of death out of Calais the better I'll be pleased. Space them well apart on the trip up to Dunkirk, sergeant and tell them woe betide any idiot I find bunching up on the one in front."

"Right Sir," said Harry, and he mounted his motorcycle and moved the first lorry out, the others following as ordered. The convoy was twice attacked, once before reaching Gravelines and again half an hour later after passing through the town, but although there were near misses, they suffered no casualties. They were not sorry to reach the ordnance dump outside Dunkirk, unload and motor on to their home park.

The next morning, the 22nd, Harry woke up wondering where David was and what the Rifles were up to. Coming from breakfast, a runner appeared and said, "Captain wants you sergeant." Harry duly presented himself and was told to take three lorries to a casualty clearing station outside Lille and bring back walking wounded to a reception area being established on the dunes at Dunkirk. He was to continue with this task until the backlog was cleared, as the R.A.M.C. ambulances were fully committed with transporting stretcher cases.

"Have we got that number then Sir?" said Harry.

"They're making a big fight of it around Lille I'm told," said the captain, "and taking heavy casualties. Operate on your own for the next few days and as the saying goes, 'I'll see you when I see you'."

"Right Sir, good luck."

"I've an idea you might be the one who will need the good luck," said the captain with a grin and a firm handshake. Harry saluted, hurried off to collect his full kit and blankets, and having got his three trucks organised, moved off towards Lille. It was a slow journey. The roads were clogged with refugees. At one point a complete brigade, or what was left of it, was moving back in good order to take up a further defensive position, the whole world seemed on the move. Harry had been issued with six large Red Cross flags, one flown at the front and rear of each vehicle. This tended to make other vehicles move over for them but it still took three hours to cover the forty miles before they met the Military Police unit to direct them to the C.C.S. Their passengers proved to be a mixed bunch, supposedly walking wounded, but since some of them had wounds to the leg, Harry suggested they wouldn't have been able to walk very far anyway. There was a number of officers, including a full colonel complete with knee-boots and red tabs but minus his hat. His uniform was badly ripped where they had cut pieces out presumably because they were stuck on the wounds when he was treated, and his right arm was now fastened securely across his chest.

"You'd better ride up front Sir," Harry suggested.

"Oh no, sergeant, I'm in the back with the others. This is your show, you run it."

His three lorries loaded with the men in the back sitting against the canvas sides, and others hanging on to the tubular framework supporting the canvas, Harry said to his corporal in the second truck, "I don't see how these blokes can hang on to the truck for three or four hours or more – some of them look all in now. The state the roads are in will shake them to pieces."

He thought for a moment. "Did you notice there was a catholic school about a mile up the road? We'll make for there and see if we can requisition some benches for them to sit on."

The corporal looked at him with eyebrows raised. "Requisition?" he asked.

"Well, you know what I mean," said Harry with his inimitable mischievous grin, which so endeared him to all the family and friends back at Sandbury in particular, and to his army colleagues in general. He went round to the back of each truck in turn and said, "We're going to pull off the road in about five minutes. I'm going to try to win some benches for you to sit on, it's a long journey to make standing up at the best of times."

Such remarks as 'good on yer Sarge' followed him as he returned to the lead vehicle. They soon reached the school, adjoining which was a small church, and as they drove into the school playground, a priest appeared followed, at a distance, by four nuns.

"How can I help you," said the priest in passable English.

"Padré, I have all these wounded to take to Dunkirk, but they have nothing to sit on. I would be grateful if I could borrow some forms from the school so they can sit down."

"I'm afraid the seats we have are all very small as this is an infants' school," said the priest. "However, you can gladly have some pews from the church; I think they will be more or less the right length for the lorry."

He took a large bunch of keys from a pocket, which seemed to stretch the full length of his arm inside his robes, and walked to the church door.

"How many rows can you get in the lorry?" said the priest.

"I reckon three," said Harry, "one down each side and one down the middle. The only problem I can see is whether they will move when we go over holes in the road or round bends, there are a lot of men with injuries that could be made worse if they were suddenly moved."

"Take the nine out and I'll be back in a minute," said the priest, and speaking rapidly in French to the sisters, told them what he was doing and to help. Harry, the three drivers and the four sisters split up so that two of the men and two of the sisters lifted and carried a pew between them out to the trucks. It was by no means light work, but they soon had them ready to lift into the lorries. During the moving, Harry noticed one of the sisters, who was particularly pretty, looking at him obliquely as she helped to carry the solid pew. Looking up, he caught her eyes, cheekily he winked at her and she immediately blushed and looked down.

"That'll be something for your confession tonight," Harry said to himself with a smile.

As they were lifting the pews into the first lorry, the priest reappeared with a tool bag in one hand and carpet bag in the other, and with the first pew slid along one side he climbed up, took out some nails and a hammer and proceeded to pin the pews down on to the wooden decking of the truck. He was obviously no slouch with a hammer and nails as in double quick time he fixed the seating in all the trucks and the men all clambered back in. The Padré then opened the carpet bag and brought out half a dozen bottles of cognac – "Two to each lorry," he said, "and some special for you, sergeant, and your drivers, but take only a little – it is very strong."

"Padré, you are wonderful," said Harry, "we shall be coming past every day for the next few days and when we do, we shall make such a

43

noise they'll hear us in Paris."

"Sergeant, if you are taking wounded back you must call in and I will give them all some cognac to help them along the way. And, by the way, what is your name?"

"Harry Chandler, Sir."

"Then I hope to see you tomorrow Sergeant 'Arry," said the Padré.

Harry saluted the Padré and the nuns and said, "Right, let's get going," and they drove out of the playground, the men in the back waving until they were out of the gate and away. Apart from the even more crowded roads, the journey was uneventful and having deposited their men at the Field Hospital, they scrounged a meal and bedded down for the night in their trucks.

The next morning they had breakfast, collected some haversack rations for the day and were off again by seven thirty. It was noon by the time they reached Lille and twice on the way there was shelling along the road, which caused havoc, particularly among the refugees. They collected their hundred odd casualties and there were many remarks about the pews they were to sit on and enquiries as to where he had 'knocked them off.'

Harry replied, "You'll see in a few minutes," and they drove off back towards Dunkirk. Approaching the school they started blowing their hooters and out into the playground again appeared the priest and his four nuns, the priest with his carpet bag as before, but this time the nuns with trays of cakes.

"Sergeant 'Arry – how are you today?" called the priest as Harry got down to go to the rear of the trucks now lined up side by side.

"Good afternoon Padré, good afternoon sisters," said Harry, with a special grin to his pretty friend of the previous day, who again blushed and looked down.

"We've stopped here," he continued, "because I wanted you to meet the gentleman who provided your seating accommodation. I can assure you it would have been a very rough ride without it." There was a spontaneous burst of clapping from inside the trucks which, by now, had had their tail-boards lowered by the three drivers. The priest stepped forward and again, from his bag, took two bottles to hand to the men in each lorry while the sisters passed up the currant buns.

"I'm sorry it is not more," he said, "but the sisters are getting low on flour."

As they drove away, the wounded men waving away to the little group standing in the playground, Harry said to the driver, "I wonder what will happen to them and people like them if the Germans take over?" Little did he know that one day the priest would be arrested by the Gestapo, would be tortured and shot for being in the Resistance like so many others of his calling throughout occupied France.

Just as they were reaching the outskirts of Dunkirk, a flight of Messerschmit fighters appeared out of the blue, and despite the fact the lorries were flying large Red Cross flags and that a large proportion of the people on the road were refugees, it made no difference to the Luftwaffe pilots, who strafed, banked and came back and strafed again. Two out of the three lorries were hit and two men killed in the rear lorry. A burst hit the side of Harry's truck but miraculously only one man was wounded, this time in his left arm, his right arm already being out of commission.

"It could have been a lot worse I suppose," said Harry, "I wonder what it will be like tomorrow?"

The next day, the 24th, followed the same pattern, but before they left Dunkirk, Harry started chatting to a Tank Corps sergeant who had come up from Gravelines. Harry asked if he knew what was happening at Calais, to which the tank man said, as he understood it, Calais was now completely surrounded with orders to fight to the last man. "Except for some Frenchmen and a few of our blokes, they're all Rifles down there," said the sergeant. "I certainly wouldn't want to be in their shoes."

"My brother and brother-in-law are there I think," said Harry. "They're in the City Rifles."

"They're definitely there." Harry went away very worried at the prospect of his young brother and Jeremy being in the thick of it.

Before they reached Lille on this day's trip, during which the flood of refugees seemed to have disappeared only to be replaced by more and more units withdrawing, Harry was stopped by the military police control point. Recognising Harry, the red cap said "The C.C.S. is back at a farm about a mile on the right, but I understand they'll be moving back again soon, we've had heavy shelling at times here this morning."

To prove his point, a salvo of four came over bursting about five hundred yards to their right, followed by another four, which were appreciably nearer the road. "I should get a move on if I were you," said the M.P. Harry needed no second bidding but drove as fast as the road and the people using it allowed, and swiftly loaded up nearly fifty people to a truck. It was heart-rending to see the agony some of these casualties were in. Those that could stand stood between the three rows of seats while the others sat as closely together as they could get, but they still left a hundred behind.

"We'll come straight back," said Harry to the C.C.S. major. "We'll be here by eight again tonight."

When Harry got back to his lorry, the driver met him and said "There's a captain sitting in your place in the cab and says he's going to stay there, he's only lightly wounded in the arm."

"Right," said Harry, "I'll sort him out."

There was no way that Harry could make instant decisions on the journey if he was sitting anywhere but at the front with the driver, as the colonel on the first trip had clearly understood. He approached the captain.

"Excuse me Sir, but I shall have to sit there. I'm sorry, but you will have to go in the back."

"I am staying here and you will go in the back, and that's an order," said the captain.

Harry thought for a moment, walked away and button-holed the RAMC major. "Sir," he said, "there is an officer up in my cab who refuses to get down so that I can control the journey."

"I wondered what the devil the hold up was," said the major, "let me sort him out." He went across to the cab, opened the door, looked up at the captain and bellowed one word "OUT." With some hesitation, the captain climbed down, "and now you can go to the end of the queue until they come back for you," said the major. Harry thought for a moment that the captain was going to strike his superior officer, but he obviously thought better of it and slouched away to where the remainder were waiting.

"Thank you, Sir," said Harry.

"Good luck, sergeant, see you about eight o'clock."

But it was nearer ten that night when they eventually got back to pick the next lot up, only to find firstly the C.C.S. was packing up and moving again and secondly the numbers to take back had swelled to over a hundred and fifty. How he crammed them in Harry never knew, but cram them in he did, and no one will ever know the suffering of some of those men on the forty mile journey, over the potholed, cobbled roads to Dunkirk. They got there at three in the morning. Harry and the drivers slept in the lorries, too tired to eat and at seven thirty were on their way again.

"I shall know this bloody road soon," said one of the drivers, but he wasn't to know anything for very much longer. Heavy shelling met them just outside Bailleul and he and his lorry were blown to pieces. There was nothing anyone could do.

Chapter Four

Back at Calais on the night of the 24th, David at last got his head down. They had been shelled heavily during the evening resulting in several more casualties in the platoon, two of them in David's section, but now the barrage had stopped on their front, although it was still going full blast on the road up from Boulogne where B and C Companies appeared to be falling back and from where there was considerable rifle fire to be heard. Suddenly the piece of wood started hitting against the wall. David jumped to his feet calling quietly, "stand-to," at which call the Bren gunners and all the men left in the slit trenches manned their positions.

Sergeant Harris suddenly appeared in David's emplacement. "What's up?" he asked.

"The lookouts have just signalled something happening out front," said David.

"Right, I'll go back and telephone company HQ." In less than a minute, the whole company was standing to and Major Grant was on his way to the forward positions to see what was happening. As he reached the platoons on the other side of the canal, Sergeant Harris' platoon being the only one on the eastern side, it became very clear what was up. Suddenly the whole sky in their sector was lit by parachute mortar flares and out of the darkness appeared a mass of German infantry to be met with a witheringly accurate fire from the newly alerted defenders. The main attack was made on the western side of the canal with probably not more than a couple of dozen attacking Two platoon.

"Hold your fire until I tell you," called David, "choose your target, make every round count." Further over to their left, Sergeant Harris was instructing the other two sections, both of whom had now lost their corporals, to do the same thing. The Germans came on in extended order, clearly visible in the succession of flares which they had put up and which now were being added to by others from Rifles, it was almost like daylight. At fifty yards, Sergeant Harris and David shouted the order to fire, and the first volley and bursts from the two remaining Bren guns wiped out half the attackers. The remainder hesitated and then turned back, but they didn't stand a chance. Not only were they being fired on from the platoon positions, but Beasley and Barclay in the forward observation post, who had been hiding in the bottom of their slit trench when the Germans had advanced, now popped up and fired at them from the flank as they retreated, and took on three of the attackers who had gone to ground behind a small ridge out of sight from David's position, but in full view of the two lookouts. Not one of the attackers got back to the boat in which they had first got across the canal from their main body. It was the noise of their scrambling up the canal bank, which had first alerted the forward picquet, and now both Beasley and the reluctant soldier Barclay, had not only made their first kills but they had also alerted the whole company to be ready and waiting, which in the event, saved them from being overrun.

The main attack on the two platoons on the other side of the canal was beaten back, though not before the platoon on the far left was engaged in savage hand-to-hand fighting until the Germans were, at last, driven out.

While the attack was taking place, the colonel, with his runner and the intelligence officer, made their way to the company headquarters where he was met by C.S.M. Ward.

"What's happening sergeant major?" said Colonel Scott-Calder.

The C.S.M. told him all he knew, which wasn't very much, but with the firing dying down the colonel said, "I'll wait for Major Grant, if I go forward I may pass him in the dark."

"Right Sir, I'll send a runner to try and find him and tell him you're here, we're having no luck with the field telephone at the moment."

At that moment, 'to make a liar out of me' as he later said to the major, the telephone shrilled out and it was the major from Three Platoon HQ. "We've beaten them off for now and I'm on my way back," he said to the C.S.M.

"Right Sir, the CO's here Sir and will wait for you."

A few minutes later Major Grant arrived and swiftly gave an account of the attack and its subsequent repulse.

"I've some serious news for you," said the colonel, "no – you stay Sergeant Major," who was going to make himself scarce if the talk was to be confidential. "I've just had a signal from the brigadier to say that the garrison here will not now be taken back to England as planned. We have to stay here literally to the last man and the last round to prevent the Germans getting up the Gravelines road to Dunkirk. It is essential to the safety of the whole of the B.E.F. that Calais is held as long as there are men alive to hold it. The last ship sails tomorrow with wounded only on it."

There was a moment of complete silence and then Major Grant said, "A complete brigade of the Rifles gone in a few days. By God, its like 1914-18 all over again isn't it?"

The colonel, nodding in agreement, stood up and shook hands with them both. "Good luck Norman, good luck Mr Ward, we riflemen do get ourselves into some pretty pickles don't we?"

"We do that Sir," said the sergeant major.

The colonel continued, "From now on then all companies will be operating independently. If you have to fall back make the final stand around battalion HQ. Good luck again," and he was off, little knowing he really was leaving them behind since when he and his two companions were a hundred yards or so from his headquarters, a shell roared in, catching them in the open, killing the I.O. and the runner and all but severing the colonel's leg. His shouts were heard by the picquets, the M.O. gave such immediate aid as he could, an ambulance raced him to the hospital ship, and within half an hour of talking with Major Grant and C.S.M. Ward, he was on the operating table being put back together again. Not that it was as simple as that, he never had the full use of the leg again despite all the efforts of the RAMC surgeons.

After the C.O. had gone, Major Grant said, "I'll make a round of the platoons and tell them the position. I think I'll bring most of Two platoon over the bridge and put them on our left where Jerry nearly got through. Sergeant Harris can leave one section on his present side of the canal to act as a forward post in case anything comes up the minor road over there, but there's no doubt when the next attack comes in it will come in on our front on this side of the canal."

The major made his rounds leaving the bad news at each platoon HQ. When he had left Two platoon, Sergeant Harris called David to his dugout and told him what the major had said. "I'm leaving you here David with the five men left in your section and Smith 24 from platoon HQ." Smith 24 had been Mr Austen's batman, a solid reliable soldier; if a little slow on the uptake. "If it gets too hot for you, you can retreat over the bridge. I've asked the Pioneer Section to come up and mine it so that it can be blown up when you're over."

"We're running low on ammunition sergeant," said David, "wouldn't it be a good idea to rescue some from the dead Germans out front, they've probably got plenty?"

"You'll need the rifles as well," said Sergeant Harris, "they're a different calibre to ours. Grab a couple of blokes and we'll go and have a look."

They searched the first two bodies and found a complete bandolier on each man. They swiftly moved further out and very quickly they had a dozen rifles and bandoliers between them. The shelling had eased a little whilst this was going on, most falling well into the town towards the docks, but suddenly it started to get closer.

"Right, back to the dugout," called the sergeant. As they ran, David heard a faint cry coming from near the canal bank.

"There's someone over there near the canal sergeant" David said.

"Get under cover and then we'll listen out," said the sergeant. They made their slit trenches in front of the platoon HQ and sheltered until the barrage moved away.

"I'll take Smith and have a look," said David.

Together they hurried the forty or so yards to the spot the cry had come from. "Go round to the left and keep your rifle at the ready," said David. Smith moved off and David moved cautiously round to the right.

In a few seconds he heard Smith's loud whisper, "Here corporal. Looks as though he's got a head wound."

"Where are you hurt?" said David in his fluent German. Not only had he an exceptional gift for the language at Cantelbury, but he had spent a considerable time in Germany perfecting it before the war.

"In the head and in the thigh, I think," said the soldier.

"Let's get him back to the dugout," said David.

They attempted to lift him but instantly came to the conclusion that it was not going to be easy. "Jesus, he's a big bugger isn't he corporal?"

"He certainly is Smithie. Look, let's stand him up, you take my rifle, and I'll try a fireman's lift." As he spoke, another barrage came over and all three huddled in the bottom of the shell hole the German had originally fallen into. When it eased up they dragged him up out of the hole, stood him up and David got him across his shoulders in the manner they had all been trained to adopt to carry a wounded comrade. By the time they got to the dug out, David's legs were decidedly wobbly. They carried him down to the cellar where they lit the Tilley lamp to see what they could do. Sergeant Harris had sent his platoon medical orderly down to help, but all he could do was to dress the wounds, give the man a drink and make him comfortable.

"Both wounds will require surgical attention but he'll be alright for now," said the orderly and went off to rejoin Sergeant Harris. A few minutes later the sergeant came back. "I'm off now David, good luck to you, see you soon I hope."

But they never did see each other again. Nor was the bridge to be a lifeline for the section. Ten minutes after Sergeant Harris and his men crossed it to take up their new positions, one of the bigger shells hit it

51

and blew it to bits. David and his men were now isolated from the Company.

It was well past midnight, no one slept, they were on permanent stand-to. The piece of wood started clonking on the wall again. A couple of minutes later he saw two figures approaching, one of them Barclay softly calling "Hold your fire." When they got closer, David could see that the one in front with his hands in the air, in one of which he held a briefcase, was dressed in civilian clothes. "I found him wandering along the road Corporal." said Barclay. "He says he's French."

"Right, leave him to me. Otherwise everything quiet down there?"

"You're joking. We've had two bloody mortar bombs almost down our rifle barrels," said Barclay, turning away and hurrying back in the curious hunched up position all soldiers seem to adopt when they are likely to come under fire.

In his reasonable school French, David said, "Please come down here," and took him down into the platoon HQ dugout that Sergeant Harris had evacuated. "Let me see your papers."

The Frenchman was slimly built, of medium height, very dirty and needing a shave. He had short grey hair and looked about fifty or perhaps a little more. He sunk on to a bench and said in excellent English, "I'm exhausted; I've been walking and dodging the Boche for three days. My name is General Strich, I am, or was, Deputy Chief of Intelligence in the staff of General Gamelin. I have in this briefcase vital information for the allies regarding dispositions of French forces both in France, as we know them and in the colonies worldwide. It is most essential we get this information back to your army headquarters." He sank back against the sandbags and appeared to go to sleep. David shook him.

"Can I have your identification?" he said. "We have had so many fifth columnists here in Calais."

The general reached inside his coat, David instantly watchful, and produced a small wallet in which was an identity card which he extended to David.

"And your identity discs," David said.

The general again rummaged inside his shirt and pulled out the discs carried on a thin gold chain round his neck. This amused David, "we have to use string," he said.

"Not when you become a general," said Strich, grinning back at him.

"Well Sir," said David, "I'm a afraid I've bad news for you. We have just learnt that we are to stay here and fight to the last man. Our communications with our company have been cut off as the bridge over the canal has been blown up only a short while ago, and we cannot go back into town as the Germans have already pushed our two companies behind us back, and have cut us off."

A further salvo of shells and an increasing number of mortar bombs started to rain in on them. Piercey fell into the dug out. "I've stopped something in the back Corporal," he said.

David took his clasp knife and cut the battledress blouse away. "It's nasty but you'll live," he said, taking Piercey's field dressing from him and tying it on as best he could, "stay in here for now and I'll try and do more later."

The general seemed to have dozed off again, so David found a blanket and covered him with it, and went up to the emplacement to make sure there were no more casualties. When he reached the opening looking out on to the slit trenches, he saw something white on the sandbags and discovered that Sergeant Harris had left his map behind. He grinned to himself saying, "I suppose he thought he wouldn't be needing that any more," and then realised that wasn't so funny after all.

The shelling stopped just before dawn. David had had his handful of men extending their slit trenches so that they were in a position to fire across the canal in to the flanks of any attackers, which might assault the main body of the company. Sure enough, as dawn broke, heavy mortaring was received all along A Company's line including smoke concentrated on the right hand side, which, with a westerly wind blowing, soon enveloped the whole company position. David could see the same thing happening half a mile to his rear where B and C Companies would soon be battling it out. Under the cover of the smoke from their vantage point on the flank, David's little group could see the German infantry moving in, supported by a troop of light tanks firing their machine guns into the smoke. When the smoke cleared a little David heard the sharp crack of the two pounder open up on the nearest tank. The anti-tank gun had only an open sight system but at a little over two hundred yards the gun layer would be very cross if he missed. He didn't. He hit the tank about two thirds down its side with an armour piercing shell which must have penetrated the engine since immediately flames shot out from the rear, as the crew bailed out. The second tank halted behind a garden wall out of sight of the two pounder except for a few inches of turret the gun crew could see above the wall. Carefully, the layer took his aim and the next shot went straight through the wall, into the tank, but whatever damage it caused, it did not disable it. It rumbled forward again, swerving away and showing its rear to the gunners and with their third shot, they hit it at its softest point and then that one too went up in smoke.

In the meantime, the German infantry in groups started making short runs then dropping to cover another group as they made their run. The smoke was beginning to clear for the final assault, and as they rose, David gave the order for his Bren gun and his five riflemen to fire. "Fire rapid, but pick your target" he yelled, which they did, to very good effect, enfilading the attackers. The confusion caused by being hit from the flank as well as the heavy and accurate fire from the main body of A Company made them halt, drop to the ground and find any cover they could until more smoke was put down and they were able to retreat, leaving two tanks and a substantial number of dead and wounded behind.

A second attack was mounted in the late afternoon, which followed a similar pattern, except that the three tanks used this time, stayed further back. Again it was repulsed. During the early evening, stretcher bearers with Red Cross armbands appeared and proceeded hesitantly to come forward to pick up the wounded. This Major Grant allowed them to do but yelling "No weapons" in appalling German, but receiving a wave of understanding from the officer in charge. A Company's strength was now down from around 130 to about fifty odd. Another assault like that and they would be finished. Ammunition was low, having started off with only just over a half of their normal quota, not as much had been salvaged from their trucks that went back on the boat as had been hoped for, and the anti tank gun was down to six rounds.

In David's section, they had an average of ten rounds each and none left on the Bren gun. David, therefore, put all the rifle ammunition into the Bren magazines and issued the German rifles and ammunition to the others.

"What do we do when this lot goes Corporal?" said Beasley.

"We run," said David with a wry grin.

"Yeah, but where the 'ell to?" asked Barclay. They all laughed but not exactly hilariously.

They had another sleepless night. David kept wondering why the

Germans didn't come up the minor road they were supposed to be defending. You would have thought they would have sent a reconnaissance unit up it if nothing more, he said to himself. What he didn't know was that where this road went over the canal, the RAF earlier in the week had conveniently dropped a bomb. As a result, nothing could get over it for the time being.

Shelling and mortaring went on all night. David could hear rifle fire almost at the docks now so the Germans had obviously penetrated the defences even more during the day. The section had had little sleep and very little to eat now except what they had been able to scrounge from the adjacent houses, some biscuits and bottled fruit, but that was running out. Strangely enough, the water was still coming out of the tap, although David had made each man fill his water bottle and under no circumstances to use it without permission, since the supply could finish at any minute.

At dawn the expected attack came in again. This time the plan was different. There was a heavy frontal fire by tanks and light machine guns and the attack proper came in from the left flank. It nearly succeeded until a unit of French troops over on A Company's left saw what was happening and fixed bayonets and charged. It was magnificent. The Germans turned to meet this new threat and the Rifles concentrated on the units giving frontal covering fire. The Rifles were all highly trained marksmen who made every shot count, as a result the German covering fire became less and less effective, the machine gunners who have to expose themselves to fire their weapons were picked off and the remainder were pinned down until the merciful smoke appeared again and they could retreat.

The Rifles did not get off lightly. They lost another ten men and their ammunition was virtually exhausted. "It's time we got back to Battalion HQ," said Major Grant, so over the next hour they filtered back in twos and threes towards the Post Office. From David's Bren position he could see the two pounder and now as he watched he saw a fifteen hundred weight truck back up to it, hitch it up and tow it away. He knew then they were on their own, with little or no ammunition, little food, and nowhere to run to, and he was the man who had to make the next decision.

By nine o'clock and with the sun well up, the shelling and mortaring had eased up mainly, David reasoned, because the Germans no longer knew where the front line was. As he stood peering out of the Bren gun position, his hand rested on the map Sergeant Harris had left behind. He studied it carefully. If we could get to the coast we might find a boat and row or sail back he thought, and then as a second thought 'that's not as daft as it sounds.' It was obvious he could neither go back into Calais because his retreat was cut off; neither could he move towards Dunkirk because the other main German attack from St Omer and Ardres was taking place on that side of the town, even if he was able to get over the canal. He saw, marked on the map, a small town on the coast between Calais and Boulogne called Wissant. There would bound to have been boats in a place like that and as it was not on the main N.I. from Boulgone to Calais, it seemed logical it would not be saturated with German troops as yet, since they would be concentrating on Calais.

Studying the map further, it became apparent that for the plan to succeed, he would first have to head inland and then go cross-country by night, hiding up in the daytime. When they reached Wissant, they would have to search for a boat or alternatively risk approaching a Frenchman to find one for them. He studied the map more closely. He saw that if he followed the minor road they were on due south for about three kilometres, an unmade road or farm track went off to the west and eventually met up with another farm track which turned north west under the N.I. main road at a point where a small river went under the road, and then on to Wissant. He estimated the total distance to be about thirty five kilometres, say 22 miles, a mere stroll for a rifleman he said to himself. The first big problem would be getting to the farm track. They had to follow the road and the canal along the left hand side for most of the way and there was impassable marshland on the right. He woke the general. "Sir," he said, "we're moving out in a little while, how are you feeling?"

"Not well at all," replied the general, "my left foot and leg are on fire."

David lifted the general's leg up, he grunted with pain. David unlaced the boot but it was some while before he could ease it off and when he had done so, the general laid back sweating with the agony he had suffered. It was immediately obvious why he was in such pain. His foot had been turned into one big blister on the edges of which were clear signs of infection setting in. "I shall never be able to walk Corporal," said the general, "so I want you to listen very carefully. I am not only a very senior intelligence officer, I am also a Jew. If the Gestapo get hold of me I cannot expect anything but a very slow death.

I therefore order you when you leave to take this briefcase and get it to the allies if you can or destroy it. I also order you to shoot me before you go."

"You are a very brave man Sir," said David.

"Not really," said the general, "I know what the Gestapo do to their own people so I have a very, very clear idea of what they would do to me."

David turned away and looked out between the sandbags. "Smithy," he called. Smith 24 looked up out of his slit trench. "Tell the others to come in here and tell the forward picquet to crawl back in."

In a few minutes they had all arrived. David addressed them. "We've got the choice of waiting here and being taken prisoner or worse, or we can try to escape. I have a plan to put to you. I will dress in the uniform of the wounded prisoner we have here and will march you down the road out of town. The general cannot walk so we will carry him on the platoon stretcher, which Sergeant Harris left behind. We shall have to get him into one of our dead man's uniforms, and bind his head up otherwise his grey hair may make any passing Germans suspicious." (The general gave a wry grin at this last remark).

He continued,

"We have to carry on down this road for a little over three kilometres and then hide up till dark when we will make a big sweep across country, under the main road from Boulogne to Calais which will be thick with Germans, and then to the coast at a place called Wissant. There we will find a boat and row back to England."

"How the hell can you row all the way to England?" asked Piercey.

"If other people can swim from Calais to England, I'm damned sure the Rifles can row there," said David. There was a pause, "Well, are you with me?" he said.

"Too bloody true," said Kenny Barclay and the others all agreed.

"Right then, you two get a uniform for the general – I'm sorry you'll be wearing a dead man's clothes – you two get the clothes off the prisoner. I hope he isn't lousy."

In under an hour they were ready to move off. David's uniform fitted where it touched but with the belt tightened up, it looked passable. He had difficulty in getting the boots on and guessed his feet would be in trouble before he had gone many miles. He commanded five men; Piercey, Barclay and Beasley the sole survivors of his original section of ten men, Smith 24 from Platoon HQ and a rifleman called Riley, the only survivor from Jeremy's old section who Sergeant Harris had left with him. The general was well swathed with bandages around his head and left foot, his left trouser leg having been cut off at calf level to make it look even more obvious that he was 'wounded.' They put his raincoat under his head for a pillow and covered it with a sandbag. They then moved off past the dead Germans on their left who had been in the first attack on their position, past the burnt out tank, with Rifleman Piercey giving a professional, quite unemotional look at the dead driver in the middle of the road and on down the little slope which would lead them into the country.

"The corporal blew that sod up," said Barclay proudly to the general as they passed the tank. The general turned his head to see the wreckage, "climbed up it while it was blasting us and dropped a grenade in it. That soon put a stop to their larks."

"That was a very brave thing to do," said the general.

They marched on. David at the rear, playing the part of the German guard, having told the men not to turn and talk to him in case they were being watched through sights or binoculars. They had been moving for about twenty minutes when Piercey, at the front, called out without turning round, "Hey up corporal, there's a vehicle coming."

David felt his stomach turn over. "Keep walking unless I tell you to stop," he said. As the scout car approached it slowed down, and a genial young man leaned out of the top. David gave the order to halt, which the men did and stood still looking down at the road.

"Where are you going," shouted the young N.C.O. over the noise of the engine.

"I'm taking this lot to the football stadium about two kilometres from here. They're getting up a prisoner collection centre there," David shouted back.

"I didn't see any football stadium."

"It lies back behind some trees by a white cottage they told me."

"I must have missed it. I don't know your accent. Where are you from?"

"Just outside Ulm. That's in the south of Germany."

"Ulm in the south? It's nearly off the bloody map," laughed the N.C.O. banging on the scout car for it to move. David shook his fist at him in a friendly fashion and started bellowing in German at the "prisoners" which they took to mean 'move off.'

"Christ corporal, you're a bleeding genius," said Barclay, and as an afterthought, "he seemed a decent sort of bloke didn't he?"

A few minutes later a half-truck loaded with infantry approached and sped past without stopping. David knew they were now getting close to where they were to lie up until their move across country. He was getting increasingly worried since there appeared to be not enough cover anywhere for a rabbit to hide, let alone seven men. If the worst came to the worst they would have to keep marching until they came to a house they could commandeer. He knew that every minute he spent on that road lessened their chances of getting away, on the other hand if they left the road and were spotted, as they surely would be, all would be up.

They came to a bend in the road and David immediately saw the track they were to follow that night about three hundred yards ahead. What he also spotted made his spirits jump. The track ran underneath the road through a culvert built to allow the cattle in the fields on one side to use fields on the other side of the road without having to be driven over the open road.

"There's the track," he said "we'll lie up in the culvert under the road until its dark."

As they approached the culvert David thought, "It will be just my luck for someone to come along just as we dive off the road," but although they could clearly hear heavy movement on the road some half a mile or more away running parallel to them, nothing approached them, and swiftly they were off the road, down the bank, in the course of which the general nearly slid off the stretcher, and into the culvert. The culvert was not quite as welcoming as they had hoped. It was just wide enough and high enough to take a cow, and therefore of a reasonable size in which to hide, and although no animals had been through it for the last few days, the marks of their passage when it had previously been used were still there in abundance. It would appear that the cows, having eaten of the grass in one field, had decided to move to the other one and had left their trademark in the tunnel on the way. Kenny Barclay's comment was illustrative of the general opinion, "Christ, what a pong." Pong or not, they had to put up with it, even sit in it, for the next eight hours or so. David organised a lookout at each end, and told the others to sleep if they could, but what with the pong, the discomfort, the particularly vicious dung flies that were around in their thousands and the occasional clatter of a vehicle overhead, nobody enjoyed more than a catnap. As they sat and waited for darkness, David wondered what the family were doing on this Sunday evening, in particular, whether poor Rose had heard about Jeremy yet, and in thinking about Jeremy his eyes filled with tears. He looked up and saw the general looking at him. "Lose a friend?" he said speaking in French.

"Yes, my best friend, he was married to my sister only two months ago. I don't know whether my family have been informed yet." He was gradually becoming more in control with the effort of finding the French words.

"I know what it's like. I lost so many friends in the last war, each of my three sisters was widowed, and now this evil man has started it all over again."

They sat in silence as it gradually darkened. "Right, let's move," said David, "keep close in behind me and if I freeze, you freeze, you know your training. Stand absolutely still if you see me stop. Oh, and don't for God's sake lose the general off the stretcher this time if we have to go down any banks." There was a little titter of amusement at this final sally, and they moved off along the track, keeping their fingers crossed that there was no one on the road to see them make their move.

Chapter Five

It was as David was talking to the general about Jeremy that Rose was lying under the eiderdown at Chandlers Lodge. She was gradually becoming more composed, although her face was white and strained and stained with the tears, which had flowed so freely. Her mother sat and held her hand doing her best to comfort her.

"I shall be like Karl and Anni, shan't I?" she said quietly.

"What do you mean dear?" said her mother.

"They have no grave to visit" (Anni's mother had died in Dachau). "Neither have I."

"You will, like us, always remember Jeremy in your heart," Ruth told her, "that will be his memorial."

There was a tap on the door. It was Moira.

"May I come in?" she said.

"Of course," Rose replied.

She approached the bed and bent over and kissed Rose on the forehead. "I'm so sorry my dearest," she said.

"You've suffered like this, haven't you Auntie Moria?" said Rose. Moira's first husband was killed in the Great War only days after they were married.

"Yes my darling, I know what you are going through. I thought those evil days were over."

"Can you and Megan stay for a while?" Ruth said, "I must go and speak to Rita."

She went downstairs and Fred booked the call for her. She was dreading this conversation, she had no idea of what she wanted to say, she was dreadfully afraid Rita would be so prostrate with grief she would find it impossible to console her in any way. When the connection was made she said, "Oh Rita, I am so very, very sorry."

Rita replied in a firm, sober voice, "Ruth, I shall carry this great sadness all my days, but now we've got to make sure that Rose and the baby receive all the love and support we can give. I want you to tell her that I am heartbroken as any mother would be, but for Jeremy's sake she must take this bitter blow with the same courage we know he faced his ordeal. We must not let him down, we must fight our sorrow as he did his enemy, and we must win." She paused.

"I think that is the bravest thing I've ever heard," said Ruth, "I shall go and see Rose immediately. Can you and Buffy come up tomorrow or Tuesday and stay a few days? We would be so pleased to have you." She heard Rita talking to Buffy in the background and waited.

"Yes, thank you dear Ruth. We will come up from Romsey tomorrow and go back on Wednesday evening if that is alright?"

"We'll see you tomorrow then. God bless you both," said Ruth.

She went back to the kitchen and told Fred and Jim how brave Rita was being, Alec having gone back to the camp for a short while. She then went up to Rose and told her almost word for word what Rita had said. It seemed to give Rose an inner strength; she regained some of her colour and sat up a little.

"I think I'll come down and hear the nine o'clock news," she said.

"You're sure you feel up to it?" asked Megan. "Slip a dressing gown on so that you don't get a chill, it's cooled down rapidly this evening after such a mild day."

There was nothing specific on the news other than the usual 'flannel' as Jack called it of British and French inflicting heavy losses on the advancing Germans. Arras and Amiens had fallen, and an orderly evacuation of Boulogne had taken place.

"God, what a mess," said Jack.

When Alec reached his battalion, and having made his rounds as Duty Field Officer, he decided to have a quick noggin in the mess before going back to Chandlers Lodge. Apart from a couple of subalterns playing billiards the place appeared deserted. "Everybody out Monty?" asked Alec of the barman.

"The colonel's in the reading room Sir," said Monty.

Alec took his Canadian Club and water and went into the reading room. "Sir," he said "we've had some bad news; Jeremy has been killed in France."

"Oh my God no," said the colonel, "that poor girl, how is she? Bloody silly question to ask of course. What happened, do you know any details?"

"No Sir, just the usual telegram. Rose, and for that matter, the whole family, are completely shattered."

"If I write a note will you take it for me Alec, you know how much I liked them both."

"Of course colonel."

Colonel Tim was rather understating the case in that sentence. He was a thirty-five year old bachelor, a career soldier, and the youngest in his rank in the Canadian Forces in the UK. When he first had met Rose it really was, on his part, love at first sight, something that had never happened to him before, but not by word or deed, despite the fact that he had been in Rose's company on many occasions, did he ever let a glimmer of his feelings be known either to Rose or anyone else for that matter. He sat down and wrote:-

'My dear Rose,
    Alec has just told me the dreadful news and I am so sad for you. I realise there is little any of us can do for you at a time like this, but if the thoughts and prayers of sincere friends can help then you can be assured that I and my officers here trust that theirs will be of some comfort to you.

I shall treasure the memory of knowing Jeremy as a fine young man and a born soldier.

Yours ever
Tim McEwan'

He read it over, sealed it, and gave it to Alec.
"Thanks Alec. I wonder how much more of this we're going to see before it all ends?"

The next day Rita and Buffy arrived. It was a sad, sombre meeting compared to all the great happy days they had all enjoyed together at Chandlers Lodge in the past. Buffy looked as though he had aged ten years overnight but Rita lived up to the brave words she had said to Ruth over the telephone the previous evening. She was particularly strong with Rose and insisted on taking her for a walk in the woods in the afternoon. "You have got to keep fit young lady," she told her and there was a wisp of an answering smile around Rose's lips, realising as she did, why Rita was being uncharacteristically bossy with her.

Fred had come home from the factory as soon as they had arrived, leaving the running of it in Ernie Bolton's capable hands. Whilst Rita and Rose were out, Buffy said, "Do you know where they were and have you heard anything from David?"

"The answer to that is no on both counts," said Fred, "but if it's all one glorious retreat inflicting heavy losses on the enemy as they shorten the line and take up new positions, as the propaganda tells us, they probably don't even know where they are themselves. You know what it was like on the Mons do in 1914; we didn't know where we were half the time." Buffy had been Fred's company commander in the Hampshires at the beginning of the Great War so that both knew a little about being in action. Little did they realise that the position the Rifles were in didn't allow for any retreat – there was nowhere to go!

That evening everyone went off to bed early, Rita sitting with Rose for a while until she became sleepy. Ruth was clearing up in the kitchen when Alec came in. Alec was twenty six and a bachelor, and it had been a standing joke that when he first was billeted with Mrs Chandler, he found himself introduced as he put it, to the four most beautiful girls in Sandbury; Rose, Pat, Anni and Megan only to find that Pat was married to David, Megan was married to Harry, Rose was spoken for and Anni was married to Ernie. He felt he had been dealt with in a most unkindly manner by the fates. Then he had met Ernie's sister Rebecca, a strikingly good-looking young lady a couple of years younger than he, and could hardly believe his good fortune. They had seen a lot of each other in the past few months and were obviously very much in love.

"Would you like some cocoa Alec?"

"Oh yes please." Alec sat at the big deal table strangely quiet for him even considering the sad circumstances prevailing in the house.

"Something on your mind Alec?" said Ruth. Her two guests were now family to her. They were quite different. Jim was a serious type of chap, married with children, whereas Alec was the extrovert of the two. "I think that's why they get on so well, they're so unalike," Ruth had said to Fred after they had first got to know them.

Alec looked up before answering her question. "Can I tell you about it?" he said.

"Of course Alec, it'll go no further," said Ruth, although her mind was racing as to what the problem might be, fortunately in the wrong direction.

"I was going to ask Rebecca to marry me," said Alec.

"Well, what's stopping you? You'll make a lovely couple."

"Oh I think we're well suited – I know darned well I am. But now this has happened to Jeremy, and Rose is left to suffer. Supposing it happens to me, how could I be responsible for inflicting the same thing on Rebecca?"

Ruth paused for a while.

"I think the way you've got to look at it is firstly it may never happen. Secondly, if it did and you weren't married would Rebecca suffer any less grief than if you were married? And thirdly, if it did happen and you were married, you would have had a great happiness together that you would not otherwise have enjoyed, which would be something she would look back on with gratitude first, and this is very difficult to say for me when all is so fresh upon us, just as Rose will in the years to come and she watches her baby growing up."

He paused again.

"I don't know what Jim and I have done to be blessed with living here these past months with such lovely people," he said.

"It's been a two-way thing. You've brought us all a fresh outlook on life. Anyway you're family now and always will be." Alec wasn't the crying type but with the emotion of everything that had gone on in the last twenty-four hours he was closer to it than he had been since he was a kid.

"I'll ask her," he said, and then with a flash of his old self, "after all, she can always say no!"

"Somehow or other I don't think she will," said Ruth with the first smile she had been able to find since the arrival of that dreadful telegram.

The next day, Tuesday, Pat telephoned her father from the shop. Normally Jack would have been going to his business in the City on a Tuesday, but he had decided to stay in Sandbury to help look after Rita and Buffy. As he had said many times, "I don't know why I go to the office, they can all do perfectly well without me," which was partially true, but at the moment because he was a specialist commodity broker, he spent half his time advising the Ministry of Supply at a very high level.

"Daddy," said Pat, "I don't want to raise mundane matters at a time like this but I need to talk to you both about my meeting with Mr Lewis at the Angel yesterday. I had to keep the appointment because I couldn't get hold of him during the morning to cancel it."

"There's no reason why you should have dear, so don't fret your pretty head about that. It is one of the sad things at a time like this, as you put it, that life has to go on. Anyhow, if I pick Fred up and meet you at the Angel again for lunch, can you manage to get away again?"

"Yes, we're not busy today and Mrs Draper can cover for me," and then, as an afterthought, "at least John Tarrant's eyebrows won't disappear into his hairline today as they nearly did again yesterday."

They met, as arranged, and were joined by Reg Church, the accountant. "Well, what happened, don't keep us in suspense," said Jack.

"I got it for four thousand three hundred, subject to his principal's final approval. About which there would be no doubt according to him, and subject to survey."

"Well done," said Fred, "very well done indeed."

"That's a hundred quid you owe me," she said with a smile. They all smiled, but inside them, both Jack and Fred had a feeling of guilt

65

that they should be carrying on normally with life in the presence of the tragedy that had hit them and was hitting thousands of others of their countrymen and allies at this moment.

"Can we leave all the details to you now then Reg?" said Jack looking at Fred for his agreement, given with a barely perceptible nod of the head. It was amazing that these two men, Jack, an upper middle class, extremely wealthy business man, and Fred an ex-regular soldier, turned farm worker, turned factory owner, were from such opposite sides of the fence, yet had the rapport almost of twins. It was the Chandlers who had shown Jack what true family life was about when David and then his family had befriended Pat when they were youngsters, following on with treating Jack as one of their family, at a time when his wife had deserted him to bring up Pat on his own. Knowing the Chandlers, he had told Moira after they were married, had kept him sane at a time when, if it hadn't been for having to take care of Pat, he had seriously thought of doing away with himself.

Having had their lunch, and afterwards having convinced John Tarrant that Pat had not found a fancy man, Jack and Fred went back to Chandlers Lodge to find Rose and Buffy alone. "Mummy and mother" (that's how she distinguished them in conversation) "have gone over to Sevenoaks on the train," said Rose, "mother has an elderly friend there who has been very poorly so she has taken the opportunity of going to see her." The four chatted on. Rose was much more composed than she had been. At four o'clock she said she thought she'd go and have a rest for an hour until the two mothers got back, which should be at five o'clock or shortly afterwards. However, they didn't return at five o'clock, nor at five thirty and at six o'clock Fred and Buffy were beginning to get concerned.

At six thirty Fred said, "I'm going to phone the station to see if anything's happening to the trains."

"Well they can't be on strike," said Buffy. "Ernie Bevin has stopped all that lark for the duration of the war."

"Yes and good for him too," said Fred, "although it is a bit ironic that a top trade union official should be the one who bans strikes. A very good example of poacher turning gamekeeper if you ask me."

As they spoke a taxi crunched up the drive and stopped at the door. Fred and Buffy hurried to meet them and while Fred was paying the cab off, Buffy was saying, "We were getting concerned – what happened?" They went into the house and Rita said, "They wouldn't allow us onto the station for over an hour at Sevenoaks when we were coming back."

"Why on earth not?" said Buffy.

"There was an ambulance train being unloaded, and all the wounded were being transferred to vehicles and being taken away," Rita replied. They were both clearly upset. Ruth turned to Fred, her eyes brimming with tears."

"They kept us waiting on the road bridge. From there, as you know, you look straight down on to the platforms through the latticework on the side of the bridge. They carried the wounded out on stretchers, dozens and dozens of them, and one man was brought out immediately beneath us, and he opened his eyes and looked up at us and he smiled. We waved to him, and he then waved back, but when he pulled his arms from under the blanket he had no hands – he was waving his stumps – and he was smiling – oh Fred, he was smiling." Both she and Rita dissolved into tears, as they were held by their respective husbands, who were incapable of knowing what to say or do. When they had regained their composure a little, Ruth said, "I'm sorry to have upset you all like that – but I shall never forget that poor brave man."

"And he'll probably never forget you two either my dear," said Buffy.

When Rita and Buffy went back, all being together had somehow welded their separate sorrows to make it more endurable to each individual. Buffy said when he left that when the circumstances of Jeremy's death had become known, in say a month or so, they would hold a memorial service in their local church if Rose would permit it. It was the church in which Jeremy had been christened and confirmed. Rose said yes immediately, and as Fred said to Ruth, whilst the service would be sad for Rose, it would be, without her perhaps realising it, the end of one tragic part of her life and the beginning of a new part for her and her baby. "She has still got a whole lot of living to do," Buffy said.

Chapter Six

When Harry reached the C.C.S. on the morning of the 25th, having had one of his three lorries destroyed by shell fire, the major in charge who had been so helpful in ejecting the captain out of his cab the previous day, called him into his tent and told him that the whole unit was moving back on to the dunes at Dunkirk and that a general evacuation was starting that day off the Mole and the beaches. He asked Harry where his unit headquarters were, to which Harry replied he had no idea, they had been at Bergues but he went there on the way through today and found some abandoned lorries and plenty of spare petrol lying around, so he'd filled up, put some cans on the lorries and left the place deserted.

"They've probably gone to the beaches to be taken off," said the major, "perhaps you'd better follow them."

"As far as I'm concerned there's still plenty to do here," said Harry. "If you're moving back I'll take the lorries as far forward as I can and bring you in the wounded stragglers. That should keep my two drivers out of mischief for a while. When will you be set up again Sir?"

"By mid afternoon I should think. We're travelling light and leaving a lot of stuff here we shan't need."

"I'll see you later then Sir," said Harry, who then saluted and went out to the two drivers.

"Looks as though we're going to be fighting a private war from now on," said Harry, going in to explain the situation. He detailed one driver to stay at the C.C.S. to take the wounded already there and to go back to Dunkirk with their vehicles and wait for him. "We'll wander forward on the Armentieres road and pick up whoever we can," he told his other driver.

Thus began four days of journeys to and from Dunkirk enduring continuous shelling, bombing and strafing as they moved forward as far as they could, their Red Cross flags flying. Harry had the unenviable task of having to select the wounded or exhausted from the other troops retreating to the beaches, those who in a snap judgement, in his opinion, would not otherwise make it on their own. There were Belgians and French mixed in with our own BEF troops, and as soon as he had both trucks full he was back to the C.C.S. set up in the dunes, itself being dive-bombed continuously. It was an amazing sight at the beaches. There were small boats coming in to the heads of orderly queues being marshalled by the Military Police, which were snaking across the dunes and stretching for a hundred yards or more into the shallow water. As the little boats, pleasure craft, fishing boats, anything that would float, picked up as many as they could get aboard, they ferried them out to the bigger craft, ferry boats, destroyers, merchant ships of all kinds where the men were packed in and taken back to the Channel ports. Mona's Isle, an Isle of Man steam ferry was one of the first to be sunk, but it was not the last by far. Altogether some eight hundred small craft took part in this miracle, for although it was the culmination of one of the biggest defeats in British Army history, Dunkirk was still a miracle. From that eight hundred, over one hundred were sunk. It was a story of unparalleled courage in the majority of cases by young weekend sailors, and a lot not so young, suddenly pitch-forked into taking part in an action, which, like the retreat to Corunna, will remain in the history books for all time.

On the 27th, Harry suffered another set back when his second truck hit a deep pothole causing the near side front wheel to literally collapse, and severely shaking up the injured men in the back in the process. They had just passed through Wormhout, about ten miles from the beaches, and there was little chance that any of the passengers could make that ten miles under their own steam. In addition, the lorry was blocking the road, so Harry got another passing ambulance to drag it to the edge of the road, which was on an embankment, and with fifty or so soldiers making their way to Dunkirk, they toppled it over and down into the ditch. "I'll be back for you in a couple of hours," he said to the stranded men, and to the driver, "you might as well join one of the queues on the beach – I'll see you back in England one day."

As Harry was returning to collect the men he had left behind, he could not know that one of the most bestial acts of barbarism was being carried out at that moment at a place called Le Paradis only a few miles away. A company of the Royal Norfolk Regiment commanded by major Lisle Ryder found itself surrounded in farm buildings by the S.S. 3rd Infantry Regiment. With ammunition exhausted, Major Ryder surrendered his eighty men to the S.S. commander who shepherded them into one of the buildings and turned machine guns on them until they had all been murdered. All but two that is. Two, although wounded, miraculously survived to tell the story. It was an isolated incident. In the main the Germans acted like true soldiers, but this would not be the last time the name of the S.S. would carry the stench of filth in the nostrils of all civilised people.

On the 29th of May, Harry delivered what was to be his last lorry load to the major at the C.C.S. Although his Red Cross flags were still flying, the truck resembled a colander, it had so many holes in it from shrapnel and the continual strafing, yet in those four days he had collected over 600 wounded or exhausted men who probably would not have otherwise reached the beaches. By some miracle not more than half a dozen of his passengers had been further wounded in running the gauntlet, but on the morning of the 29th, his driver was wounded in the shelling, and he too had to join the long, long lines of men patiently queuing. The C.C.S. major button-holed him when he took the driver in. "Sergeant Chandler, you've done more than your fair share, why don't you get in a queue?"

Behind his grime and stubble Harry grinned. "When are you going Sir?" he asked.

"When I'm no longer needed or can't do anything more," said the major.

"I'll come with you when that time comes," said Harry, saluted and turned away.

He drove his truck back to Bergues to fill up from his hidden supply of petrol, and while he was in the process of funnelling one of the four-gallon cans into his petrol tank, a cheery voice behind him said

"Where is everybody sergeant?"

Harry swung round, put the can down and saluted the fresh faced young Royal Engineers captain who, smilingly, returned his salute.

"They moved out several days ago Sir, I've been on detachment collecting wounded and bringing them in for about a week now."

"Well, will you take your flags down and give me a hand for a couple of days, it's very important?" said the captain. "I'm Captain Osbourne."

"What have we got to do Sir?" Harry asked.

"I've got a broken down truck full of gelignite, I had a driver who got himself wounded and I've got two bridges to blow, over on the road to Poperinghe. They're both minor roads but Jerry could sneak up behind us on them while we are holding the main roads from Lille and Ypres."

Harry knew these roads by now like the back of his hand.

"Where's your truck Sir?"

"It's about a mile down the road to Wormhout," said the captain.

"Right, I'll finish filling this up and I'll be with you," said Harry and having done so and having also removed his Red Cross flags and put them in the back of the lorry, they climbed into the cab and drove off. When they reached the RE truck, Harry at once detailed half a dozen passing soldiers to help transfer the explosive and detonators on to the back of his three tonner. They weren't exactly enthusiastic about the job but Harry was standing no nonsense. He realised, of course, these men were demoralised, the idea of moving explosive around when they were getting close to what they hoped would be a passage to safety, wasn't exactly appealing, but by a combination of firmness and his irrepressible humour, they soon had the job done.

The journey to the first bridge was dreadfully slow, with the road crowded with troops having to constantly throw themselves into the ditches at the sides as fighter planes flew over strafing them. With more and more shell holes having appeared since the last time Harry had been along this section only two days before, and above all with the knowledge that if a stray shell hit the load on the back of the three tonner, they'd pick Harry and the captain up from all over the Belgian-French border in little pieces, made it a trip Harry would not like to repeat too often. The captain however was jolly good company and like most sappers, a down to earth, practical man. When they reached the minor road where the first bridge was to be blown, they passed a group of farm buildings.

"Let's park the vehicle under those trees and sleep in the farmhouse tonight," said the captain, "my orders are to blow the first bridge anytime after first light tomorrow, and the second one as soon after midday as possible."

Harry pulled over and they got down from the cab, locked it, and made their way to the main farmhouse. All the buildings had suffered from the shelling but were still in reasonable condition. Having found the front door was locked; they made their way around the back, and found to their surprise the back door was unlocked. They really shouldn't have been surprised, the front door of a dwelling such as this was only used for weddings and funerals, everybody used the back door for all other occasions. They walked into the kitchen and Harry called, "Anybody there?" There was no reply but Harry then noted the black lead kitchen range had the remains of a fire in it. He pointed to it and said, "Someone's been here, Sir."

"Could have been passing squaddies," said the captain, but at that, a door creaked from the stairway, and from what was obviously a cellar, emerged a middle-aged lady dressed all in black. Harry immediately removed his cap and the captain saluted.

"Good evening Madame," he said in passable French, "we were hoping to be able to spend the night here."

"You are very welcome," said the lady, she called down the stairs and two young women in their early twenties appeared, probably her daughters Harry thought.

"If you have any hot water we would very much like to wash and shave," said the captain, neither of them had been able to do either for the past three days.

"The girls will get you the water and I will heat some soup for you and get you something to eat," said the lady. "I am Madame Duchesne and these are my daughters Veronique and Jeanne." They both bobbed little curtsies. "My husband died a year ago, we run this small farm on our own now, the man we employed has had to join the army."

The girls bustled into the scullery and filled a large two handled cauldron, which they put on the range, this, in the meantime having been liberally stoked up with what smelt to Harry like the wood from an apple tree. Apple tree wood has a distinctive sweet smell when it is burnt, it reminded Harry of his days at Home Farm when he was a boy and when, from time to time, they burnt some of the branches from the orchard around the house.

When they had strip washed, shaved and put their clothes back on, they went back into the kitchen where the table was already laid, and at which their seats were indicated by the two girls. There was a large tureen of soup at Madame's place and a pile of large plates beside her and when they were all seated she bowed her head and said a grace, which included a prayer for the safety of their two welcome guests. Harry's mouth started watering at the smell of the soup to the extent he would never have believed possible.

"This is the first hot food I've had in five days," he said to the captain. Madame looked at the captain for a translation. "The sergeant says this is the first hot food he has had in five days," he repeated.

"Then you must eat slowly and enjoy it," said Madame, with nods of agreement and smiles from the two girls.

They had their soup with fresh made bread, which Madame Duchesne followed with cold chicken and potato salad and some more bread with homemade cheese to end the meal.

"We have to start very early, before dawn tomorrow," said captain Osbourne, "so I think we should get some sleep now and say good bye so as not to wake you in the morning."

"We get up early to see to the cows," said Madame, "so we shall see you then."

"Thank you Madame for all your kindness," said the captain, taking Madame and the two girls in turn and kissing them on both cheeks.

Harry followed suit, thinking to himself, 'I've not had much practice at this lark' but doing well all the same.

They were shown to their room where there was one large double bed. "I will call you at four o'clock," said Madame and departed.

"Thank God for that," said the captain "once I sink into this bed I shall never wake up."

"Well I was just wondering about that Sir. If I get back to the unit and tell them I've slept with a captain, my mates will never speak to me again."

"I don't know what you've got to worry about. I've always understood that if you have to sleep with someone from the Service Corps you make sure you keep your trousers on."

They both sank into the mattress, and with the faint smell of lavender from their pillows they were asleep in seconds. There was heavy shelling in the night, landing about a mile away – they didn't hear a thing.

Madame woke them as promised. They dressed quickly and went downstairs where the girls had laid out two plates of sausage and some cheese and were filling huge basins of coffee. Harry put his arm round the mother and hugged her and said, "You're an angel," which, after being translated by the captain, brought blushes from Madame and laughter from the girls. Whilst they were eating Madame said to the captain, "When do you think the Boche will be here?"

"With the Belgian Army just surrendered, I don't think we can stop them," said the captain, "but we'll be back one day, that I promise."

The three women looked sad and bewildered, and as they finished their meal again Madame bowed her head in prayer for the safety of the two young men who had been with them for such a short while but who would always remain in their thoughts and their prayers.

Dawn had broken by the time they reached the first bridge. The captain showed Harry how to tie the correct number of sticks of gelignite into a bundle and on to which of the supports to fix each bundle. This work took about an hour during which a number of stragglers came along the road making their way to Dunkirk. At last the detonators were all in, the wires connected to the main wire which was then paid out to a ditch about fifty yards away and screwed on to the plunger terminals.

"I'm ready now," said the captain, "climb up on the bank and see if there are any more coming."

Harry climbed up, saw the road was empty, ran down the bank and along to the ditch and gave the captain the all clear.

"Keep your fingers crossed," he said, "and lie low until all the bits have come down."

He pressed the plunger and there was an instantaneous roar from the bridge. Harry was tempted to look up out of the scanty cover they had on the side of the ditch but when a piece of metal landed with a clonk and a shower of sparks, only a couple of yards away on the cobbles, he understood the reason for the captain's warning.

"Alright now I should think," said the captain with a grin, "bit of a bang, what?"

They made a quick inspection of what remained of the bridge. It had been neatly sliced into two sections now lying one partially on top of the other fifteen feet below in the river.

"They'll get no vehicles over that for a while," said Harry.

"The trouble is neither shall we – if we've got any left that is," said the captain thoughtfully, and continued, "Come on, let's find our way to Poperinghe."

They reached the second bridge at about midday having several times to partially fill in the road where shells had hit it before they could drive the lorry further. "The trouble is, this stuff," said the captain indicating the explosive in the back, "doesn't travel very well at the best of times and this batch is a bit weepy so we'd better not bump it about too much.

"This is a nice time to tell me," said Harry with a smile, but it was noticeable he dodged as many of the smaller potholes as he could from then on.

As they approached the second bridge they saw a lance corporal with a motorcycle standing at the side of the road.

"He's one of our unit," said the captain as they got nearer and when they came alongside the lance corporal came up to the cab, saluted, and asked, "Captain Osbourne Sir. I've been told to wait here until you arrive and give you this, then I can go to the beaches. All the

rest of the unit have gone." He handed the captain an envelope. The single sheet of message pad read: -
  DELAY ACTION PLANNED TODAY FOR TWENTY-FOUR HOURS.
  SIGNED T HARCOURT LIEUT-COLONEL
And then scribbled underneath,
"Then bugger off to Blighty – see you there – T.H."
"Right Corporal, you can go, good luck."
"Thank you Sir." The corporal saluted, got on his bike and roared away in the direction of Dunkirk. The captain handed the message over to Harry.
"We'd better go back a bit into that copse we passed and hide up," said Harry.

When they reached the copse, they reversed into it and Harry cut some branches down to put on the truck and to stand against it, particularly against the windscreen. The last thing they would want would be to attract the attention of some eagle eyed Luftwaffe pilot circling around for an easy kill. At three in the morning, they understood the reason for the postponement. They were wakened by the stomach churning, clanking noise of tanks moving along the cobbled road towards them. No one who has not experienced it can ever know the feeling a soldier on foot, in the open, or in the bottom of a slit trench has at the hideous threatening noise of tank tracks and the low geared, ever changing, roar of the engine exhaust of this brutal monster able to engulf him without even knowing he existed.

"They must be ours," said the captain. "Jerry wouldn't move in those numbers in the dark."

That they were 'ours' was quickly confirmed by the approach of a British sergeant on a motorcycle, which, as it slowly passed, was showing a dim white light on its rear mudguard by which the first tank was being guided. There were ten Matildas – medium tanks, followed up in the rear by two light French tanks, which had presumably tagged along. The two bridge blowers climbed out of the ditch in which they had been hiding and gave a wave to each of the tank commanders standing in their turrets as they rumbled past.

"They've only an hour or so to get hulled down before daylight," said the captain. "I wonder what their plan is?"

"I suppose they must be the rear guard," said Harry. "I don't fancy their chances if the Stukas find them when it gets light."

And find them they did. Harry and the captain were dozing in the cab when the first flight of Stukas roared over them, climbed and started their screaming descent one after the other. As they ran to the edge of the copse, they could see a second flight coming in and could hear the bombs bursting from the first flight. The tanks were no more than three or four miles away, a pillar of black smoke was already billowing into the sky from a stricken Matilda, when yet a third flight attacked. This time they didn't get it all their own way. From the north, flying at very low level, they saw a flight of fighters hurtling towards the Stukas. It was difficult to tell whether they were German or British until they saw one Stuka at the top of his dive literally blown out of the air by what they discovered to be a Hurricane. A second Hurricane hit a Stuka, which had delivered its bombs, and the two remaining Stukas broke off the engagement in an endeavour to escape. They were no match however for the much faster Hurricanes and as they flew east to find safety in some clouds, they were mercilessly picked off. The complete action had taken no longer than fifteen minutes.

"We do see life in our own quiet way Sir don't we?" said Harry as they made their way back to the truck to wait for midday to come.

But Harry was going to see a lot more life – and death – over the next four or five days than he could have thought possible.

Chapter Seven

When David made his move across country on the night of 26th May on the second stage of his escape plan, he wondered again whether Rose and the family had yet heard about Jeremy. In fact Rose had, that very evening, received the telegram and was lying shocked and heart broken in her room at Chandlers Lodge. He wondered too what Harry was doing, whether he was even alive, and at this said to himself, "Don't worry about Harry, if anyone can look after himself it's him." But he got little comfort from this thought.

The track they were on was quite clear and it was a light night so they made good progress without incident, hitting the junction where they were to turn right to go towards the main road. They stopped to give the lads carrying the general a breather.

"All right corporal?" whispered Rifleman Barclay.

"These bloody boots are killing me," replied David "now, no more talking."

Barclay said no more, but he reasoned that the corporal must be in some pain to talk like that. In an environment where a swear word was used in every phrase or sentence they rarely heard David say anything out of place.

"Prepare to move," he whispered, and then got up to lead the way again. After another hour and a half David suddenly stopped. Immediately the men behind froze and each involuntarily opened his mouth to try and hear better what it was that had caused David to come to a halt. He turned and beckoned them to move on when suddenly they all moved in different directions, nearly tipping the general off the stretcher again. The cause of this chaos was none other than a fox, which had caused David to stop when he heard rustling in long grass beside the track and which then he had almost trodden on. The startled animal running from David, and then through the others, disappeared, leaving Beasley with a fit of the giggles he could barely suppress. David came back to them, "Quiet," he whispered, "the road is about a mile or so ahead. When we get closer to it I'll go forward to see if we can hide up under it somewhere. It will be light in an hour or so. Right, move on."

Gradually the elevated road came into view. To David's

satisfaction there appeared to be little traffic on it but he knew that that situation would rapidly change as it got light. Some little way from the road there was a tall patch of rushes.

"Hide in here, I'll be back in 20 minutes," he had told them, and went on down the track feeling terribly conspicuous because of the lack of cover, though fortunately the night was getting darker as it approached the dawn. He got to within a hundred yards of the road and then laid flat on his stomach. The road had an upward gradient in front of him towards Calais, and directly in front of him he could see another culvert under the road much larger that the one in which they had sheltered the previous day. He turned and moved back to the rushes. "Right, come on," he said quietly, "I think I've found another culvert."

When they had nearly reached the road they were startled to hear a number of vehicles coming up from Boulogne. It was too far to make a run for it, so David immediately ordered, "Down – and keep your faces down." This they did, in the process dropping the stretcher with a most inconsiderate thump which produced an involuntary grunt of pain from the general and a few very well chosen words from David, drowned fortunately by the noise of the lorries. In five minutes they had all passed and the little party made its way quickly to the culvert. Although the culvert was some twelve feet wide and eight feet high, the path itself was very narrow most of the width being taken up by a small river, which funnelled into it. There were plenty of rushes to be had so David quickly organised the collecting of a couple of bundles with which they were able, partially, to mask each end of their hideout, it would not pass close scrutiny, but he reasoned, it gave a little protection.

They laid up all day eating what remained of their meagre supply of food and being allowed to drink twice from their water bottles. David himself was in pain where the undersized boots had rubbed him but he decided not to take them off on the premise that he might never get them on again. Despite the vehicles rumbling overhead, they all got a little sleep. At dawn the sound of mortaring and furious small arms fire carried to them from the direction of Calais, the battle there obviously was not yet over. They had two experiences of being on the receiving end of their own fire during the morning, the first occasion being when a flight of Blenheim bombers flew along the road first bombing and then strafing the traffic on it. Later in the morning heavy shelling took place landing a mile or so up the road towards Calais. David could only surmise this would be from a Royal Navy warship lying off the coast. His biggest fear was not in being on the receiving end of this activity but that Jerries caught out in it might spot his hideout and use it as a temporary place of safety. Fortunately that didn't happen.

During the afternoon the noise of firing from Calais died down, and by early evening stopped altogether. "They've been overrun," said David in a whisper to the general, with tears again showing in his eyes. The general clasped his hand.

"The Boche paid dearly for it," he replied, "but mark my words – we'll be back." But it was to be more than four long years before that happened.

David was shaken out of his sadness by an urgent whisper from Piercey, on lookout at the Wissant end of the tunnel, "Someone coming along the paths."

David crawled towards him. "Everyone down, keep quiet," he said quietly, and then, peering through the screen of rushes saw that a young male civilian was making his way towards them, looking in the rushes at the side of the river as he came. "Let him come in and we'll grab him. I'll take his top half and stop him shouting, you grab his legs."

The intruder had a little difficulty in getting around the screen without slipping down the bank into the river, and the minute he had done this, David and Piercey pounced, and quickly dragged him into the cover in the culvert. Still holding his hand over the young man's mouth he whispered, "We are English, keep quiet and we will not harm you." The young man stopped struggling and nodded his head. They took him to the general who, in a kindly voice, asked him who he was, where he came from and whether there were any Germans in Wissant. The young man said his name was Jean-Pierre Chabran and that he lived on the outskirts of Wissant. He was eighteen.

"Why are you not in the army then," asked the general. Jean-Pierre said that he had received his papers to report to Beauvais but since the Germans had overrun that district he couldn't get there. He had a twin brother, Claude, who was similarly placed. He went on to say that there were Germans in Wissant but none in his little village on the outskirts.

"Do you know where we can get a boat?" said the general. The lad thought for a moment or two.

"All the motor boats are under guard in Wissant," he said. "Monsieur Mayer has a holiday cottage about two kilometres along this little river where he kept a large rowing boat he used to go fishing in with his friends, but he's not there now. He is Jewish so he left with his family for the south when the Boche attacked Belgium."

David understanding most of what was said smiled to himself. All small villages are the same whatever the country he thought, remembering his own childhood back in Mountfield where everybody knew everything about everybody else.

"Is the boat still there?"

"I would think so, the Germans have not searched any houses yet except on the coast."

"How many would it take?"

Jean Pierre thought for a moment.

"If the sea is reasonably calm it will take all of us."

"What do you mean, all of us?" said the general.

"I mean all of you and Claude and me, we can then report for service in England and anyway, we're used to handling boats, these people," waving a hand at David and the others who were listening intently but understanding little, "have probably never rowed anything in their lives."

David looked at the general. "You spoke so quickly Sir, I didn't understand all that."

"He wants he and his brother to come with us."

"Is the boat big enough?"

"He thinks so."

David paused in deep thought, and after a short while said, "Do you think we can trust him?"

"Yes, I think so."

"Then this is what we do. When it is dark he can leave and collect his brother. Bring what food he can manage and wait in hiding for us on the path nearest to where the boat is. We will leave an hour later. The big question is where does this river come out, if it comes out in Wissant, we will almost certainly be seen by sentries."

The general translated and Jean Pierre replied.

"He says the river flows into the sea about a kilometre north of Wissant so you should be O.K. It will have to be pulled along the river for one kilometre from the path with a rope until we get to a little jetty. The river is neither wide enough nor deep enough up to that point to be able to sit in and row."

"Sir, will you ask him to bring a couple of small buckets, a map of the channel with England on it and a compass if he has such a thing, no matter how basic, oh, and a flashlight."

Again, the general translated and replied, "Yes, they have all those things."

As soon as it was dark, Jean Pierre moved off, and exactly one hour after that David gave the order to get ready. He was concerned about the general whose foot was looking very nasty indeed, and who was beginning to perspire with every movement. "You be careful with him," he said to the four carriers, "or I'll have your guts for garters." Piercey was in considerable pain from his back wounds with the dressings now all congealed and every movement causing them to rub on the wound themselves. Finally David found the first few yards to be absolute agony. There was no doubt about it, his feet were either in, or going to be in, the same state as the general's before very long.

They moved slowly along the path and after half an hour or so were greeted by a low call from Jean Pierre.
"Where is the house?" said David.
"Down here," replied Jean Pierre and started to lead them off on a side track, which, after about a hundred yards, brought them back alongside the river. They moved slowly and quietly as they approached the single story building set against the riverbank. Their guide led them around the house and on the far side they were shown a double door with a cobbled slipway leading from it down into the river, which, at this point, was a little wider than it had been at the culvert but as David could readily see, would not allow the boat to be rowed.

Barclay slowly drew his bayonet from its scabbard, which he had concealed inside his uniform when they first left Calais and very efficiently removed the padlock, hinge and all, with the very minimum of noise.
"You've done that before," whispered David.

Barclay grinned at him in the pale moonlight. Inside they could make out the dim shape of the rowing boat. Keeping the torch dim by wrapping a handkerchief round it, Jean Pierre explored the interior of the boat house, found the oars which he put in the boat, put the buckets and a small sack in and having put the general on the ground, they lifted the boat and carried it outside. It was very heavy, but they couldn't afford the noise they might have made if they had dragged it. When it was outside ready to be placed in the water, David examined it. There were two cross-seats with rowlocks for four oars. There was a seat at the front to take two people and a seat at the tiller end to take three. They all stood looking at it.
"Not much like the Queen Mary is it Corporal?" Barclay said.
"It'll do," replied, David, "now lets lift it in and once it's in,

Piercey, you take the tiller, you won't be able to row with that back."

They carried it into the river, the two French boys took the tow line and the boat began its journey. They soon reached the jetty where they transferred the general and his briefcase into the front of the boat, which was done not without some considerable pain to him despite their careful handling. David sat the two brothers together on the rear rowing seat and told them to start the rowing on their own, the last thing he wanted was the noise of two of his men catching crabs or knocking against the brothers oars accidentally. Soon they heard the soft noise of the waves breaking on the approaching shore and then suddenly they juddered to a halt. Where the river had widened at this point it was very shallow and they were obviously on a mud flat.

"Right, Beasley, Smith, Riley, over the side with me, we'll have to push it."

The four went slowly over the side, and with the combination of lightening the boat and its being pushed, it slid along the bottom for about forty or fifty yards until, once again, it floated freely. One by one the four climbed back in.

"Bloody hell Corporal, what a pong," said Piercey, and there was no doubt about it, whatever the four had been walking in, in the bottom of that stream, it certainly wasn't Chanel No.5. The river swung round to the right and then they saw the sea in the near distance. When they reached it however, it disappeared. In fact everything disappeared. A fog blanket had drifted in from the sea and in seconds they were enveloped in a damp cold mist so that they could hardly see each other.

"Right," said David, "Barclay and Beasley take the other two oars and keep in time with two French lads. Piercey, I'll show you which direction to point us," and in checking the school atlas the boys had brought with them and then setting which way the arrow should point, he said "Right, let's go, next stop England," and then, with help from Smith 24, he took his boots off.

They moved steadily until it got light and as the dawn came so the fog thinned and gradually lifted. The two brothers voluntarily bore the brunt of the rowing as it was quite plain to them that the soldiers, weak with lack of sleep, with the exhaustion of combat still with them, the twenty-two mile march across country all combining together had made them all in. Added to this, whilst their hands were not soft they were certainly not used to pulling on oars for hours. As a result, they all developed blisters. David was a tower of strength. As soon as one man flagged he took over for half an hour, but the two French boys steadily and rhythmically set the pace, and Piercey kept himself awake to steer by pushing his back against the tiller seat everytime he felt sleepy and was instantly awakened by the agony of his wounds. They were lucky that the sea was dead calm, there was very little freeboard on the boat, had there been waves, they could well have been in trouble.

"How far do you think we've come?" said Barclay.

"It's difficult to say because we don't know what the currents have been doing to us," said David, "but I reckon about twenty miles, so we should be about half way."

They rowed on. Suddenly the general, who had been dozing, said "Aircraft at the rear Corporal."

David turned from looking to see if he could get a glimpse of the white cliffs of Dover, or anywhere else on the south coast for that matter, and said, "It's a Jerry." The aircraft approached and flew at low level past them, banked and turned and flew back again. He then banked to the left having obviously decided the boat was a legitimate target, turned and came straight for them firing his machine gun as he dived.

The first burst was well short but the second straddled the tiny craft. One bullet hit Riley in the shoulder and in addition to taking a lump out of him, knocked him clean off his seat into the sea, and a second put a hole in the side of the boat through which water started spurting. Having made his first run, the plane again banked and turned coming back for the kill, but to the total astonishment of the men in the boat, currently engaged in hanging on to Riley until they could drag him back in, it continued to turn downwards until the pilot managed to right it and as he levelled off he hit the sea, went up on to his nose, slid across the surface until he was only fifty yards away and then stopped with a loud plop as the tailplane fell back making the plane float on the calm water. They could plainly see the pilot slumped over his controls obviously unconscious.

"Row towards it," said David standing up and taking off his tunic, and as they pulled along side the wing he jumped on it, nearly capsizing the boat as he did so.

"Pull clear," he said, "in case she sinks and turns over on you."

"Why not let the bastard drown in it Corporal," called Beasley, but David was already running along the wing and climbing up on to the front of the cockpit. He pushed the canopy but there was no way he could move it. He called to Piercey, "Bring the boat in and throw me up the rifle." The rifle was the German one he had 'guarded the prisoners' with, and which some strange whim had made him carry when he could have ditched it and not had its weight to worry about. This was to be his souvenir he had thought. Piercey lengthened the sling and then carefully judged his throw up to David. It was a little high but David caught the sling and immediately started to hit the framework of the canopy to slide it back. Although it was a German rifle it went against all his feelings and training as a Rifleman to ill treat the weapon in this manner. Dropping a rifle, even accidentally, was a major offence in the Rifles, to deliberately mistreat it was criminal. After several heavy blows the obstruction to the canopy gave way and David slid it back. He threw the rifle back to Piercey who deftly caught it, and the boat pulled clear again.

When David looked into the cockpit, he could see that the impact had jammed the pilots' feet under an obstruction on the floor. He leaned in and was just able to reach his boots. There was no doubt the boots were really stuck, he would just have to try and get him out of the boots. He undid the retaining harness of the unconscious flyer and then sat on the canopy and attempted to pull him out of his seat. It was then that he began to realise how terribly weary he was and started to tremble. It was a peculiar feeling. He was almost crying, his lower jaw had an uncontrollable tremor and a feeling of sickness in his stomach and of complete desperation came over him. He wiped his eyes and forehead with the back of his hand then, looking up, saw Jean Pierre and Claude running along the wing towards him. With one on either side and David pulling from the rear, they managed to get the flyer out. David sat on the fuselage, leaned backwards and slid back into the water clasping the pilot to him. It was not the end of the incident. As he slid back so he caught his buttock and the top rear of his leg on the projection, which had caused the canopy to jam in the first place. It was as sharp as a razor. It ripped his trouser leg and gave him a deep agonising cut for nearly nine inches causing him to cry out in pain.

The boat was quickly alongside and David, bleeding profusely, was hauled in closely followed by the pilot who was beginning to regain consciousness. They pulled away quickly from the aircraft which was settling deeper in the water until, when they were thirty or forty yards away, its tail went up and it sank slowly under the surface.

"Search him for weapons," David said to Piercey which he did and removed a Luger from a holster on the pilot's belt and a sheath knife from a pocket in his trousers below the knee. In the meantime, Smith 24 and Beasley, who had been binding Riley's wound and strapping his arm against his chest, were cutting David's trouser leg away at the crotch so that they could get the two dressings that remained between them on to this very ugly and jagged cut from which blood was literally flowing out. The general took his raincoat off.

"Cut the dressings in half," he said, "and lay them endwise on the wound. Then cut the lining of this coat, it is silk and very strong, and bind it around as tight as you can to stop the bleeding. That's as much as we can do for now."

As David lay there being attended to, the day flashed through his mind when he, as a thirteen-year-old schoolboy on Home Farm at Mountfield, had heard a scream of pain from the direction of the bull pen and had rushed across to find George the cowman being gored by the bull. He had managed to drag George out although he himself had been attacked and injured by the bull. He had plugged George's wound with his shirt and tied it in with string before running to the local pub to get the ambulance. They said afterwards his prompt action in plugging the wounds had saved George's life. He wondered how George was getting on. I must go and see him when I get leave he thought.

The German had regained consciousness and was watching the aircraft disappear. He looked at David, "Thank you," he said, it was obvious this was probably the sum total of his English vocabulary.

"Why did you attack us when we are unarmed?" asked David in his fluent German.

"You were obviously soldiers escaping to England. I had no means of making you return to be taken prisoner; I therefore had to sink you."

David translated for the benefit of the others, thought for a moment, and said to the general "Do you think he was justified in doing that Sir?"

"He might have a point," said the general "I'm sure he could make a case for doing what he did, but then I'm not a lawyer."

The pilot continued. "I would like to commend your honour in rescuing me from the aircraft; you could easily have left me to drown. Why did you not leave me to drown?"

"One does not do that sort of thing," said David and they left it at that.

After half an hours' steady rowing, Piercey still awake and steering although he had complained on several occasions that his bum had kept going to sleep, suddenly called out, "Another plane corporal," pointing over David's shoulder. As it approached, David said, "It's a Spitfire; Barclay, Beasley, stand up and wave, but for God's sake don't tip us over." The two men did as they had been told, facing the pilot, who throttled back and came down within a hundred feet of the water slowly circling them. At last, he speeded up again, climbed and banked and then flew over them with his wings waggling. "He's going to tell them we're here," said David and then thought, 'but who the hell 'them' are I haven't the faintest idea.'

About an hour later they found who 'them' was when they heard the gradually increasing deep-throated roar of an RAF rescue launch coming towards them. Reaching them, it did a big sweep and slowly came alongside. "How many of you," a man with a deep West Country accent called across.

"Ten, including a French General, a German pilot and two young Frenchmen."

"Proper League of bloody Nations aren't you?" the cheery voice called back, and then after a consultation with a colleague in the wheelhouse, "We'll take four off and tow the remainder in to Folkestone."

They transferred the two French lads, along with Barclay and Beasley and with a tow line attached to them were quickly under way. An hour later they arrived in Folkestone harbour and pulled up against a flight of steps. Here willing hands moved in to lift the general on to a stretcher and carry him carefully up on to the dock. A military police vehicle with a sergeant and two corporals was standing by, and as the pilot reached the dockside he turned, stood to attention and saluted David before turning away to be driven into captivity.

David got his five men together and wearily climbed the steps. Standing on the dock was a red tabbed full colonel with a young lieutenant in attendance. David immediately whispered, "Smarten up," and when they all were on the dockside, he called out, "Fall in A Company." The five men fell in, in line. "Stand to your front – A Company," commanded David which is the Rifles' way of bringing men to attention. They stood there, swaying a little, as David turned to the colonel. "A Company, City Rifles, reporting for duty – SIR."

They were a sorry looking lot. Unshaven, dirty, Piercey unable to stand up straight because of the pain of his wounds, Riley with his right arm tied across his chest, Barclay, Beasley and Smith 24 encrusted still with dried black mud from the river and David in a pair of German trousers with one leg cut away completely, showing bloodstained bandages and wearing no boots. They were the remnants of two and a half thousand riflemen who had crossed to France only a few days before. It seemed like a lifetime.

When David reported, he could not salute, he had no cap. The colonel however did salute and David saw that this hoary old warrior, probably dragged out of retirement for the duration, this old soldier with the '98 Frontier Medal, the Queen and King Boer War medals, Pip Squeak and Wilfred medals from the Great War and in front of them all the D.S.O. and the M.C., this man who had seen more valour probably than anyone else could ever have experienced, stood there as the salute with tears running down his face at the sight of these young men, beaten in battle, but still standing in front of him as soldiers, ready to battle again. He turned abruptly to the lieutenant and bellowed, "Get those bloody ambulances down here," at which the lieutenant, galvanised into action, repeated his bellow, the three ambulances reversed along the jetty to collect the six men and the two French boys and they were all driven away. David's last thought before he fell asleep on the ambulance bunk was, "I wonder what will happen to the boat."

Chapter Eight

When Rita and Buffy left on the morning of the 29th, Fred and Ruth walked slowly back into the house, both deep in their own thoughts.

"Would you like some tea before you go back to the factory dear? I'll ask Rose if she would like one."

"Yes please – another ten minutes away from the hive of industry won't make a lot of difference to the war effort I suppose."

As Ruth went through the hall to go up to Rose the telephone shrilled and quite startled her. 'Goodness – my nerves must be on edge', she thought as she picked up the earpiece. It was Megan.

"Mum, wonderful news, David is back and safe."

"Oh Megan," she began to cry "Megan dear, how do you know, where is he, is he alright?"

"I'm at home but apparently a sister who knows me at Ashford Hospital where they've taken him, phoned me at my hospital with the news, and they in turn got me at home. I'm on nights now," she added in explanation. "Anyway, he's wounded but comfortable and Pat will be hearing officially in a day or so. I haven't been able to get hold of Pat, she's not at home nor at the shop so if you see her or can get in touch with her will you tell her?"

"Yes dear of course I will. But Megan, have you heard anything from Harry?"

"No, nothing, but I keep thinking the phone will ring at any minute and he'll be on the line."

"Oh Megan dear, I do hope so, no one can know what you must be suffering, you are always so very, very brave. Anyway, I'll ring around and try and locate Pat. Bye bye dear, love to the twins."

She went back into the kitchen and Fred, seeing her face wet with tears, immediately jumped to his feet and said, "What's the matter, what's happened?"

"Megan has phoned, David is back, wounded, in Ashford Hospital."

"Will he be alright?" asked a voice behind them. It was Rose who had come down having heard the telephone ring.

"They say he is comfortable," said Ruth putting her arm around Rose. "We'll phone the hospital and see if we can go and visit him. Now sit down and I'll make the tea." As she busied herself putting the kettle on the Aga and laying a tray, the front door bell went. "I'll go," said Fred and a few seconds later they heard him say, "Pat – we were just going to try and locate you." Pat hurried in without replying holding a sinister looking buff telegram in her hand. "This came as I was leaving home" she said, her face pinched and her eyes shining with unshed tears. She gave it to Ruth. It said, "The War Office regrets to announce that your husband, Corporal Chandler D, is missing believed prisoner of war."

Ruth folded her in her arms and as Pat looked round and saw they were all smiling at her she said, "Why are you smiling – please tell me."

"Megan has just phoned. David is safe in Ashford Hospital. He is wounded but comfortable. We are going to phone to see when we can go and see him." Pat dissolved into tears of relief until Fred said loudly "Well then, what about this tea, one of us here at least has got work to do."

After Fred had gone back to the factory they took it in turns to phone the good news to friends and relatives, Ruth keeping a watchful eye on Rose in case the emotion of the moment had any adverse effect on her, but Rose loved her brother very deeply and the fact that he was safe helped to balance the sadness of knowing that her beloved Jeremy would never return.

When they at last got through to the hospital, Pat was told that all calls involving returning soldiers were being put through to the Almoners Department where, after a lengthy delay, a Royal Army Medical Corps sergeant answered her. "Sergeant Rance here, can I help you?" Pat explained who she was and that she was enquiring after Corporal Chandler, City Rifles. He asked her to hold the line. Impatiently they all waited for the sergeant to come back to Pat.

"He's comfortable. He's sleeping. He's going to be alright," the sergeant said.

"When can we come and see him?" said Pat.

"Visiting days are tomorrow, Thursday and Saturday and Sunday, two till four," replied the sergeant. "We are laying trucks on to and from Ashford Station for service families from one-thirty onwards."

"Thank you very much sergeant." Pat turned and told the others. "We can go tomorrow."

"Let me phone Fred," said Ruth, "he may well have some petrol and can take us in the Rover." She phoned Fred who said he had enough in the tank to get them to Ashford and back, and the new ration was due on Saturday.

Pat awoke early the next morning, disturbing Susie the tortoiseshell they had inherited when they bought the bungalow. She slept on the foot of her bed and looked at Pat crossly as much as to say, 'It's not time to get up yet.' Pat leaned forward and stroked her. "I'm going to see your Daddy in a few hours and soon he'll be here to stroke you as well." Pat swore that the cross expression disappeared immediately and that she started to purr fit to burst her boiler, as David would say, when she related the story to Ruth later. "You're as daft about that cat as David is," Ruth laughingly said.

They ate an early lunch at Chandlers Lodge and then climbed into the Rover. "I wonder what Harry's doing," said Rose. "I do hope we hear soon." Harry, at that moment, had just helped to blow up his first bridge and was on his way to the second. It would seem like an age before the family would hear of what happened to Harry.

When they arrived at the hospital and established which ward David was in, they had a few minutes to spare before they were allowed in. Fred had said that Pat should go in for a few minutes first, and as only two people were allowed at the bedside at any one time, Ruth would then go in, and then they'd change over with him and Rose. Pat was very nervous as she asked the sister which bed corporal Chandler was in, and was pointed to one in the corner. As she approached, she saw that David was lying asleep almost on his stomach facing the wall. She was being watched by a thin faced young man sitting up in the next bed, but as Pat was used to being looked at by young men she took no notice until the man asked, "You Mrs Chandler?"

"Yes," she replied.

"Give 'im a shake. Wake the blighter up. You know he's a blooming hero don't you?"

It was Kenny Barclay, one time deserter. Barclay, who'd spent more time in the Glass House than he had spent with the colours, later to be a brave and resourceful Rifleman Barclay, City Rifles and proud of it. Pat smiled at him, "Were you together over there?" she asked.

"We all were," he replied indicating two beds next to him and four opposite to them, and repeated, "'E's a blooming hero – ask any of them."

Pat gently laid her hand on David's face and slowly he awakened, turned partially, tried to sit up, fell back in pain and in a second she said, "Don't move darling, don't move" and bent over and kissed him on the forehead, on the cheek, on his lips and then took his hand and kissed that. She was crying very quietly, the other lads nearby studiously looking away.

He managed to manoeuvre himself into a more comfortable position so that he could look at her. "God, you're beautiful" were his first words.

"I bet I am, blubbing like a five-year-old," she said, smiling through her tears. He put his arm out and pulled her head down to kiss her properly. The first minutes of any hospital visit are always the worst, not knowing what to say, not knowing what to do. "Where are you wounded?" she said at last, and the answer he gave broke the first tension.

"Nowhere that matters," he said cheekily, looking a little more like his old self for a second or two, "and anyway I wasn't wounded – I got a bad cut."

"You got cut – how did you get cut?"

"On an aeroplane," came the unlikely answer.

"This becomes more like Alice in Wonderland every second," said Pat clasping his hand, and then saw David looking over her shoulder as he saw his mother approaching. Pat moved aside as Ruth bent over the bed and held David in her arms.

"I'm so pleased to see you," she said, "we've all been so worried. Dad and Rose are outside."

"Bring them in," said David.

"You're only allowed two visitors at a time," replied his mother.

"Then they can come and visit Barclay, then we'll all be together." He pointed to the young man in the next bed.

"So you're my new adopted son Kenny are you?" said Ruth, turning and standing up. She took Kenny's face in her hands and kissed him on the forehead. "Pleased to meet you Kenny Barclay – next of kin." They all laughed, but inside Kenny Barclay had a warm feeling he had never experienced before and if he had been asked to analyse it would have found it impossible to describe. Pat went and called the others in, and for the next two hours they visited the other riflemen and the two French boys. Rose spoke very good French and was able to establish that they would be moved to the provisional French depot in a day or so to be sworn in. She gave them the address and telephone number at Chandlers Lodge and made them promise they would write and tell the family how they were getting on and offered a warm and sincere welcome to them to come and visit when they were given leave. Barclay, Beasley and Smith 24 were all being posted to the depot at Winchester after the weekend and would then go on leave, Beasley and Smith 24 to their families. Piercey would be in hospital for a while with David until his wounds healed. "Where will Kenny go?" asked Ruth.

"I don't know," said David. "Barclay, where will you go on leave?" There was a pause.

"Oh, I expect I'll stay at the Y.M. or the Union Jack Club or somewhere."

"What's it like there?" asked Ruth.

"Well, it's alright," said Barclay, not very convincingly. "As far as I know, I've never been on leave before." His mates laughed, knowing well the reason for that.

"Look Kenny lad," chimed in Fred, "if you feel like it you can come to us, then you can tell us everything that happened – we shan't get much out of this lummock I'll be bound."

"Do you mean that?" asked the incredulous Kenny.

"Of course," chorused Ruth and Rose.

With all the strain, the emotion, the total exhaustion they had suffered over the previous ten days, Kenny Barclay was close to tears.

"That's settled then," said Fred, "I'll have a quart of Whitbread's waiting for you."

Riley was the only one who would not, eventually, be going to the depot. They had operated on his shoulder as soon as he arrived, but there was no doubt he would never be able to soldier again. It was civvy street for him.

The two hours up, they said their goodbyes all round and drove back home to Sandbury.

"Did you find out what happened?" asked Ruth of Fred.

"I picked up bits and pieces – it seemed they got a boat and rowed back from France. Someone said they got shot up by a German plane but they took the pilot prisoner. Someone else said they saved the life of a French general. Someone else said they walked through the Germans and David wore a German uniform as if he was guarding them and spoke German all the time. They all said he's a bloody hero, but what happened in Calais nobody would talk about except they were the only ones as far as they know who got away, and it was David that did it. I'll get young Kenny Barclay on one side when he comes on leave and I'll get it all out of him, day by day. He worships the ground our David walks on." He paused for a while and then continued, "How can you take the pilot of an airplane prisoner?"

They all agreed David looked thinner and very tired and strained, but as Ruth said to Pat, "When he comes on leave we'll break into the store cupboard and you'll soon fatten him up again."

When they reached home and had tea, the telephone went into full use, phoning relatives and friends with the news. One person contacted was Lady Earnshaw who lived in the small village of Mountfield about five miles from Sandbury where the Chandlers had also lived until they moved to Chandlers Lodge. Lady Earnshaw was a wealthy woman in her own right who as Miss Parnell, as she was then, played the organ at the village church and had got to know and like David over a number of years. She had married Lieutenant General Sir Frederick Earnshaw when she was in her forties in December 1939, he by coincidence being a very good friend of Jack, Pat's father. "The general will be delighted to hear David is alright," she said, "and please let us know as soon as you hear from Harry."

At nine o'clock they switched the wireless on to hear the news. The first item was by a solemn announcer stating that the battle for Calais had ended and that the War Office had issued the following communiqué. The announcement explained how a British brigade of two and a half thousand men, one thousand French soldiers and tanks from the Royal Tank Regiment, the combined force commanded by brigadier Claude Nicholson, opposed two complete armoured divisions of the enemy. The announcer continued:-

"This action will count among the most heroic deeds in the annals of the British Army. In spite of repeated attacks by the enemy and of continuous air and artillery bombardment the garrison held out for several days. By its refusal to surrender, it contained a large force of the enemy and gave invaluable time to the BEF in its withdrawal from Dunkirk." Communiqué ends.

"So it wasn't just a waste of a brigade after all," said Jack. "I wonder when we'll hear the full story. Not for years probably."

At Ashford Hospital on Friday afternoon the nurses on the ward started bustling around, straightening sheets, putting bed pans out of sight, smoothing counterpanes and doing all the other little unnecessary things that nurses do in a ward when the word has been telephoned that the matron was on her way over with a general in tow. The general to them was not important, but Matron was next only to God, hence all the scurrying around. The door was held open by one of the probationers as Matron swept in, followed by the general, but whereas Matron moved more or less silently on her rubber soled shoes, the general in his polished knee-high boots, a formidable figure wearing a Sam Browne and at first sight covered in red tabs, clumped along. As sister said to David later, "Isn't it funny how generals always clump along, they never walk like everybody else."

A quick word from Matron to sister and they were led to David's bed under the open mouthed gaze of the rest of his little party who, with the exception of Riley, were sitting up in their beds. David was dozing but woke up with the light touch from sister. "You have a visitor," she said.

David immediately spotted the general. "Sir," he said, "how nice to see you," but with the effort of trying to turn and sit up bringing on a spasm of pain, had to lie back again.

"Don't move David," said the general, "I'm on my way through Ashford from Dover and Lady Earnshaw said I must come and see you and bring you her love." Barclay who had got out of bed, found a chair and put it beside the general who thanked him graciously.

"David, I was so terribly upset to hear about poor Jeremy. Lady Earnshaw tells me that Rose is being extraordinarily brave, she talks to your mother quite regularly you know. It seems only yesterday that I was escorting your mother at the wedding, to think it should end so soon is utterly beyond belief." He was silent for a few moments. "Now what's all this about your rowing from France and shooting a plane down and God knows what else?"

"We got a boat, that is Barclay here, Smith, Riley and Beasley and recruited two French boys over there," indicating Jean Pierre and Claude, "who are going to join the French Army as soon as they get released from here. Oh and then there was Piercey." Piercey had just returned to his bed from the toilet. "Piercey was wounded before we left."

"What about this aeroplane?"

"Well we were rowing away quite merrily until it attacked us. Riley got hit and the boat got a hole in it, which we managed to bung up, but then the plane got out of control and it crashed into the sea. The pilot was unconscious before we got him out and brought him back with us. Then the RAF spotted us and we got a tow from one of their rescue boats for the last hour."

"David, as far as we know, apart from the wounded ones who came back on the hospital ship, you are the only ones that got away. As soon as you are able I want you to write a full report, day by day, of everything that happened to you and your platoon and send it to me marked "Top Secret" to Corps Headquarters. Is that clear?" He turned to the others, "and you people make sure he leaves nothing out through false modesty – right?"

"Yes Sir," they chorused.

"Right, I'll be gone then. Get well soon and we'll see you back at Mountfield."

"Thank you Sir and my very kindest regards to Lady Earnshaw."

The general stood up, shook hands and then to their surprise, shook hands with each of the riflemen and with the two French lads, saying, "Well done, credit to your regiment, good luck in the future." Platitudes spoken by all generals to the lower orders but, in this case, sincerely meant. He shook hands with sister and clumped out. There was silence for a few seconds after he had gone broken eventually by Rifleman Piercey saying, "You don't know Winston bleeding Churchill by any chance do you Corporal?"

All the family came to visit David either on Saturday or Sunday. Megan, Pat's father Jack, Anni and Ernie Bolton with Fred, Ruth, Rose and Pat of course both days. They spread themselves around talking to the other lads so that it was one big party at that end of the ward. Under normal circumstances sister might have put her foot down knowing that all the visitors were really for one patient, but as David was by now a bit of a celebrity she turned a blind eye. He told them of the general's visit and that he had to write an account of everything that had happened to which Fred said, "Do a copy for all of us won't you?"

"It's supposed to be Top Secret," said David mischievously.

"Top Secret my..." he stopped just in time from saying what he was going to say and continued "my Aunt Fanny. Everything's Top Secret in the army, you order a gross of toilet rolls for the company latrines and its Top Secret. This way we'll get the real story, so you make us a copy. You watch he does it Kenny, alright?"

"We'll make sure he does Mr Chandler," said Kenny.

When the visitors had all left on the Saturday and Sunday, the lads got together and went over between them what had happened from the day they had landed at Calais and Mr Austen had been killed until they landed back at Folkestone, and when it was all roughed out, Riley spoke the understatement of the age "We had a bit of excitement there one way and the other in a short space of time, didn't we?"

"I wonder what happened to Sergeant Harris and the others," said Beasley.

"I expect we'll find out some day," replied Smith 24, but in some cases it would be several years before the full story was told. David thought constantly of Jeremy. Rose was so brave, he had held her hand trying to tell her how sad he was for her, but except for a couple of times when inadvertently the name of Corporal Cartwright was mentioned by one of the lads she concealed her anguish and showed only serenity to the outside world despite the deep, sickening feeling of loneliness inside her.

When the family got back to Chandlers Lodge on Sunday afternoon, Alec and Rebecca were in the sitting room and came out in to the hall to ask after David and 'the boys,' as his little party had become known. Ruth's first words were "Right, who's for tea?"

But Alec broke in and said, "Could I have a word first?" Ruth immediately knew what he had to say, and looked at the slightly flushed, happy face of Rebecca as she stood at his side holding his hand. There was a momentary hush and he continued with, "We want you all to be the first to know, except for Rebecca's parents, that I have asked Rebecca to marry me and for some outlandish reason that I am still not able to fathom she has said yes."

Ruth was the first to congratulate Alec, Rose was the first to hug Rebecca. When the commotion died down a little, Jack said, "You know what you're letting yourself in for don't you Rebecca. All those oil lamps and log cabins and grizzly bears and so on."

"And snow forty feet deep," said Fred.

"Now stop all that ribbing," said Ruth. "We all wish the pair of you the very best of luck – now have you set a date?"

"Last Saturday in July at Mountfield Church with the reception here at the Angel. Rebecca's mother and father will be sending the invitations out in due course."

"Well what about this tea?" said Fred. Ruth, Anni and Megan hurried off to the kitchen to get everything started. Pat looked round for Rose and saw her standing wistfully by the radiant Rebecca. She moved round to her and put her arm round her waist, saying nothing.

They stood for a while, watching the animated conversation of the others, until Rose said, "It seems so many years since Jeremy proposed to me." It was the first time Pat had heard Rose mention Jeremy by name. She said nothing and Rose continued, "and yet it was only five months ago, on Boxing Day. There was a rumour going around that they might be posted to the Middle East and he asked me if we could get married before they went." Pat remained silent. Rose paused for a moment or two. "I'm so glad I said yes," she said. Pat saw that these memories had been spoken of without tears and was gratified to see that gradually Rose was coming to terms with this tragedy in her young life.

In a private moment or two with David at the hospital, Rose had asked if Jeremy had suffered and David had truthfully been able to tell her he was killed instantly. It was only minute consolation to the heartache they were both to endure for many years to come, but consolation it was.

Their little private world was interrupted by Jack calling out, "When are we going to see the ring then Rebecca?"

"We're going to Maidstone on Wednesday – we've both got a day off," said Rebecca.

"Its early closing day in Maidstone on Wednesdays," said Fred, "so make sure he gets you there during the morning. We've heard that excuse before from blokes saying they couldn't buy the ring because the shops were shut." They all moved into the kitchen for tea.

At a few minutes after seven, the telephone rang. Jack was nearest so he answered it, "Chandlers Lodge." A solemn, cultivated voice on the other end said, "Would it be possible to speak to Mrs Cartwright?"

Jack said, "Yes, of course. May I ask who's calling?"

"It's Scott-Calder here."

"Oh colonel, this is Jack Hooper, how marvellous to hear your voice. Where are you?"

"In the Herbert Military Hospital at Woolwich I'm afraid. I got myself wounded and was brought out in the last vessel to leave." I take it Rose has heard about Jeremy?" The colonel, then a major, had been one of the guests at Rose and Jeremy's wedding and had been Housemaster to him and David at Cantelbury before the war.

"Yes she knows and she's being incredibly brave." I take it you've heard about David?"

"No, I haven't. I was afraid almost to ask. Was he taken prisoner?"

"No, he got a little gang of survivors together and they stole a boat and rowed back to England. He's in Ashford Hospital. We've just come back from visiting him."

"That's marvellous news. I must hear the full story as soon as we can arrange it."

"I'll get Rose for you."

When Rose came to the telephone the colonel was so kind to her. "I knew those boys since they were eleven-years-old," he said to Rose, "of all the boys that went through my hands at Cantelbury and in the Rifles, I always felt they were extra special. I do hope I'm not distressing you by saying all this but being a confirmed old bachelor and not having a family of my own, those two were like surrogate sons to me, not that I ever showed them favouritism in any way. Jeremy was a brave resourceful soldier and I shall always be proud to have known him and if, at any time, I can be of service to you in any way, you have only to command me – sounds a little stilted but I mean it."

Rose paused for a moment, "Thank you Colonel Scott-Calder. It's having friends like you that gives me the strength to carry on. By the way, if you're not flooded with visitors may we come and see you? Uncle Jack said you were at Woolwich."

"I'm afraid I'm far from flooded with visitors. I have no family except an ancient uncle and aunt in Rhodesia. Doctor Carew came today. He's the only visitor I've had."

"When are visiting days?"

"Well when you reach the exalted rank of lieutenant colonel you're allowed people to see you any day after two o'clock."

"Then we shall see you soon."

She went back in and told the others of her conversation. As a result Ruth and Pat suggested the three of them went up to Woolwich on Tuesday. "Mrs Draper can look after the shop for the afternoon, she'll have to get used to it any way for a while when David comes home" and then with a sickening feeling in her stomach, thought how inconsiderate and unkind she had sounded standing as she was next to Rose, whose Jeremy would never come home. But Rose put her arm round her to reassure her, no words were necessary.

Jim had to go back to camp that evening just to make an appearance as technically he was on duty. He spotted Colonel Tim in the reading room and went in to tell him the up-to-date news from Chandlers Lodge including the proposed visit to Woolwich.

"On Tuesday did you say?" said the colonel, "I've got to go and see the C.R.A. at Woolwich on Tuesday afternoon to discuss this exercise we're having with the Gunners next month. I could take them in the staff car, save them a lot of mucking about on trains."

"I'll tell them when I get back Sir. Why don't you pop in for a drink tomorrow evening and fix it all up?"

"To be truthful Jim, I've had this cowardly feeling about facing Rose. I wrote to her but I haven't been able to summon up the courage to meet her face to face."

"She was very proud of and grateful for your letter Sir, and showed it to us all. You've nothing to worry about there. She's shattered of course but she's very composed. She'd like to see you I'm sure."

When Jim got back to Chandlers Lodge, only Ruth and Fred were there, the others had gone home and Rose had gone to bed. "What's this C.R.A. he's going to?" asked Ruth.

"The C.R.A. is the Commander Royal Artillery. He's the chap who co-ordinates the artillery support in a division. On this exercise we're going to have live ammunition firing over our heads as we carry out a battalion attack. It's supposed to get the men used to advancing under a barrage, get them used to the noise shells make when they go off near them and so on."

"I can tell you it's an experience most sane people can do without," said Fred. "Still, as long as you haven't got rookies firing them and dropping them short you should do alright."

Jim grinned. "I'll remember to hang back a bit," he said.

Colonel Tim called on Monday evening and was persuaded – though as he himself said, he didn't need a lot of persuading – to stay to dinner. Fred had to excuse himself early as he was on LDV patrol that evening, Alec and Jim had to go back to camp, which left Tim, Rose and Ruth together. After a slow start Ruth said, "What can Rebecca expect to find different in her life when she and Alec arrive in Canada?" Tim thought for a while and came to the conclusion that the main difference would be not having a place like London nearby, the cars are bigger, mainly from the United States, most people have one, and the distances between towns are vast. From Toronto to Calgary for example is roughly the same distance as London to Moscow.

"Where is your home town?" said Ruth.

"It's a place called Cochrane, a small but very pleasant town up towards Hudson Bay in Ontario. I will bring you some photographs of it when I see you again, if you'd be interested that is."

"I'll get the atlas," said Rose and ran upstairs returning with the huge Times Atlas of The World under her arm. They poured over it together. "There we are," he said, "miles from anywhere," and laughed.

"Now lets look at this distance between Toronto and Calgary," said Rose.

"Well, I only took that as an example because I happened to know the mileage," said Tim, "but when you look at a map like this and consider from here upwards," he ran across the page with his finger, "hardly anyone lives, it's mind-boggling."

They closed the book and Tim looked at his watch "I'd better be getting back or I'll have the Orderly Officer putting me on a charge," he said. "Thank you again for a lovely evening, and I'll pick you up at 12.15 as arranged."

As the colonel left, Alec and Jim returned, to be followed shortly afterwards by Fred. "What a charming man the colonel is," said Ruth, "he looked so young here this evening to be in command of six hundred odd men, it must be an enormous responsibility."

"Well, not really," said Alec "he leaves it all to us – doesn't he Jim?"

"Of course," said Jim, "he'd be lost without us I can assure you."

"Jim," said Rose, "you are getting as bad as Alec, you really are," and she smiled, it was the first real smile they had seen her give since the tragedy struck. It only lasted a short while but a smile it was, and it made them all very happy for her.

Chapter Nine

At noon on 31st May, Harry reversed the three tonner on to the bridge they had come to blow. They discovered that as a result of the riverbanks being much higher than the road, and the road having a dog-leg immediately after crossing the river with again a high bank along one side, it was impossible to have a direct view down the road leading away to Poperinghe. Harry said, "I think it might be a good idea if I mount the Bren gun up on that bank so that we are able to fire down the road. If any stray Jerries do come along, a few bursts might put the wind up them long enough for us to get finished and be away."

"Jolly good idea," said Captain Osbourne.

Harry jumped into the back of the truck and reappeared with a Bren gun and a box of magazines. Strictly speaking he shouldn't possess such a weapon but it 'arrived' in his possession when he 'discovered' it in an ack-ack fifteen-hundredweight truck designed for use to protect convoys from low flying aircraft. At the time he had said, "This might come in handy one day" and hid it away under a spare tarpaulin. He climbed up on the bank, sited the Bren gun so that it would be in a position to fire straight down the road, and ran back to help unload and position the explosive. They worked steadily until the captain said, "That sounds like a vehicle in the distance."

Harry immediately jumped to his feet and ran up on to the bank while the captain steadily and unhurriedly inserted detonators and ran the wires back. When Harry carefully looked over the top of the bank he saw, firstly, a British soldier hurrying along the road towards them. He would have been about five hundred yards away. The second thing Harry saw was a German motorcycle and sidecar unit carrying two Germans rapidly catching up on the soldier who, hearing the engine, had broken into a trot. It was obvious that he must have immediately decided he had no chance whatsoever in getting away, or perhaps he was totally exhausted, in any event, he stopped, faced the Germans with his hands in the air and turned as they pulled up beside him.

The distance was too great for Harry to have done anything to help the luckless soldier, added to which he had never fired a Bren gun in his life, so the chances of killing the Germans and missing the soldier were remote. He resigned himself to the fact that the man would be taken prisoner. Whilst all this was going through his mind, the German in the sidecar had climbed out. He was carrying a Schmeisser sub-machine gun slung across his chest. To Harry's horror, changing rapidly to rage, he saw him aim it point blank, there was burst of fire, the soldier doubled up and fell back into the ditch. The German took his seat back in the sidecar and they drove slowly on towards the bridge. Harry judged the distance to the first part of the dog-leg in the road to be about a hundred and fifty yards, and set his sights accordingly. "Even I can't miss at this distance," he said encouragingly to himself. They slowed a little more and Harry began to have fears they might turn round and go back, but they came on. Fifty yards to go and Harry's vision was getting blurred through concentrating on sighting his target along with the anger boiling inside him. He blinked rapidly to clear it and they were there. He let off a burst of fire, much too long in fact, the bullets go all over the place if you fire too long a burst, but he hit the driver causing him to slew round in the road, stall the engine, and slowly topple sideways off the machine, lifeless into the middle of the road. The soldier in the sidecar jumped out, looked around for somewhere to hide, but immediately realising there was nowhere for him to go, put his hands in the air and faced the direction from which the burst of fire which had killed his comrade had come. Harry was still so consumed with rage at the killing of the British soldier only minutes before, that he took careful aim and summarily despatched the murderer and when he had carried out the sentence, ending a trial in which he had in the space of only a tiny fraction of his life been a witness, prosecuting counsel, jury, judge and executioner, he laid the gun on its side and said out loud, "An eye for an eye, old son, an eye for an eye."

He started to walk down the bank to help the captain. "What happened?" asked the young sapper. Harry explained quickly as they continued to position the explosive.
"I think that will be enough," said the captain, "if they're as close as those two it's about time we weren't here. Will you take the lorry back and then come back to finish off?"

Harry took the lorry some distance along the road and parked it. There was still a fair quantity of explosive on it and he made a mental note to ask the captain whether they should dump it or not, he'd got a little jumpy about riding around on a time bomb. As he hurried back to the bridge he heard the roar of a fighter engine and looking over to his left, saw what looked like a Messerschmitt following the line of the river and rapidly closing on the bridge. He dived into the ditch and as he went, he saw the captain hiding behind a steel upright. The pilot saw nothing suspicious on the bridge but he did see the truck. He banked and turned and in a low shallow dive headed straight for it. At five hundred yards he fired a long burst into the target, which in the second he flew over, it exploded with a terrific roar, blowing the aircraft over on its side and plunging it cartwheeling in a mass of flames across the lush farmland. Harry ran to the bridge, "Does the Service Corps or the Royal Engineers get the credit for shooting that one down?" he yelled to the captain.

"We'll share it," replied the captain, "The only thing is we've got to walk all the way to bloody Dunkirk."

"Not if I can help it," said Harry and ran on across the bridge, round the bend and out of sight. A couple of minutes later the captain heard the roar of a motor cycle engine approaching, and then Harry stepped beside him calling out, "My Lord, your carriage awaits."

"Right, take it down the road and I'll set this little lot off. Then you can come back for me." Harry roared away and waited close to the shattered and burning truck, facing the way he had come, waiting for the big bang. As he idly looked into the ditch beside the road, he spotted one of his Red Cross flags, looking a bit tattered from being blown out of the truck but otherwise in one piece. He scrambled down and retrieved it and returning to the bike, he saw there was a vertical tube welded to the drivers' side of the sidecar obviously for the sole purpose of carrying a flag or banner of some sort.

He fixed it in, thinking that it would possibly deter anyone shooting at them. After all, if a German motorcycle combination was spotted, it would be assumed there would be Germans on it, particularly by Belgian or French soldiers not necessarily familiar with British uniforms. He began to have doubts as to the wisdom of riding around in German equipment, but the thought of walking all the way to Dunkirk swiftly outweighed his fears. As he mulled these points over, there was a tremendous roar and when the dust settled he moved forward to collect the captain. There was no sign of him. He raced forward to the point where the plunger had been positioned, and lying half in and half out of the water in the bottom of the ditch he saw the young sapper either dead or unconscious, having a nasty wound on the side of his head, his steel helmet lying in the ditch beside him. Harry dragged him up on to the bank and took the field dressing from the officers' pocket and tied up the wound. It was obvious that a bit of the steelwork of the bridge had hit him, only his steel helmet having saved him from certain death. He loaded him into the sidecar, and when they reached the lorry, Harry found some rope from off its canopy, which had been blown clear. He tied him in and pointed his nose towards Dunkirk. He had only travelled a mile or so when he saw a figure some four hundred yards from the road, staggering along, still carrying his rifle, but obviously all in. He turned down the rough track to meet him, but before he reached him the boy, for that's what he turned out to be, collapsed motionless on the bank at the side. Harry pulled up and shook the lad. "Wake up son, I've got you." The young man came to. "Come on, let's get you aboard" he continued half dragging him into the sidecar and wedging him in against the captain.

"How old are you?" said Harry.

"Eighteen," said the lad slowly coming round.

"But no one is supposed to be in the BEF under twenty," said Harry.

The young man grinned slightly but said no more, Harry never did find out how an eighteen-year-old had ended up at Dunkirk. They picked up two more walking wounded on the way sitting one on the pillion and the other precariously perched on the bank of the sidecar, hanging on to the flagpole. Harry made his way to the major at the C.C.S. who was still on the edge of the dunes patching people up for the journey back to England. A mile or so from Dunkirk, captain Osbourne had regained consciousness and when he had been seen by the major, had a final talk with Harry as to the success or otherwise at the bridge, during the course of which he took Harry's name, rank and number and, in addition, asked for his home telephone number or address so that he could get in touch with him one day. Little did they realise to what this exchange would eventually lead. They shook hands, Harry saluted and a medical orderly led the captain to the walking wounded queue, snaking its way out into the shallow water and moving oh! So slowly. He went back into the C.C.S. and realised he was very hungry.

"Any food going?" he asked one of the sergeants.

"There's plenty of bully and biscuits, but not much else – help yourself."

He tucked in to a feast, which if not cordon bleu, was very, very welcome indeed. He borrowed a couple of blankets and curled up in the back of the tent and although it was not yet eight o'clock in the evening, he was fast asleep in seconds.

The next morning he inspected his motorbike. It was a Zundapp and to his surprise had a British engine, a Rudge Python four stroke, he guessed about 500cc. The major came over to him.

"I thought you would have been away by now," he said, "what have you got there?"

Harry described how he had come by this piece of equipment and how their lorry had been blown up. "It was just as well we did have this," he said, "we would never have got through on the lorry, the road has so many shell holes and bomb craters in it. At least in this you can usually get round them. How long are you going to be here Sir?" he asked.

"Oh another couple of days at least," said the major.

"Right, well I'll go out on this for a couple of days and round up some more stragglers, then I'll get in a queue."

And so he did. Harry's German bike with its Red Cross flag became a familiar sight up and down the approach roads to Dunkirk, loaded to the gunwales with wounded, exhausted men who would not otherwise have reached the beaches. On the 4th he had had a particularly hair-raising time having been strafed, bombed and shelled running the gauntlet back to the C.C.S. all in the space of under an hour. He seemed to have a charmed life. When he finally got back at about four o'clock, one of the RAMC sergeants said, "The major wants you."

Harry duly reported himself to the major who just said to him, "No more – OK? We're off tonight."

"Right Sir, I'll come with you."

Later that evening, they were ferried aboard HMS Shikari, she was the last ship to leave Dunkirk. Over 350,000 men had been evacuated, but on the debit side all their equipment had been lost, 40,000 men had been left behind including the 51st Highland Division and the 3rd Armoured Division who, as rear guard, held off the might of dozens of Panzer Divisions, and 68,000 had been killed, wounded or missing. Despite the euphoria over the deliverance of those who got away, it was a monumental defeat.

It was around six o'clock on the morning of the 5th June when Harry, at last, set foot in the big customs shed at Dover, was recorded, given a rail warrant to his depot unit at Bulford and directed to a train waiting to go to London. He was totally exhausted having had to stand up all night against the ship's rail, the deck had been so crowded. The train too was packed and again he found himself standing in the corridor. It was two hours before it moved off and steadily made its way through Kent until it reached Tonbridge. At this point they were shunted into a siding where they stayed for over half an hour. When they again got under way, it soon became apparent to Harry that they were not on the direct line to Sevenoaks but were being subjected to a detour, which, as far as he could tell, would take them through Sandbury. The thought of his almost passing his own front door was infuriating, and became more so as they picked up the line from Maidstone and Harry began to pick out the familiar landmarks you look for to establish how near you are to your own station. As they approached Sandbury they slowed. Harry assumed this was to go through the station but to his delight they pulled off the main road and moved into the slow platform and stopped, obviously to let a fast train through. Without thinking further, Harry opened the door, got down on to the platform and walked to the exit. "Ticket, sergeant?" asked the elderly porter on the gate.

"I'm sort of breaking my journey for a couple of days," said Harry, showing him his travel warrant. "Any taxis around?"

"There's one outside," replied the porter, "but whether he'll take you the state you're in I don't know."

It was only then that Harry realised the state he <u>was</u> in.

The taxi man was an old soldier from the Great War. He did take him, guessed he had come direct from Dunkirk, and wouldn't charge him a farthing, which was just as well as Harry realised when he climbed in that he had no English money anyway. He told Harry how he came on leave once, direct from five weeks in the trenches without a break, and he was so lousy his wife wouldn't allow him in the house. She made him strip off in the front garden and then get into a tin bath in the outhouse with the water liberally laced with carbolic before she'd even kiss him. "Mind you," he continued with a salacious grin, "I didn't half make up for it afterwards!"

The taxi pulled into the little lane where Harry's cottage backed on to the river and pulled up.

"I'd better wait a minute to see if you can get in," said the driver.

"I'll break the door down if I can't," replied Harry. He knocked on the door, which was opened by a lady he had never seen before, but who looked at him with open mouthed, wide eyed surprise for a second or two before yelling, "Megan, look who's here."

Megan covered the distance from the kitchen through the hall to the front step in three bounds and threw herself into Harry's arms, laughing and crying and kissing his dirty, unshaven face. The taxi driver gave a friendly toot and, with a wave, drove away. The unknown lady muttered something about, "Well, I've got things to do," and made her way into the house next door, Harry assuming she was obviously a new neighbour, leaving them both hugging on the front step.

"Well, do I get asked in?" said Harry.

Megan, holding his hand tight, led him in.

"Let me look at you," she said, and when she had taken a long look at his filthy clothes, his face much thinner than when had been home at Christmas, his red rimmed eyes and five days growth of beard, she started to cry.

"Now come on my love," Harry said to her. "I know I look a wreck but a bath and a shave and a change of clothes and I'll be a match for Errol Flynn himself." She smiled through her tears.

"I must phone your mother and Mum and Dad at Carmarthen, but you must have something to eat, are you hungry?"

"I'm starving. They gave us the usual two thick sandwiches and a piece of fruitcake at Dover, but I couldn't get it down somehow. I'm so tired, I've had four hours sleep in the last three days, I slept standing up in the train. Now tell me, have you heard anything of David and Jeremy. I was told they were all either killed or captured."

Megan started to cry quietly again. "Jeremy was killed."

"Oh no, poor, poor Rose. Is she alright – how has she taken it?"

"She's been marvellous. David is safe in hospital at Ashford."

"Where are the kids?"

"They're with Nanny at The Hollies. I'm on duty this afternoon, at least I was, I'll phone them too."

Harry stood for a minute, holding her close.

"I'd better let you go – I smell."

"It's the loveliest, loveliest smell I've ever experienced in all my life," she said, and kissed him again. "Look, I'll do you a big fry-up, you go and have a quick bath, get into bed and you can have a meal on a tray. I'll do the phoning in the meantime."

She phoned Ruth at Chandlers Lodge who, in turn, passed on the good news to the rest of the family. She phoned Carmarthen, and then the hospital, where matron said, "We'll expect you when we see you," which was quite the most magnanimous and unprofessional sentence she had ever heard the matron utter. When the food was ready and she had taken a minute or two to straighten her hair and take her pinafore off, she took it up to their bedroom.

"Here we go," she said, but there was no answer. Her Harry, her exciting, wonderful lover Harry, who had brought her delights she hadn't dreamed existed, was curled up on his side, a little frown on his puckered up face, fast asleep and breathing deeply. She didn't know whether to laugh or cry. Instead, she put the tray on the chest of drawers and tip-toed to the windows and drew the curtains. As it was, she needn't have tip-toed, she could have thumped around in army boots, nothing would have awakened Harry from his sleep of utter exhaustion. She went back downstairs with the tray, came back for the pile of dirty clothing and for the next three hours washed, dried and ironed them. She then phoned Nanny to ask her if she could keep the twins overnight as she was afraid they would wake him up. She had had so many wounded at the hospital in the last few weeks who had slept the sleep of total fatigue that she knew it could be many hours before he surfaced, but he was here! He was here! – That was the main thing.

Megan made a bed up for herself on the sofa so as not to disturb him and woke early on the Thursday morning. When she crept upstairs and opened the door, to her surprise, he was lying back on the pillows awake.

"How long have I been here?" he said.

"Well, it's about half past six," replied Megan.

"And I got home about midday. Those six hours sleep will do me good."

"It wasn't six hours, its half-past six in the morning, so you've been there eighteen hours." She had reached the bedside by now.

"Do I smell any better?" he said, holding on to her hand. She bent over to pretend to make the necessary test in order to answer his question, he put his arms around her and pulled her to him. At half-past nine the phone rang continuously. They disentangled themselves deciding, with a great deal of reluctance, it had better be answered.

Chapter Ten

The visit to Colonel Scott-Calder, at the Herbert Hospital on the 4th June proved to be very interesting indeed to Ruth and the two girls. Colonel Tim picked them up as arranged but as he had discovered his meeting would not end until five o'clock, he had brought with him a pass letter to enable them to obtain entry to the officers' mess at the Royal Artillery depot about a mile away where he would arrange for them to be served tea, and where he would meet them to bring them home. After he had been dropped at the CRA office, he would send the staff car back to the hospital to wait for the ladies. Although they protested they could easily walk, he wouldn't hear of it, saying they could easily get themselves accosted with all those gunners around.

"My father was a gunner," remonstrated Pat.

"Well, it just proves my point doesn't it?" said Tim in a totally uncharacteristic cheeky reply. The girls looked at each other.

"Now we know where Alec gets it from, don't we? Said Ruth.

"I'm beginning to believe its all part of their training," continued Rose, "you know Manual of Saucy Remarks Canadian Officers for the use of."

They all laughed at the riposte. Rose was gradually coming back into the world, and Tim was so infinitely happy that he had, however inadvertently, been the cause of this tiny step she had taken.

The journey to Woolwich was uneventful. They were stopped at a check point on the A20 near Swanley but the ladies, having shown their identity cards, were quickly on their way again. As they pulled up at the huge hospital Ruth said, "Did you know that my husband was in this very hospital in the last war? It was founded by Florence Nightingale you know after the Crimean War."

"I didn't know either of those facts," said Tim, "but that's the problem I've found in England, you drive past history every day and it's not until you stop and start asking questions you find out all you've been missing. Take Sandbury Church for example. There's not only a Crusader buried in there, but people are actually buried under the floor in the nave. You go to a service there and you're sitting on top of Sir Roger de Everly or someone – it's fascinating. Anyway, I'll be off and I'll see you in the RA mess at about five o'clock. Give the colonel my regards – hope to see him about soon, and tell him its open house in my mess when he's next in Sandbury." He gave a cheery wave as he was driven away.

"We're to see Colonel Scott-Calder," said Ruth to the sergeant at the main gatehouse.

"Yes ma'am," replied the sergeant. "Orderly!!"

At the sergeant's bellow a young RAMC private almost ran into the room.

"Take these ladies to Colonel Scott-Calder in the senior officers' block."

"Yes sergeant. This way please ladies."

He led them to one of the massive blocks in the centre of the hospital, up four flights of stairs, along a seemingly endless corridor – "Bit of a route march ladies I'm afraid" – and eventually arrived at a desk where an extremely attractive sister wearing the uniform of the Queen Alexandra's nurses was seated.

"These ladies to see Colonel Scott-Calder," said their escort, and turned away with the thanks of them all following him. The colonel was in a pleasant room with a large window looking out over a kitchen garden well stocked and cultivated. He shook hands with each in turn and thanked them profusely for coming to see him. He was sitting up, with a frame over his legs covered by the bed clothes and looked thinner and a good deal paler than when they had last seen him at Rose's wedding – was that only four months ago?

"When will you be able to leave the hospital?" asked Ruth.

"Well, they tell me they've saved the leg, but I shall be here for another month, then I'll have a period of sick leave, during which time I shall have to put my mind to what I'm going to do next. Anyway, enough about me, have you heard about your other son Mrs Chandler?"

"No, we've still heard nothing at all, we're all very worried."

Harry, at that very moment, was just getting ready to join the queue to come home, and in a few hours would be back with them again.

They chatted on together. An orderly brought in tea and biscuits and when he had gone Ruth said to Rose, "You can be mother," and then looking at the colonel said "we can then see how good she's going to be at it."

"Is this so?" replied the colonel and took her hand "Oh, I am so happy for you. Now you must take care you know, don't overdo things, I really am delighted."

"You sound as though you're an expert in these matters," said

Ruth. "I'm sure we're all most surprised," looking at the other two smiling faces.

"It did sound a bit like that didn't it?" he said. "All the same, it's marvellous news."

They had finished their tea when a knock came on the door. When being bidden to enter a grey haired man in a wheelchair appeared in the doorway, dressed in a Government Issue dressing gown, with his legs covered in a blanket.

"I am very sorry colonel. I did not know you were entertaining visitors," he said in good English with a positive French accent.

"Oh please, do come in, how can I help you?"

"Well, matron told me you had come from Calais and as I have just come from there as well, I thought I would call on you. You were, I believe, the commanding officer of the City Rifles?"

"That is correct – yes."

"I owe my life to men of your command. Please allow me to introduce myself. I am General Edouard Strich."

"I think we already know of you, general. Do you know the name, or names of these men?"

"I shall never ever forget them. They were Piercey, Barclay, Beasley, Riley and Smith. They were led by a very brave and resourceful young man, Corporal Chandler."

The colonel smiled. "May I now introduce my guests General. Firstly Mrs Ruth Chandler, David Chandlers' mother, secondly Mrs Pat Chandler, David's wife and thirdly Mrs Rose Cartwright, David's sister. Rose lost her husband in the fighting in Calais," he added, the sadness showing in his voice.

The three ladies approached the general who suddenly was overcome with emotion. He took the face of Ruth and then Pat in his hands and kissed them on both cheeks, and when finally Rose approached him, he put his arms around her and just said, "I am so sorry, so terribly sorry."

There was a silence for a short while until the general recovered himself, and said, "You know the story then?" addressing his remarks both to the colonel and to the ladies.

"We know very little," said Ruth "please tell us what happened."

The general started by telling them how he had walked for a hundred and fifty kilometres to reach Calais evading Germans all the way, how he had been challenged at the outskirts of Calais and brought in to David's dugout, where he had to undergo critical examination before David would accept he was not a Fifth Columnist. He told them how they carried him for twenty-five miles, of the attack by the German plane and David's rescue of the pilot, and their final rescue by the R.A.F. He ended by saying as he had originally said to David, "You see, I was not only a very senior intelligence officer, but I am also Jewish. If therefore, I had fallen alive into German hands I would have suffered unspeakable torture. David therefore promised that he would make sure that would never happen."

"You mean…" said Pat.

"Yes, he is a very courageous young man."

They were all silent for a while at the conclusion of the story until, at last, the colonel said, "I speak for all of us when I say that you too are a very brave man General. Now tell me how are you progressing after all your experiences?"

The general told them that the specialists had been very worried about the infections in his feet, but they were now much happier and expected him to be able to resume duties in two to three weeks. "And now," he said, "I have intruded upon you for long enough. I will come and see you again tomorrow Colonel if I may, in the meantime ladies, I will say au revoir, which means that we shall most certainly meet again."

Rose held the door for him so that he could propel himself through. When he had gone Ruth said, "I shall have a word or two to say to our David when I see him. He didn't tell us a quarter of what the general told us."

"Would you have expected him to?" said the colonel with a smile.

The afternoon sped past until at four thirty Ruth said they would have to be making their way to the R.A. depot. The colonel rang for an orderly to take them back to the front vehicle park for pick up in Colonel Tim's staff car. With promises to come and see him again in a week's time they said their farewells.

The officers' mess at the R.A. barracks was a magnificent building. They were met by a young lieutenant, who told them he was the assistant adjutant and that he had been instructed to take good care of them, adding in a most engaging manner that the instruction was most certainly unnecessary. They had tea in the superb ante-room, served by white-jacketed mess waiters, during which colonel Tim arrived, causing the young lieutenant to spring to his feet and to call for another chair.

After asking whether 'Tony' (obviously the young lieutenant) had been looking after them properly and enquiring after the health of Colonel Scott-Calder, Tim looked around and said, "This is a bit different to our Nissen hut don't you think?"

The room, and the adjacent room leading into the bar which could by glimpsed through the open doorway, were high ceilinged, with beautifully sculptured cornices, the walls panelled and carrying large original oil paintings of battles past and of their commanders. The furniture was solid mahogany and the deep armchairs were superbly upholstered in the finest leather. Solid brass door and window fitments, and highly polished parquet floors covered in places with deep oriental carpets, all gave the impression of a very expensive gentleman's club, which of course, was exactly what it was.

"How long has the Regiment been here?" asked Tim.

"Well Sir," said Tony, "we have been at Woolwich since 1672, although of course, regiments of artillery have been used in the British Army for centuries before that. Edward III was the first commander to use artillery in 1344, although of course it was all very basic and cumbersome in those days. In 1716 the establishment here was renamed 'The Royal Regiment of Artillery' so we have a history in Woolwich of nearly three hundred years. We are, of course, very proud of that."

"And rightly so," said the colonel.

"I do hope I haven't bored you with all that guff," said Tony turning to the ladies.

"Far from it," answered Ruth, "we're most impressed with your knowledge of the regimental history. I take it you are a regular officer?"

"Yes I am, and as such, Regimental History is like learning the catechism all over again!"

They said their goodbyes to Tony who escorted them to the staff car and saw them off with an impeccable salute. Tim remarking that there was no doubt it was intended not so much for him but for his most attractive companions. "Very impressionable these young lieutenants," he added.

"You were one yourself once," teased Rose, and once again they were all secretly pleased to hear her taking part in the banter.

They arrived at Chandlers Lodge at shortly after seven to find Moira, Jack, Anni and Ernie there.

"We wanted to hear every word the colonel told you," said Jack "then perhaps we can get a proper picture of what happened. Added to which Mr Churchill is speaking on the wireless tonight – it will be a momentous occasion. I thought we all ought to be together to hear him."

"You will stay too, won't you Tim?" said Fred "if only to keep your two layabouts in order."

Tim needed no second invitation, despatched his driver, arranging for the duty driver to come and collect him when he telephoned. They had a cold supper preceded by a delicious marrowbone soup made by Ruth that morning and left to keep warm in the Aga, and by the time they had finished it was time for the speech. They knew it would be a sombre occasion, we had our backs to the wall, we were the only ones now able to fight the might of Nazi Germany, and only a tiny strip of water, the Royal Navy and the R.A.F. were preventing our being overrun.

And sombre Winston Churchill was. He did not seek to minimise the great crisis we were now having to endure. He spoke of the heroic resistance of the men of Calais, a brigade of Riflemen, a handful of tanks and a thousand gallant Frenchmen were opposed by two complete German armoured divisions. For four days the men of the Rifles with their brave allies prevented the Germans from moving towards Dunkirk. With this time gained, the Gravelines waterlines were flooded which finally prevented any advance against the Dunkirk perimeter from the south and enabled the evacuation of nearly four hundred thousand men able to fight another day. He concluded this growling, proud, and defiant speech, the greatest speech he ever made, possibly the greatest speech anyone, anywhere ever made by saying,

"Whatever the cost shall be, we shall fight on the beaches, we shall fight on the landing grounds, we shall fight on the fields and on the streets – WE SHALL NEVER SURRENDER!"

There was a silence as the speech finished. Each and everyone in the room were profoundly moved in his or her own way. Rose was quietly crying with Ruth and Pat holding her close, Anni and Moira too were overcome with the emotion of it all, whilst the men stood grim visage realising what a desperate plight the country was in. Fred broke the silence.

"I give you a toast – our Winnie."

They raised their glasses and drank.

"And thank God we've got him," said the realistic Jack. "God knows what would be happening now if Chamberlain had still been there."

There followed another short silence broke by Ruth saying "I wonder where Harry is tonight," but as no one there could answer her question it remained unanswered, while Harry himself was at that moment, up to his waist in water and just about to tumble into one of the last of the little boats which would ferry him out to HMS Shikari, and then the little boat would itself sail off to Dover at the end of ten days of heroism which would remain for the rest of their days in the memory of the two young seventeen-year-olds who had manned it during that time.

The speech over, they went their various ways. Ruth and Fred went up to bed, but it was a long time before either of them got to sleep.

"It's the not knowing," said Ruth. "It was the same when you were in France. Day after day after day looking to see if you were among the names on the casualty lists. If Harry had got away we would surely have heard by now."

"He might have been among the last," replied Fred, "in which case we could still hear." He said this more to ease Ruth's pain and misery rather than any firm belief in what he was saying.

Ruth gave a little sob "Poor Megan – what must she be going through." Fred held her close and in a while they slept.

Ruth was about again as usual in the morning, getting the various members of her flock about their daily business. At half past twelve, the telephone shrilled and with her usual, "Who's that I wonder," to Rose she walked into the hall to answer it. In seconds she was back in the kitchen hugging Rose up and saying, "Harry's back, Harry's back," to a delighted Rose. Mother and daughter laughing and crying at the same time, did a little jig in front of the Aga until Ruth said, "We must phone the factory, you can then phone the hospital to ask sister to tell David, Ernie will tell Anni. I will phone Jack – he's home today and he will phone Pat and Moira and you can phone Colonel Tim if you will so that he can tell Jim and Alec."

Rose looked amusedly at her mother through her tears. "You've really got things organised haven't you?"

Ruth laughed and ran out into the hall to make the first call leaving Rose on her own. She sat down looking across the deal table to the glistening black surface of the Aga and the thought suddenly struck her – "But no-one is coming back to me." Her sadness was so acute, her despair so overwhelming that for a few moments she felt near to fainting and fleetingly closed her eyes. When she reopened them she saw clearly across the table, standing in front of the Aga, her beloved Jeremy. He was smiling at her, that gentle smile she knew so well and loved so much. She whispered his name, "Jeremy – is it really you?" She sat absolutely still, looking into his eyes, trying to find if there was

115

sadness there, or pain, but there was none. The eyes that met hers showed only love and tenderness and, at the same time, seemed to be willing her to forget the despair so recently felt. At last, after making small movements with his hands he gradually faded from her sight, leaving her with an inner happiness she could not describe, and although she visualised her great love many times over the years that followed, never was the picture so clear, distinct and near to her as it was that morning. She treasured that moment all her life, and despite the fact the heartache would never ever finally leave her, from then on, she was able to think about and talk about, Jeremy without the sick feeling of hopelessness she had endured since receiving that dreadful telegram. She knew he had been with her and would always be with her.

Ruth bustled back in. "I've phoned your father and Uncle Jack," she said, "now you do your calls." Rose smiled at her.

"You look ten years younger," she said.

"Away with you, how can I possibly look twenty-one with a daughter your age," she joked back, and picking the kettle up, continued, "we need a cup of tea."

It took a little while for Rose to get through to the sister at the hospital but eventually she was put through and was assured the message would be passed to David straight away. There was no delay when she phoned Colonel Tim.

"There's a Mrs Cartwright on the line for you Sir, says it's personal," said the operator with the 'personal' heavily accentuated.

"Put her through you idiot, don't hang about," replied Colonel Tim. The operator grinned a knowing grin to himself. The colonel was changing his spots was he? A married woman too, "Sounded very dishy she did," when he recounted the incident to his relief later on.

"Don't you say a bloody word beyond these walls or he'll have you bloody shot," was the relief's warning, "what you hear on this phone you keep to your bloody self." He'd obviously got to like the sound of the 'bloody' since he had been in England.

"Rose, how nice to hear from you? I know, I spilled some Whitbread's on the carpet last night and you're phoning to give me a rocket."

"No, nothing as mundane as that. I'm phoning the good news that Harry is back, and I wondered if you'd be so kind as to tell Jim and Alec."

"I say, that's great news, I bet you're all so relieved."

They chatted on animatedly for several minutes, the call being carefully timed by the operator so as to lend weight to his intended story to the relief later on.

"Does David know yet?"

"I hope so; I've asked the sister in his ward to pass the message on. Mum, Pat and I are going to see him this afternoon. We're going on the train, in fact we shall have to leave very shortly now."

"I tell you what, I've got to go to Shornecliffe some time in the next few days, why don't I pop in and give you a lift. I've nothing important on here today so I could come to the hospital with you and then pop off to Shornecliffe for an hour while you're still visiting, and then give you a lift back."

"Oh, you are kind. That would be marvellous."

"See you at one-thirty then, bye, bye."

He sat back smiling with satisfaction at the turn of events while Rose hurried in to give the news to her mother and to Pat who had just arrived. "The only problem now," he thought to himself, "is finding someone at Shornecliffe that I can visit with good enough reason at this short notice." But Colonel Tim had not become a lieutenant colonel in his mid thirties without being possessed of a certain amount of initiative which he now put to what, in his opinion, was very good use.

David was sitting up when they arrived and looked a lot brighter than he had when they last saw him on the previous Sunday. Piercey was still there, but Barclay, Beasley and Smith 24 had been sent off to the depot the day before, the French boys had gone on Tuesday and Riley had been sent off to a hospital near his home in Darlington, from which he would be discharged.

"It's a funny thing – war," said David. "Riley's gone and I'll never ever see him again." He was silent for a moment. "Now," he said, "I want to know everything about Harry and Colonel Scott-Calder."

The afternoon sped past. Colonel Tim came back and chatted with David for a few minutes before he, Rose and Ruth went out to the staff car leaving Pat with David for a while. After Pat had left and David leaned back on his pillows, feeling strangely drained, Piercey looked across and said, "I thought you only consorted with generals, Corporal. I didn't think you'd lower yourself to hob-nob with a mere colonel, and a Canadian at that."

"Oh, I'm not proud," retorted David, "as long as they keep their place." They both laughed. It's funny what you laugh at when you're stuck in a hospital bed – if you feel like laughing at all that is.

The telephone call that disturbed Harry and Megan the next morning was, of course, Ruth enquiring after Harry's health. Megan, who had a wonderful understanding with her mother-in-law said that she was very pleased to report that despite what Harry may or may not have been through recently, there was definitely nothing wrong with his health. Ruth laughed and laughed, and asked whether they would come round for lunch, to which Megan replied that they would be delighted to join them, and that Harry was going on to Bulford on the four o'clock train that afternoon. "Though how he will explain a clean uniform when he gets there I don't know."

"They'll be so pleased to see him they won't even notice it," said Ruth.

When Megan and Harry arrived, all the family, along with Jack, Anni and Ernie and the two Canadians were there to greet him! Ruth looked at him closely and saw one or two lines particularly around the eyes, which weren't there before. He was thinner too. She made no comment on her observations.

"We've found out David's story, now we want yours," said Fred.

"Wait till he comes on leave," said Ruth, "he'll have more time then."

"When do you think that will be?" asked Alec.

"As far as I know, once I've been documented and so on and issued with new kit, I get fourteen days – at least that was the talk going around at the sheds at Dover. So hopefully, I should be home sometime next week."

It was soon time for him to go and before he went he held Rose very close to him away from the others and said, "Now you remember this young lady, if you want to talk to anyone at anytime, day or night, you come on to me. I'll let you have my mess number as soon as I get to Bulford or wherever I'm posted after that."

Rose hugged him back. "Thank you dear Harry, thank you so much – and I'm so happy and grateful you are back with us."

They had said all they both needed to say.

Chapter Eleven

The following Saturday was Cup Final day. Jack and Moira took Pat and Ruth to visit David, Jack having enough petrol in hand to get Moira's little Morris Eight to Ashford and back. They took with them a portable second-hand wireless set for David that Jack had picked up in a radio shop in Sandbury. It was a Vidor set made only the previous year using the new type dry batteries, which replaced the normal accumulator. "The lads can hear the match on this and then David can eventually bring it home with him," said Jack. In the event it brought a lot of pleasure to those who had no visitors, those that did, being able to listen to the second half after the visitors had gone. Piercey was particularly pleased to hear his home team, West Ham beat Blackburn one-nil, much to the annoyance of a couple of Lancashire Fusiliers in nearby beds who had had five-shilling bets on with him.

During the visit, David was able to tell them that he had been told he would be having his stitches out on the following Monday, and that a couple of days after that if there were no problems, he would be sent on hospital leave for seven days. "The same applies to Piercey," he said.

"But you've no uniform," said the ever practical Ruth.

"We're issued with those 'Hospital Blues' you see chaps walking around in," said David. "They're pretty ghastly, but I can put my civvies on when I get home."

'Hospital Blues' were a pale blue flannel tunic and trousers, a white shirt and bright red tie. As they were used and re-used they could hardly be called made to measure, and being flannel they crumpled the minute they were put on.

"Can you bring me a pair of shoes tomorrow?" David asked Pat. "I could get a pair of boots from the stores here but my feet are still very tender so I didn't fancy breaking a pair of boots in at this stage. Oh, and will you bring me a cap badge from my old terrier uniform. They'll give me a forage cap, but I shall feel naked without the Rifles badge on it."

"What a lovely thought," said Pat, mercifully out of the hearing of the others.

And so it happened that all three came on leave on Wednesday 12th, Harry from Bulford, David from Ashford and Kenny Barclay from Winchester, who had telephoned Chandlers Lodge on the Monday morning and spoken to Ruth saying, "Did you really mean I could come and stay with you when I'm on leave Mrs Chandler?"

"Of course we did – your room is all ready, we're looking forward to seeing you."

When he arrived, kitted out in an immaculate new uniform, he presented his ration cards and said, "I've been paid, so how much can I give you for my board and lodging?"

Ruth hugged him to her. "You're our guest and a comrade of our son, we couldn't dream of taking anything from you, we really are very, very pleased to have you. Now, you're to treat this place just like your own home – isn't he Rose? You come and go as you please but let me know if you're not going to be in for meals. I'll give you a key in case we're out or you're in late."

There was a pause until Kenny said, "This will be new to me, you see I've never had a home, not a proper one." Another pause, "But I'll make myself useful, you want anything done, you just say. Cleaning windows, washing up, garden jobs, anything, you just say the word. The only thing that worries me is living with those two officers – how are they going to take having a buckshee rifleman floating around?"

"They'll call you Kenny; you call them Sir, just as you would normally. You'll find it will work itself out; they're very nice people and will treat you as one of the family. David calls them by their Christian names, but even he calls the colonel Sir and the general too when he's here. It'll all work out, you'll see."

And work itself out it did. Kenny found he was readily accepted by all the family and, in particular, by young John and the twins who Nanny had to bring every morning to Chandlers Lodge to play football with a tennis ball on the lawn with him or to play soldiers in the spinney at the end of the kitchen garden. Kenny ended up getting shot every time, much to the delight of Elizabeth who then became a nurse to look after him.

When David arrived home at the Bungalow, having got a taxi from the station, he was given a rapturous welcome, not only from Pat but also from Susie whose 'purr could have been heard a mile away.' As soon as he sat down she jumped on him, rubbed against him, jumped down and crazily raced round the room only to jump back on him again. It was a full ten minutes before she eventually settled on his lap and looked up at Pat as much as to say 'Don't you dare take me off!'" From then on until David went back off leave she was never more than three or four feet away from him as he moved about the house and garden, and had to be forcibly removed into the conservatory when they went to bed at night (or in the afternoon).

David's leg was still very sore and badly bruised which considerably reduced his mobility. He found it impossible to ride his bike. They used the hourly bus to get into Sandbury but this meant having to leave either the Hollies or Chandlers Lodge by nine o'clock to catch the last bus back. As Harry said to his father with a grin, "Having to have an early night every night won't worry David I don't suppose!" During his leave, he and Pat took the train to London and then out to Woolwich to visit Colonel Scott-Calder and General Strich, although the sergeant at the main gatehouse at the Herbert Hospital was more than a little surprised that a corporal, even if not in uniform, should be visiting a colonel and a general. Even so, he bellowed again for the orderly to take them to the senior officer's wing, the orderly setting off at such a pace that David had to say, "Hey, hold your horses, I may be a rifleman that I can't keep that pace at the moment." The orderly grinned and slowed down. Both the colonel and the general were delighted to see them both, the general making much to two of his colleagues visiting him of the fact that this was the young man who saved his life. However, it has to be said that the two colleagues both being Frenchmen in their middle forties were far more interested in Pat, who looked particularly fetching in a lemon and black spring suit, on the lapel of which was proudly displayed a Rifles badge made into a brooch. They asked the general when he would be ready to leave the Royal Herbert and he thought in about a week or so. Pat immediately invited him to stay at the Hollies during his convalescence if he would care to do so.

"You are very, very kind to me," said the general taking her hand. "I would very much like to take up your kind offer. I'm sure I shall get fit again much more quickly in the country than in a hotel in London," but as they were talking, an interruption came in the form of another French officer coming into the room. He was in tears.

"The army has evacuated Paris," he said. "I have just heard it on the radio. Paris has fallen to the Boche and they are, at this moment, marching down the Champs Elyseés."

There was a stunned silence, broken eventually by the general saying, "It was inevitable," and then, "but we shall be back don't ever doubt it – we shall be back." But it was to be four long years before that prophecy became reality and the general again saw his beloved Paris. An awful lot was to happen in the meantime to each of those people in that room on that lovely day in May, as it was to millions of others throughout the world.

David went back off his hospital leave on the following Tuesday night, but was able to get a 48-hour pass at the weekend while Harry and Kenny were still on leave. Ruth had suggested to Fred they might have a few friends in on the Saturday evening and invite Buffy and Rita up for the weekend.

It was still only a month since Jeremy was killed which prompted Fred to say, "Well as long as we don't make a party of it."

Ruth squeezed his arm "No-one will do that, and it will, perhaps, help Rita and Buffy to be with others for a while." When she phoned Romsey, Rita said they would be most pleased to come and, in addition on the Thursday, General Strich telephoned Pat to ask whether he could take up her kind offer for him to stay as he was now convalescing. He was therefore, installed in The Hollies on the Friday where he told Ruth later that he was being thoroughly spoilt by Nanny and constantly amused by young John and the twins.

The Saturday evening went off well. Rose made a point of having cheerful conversation with everyone, which set all at ease, the general was genuinely delighted to see Kenny Barclay again telling everyone, with his arm round a slightly embarrassed Kenny's shoulder, that "this is the young man who helped to carry me nearly forty kilometres to avoid capture," and above all, the general atmosphere slowly brought Buffy back to something approaching his old self.

At nine o'clock they listened to the news to hear that general DeGaulle, with the agreement of the British Government, had announced the formation of the French National Committee in London with the object of carrying on the war against Germany. Everyone pressed forward to congratulate the general who was close to tears with the kindness being extended to him, and with the emotion of realising that, from now, it could be Frenchman fighting Frenchman, a circumstance the thought of which filled him with horror.

On Sunday morning they all went to church – even Kenny, who said jokingly to David, "Do you think they'll let me in?" It was his first visit to church and it affected him quite deeply, more so than he would have admitted to anyone, except perhaps David.

In a couple of days the lads had all gone back off leave, the Canadians were away on a seven day exercise and Rose had gone back with Rita and Buffy for a few days, taken from her holiday entitlement. Ruth and Fred suddenly found they were in the unusual state of having themselves to themselves. "Crikey, we could walk around with nothing on if we want to," Fred exclaimed. "Now that's a turn up for the book."

Ever practical Ruth replied, "Since no one's going to be here for the next week, why don't we have a little holiday. I've always wanted to go to Chester – it's a beautiful city – let's go on Thursday and come back on Monday – can they manage at the factory?"

The whole of this sentence was said with one excited breath which so took Fred by surprise that he could only say "of course they can – hey, wait a minute," he paused "maybe it's not such a daft idea," another pause, "OK, you're on, go and get the things ready, cancel the milk and so on and I'll organise the factory."

They had a lovely time at Chester. They stayed at the Grosvenor and were looked after in a manner, which would very soon disappear for many years to come. They walked the Roman walls around the city, visited the Cathedral, went shopping on The Rows and found a lovely little 16th century pub where they had a noggin before lunch each day. Monday came all too soon – it had been a wonderful break but it would be two long years before they got another.

When they arrived back at Chandlers Lodge on Monday evening, they found the four girls waiting for them with a light meal all prepared. After they had eaten Fred said he would have a quick run down to the factory to see Ernie, who would be there until ten o'clock. When he had left, Rose led the questioning as to, as she put it, did anything unusual occur? Put in a very casual way but with a wealth of meaning.

"Well," replied Ruth, "I have to tell you that in the hurry in packing before we went away, I found that I had forgotten to put a nightdress in," she paused.

"Well go on," said Megan, "don't keep us in suspense."

"Well," – another pause – "I said I shall have to sleep without one, and buy one in the department store next door tomorrow," another pause, "but somehow we didn't get round to it at all." There was much laughter at this. She continued, "But we did buy this and from her handbag she took a burgundy coloured box which she opened to show the most exquisite antique Cameo brooch the girls had ever seen. There were gasps of admiration, broken by Anni saying, "But Auntie Ruth, what did you have to do to get that?"

"Ah – now that would be telling wouldn't it?"

Pat kept the ball rolling, "Now, mother, you must tell us, then we'll know how to play our own cards when the opportunity arises."

In the midst of the general laughter, Alec and Jim arrived, and each having given Ruth a hearty kiss and welcome home hug, demanded to know what the general merriment was about.

"It was girls talk really," said Megan, "we were shown a most expensive present our mother was given whilst away on her second honeymoon and we were hazarding guesses as to how she came by it."

"May we see the item in question?" said Alec. The brooch was produced. Alec and Jim looked at it in silence for a moment or two. "It is obviously very valuable," Alec said. "Do you think, Jim, it represents a reward perhaps, or maybe a gift to celebrate an anniversary of some sort, or…"

"Or an appreciation of having forgotten her nightie," broke in Rose. The Canadians were convulsed with laughter when this was explained to them.

Finally, Jim came up with the answer, "There is no doubt in my mind that this decoration to Mrs Ruth Chandler was awarded for conspicuous service for several days over and above the course of duty." Loud clapping followed this announcement, which he interrupted by saying "Or should it have been for several nights?"

On the day that his parents returned from Chester, David was posted to the Rifles depot at Winchester. He travelled in his civilian clothes, arriving at the depot guardroom soon after 2.30. The sergeant of the guard was in conversation across the guardroom table with the provost sergeant as he entered, so he stood to one side until such time as their business would be concluded. Suddenly the guard sergeant grabbed his hat off the table and jumped to attention as through the doorway appeared the immaculate figure of the depot RSM.

"Sergeant Martin," he said, addressing the provost sergeant, "I've been looking for you about these deserters they caught at Andover." Glancing around, he saw David standing there rigidly to attention, although in civilian clothes.

"Why aren't you in uniform?" he roared.

"I'm afraid I lost it Sir," replied David.

"What? You lost it? How did you lose it?"

"I lost it at Calais, Sir. I've just come from Ashford Hospital."

"Calais eh? What's your name?"

"Corporal Chandler Sir."

The RSMs attitude changed immediately.

"Yes, that's right Corporal, I've got all your details, I'm sorry I bellowed at you, it's been a bad day. Wait there a minute will you?"

The two sergeants, both old regulars, looked at each other wide eyed. The RSM apologising to a corporal – what was the bloody world coming to they wondered. Perhaps the old man was going soft in the head. After all, he had done twelve years in India and another three in Palestine, all that bloody sun must have affected him somehow. They were brought to earth by the RSM asking whether the escorts to Andover had been organised to which the provost sergeant said that they had just left and he was checking with the guard sergeant that the cells were ready. He then left.

"Right," said the RSM, "now let's get you organised. Sergeant Betts, can I borrow your stick man for an hour or so?"

"Of course Sir, he's got nothing special on until he gets the guard's tea at half-past four. Lawson! Cap on and double forward." Lawson appeared from the back of the guardroom.

"Now, my lad, take the corporal here first to the quartermaster's stores. Present my compliments to the RQMS and ask him to fit him out with a complete kit. Oh, and ask him from me to make sure that at least one of his battle dresses is a good fit. Ask him, as well, for two sets of sergeants' stripes for his blouses and one for his great coat. When you've got all the kit, take the corporal to the sergeants' mess and see Sergeant Willis there. He knows what's going on and has got a bunk ready. Dump all the kit, except the battle dress blouses and great coat and then go to the regimental tailor. Tell him, from me, to drop what he's doing and sew the stripes and badges on the battle dress and check the collars fit properly. Then go to the barbers' shop and make sure the corporal gets a haircut, he bloody well needs it. Then dump his tunics in his bunk and bring him to my office. Now son, can you remember all that?"

"Yes, Sir, I've got all that."

"Right then, off you both go."

By four o'clock or a little after, David found himself in the RSMs office, next door to the adjutant's and the C.O.'s offices, having been kitted out and shorn a bit closer than he really would have preferred.

"Sit down," said the RSM, looking a great deal less fierce without his cap on. "Now you're probably wondering what the hell this is all about. First of all as from six o'clock this evening, Part Two Orders will announce you are promoted to lance sergeant. As to why and what's happening after that, the CO will see you and explain, so you'll present yourself here tomorrow morning for C.O.'s orders at ten o'clock, though with what we've got on it'll be probably nearer eleven before you go in – he'll deal with all the rubbish first." (The 'rubbish' would be the defaulters, remanded to be dealt with by the CO by company commanders for more serious crimes than they would normally award sentences).

"Now my lad, I want you to tell me hour by hour what happened over there. Two very old friends of mine were in your lot, CSM Ward and Sergeant Harris. What happened to them – do you know?" David went through the day by day story and when he had finished the RSM sat back in his chair and there was such sorrow on his face. "Fancy losing a whole brigade of Riflemen, it just doesn't bear thinking about. Wardie and me were together in the last lot you know. By Christ, we had some close shaves."

There was a silence for a while, broken by, "Well then, it's no use moping, it's nearly six o'clock so we'll go to the mess and have a quick drink then I must get home to the Duchess or she'll have my guts for garters."

The thought that there was someone, somewhere who could instil fear of any description on the most fearsome RSM of all the RSMs in the regiment made David almost laugh out loud, but he just grinned at the RSM and said, "Thank you for all you've done for me Sir."

"That's alright, son, we're proud of you, you know."

David didn't know and decided not to comment further. Whatever the hell was happening, he'd find out in the morning. The RSM bought David a beer, introduced him to a colour sergeant and another platoon sergeant and then departed to present himself to the Duchess. David ate his supper and then telephoned Pat. After the usual introductory pleasantries David said, "Oh, by the way, you are now talking to Sergeant Chandler."

"What do you mean, is Harry there?"

"No, you nut case – I am now a sergeant."

He went on to explain what had happened since he arrived and that he was to see the C.O. in the morning – "A lieutenant colonel and a Lord to boot," he added. "His full method of address is Lieutenant Colonel The Lord Gravely – I understand he is more commonly known in the depot as 'Old Gravy Face'."

Pat was excited and curious about the forthcoming meeting and made David promise that as soon as he possibly could, after it finished, he was to phone her at the shop – "Get the operator to reverse the charges so that you don't have to mess about with coins," she added.

"God, if you're offering to pay for the call you must be keen to find out what's happening. Are you sure it won't break the Country Styles' bank?"

They went on chatting for a few minutes until Pat said, "Well, I must go now and tell everybody the news. Susie sends her love – so do I, bye, bye darling – sorry – sergeant," and with that, she rang off.

David, grinning, went back to his bunk. The room was spacious and comfortable. It was, of course, a peacetime establishment, the general décor and fitments of the mess bar, dining room and living quarters reflected the comfort that senior NCOs and warrant officers in the Rifles in peace time would expect. He tried his uniform on to ensure he would make a good initial impression on 'Old Gravy Face' in the morning. The boots were not up to the standard he would have liked so he set about spitting, polishing and boning the toe caps with the handle of a toothbrush for over half an hour to get some degree of shine on them. Both his blouses were a good fit after the tailor had taken the collars in a bit, and the huge black stripes separated and surrounded by gold piping and worn only on the right arm, unique to the Rifles, gave him an intense feeling of pride. He spent another quarter of an hour burnishing his cap badge and then deciding he could do no more, carefully hung up the uniform in the wardrobe ready for the next day.

At five minutes to ten precisely, Lance sergeant David Chandler presented himself at the anteroom housing the various bodies waiting to be seen for one reason or another by the commanding officer. At precisely ten o'clock the C.O.'s door opened and the RSM appeared.

"Railton," he bellowed.

"Here Sir," said a regimental provost corporal; bringing forward a miscreant to whom he was handcuffed.

"Take those off then. Escort and accused Attention! Quick March, left, right, left, right, party halt, left turn, Rifleman Railton Sir." The door closed, but whilst the defaulter was being marched through, David caught a quick picture of the colonel sitting at the desk. He looked quite old, probably brought out of retirement David thought to do a desk job.

The defaulter was marched out and promptly re-handcuffed – they were obviously taking no chances with him for some reason. "Right my lad" said the RSM. "Fifty six days in the Glasshouse will teach you that you can't go round bashing NCOs. Take him away."

And so the various parties were dealt with until, as the RSM had guessed, at just after eleven o'clock, he appeared again through the door. "Sergeant Chandler!"

"Sir."

"Fall in here. Attention!" David saw he was given a quick look over before the RSM continued "Quick March, left, right, left, right, party halt, left turn. Salute the officer. Sergeant Chandler, Sir!"

"Stand at ease sergeant," said the Colonel.

David studied the noble Lord, who equally was studying him intently.

"Tell me, sergeant, are you now recovered from your injuries?"

"Yes Sir, fully, thank you Sir."

"Good, well, there are several things I have to tell you about. First of all we all would like to congratulate you on your initiative in getting yourself and your men back from France." He looked round where the adjutant, R.S.M. and field officer of the day were standing nodding in agreement. "Secondly, your saving a very senior French Officer from capture and eventual death has brought great credit to you and to this regiment, since its repercussions have been felt not only with the French forces, but also in very high circles at Horse Guards and in Southern Command. Thirdly, we have had a report of your gallantry from your commanding officer, Colonel Scott-Calder whilst you were in Calais."

David had an irreverent thought at hearing all this – 'they're going to make me a general.'

The colonel continued, "Finally, I understand your application for a commission was approved before you went to Calais. I understand you and your friend, Corporal Cartwright, whose family are friends of mine at Romsey and who, sadly, did not come back, asked that these approvals be 'lost' until you came back." David still kept quiet working on the old army adage 'never admit anything'.

"This is why we had you promoted to sergeant so that you didn't have to go back into the barrack room. Until you leave here you will at least have a room to yourself. Now, a place has been found for you at the new cadet unit at Worcester, the course commencing Monday 5th August, the adjutant will be giving you joining dates in due course.

The next thing is that Colonel Scott-Calder recommended you to receive The Distinguished Conduct Medal for your gallantry in destroying a tank. I am pleased to tell you that this has been approved and will be on Part Two Orders tonight. You will then have to go to Southern Command Headquarters in a couple of weeks' time to receive the actual decoration. In addition to that you and all your men, Riflemen Piercey, Barclay, Riley, Beasley and Smith 24 have been Mentioned in Despatches. These awards too will be on Part Two Orders tonight. Now, lastly, which regiment do you wish to join after OCTU?"

"I would very much like to come back into the Rifles Sir – I can't imagine being anywhere else."

"It's not a cheap outfit you know, even in wartime. Have you got any money?"

"Yes Sir. I have my own money and my family are reasonably well off."

"Well, I'm sorry to have to ask you that, come to that, I wish I could give the same answer to the same question!" David was beginning to warm to this somewhat dandified peer of the realm.

"Right then, that's settled. When you return from OCTU where you will be doing all that arms drill, square bashing red coat rubbish, you will come back for a month under the eagle eye of RSM Forster here who will teach you again how to be a Rifleman, then we'll post you to a battalion somewhere where you will quickly learn that as a second lieutenant you will be the lowest form of life – is that not true Algy?" (To the adjutant).

"I think he'll survive it Sir," said a smiling captain the Hon. Algernon Cotherington, whose father, grandfather and his father before him had all been in the Rifles.

"Right then, we'll leave it at that."

The RSM sprang into action. "Attention! Salute the officer, left turn, quick march," and David found himself halted outside the door.

"Go into my office, I've got a couple of things to clear with the adjutant then I'll be there. Tell the orderly room clerk to bring two mugs of tea and not to forget the bloody sugar in mine today for a change."

David went to the Orderly Room and gave the clerk the RSM's message verbatim, to which the response was "He was too long in India – he likes a little tea with his sugar does that one." The orderly room clerk was a time-served soldier – he'd been managing RSMs for years, he was one person in the depot that none of the hierarchy could do without.

When Mr Forster arrived back he said, "Well, congratulations – it looks as though I shall be calling you Sir soon doesn't it?" He said this in the most friendly of tones. "Anyway it's for the good of the regiment as I see it; I reckon you'll make a good officer. Incidentally, who was this corporal the C.O. was talking about from Romsey?"

"Corporal Cartwright Sir, he was my brother-in-law."

"Oh no! How old is your sister?"

"She's eighteen Sir, they were only married for two months, he was a wonderful chap. We were at school together and then in the Terriers together. I still can't believe it's all happened."

"I know what its like," Mr Forster said after a pause. "I lost two of my older brothers in the last lot." He paused again.

"Right now, back to business. You're entitled to leave but we can't let you go until we know when you've got to go to Command HQ. I understand they've got a new G.O.C. coming, then they will notify us. In the meantime, anything you want to do here?"

"Yes Sir, I'd like to get fit again. All that lying around in hospital and sick leave and so on has softened me up."

"Well, have a word with the P.T.I. CSM – he'll fix you up, although he's a bit short-handed at the moment I believe."

"Right Sir. I'll go over to the gym and have a word with him and thank you very much again."

David stood up, put his cap on, came to attention, did a smart about turn and marched out of the office. The RSM noted the courtesy and respected him for it.

When he arrived at the gym, the CSM Instructor was seated at a table filling in some returns. "Yes, sergeant, what can I do for you?" he said affably adding, "You're new, where have you come from? And talking about policemen getting younger all the time, I don't think I've ever seen a younger sergeant than you."

"Well Sir," said David, dodging the question as much as he could, "I've come from hospital and the RSM said you might be able to help me get fit again – I'm pretty flabby at the moment."

"I've only got one other instructor at the moment. I've got one who fell off the parallel bars and broke his arm, another on a course up at Retford for two weeks, another on leave to get married, silly sod, and the last one in the nick today for bashing a corporal in a pub in the City. How are you on taking P.T? We're getting rookie platoons in one every two weeks, so we're up to our eyes in getting them fit enough to even put their bloody boots on, without being able to play as soldiers. It's all simple P.T. drill you've done hundreds of times and road runs every day getting longer each day. You can kill two birds with one stone, shake these blighters up and brighten yourself at the same time. If you can do three or four mornings a week for the next couple of weeks that would really help me out."

"Right Sir, you're on."

"OK. They're here 10.30 in the morning till 12 o'clock – there's a list of exercises, there's a list of runs, they're on Number Four at the moment so it will be Number Five tomorrow. Now, if you get puffed allow them to walk because you don't want <u>them</u> to over do it – OK?"

"Yes Sir, all understood." and then, thinking, 'Crikey, what have I let myself in for?'

He went back to the mess and had lunch and then, estimating that Pat could by now be in the shop having had her lunch, booked a reverse charge call from the coin operated box in the mess entry hall. After ten minutes the bell rang and he spent the next fifteen minutes telling her some of the happenings that morning at the C.O.'s office and with the P.T. sergeant major. He concluded with, "Oh and by the way I nearly forgot, I shall be coming on leave in a week or so."

There was a squeal of delight from the other end. "How wonderful, oh you devil, why did you leave that while last?"

"Well I didn't actually."

"What do you mean, what else is there?"

"They've awarded me a medal. It's being announced on Orders tonight so it's not official until then."

"A medal," more excitement in her voice "what sort of medal – what for in particular?"

"It's called the D.C.M. – Dad will explain it to you – and we've all been Mentioned in Despatches although the lads won't know that till tonight."

"What – Kenny as well?"

"Yes, Kenny as well. From glasshouse to hero – real Boys Own Paper stuff isn't it?"

They laughed together.

"Oh darling, I'm so proud of you. I'm going to phone everybody now and bask in your reflected glory. Won't your father and Harry be thrilled? Oh, and please phone me again as soon as you can, darling, please do."

"I will, bye bye."

Chapter Twelve

At Sandbury the news of David's medal was flashed around all the family and friends, as a result everyone came to Chandlers Lodge that evening to drink his health. Alec made the pronouncement that 'it was the next award to the V.C. you know' and there was general speculation as to how and where David would receive it.

"How did you have your military medal delivered to you Mr Chandler?" asked Jim. "You know you've never told us anything about it."

"They stuck it in an empty bully beef tin, mind you I'll say this, they washed the tin out first, and sent it up by company runner."

There was general laughter at this, interrupted by Ruth saying, "Clout him somebody."

Fred continued. "Actually we were taken out of the line and the corps commander came up and dished them out. I remember I had to spend half the night before the parade cleaning all the mud off my kit to look presentable and the general dishing out the medals looked as bored as hell with it all and dashed off in his Daimler the minute it was all over. A bit later, Buffy Cartwright sent his batman over to my hut with something wrapped in a sandbag – it was a bottle of Johnnie Walker, he said afterwards he wouldn't have insulted me by sending a John Haig knowing how everyone felt about the brass hats."

Life at Chandlers Lodge was beginning to settle down after the trauma and tragedy of the last two months. Rose had restarted her job, which the rest of the family agreed among themselves, was a very good idea. Everyone at the office was most kind without being over-attentive. She met Anni each day for lunch when they compared 'bumps' together and discussed the news from Anni's father – he always had something cheerful and interesting to report even though he was in the internment camp. Ruth was kept busy, although she had daily help in the house from a lady whose husband had been posted to Palestine, leaving her with two young children to look after. Megan was less busy at the hospital as many of their wounded men had either been discharged or moved on to military hospitals, however, they would soon be busy again catching up on the civilian entries which had had to be delayed to accommodate the servicemen.

Harry had, of course, been told of David's decoration about which he was utterly delighted. On the Thursday evening after getting David's news, he phoned Megan and received no reply. He knew she was not at the hospital during the evenings that week so he booked another call to Chandlers Lodge and, by chance, when the ring came, it was Megan who answered it.

After enquiring after the twins and the rest of the family Harry went on," The main reason I phoned was to tell you that I went to the C.O. and told him that as my brother had got a medal, I wanted one or else there would be trouble so they've given me one."

"Harry, stop messing about, what are you gabbling on about?"

"Apparently the major I worked with at the C.C.S. at Dunkirk recommended me for a decoration. I've got the MBE. At the same time for working with Captain Osbourne on those bridge blowing larks, I've got a mention."

"The MBE – I thought that was a civilian medal?"

"Oh no, there's a Military Division right up to KBE – they offered me one of those but I said I'd wait a year or two for that, I didn't want to be greedy."

"Oh Harry, Harry you are a lovely, lovely loveable fool, you really are."

"I know, all the girls tell me that."

Megan was laughing and crying at the same time in a mixture of excitement, pride and love of this brave, caring husband of hers.

"Are you still there?" she heard Harry say.

"Yes my lovely darling and I always shall be. Oh, won't your mother be proud of you. I must go and tell them all the news. Please telephone again soon."

She went back into the kitchen. Rose, seeing the tears on her face, instantly got up and came towards her. "What's wrong Megan dear, what's wrong?" The conversation around the big deal table ceased immediately.

"Nothing's wrong – Harry's been awarded a medal as well," and excitedly repeated to them all that Harry had told her.

"Talk about a family of heroes," said Alec "you'll all be in the papers next." And so they were. The local reporter of the Mid-Kent Gazette was around the next day asking for photographs but as he had missed this week's publication day he passed his article on to the Daily Mail and in the Saturday edition, Alec's caption appeared 'A Family of Heros' with the photographs of the three soldiers. Fred, in his uniform from the Great War, and Harry looking so alike it was uncanny, and on the Monday Chandlers Lodge was deluged with mail from people they 'didn't know from Adam' as Ruth put it, sending congratulations from all over Britain, to be followed in the next days with parcels of all sorts of gifts from knitted gloves and socks to home-made cakes. Ruth and the girls sat down each evening and acknowledged every letter and gift, Fred making himself responsible for the postage. Many of the letters were heart-rending, mothers, wives, sisters or sweethearts asking whether David or Harry had seen their loved-one who had been posted missing and about whom they had no further news. They enclosed photographs in the forlorn hope that either of the boys might have seen them, the girls replying that as soon as Harry and David came on leave they would get them to thoroughly examine the pictures of their son or husband and they would write to them again. Everybody knew how much of a forlorn hope it was but in tragic circumstances such as these, hope is all you have.

David found his first two days of P.T. exhausting to say the least, he hadn't realised how unfit he had become. On Friday, he dismissed his squad with the comforting thought that he had a whole weekend to nurse his aches and pains. There was a battalion parade complete with regimental band on Saturday morning at which he would be a spectator, but after that, he would be free until Monday morning. He planned to look around Winchester on Saturday afternoon and to get the bus to Romsey on Sunday to visit Rita and Buffy.

The Saturday morning parade was the first occasion on which he had ever seen a complete battalion drawn up in line. Each Company, in turn, had marched on to the huge barrack square at rifleman pace in time to the band, had halted, turned in to line, dressed to the right so that there was not a whisker out of place, and then were stood at ease to await the adjutant and the colonel. At a signal from an orderly posted on the edge of the parade ground, the RSM called the battalion to attention.
"Stand to your front."
Each man braced himself and looked straight to the front.
"CITY RIFLES."
At this command, they sprang to attention as one man and stood perfectly still. The RSM was not a big man but those words of command were so clear and piercing and carried such authority that not a man blinked as the RSM turned about to await the adjutant. To David's surprise both the adjutant and the colonel came on to the parade on horseback, the adjutant leading and riding up to the RSM.
"Parade ready for inspection Sir."
"Thank you Mr Forster."

The adjutant rode forward, turned facing the C.O. and commanded "Parade present arms."

Six hundred men moved as one, presenting arms direct from attention, as is the way in the Rifles. Six hundred boots hit the parade ground on the final movement with a sound as clear cut as crystal and as they did so, the adjutant and the officers in each company brought their arms up in salute. David, watching from the sidelines, was fascinated by the perfection of the choreography of this ballet – a heavyweight ballet perhaps but a ballet all the same.

"Parade, order arms," commanded the adjutant and then trotted to the C.O., halted, saluted, "Parade ready for your inspection Sir."

Whilst the inspection took place, the band played music in waltz time, as is the custom until eventually having completed his traverse of the complete battalion, the colonel returned to his original position.

David was then to witness the stirring sight of the advance in review order. In this, the whole battalion in line advances for fifteen paces at the double and halts without a command. It is a magnificent spectacle, which can easily be completely ruined by some idiot losing count of his paces and halting too soon or even worse one pace too late. Fortunately, this rarely happens, but David knowing from what old soldiers had told him in the past of the catastrophes that had occurred in places as far apart as Palestine and Poona, kept his fingers crossed for the rookies, in particular, on the far left of the parade. However, all went well, the adjutant was told to march them off by companies, which they did to the music of the regimental march, the colonel taking their salutes as they departed. Another Saturday morning was over.

After lunch David wandered off on his own into Winchester. As he strolled around the city he thought of those carefree days before the war when on one of the occasions, his German friend, Dieter, had come to stay with him at Sandbury. They had made a cycle trip from Sandbury in Kent down to Portsmouth and up to Winchester, finally staying with Jeremy's parents at Romsey. There were six of them, Dieter, Rose, Pat, Anni, Jeremy and himself, they all had such a great time. Dieter came from Ulm, whose Cathedral has the highest spire in Europe and he remembered as clearly as if it were yesterday as they approached the Cathedral at Winchester Jeremy saying, 'You have the highest spire in Europe and we have the longest nave' – poor Jeremy, and what has happened to Dieter who was called into the German Army the year before war broke out. Dieter was such a committed anti-nazi; on the other hand, he was as patriotic about his Fatherland as David was about his King and Country. David wondered how he balanced his inner conflicts and came to the only logical conclusion he could, namely, that Dieter would consider himself a true soldier and act like a soldier at all times, holding himself above the politics of the moment.

On Sunday he got the bus to Romsey. As he was driven through the quiet Hampshire countryside it seemed to him impossible that massive armies were being assembled at that very moment ready to be ferried across the English Channel to invade those lands which had not seen the foot of a conqueror for nearly a thousand years, and a massive anger swelled in him. For a moment he caught a glimpse of his reflection in the bus window as they passed close to a dark hedge. He saw his lips fixed in a thin, white line; his eyes set rock hard and his jaw firm and resolute. Laughing inwardly at himself he thought, punning the illustrious Duke of Wellington, 'I don't know if that face would frighten them but by God it put the wind up me!' which thought brought him back to enjoying the beauty of Hampshire again.

He spent a pleasant day at Romsey, arriving just in time to join Rita and Buffy for Mattins. He was relieved that they both were able to talk about Jeremy, they had obviously reached acceptance of his death, even if they were not yet reconciled to it. After lunch, they spent a pleasant hour in the quiet of the riverside, it seemed impossible to David that only six weeks ago, he was slogging it out at Calais. Then it was back to tea and the 6.30 return bus to Winchester.

An amusing incident took place on his Monday morning run. His squad was doubling down the Worthy Road, David at the rear offside. Coming towards them, he saw an attractive young woman, thirtyish he guessed, on a bicycle. She was struggling against a strong head wind which, when she was a dozen yards or so away, took her skirt and lifted it almost to her waist. The young soldiers naturally made a meal of this with wolf whistles and good-natured repartee, which David quickly silenced, but in the meantime, the young woman in the effort to hold her skirt back down, steer the bicycle and fight against the wind had come to a halt. David let the men pass her and then bellowed, "Mark Time." With the men running on the spot, David stopped and apologised to her. "I'm sorry about that Ma'am," he said, "they meant no offence."

"Oh that's alright sergeant – it's when they stop doing it I'll be offended. You're from the Rifles aren't you?"

"Well I shouldn't tell you Ma'am since you may be a German spy, but yes we are."

"I know someone in the Rifles."

"If I may say so Ma'am, you look far too respectable to know anyone in the Rifles, good-day Ma'am," and with that, he doubled his squad off to the barracks, such remarks as, "you get a date sergeant?" "What's he got that we haven't got more of," and other such subtleties drifting back to him as they ran.

When he returned from his run on the next morning, the CSM said, "The RSM wants to see you, he said to come as you are." A surge of excitement gripped him as he considered this might be news of his leave. He had to wait for ten minutes or so outside the RSMs office, there being a conference on with the Band Master and the Drum major. When eventually he was sent in, he stood smartly to attention and was told to sit down.

"Well things are moving at last. The new C in C Southern Command, General Sir Alan Brooke has now been appointed, so the medal ceremony will take place on Friday 12th at Aldershot. You can invite up to four guests if you want. The C.O., the adjutant and I will be going and taking our wives, a fifteen hundred weight truck will take you and three other medallists and you can go on leave straight from Aldershot – the documents are being processed."

David listened without interruption as Mr Forster continued.

"Now, there are two other points. It was brought to my attention that a photograph of yourself was seen in the Daily Mail at the weekend. We have a strict 'no treating' rule in the mess, but this is broken automatically if a member gets his picture in the papers. It will, therefore, be drinks all round on you tonight." David grinned acceptance of the fine. "The next thing is I understand you have not only been chatting my wife up but you insinuated I was not a respectable person."

"Oh Lord, was that lady Mrs Forster?" said David "I must say Sir, she was utterly charming and very attractive if I may be allowed to say so."

"You may sergeant. I suppose RSMs wives are generally expected to look like the back of a Mathilda tank but she is rather special. I'm older than her of course, by eleven years. I married late only four years ago and we have a boy eighteen months old."

"I shall be asking my wife, parents and sister to come on Friday Sir, I would be most pleased if you will come and meet them."

"Consider it done," said the RSM "and I think it highly probable the C.O. and adjutant will want to meet them too."

David was kept busy for the next few days getting his uniform and particularly his boots in apple pie order, getting his family passes from the orderly room, as well as carrying out his normal P.T. commitment. The family had decided to travel by train and would meet him either at or after the ceremony. He then had two weeks leave to come, returning to barracks on Sunday 29th July.

The medal ceremony was most impressive. There was a guards' band over from Pirbright, dressed in wartime khaki but as superbly melodious as ever. There was a veritable throng of red-tabbed colonels, brigadiers and upwards, all anxious, presumably, to catch the eye of the new G.O.C. Southern Command. David found himself thinking, "What the hell do they all do? Push paper to one another I wouldn't mind betting." As he was musing this point, the general's staff car arrived.

The Garrison Sergeant major commanded the guard of honour, "General salute. Present arms." A bugler sounded the general salute followed by the guard being ordered to slope arms, was inspected by the general who then wasted no time in ascending the dais.

Most of the awards for gallantry were for the actions up to and including Dunkirk, but there were two other Riflemen from Calais as well as David, both of whom had been wounded and repatriated. One was an officer who received an M.C. and the other a sergeant who was awarded an M.M. Neither of them had been in David's battalion. There were several awards to guardsmen who fought so savagely at Abbeville thereby keeping the Germans out of Boulogne and enabling the evacuation of that sector to be successfully concluded. As David's turn to be called approached, he studied the general carefully. He thought he looked more like an Oxford Don than a warrior, but warrior he was. He was one of the few generals in the B.E.F. who had emerged with any credit from the catastrophe and who, after only twelve days in his present command, would be whipped away to be Winston Churchill's right-hand man in planning the conduct of the rest of the war.

"Sergeant Chandler," the Guards RSM in charge of the medallists called. David marched forward in Rifleman's time, halted and saluted. The general took the medal from an aide and pinned it on his tunic. "That was a very brave action Sergeant Chandler. Very well done."

"Thank you Sir." They shook hands and David stepped back a pace, saluted and marched off. The ceremony lasted another ten minutes or so before the general was whisked away to the sound of another general salute and much shouting from the direction of the guard of honour. David turned to look for his family and soon found them already talking to Mr & Mrs Forster. David kissed his wife, mother and sister and shook hands with Mrs Forster. They all congratulated him and examined his medal having its crimson ribbon with the navy blue stripe down the centre and the wording on the back, which Pat read out. "For Distinguished Conduct in the Field" she said excitedly. David's face was quite serious.

He said, "I've done nothing compared to these two," indicating his father and the RSM.

"What we've done or had to do doesn't lessen your achievement son, in any way at all," said the RSM.

"Thank you Sir."

"Now we've booked a table for lunch at the Victoria. Mr Forster, would you and your wife care to join us?" Fred looked from one to the other, "And if I may be allowed to say so Mrs Forster, RSMs wives are vastly superior to those I knew in my day."

"You can certainly say so Mr Chandler and" (looking at her husband for agreement) "yes, we will be most pleased to join you."

They had a most convivial meal even if it was hardly a gastronomic experience, and having said their goodbyes to the Forsters, they caught the 3.10 back to Waterloo and then on to Sandbury where everyone was waiting at Chandlers Lodge to see David's medal. Whilst Anni and Megan, Ernie and Jack were scrutinising it, David stood back a little, a great sadness having come over him. Rose noticing this put her arm round his waist and said, "Anything wrong?"

"I was just thinking that if I'd got to that tank five minutes earlier Jeremy would probably still be here."

"You mustn't think like that dear, you really mustn't. What you did saved many other lives, Colonel Scott-Calder told us that and anyway, I want you to know Jeremy is here, he's here with us all the time. I can't expect you to know that, but I promise you I do know it, truly I do."

David hugged her.

When the Canadians arrived and had duly inspected the medal, they all sat down to supper, but they had hardly taken a first mouthful when the telephone rang. Megan was nearest so went to answer it. She was gone for several minutes and then came back in and said, "It's Harry, he wants to have a word with you mother."

Ruth got up quickly and hurried in to the hallway. "Harry sends his regards to you all," and when Ruth returned she continued with, "Harry's presentation is at Tidworth next Thursday. He would like

Mum and Dad and Rose to come with me and we can take the twins. Could we get there alright do you think?"

"Let them try and stop us," said Ruth, although who exactly 'them' was was not clear.

"All I hope is that you both don't keep on getting medals. I can't afford to keep taking time off and paying fares and buying meals and all that caper," complained Fred.

"You know guv'nor," said Ernie, he had taken to calling Fred 'guv'nor' for some time now. Anni of course, called him 'Uncle Fred.' He could hardly call him Uncle Fred in the factory so he had hit upon guv'nor, which seemed to fit the bill in all directions. "You know guv'nor, you should have been on the stage. You said that really as if you meant it."

"Well, when I come to you to borrow a few bob next Wednesday you'll know that I did," retorted Fred.

A sadness descended on Chandlers Lodge at breakfast the next morning. Jim and Alec came down together and sat down. "Are you going to tell them or am I?" said Alec.

"I will," replied Jim. "We have very reluctantly to tell you dear Mrs Chandler that you are losing us. The officers' quarters have now been completed at the camp so we've been told we've got to re-join the battalion."

"Oh, how dreadful," said Ruth. "I knew, of course that it would happen one day but now the time has come it's like losing more of our family. When will you have to go?"

"Next weekend I'm afraid. We knew last night of course, but we thought we'd leave it until this morning to tell you. Alec said you'd be giving three cheers anyway for getting rid of us."

"Oh no I shan't and neither will the others. The place won't seem the same without you – you will come and see us regularly won't you?"

"Try and keep us away – where else shall we get Whitbread's Light Ale except from under your stairs?"

"Alec dear, with everything all organised for the wedding, I mean, this isn't going to interfere with it, is it?"

Alec replied that everything certainly was organised and there were no problems. In two weeks time from this very day Rebecca will become Mrs Fraser, "provided she doesn't have last minute thoughts and change her mind." And then they would be going to Cornwall for the honeymoon staying in London overnight on the Saturday.

"Well, in the meantime, Alec and I are throwing a lunch next Sunday at the Angel to go some way towards thanking you all for all you've done for us and been to us during these last seven months. And if John Tarrant is short of food, I'll personally raid our cookhouse stores to make sure we don't go hungry."

"Oh and Jim, don't forget to warn them of my stag night on Thursday week."

"Not on Friday?" queried Ruth.

"He wants to be sober on Saturday – that's why he's making it Thursday," replied Jim. "I think that illustrates the degree of efficiency in forward planning now achieved by the Canadian Army don't you?"

"In which case, we'd better warn the factory staff not to speak too loudly in a certain person's hearing on Friday morning," said Rose. "Come to that, we'd better muffle the cat's feet as well."

David and Pat had such a wonderful leave. In addition to being with family and visiting friends including Colonel Scott-Calder and Dr Carew, they had hours and hours together walking on the Downs, doing chores in the house and garden and above all, revelling in their passion together which, in its fervour and excitement, made them marvel as to what they had done to be so blessed. Late one night as at length they laid still in each other arms, Pat whispered, "You will take care won't you darling. I know I would never survive if anything happened to you."

Normally David would have made a jest in reply, but he sensed the deep-seated fear in her voice and just said. "I promise, and you must do the same." But the leave was soon over. The family had returned from Tidworth and reported that Harry was the 'smartest one there' – naturally – the thank you dinner at the Angel provided two hilarious speeches from Alec and Jim, both three sheets in the wind, and the less said about the stag night the better. It was held in the officers' bar at the camp – fortunately positioned on the outskirts of the camp or the party would have kept the whole battalion awake. The wedding was magnificent, photographers from everywhere to capture pictures of the first Canadian officer's wedding in the UK.

David and Pat, Moria and Jack, Anni and Ernie all joined Ruth, Fred and Rose for Sunday lunch and soon it was time for David to go. He changed into uniform and said his goodbyes to Pat in the drawing room, rejoining the others in the hallway as the taxi arrived. Looking out of the rear window as the taxi crunched down the drive, he saw Pat standing waving to him being comforted by the arms of Ruth and Moira around her. They had planned the parting like this, neither of them liking tearful partings at the station.

The journey back to Winchester was a blur. He looked to see whether he had any post when he arrived back at the mess and found a number of congratulatory messages including one from each of his little band. Even Riley had found out about the D.C.M. presumably because he would have been notified of his Mention and made further enquiries. Despite the congratulatory messages, he still went to bed that night desperately sad and lonely.

The next few days he spent his mornings with the P.T. squad. His afternoons were spent in the City buying odd things that he thought would be useful at OCTU, and investing in a pair of black oxford shoes. They always wear black shoes in the Rifles. On Friday the RSM called him in. "All packed and ready then sergeant?"

"Yes Sir, but Sir, how do I travel? I mean do I arrive as a sergeant or do I take the stripes down or what?"

"You are a sergeant until you get to the new unit. Then you take your stripes down and put on the white flashes of a cadet. Oh, and don't forget to hang on to your stripes, if you fail the course you'll have to put them back up again, but not for long because if you fail the course, I'll get you busted when you come back for failing it – understood?"

"Yes Sir," said David with a grin. "I'll try not to fail."

"Well, good luck lad. The orderly room sergeant has got all your travel tickets and documents ready, so I'll see you in a few months time." He shook hands with David warmly and David smartly turned about and marched out.

It was a tedious journey to Worcester. Outside the station was a three-tonner with a sign "OCTU" on it so he gathered his kit together and bundled it on to the truck and climbed aboard. There was considerable interest in his stripes from a number of the prospective cadets, most of whom seemed to him to be very wet behind the ears. They registered, were given their flashes and shown to their rooms by A.T.S. orderlies. The camp was a new hutted affair, fairly basic but quite comfortable and David was pleased to see there were sheets on the bed. The rooms were shared between two cadets and since David was the first in his room, he pondered on what sort of bloke his roommate would turn out to be. Having taken off his stripes and slipped his white stripes over his epaulettes, he decided to wander off and get some tea. The A.T.S. girl had told him running buffets were being provided today for tea and supper to accommodate the arrivals of the cadets on the course, and there would be a parade at ten o'clock the next morning in the main hall to be addressed by the commandant, this to be followed by a short service.

Having taken tea and spoken to a couple of the new arrivals he made his way back to the room and as he approached the doorway, which was partly open, he could hear what he thought was two girls talking. "God, my luck's changed at last," he joked to himself, however, when he pushed open the door and walked in, he saw that the young A.T.S. girl who had brought him to the room was talking to a very young, fresh faced fair haired boy who looked and sounded like a sixteen-year-old girl.

The lad spun round "Oh, so you're my room mate are you, my name's Charlie Crew."

"I'm David Chandler, pleased to meet you."

David regarded him closely. He was shortish, very slimly built, his shoulders, David thought, not exactly constructed to carry a 60-pound pack or a Bren gun for that matter.

"Where have you come from," asked David.

"I've been two months at a basic training unit. I joined when I was exactly eighteen."

"So you've had two months service and now you're going to be an officer?" asked David.

"Yes, I'm going in the Rifles, my father and grandfather were both in the Guards, but I'm not tall enough, so I'm going in the Rifles. Why, does that surprise you?"

"Nothing about the army surprises me any more, but it looks as though we're stuck with each other for a while because I'm going into the Rifles as well, so it's up to us to show the rest of these people that one rifleman is worth two redcoats any day. What work did you do before you joined up?"

"Well I didn't actually." His voice rose even higher. They're bound to think I've got a girl in here thought David. "I left Eton where I didn't do all that well and decided against university. I wanted to get into the war, so I joined up."

"Where do you live?" asked David.

"We live on my grandfathers' estate not far from here. He's the Earl of Osbourne, my father is Lord Ramsford."

"So you're an 'Hon'," said David.

"I'm an 'Hon' – but don't let it worry you," replied Charlie cheerily, "it never does me."

"We'll cope with it somehow," said David beginning to quite like this young innocent.

"How did you like Eton?" asked David.

"Not much. I got chased a lot during the early years – seniors fancying me and wanting me to shack up with them. It was a bit nasty at times, but my father had warned me about it so I just told them to sod off, which was a bit of a pun really when you come to look at it."

David continued to unpack his valise and from its depths withdrew a large chunky pullover inside which was wrapped a silver photo frame. He carefully removed it, examined it to see it had not been damaged and placed it on his chest of drawers.

"By jove," exclaimed Charlie, "she's a real hundred per cent copper bottomed corker if ever I saw one. She your popsy?"

"She's my wife," said David, "and any more familiar remarks about her will land you with a walloping."

"No offence dear old boy, but you can't blame me if I stand here drooling away at such a gorgeous piece of pulchritude can you now? I mean, such elegance, such grace, such glamour I've never before seen! She wouldn't have a younger sister by any chance I suppose?" David shook his head. "Oh well, just my luck. I shall just have to venerate from afar I suppose."

David went to bed that night after having telephoned Pat and telling her she had yet another admirer – and an 'Hon' at that. As he drifted into sleep, he thought of the things that had happened to him so far in his life. He had been to college, had travelled over Europe, had married a beautiful girl, had been into action, won a medal, and was now going to be an officer – not bad for a farm boy he thought, and then with a little sob came back to earth with the thought that he had lost his best friend. And if he felt sick in his stomach at that thought tonight, how must poor Rose feel when she went to sleep every night. Yet she seemed convinced that Jeremy was still with her, it seemed to give her consolation he just couldn't understand. Thinking of it all, he drifted off into a sound sleep.

Chapter Thirteen

At Sandbury, Fred found himself back in uniform again. Up until now the LDV wore just an armband, but now it had been decided to put the million odd men who had volunteered for the LDV into uniform and rename them the 'Home Guard.' This meant they would have to be given army ranks, as a result he found himself provisionally a lieutenant with Jack Hooper being made a captain and in charge of the Sandbury unit, all ranks to be confirmed later in the year. They had a hotchpotch of weapons, mainly American, along with some Lewis guns, but now the emphasis was to be on training and field craft, intended to meet the threat of invasion which increased daily.

During the summer, the men at the works had been building a mobile canteen for the Sandbury Rotary Club. Jack and Fred had donated a Morris Commercial chassis, which had been standing in the works, the result of a cancelled order by a firm, which among many hundreds went bust after the war started. The Rotary Club paid for the material and canteen fittings and the men worked on the vehicle in their own time. It was to be used to visit all the outlying anti-aircraft posts, searchlight units and dispersal points around Sandbury RAF aerodrome, personnel who otherwise would never get a chance during their turns of duty to visit a canteen. Rotary organised a schedule of drivers from their wives and families, and with other volunteers like the brigadier's wife, were able to give a twice daily visit round all the posts, visits which were greatly appreciated and looked forward to. Pat and the brigadier's wife decided to team up and do the Monday and Wednesday morning shifts, these being the most convenient times for Pat to be away from the shop.

On the Monday after David's arrival at Worcester, Ruth was talking to her daily lady who had just arrived, when there was the scrunch of wheels on the drive followed by a knock on the front door. Ruth slipped her pinafore off and went to the door to find the major there who had first visited her back before Christmas to ask her if he could billet the two Canadian officers on her.

"Hello again major, please come in."

He came into the hallway. "Just another quick visit Mrs Chandler. Are you still able to take a couple of officers? I understand your Canadians have now deserted you."

"Well yes, of course, we'd be delighted."

"Well to ring the changes a bit, these two are Australians, you probably know there are some Australian personnel on Sandbury airdrome. These two gentlemen are both squadron leaders but not, I believe, aircrew, so if it's OK by you, they'll be here in the morning."

"That will be fine, we'll look forward to meeting them."

The family were intrigued as to what the new arrivals would look like. Tall, lean, fair, tanned and brash was the general view of what they should expect. In the event, Sammy Goldman was short, tubby, sallow complexioned and taciturn and Bill Greaves was medium height, stocky, possessed of a melodious voice albeit with a strong Australian accent. Sammy came from Sydney and Bill from a small seaside town north of Brisbane called Caloundra. They were engineer officers and had come to Sandbury to set up an emergency workshop. They soon settled in and became part of the house, but they never became family like Jim and Alec, probably because they spent long hours at the airfield and when they came back to Chandlers Lodge brought their work home with them and generally closeted themselves in the drawing room, whereas Alec and Jim had more or less lived in the kitchen with all the others.

On July 31st, a White Paper was presented in Parliament, which gave the right to internees to go before a tribunal to apply for release. The House was disturbed to hear that some internees were still sleeping on bare boards or under canvas and it was felt that this was not to be expected from a civilised country. The main criterion for consideration for release was that the applicant 'consistently over a period of years had taken a public and prominent part in opposition to the Nazi system.' Anni and Ernie visited Karl's solicitor in order to get the appeal organised. As the solicitor said, the wording of the main requirement showed very little appreciation by the powers that be of the true nature of things inside Nazi Germany. Those people who had managed to get out were able to shout their heads off about the Nazis from the safety of London but to do so while still living in Munich or Dresden or wherever meant instant incarceration. However, with regard to the fact that Karl's daughter was now English, his wife had died in Dachau and that he had a number of influential friends in the community who could vouch for him, should be enough to secure his release. Nevertheless, since tribunals of this nature moved very slowly, he suggested they should not hope that anything would happen before the end of the year. Anni and Ernie went back to the family with mixed emotions, although as

Fred said, "It's a step in the right direction."

Rose and Anni were both going regularly to the clinic to 'have their bumps checked' as they laughingly described the purpose of the visits. They both looked extraordinarily well, and as Anni said to Ernie one night when they were lying close together, "Rose always took to me with open arms from the time I arrived, but I feel we're even closer now. She is so good and kind and brave." She gave a little sob and Ernie held her close saying nothing but knowing how sad she felt for the one who was more to her as a sister than many people feel for their natural sisters.

On the evening the Australians arrived, Megan had just settled down with her feet up, having put the twins to bed when the telephone rang. A cheerful, friendly voice asked if that was Mrs Chandler and on being told it was, asked if there was any chance that Sergeant Chandler was home, adding he was Captain Ray Osbourne, and had been with Sergeant Chandler for a short, but not uneventful, time in France. "In fact," he continued, "he saved my life – I wouldn't be here today if it hadn't been for him."

"You're the officer he helped to blow up some bridges aren't you?" she asked. "He told us he had been involved in this but said nothing about saving your life, I shall have words to say to him when he telephones next."

"Not only that, but to get me to the Aid Post quickly, he put me on a motorbike and sidecar which he had won."

"What do you mean – won? How can you win a motorbike and sidecar?"

"By the simple expedient of bumping off the two Germans who were previously on it."

"You mean Harry killed two Germans? He has never said a word about it."

"Well he wouldn't – would he? He's not the sort. They deserved to die though, Harry had just seen them murder a British prisoner so they got their just deserts."

"So that's where he got the motorbike from. Did you know he got the MBE for bringing in dozens of walking wounded and exhausted men to the beaches? – He was on the last ship to leave."

"Doesn't surprise me. I recommended him for a gong – I believe they gave him a mention. I can tell you this, if ever I was in a tight spot again, there's nobody I'd rather have with me than Harry Chandler."

"Well look, Captain Osbourne, I can give you Harry's mess

number, he may well be there now. Now tell me, have you recovered from your wounds?"

"Yes, it was a long job but then I believe you're a hospital sister so you'll know all about these things. I'm still getting some double vision but the quacks tell me that will gradually clear."

"If you're nearby, perhaps you could come and see us and the family."

"Yes, I'd love to. I'm at the RE Depot at Chatham, not far away. Perhaps when I've spoken to Harry I can contact you again?"

When he had rung off, Megan immediately got on to Chandlers Lodge where Fred answered the call. "What do you think I've heard about that blinking Harry?" she said.

"Harry? He's gone off with another woman," Fred replied. At this, the heads of Ruth, Rose, and Anni who was waiting for Ernie to pick her up when he finished the long day shift and Pat and Jack, who had just called in, spun round in astonishment. When Fred rejoined them Ruth said,

"Was that Megan?"

"Yes, she's had some news about Harry."

"What do you mean 'he's gone off with another woman'?"

"Another woman? What are you talking about?"

Jack joined in – "I think you've just done another 'they've invaded', clanger Fred old boy."

"Oh crikey, have I done it again? No, he hasn't gone off with another woman," and he told the story of Captain Osbourne's phone call ending with, "Anyway this Captain Osbourne's only at Chatham so he's coming to see us – we shall get the full story out of him then just like we did about David from Kenny. It's a problem with we men you know, we're all so modest and what do they call it, oh, I remember, self-effacing. Yes, that's what we are, self-effacing."

"I'll efface you altogether if you pull another trick like that Fred Chandler, you see if I don't," threatened Ruth.

They talked generally around the table about the war situation. It was Jack's view that the present quiet period was the calm before the storm. "If he's going to invade, and there's no doubt in my mind he'll try," said Jack, "it's generally agreed he's got to do it by September, and if he's going to soften us up first, he'll have to start soon."

The family all had a great respect for Jack's opinions. Not only, like Fred, did he normally only venture views that had been well thought out, but also he had the ear of many knowledgeable people in the City as well as the several ministries with whom he came into contact during his Ministry of Supply duties which gave his statements added substances. "It's too damned quiet for my liking," he went on.

"I think the Government have got the wind up too," Fred added, "at least the Tory part of the Government. Did you read they have made an Order in Council to bring forward grouse shooting from the 12th August to the 5th and then pheasant shooting forward from October 1st to September 1st. I ask you, a war on and they have to have an Order in Council to shoot blooming birds."

"I wonder if anyone has told the birds," mused Pat, "it would be very unfair if they haven't. Anyway, I must be away. I'm meeting Lady Agatha first thing in the morning to do our good deed for the day."

"How does a brigadier's wife get on with the squaddies?" asked Ruth.

"Well, they don't really know she is a 'Lady' or a brigadier's wife, so most of them call me sweetheart or ducks or the shyer ones say Miss, but they all seem to call her 'love,' she hands them a mug of tea and they say 'thank you love,' and she enjoys it tremendously. But I must say they do so look forward to our visits, there's never any bad language used while we're there, and when there has been the occasional familiar remark made, the person concerned has been jumped on very swiftly by all the others. We're so pleased to be able to do something. I know it's not much but at least it's something."

As she finished talking, Ernie arrived and the gathering broke up, but the significance of what Jack had said and the words that Pat had used about 'not doing much' would remain with all of them for the remainder of their days.

Chapter Fourteen

On the Sunday after their arrival, David and Charlie Crew made their way to the gymnasium, which doubled as the main assembly hall having been provided with a small stage at one end. They were interested to know what the commandant was like and to see, for the first time, their officer and senior NCO instructors who would be running their lives for the next four months or so. At two minutes to ten the officers, company sergeant major and four sergeants filed on to the stage. The CSM and sergeants were all old sweats, immaculately turned out and all possessing ribbons of one sort or another. At precisely ten o'clock the CO and adjutant arrived. The CO was a Great War veteran, a lieutenant colonel of the Durham Light Infantry; another old soldier brought back for the duration to do a most essential job. He started by welcoming all the cadets and went on to say that he was pleased to see several Light Infantry Bobs, including a couple from the D.L.I. At this, Charlie Crew thrust his hand up saying "Sir?"

David was astonished, people in the front looked round, officers on the stage looked on in disbelief, NCOs glared – nobody interrupts the C.O. when he's giving an address. The C.O. was so taken aback that instead of bawling Charlie out he just said, "Yes, Cadet, what is it?"

"Sir, I'm a very young soldier," he explained in his high piping voice "but this D.L.I. lark, is that a sort of laundry unit?"

There was a dreadful silence, broken only by gurgles and gasps from those doing all they could not to explode with laughter. Two of the officers on the platform had to turn their backs so that their laughter couldn't be seen by the cadets, and the company sergeant major's face was an absolute study. He was from the Royal Berkshire's - as red-coated an outfit as any to decorate a parade ground. He didn't hold much with the Light Infantry 'Running around at a 140 to the minute like blue arsed flies and getting nowhere most of the time' was his view of them, as a result he thoroughly enjoyed someone 'taking the piss out of them'. On the other hand, discipline is discipline, so cocky young farts; straight out of college didn't come on his parade and bugger about with the C.O. in the middle of an address. He was just about to bellow 'Take that Cadet's name' when the C.O. recovered sufficiently to say,

"I think cadet, that as you are as you say a very young soldier, I shall forgive you for interrupting me and to warn you not to chance your arm a second time. As regards the D.L.I. I shall leave it to your fellow cadets, who are privileged to belong to that illustrious regiment to acquaint you forcefully of its history and achievements."

They all simmered down. He went on to explain what their course comprised. The first month was a pre-OCTU course designed to get them thoroughly fit, to learn to drive a truck and ride a motorcycle, to learn basic foot and arms drill and to carry out certain initiative tests. At the end of that month they would have a forty-eight-hour pass before they started the full course to learn how to be a platoon officer. If they did not satisfactorily pass the pre-OCTU they would be returned to their units – or as it was known with dread – RTU'd. On the OCTU course they would have a seventy-two hour pass at the halfway mark and seven days leave on completing the course and becoming commissioned. He ended by saying, "I wish you all good luck, work hard, read, mark, learn everything your instructors tell you, you have my word they are the best there are." He turned, everyone stood up, and the platform cleared leaving only the padré to conduct a short service of prayer.

When it was all over and everyone was making a move towards the NAAFI, David grabbed Charlie's arm and said "You silly sod – what did you say that for to the C.O?"

"Now you mustn't swear when you've only just come from Church today – you know that."

"Do you know you lunatic, that a couple of ex-Durham miners complete with steel toe caps will be coming after you – don't expect me to be your bodyguard."

"Well I had to say it didn't I? I mean, fancy his having the cheek, even if he is a colonel, and I've met a lot of bloody stupid colonels in my short life already, fancy having the cheek to single out the blooming Light Infantry that nobody's ever heard of. I mean if he'd singled out the Rifles or even the Worcesters, I wouldn't have said anything."

"All I can say to you Charlie lad is that you are in the army now and no matter what parade you're on, you keep your mouth shut or you'll end up either with your own or at the worst, somebody else's foot in it. You're going to find this isn't a bit like Eton."

Charlie squeezed his arm. "Thanks a lot dear old boy – I'll remember every word you've said."

Because Charlie had the backing of most of the cadets, either because of their views on the Light Infantry, the fact that he'd had the absolute gall to ask such a question from the C.O. or the fact that his new pal was obviously very much on the bulky side, he did in fact get no trouble from the D.L.I. contingent. The amusing thing was that though he sounded such a cissy and would normally have been considered one by anyone listening to him, he was now considered a bit of a card and therefore should be nurtured.

They started their training on the Monday, on the Tuesday they had their first motorcycle lesson, round and round the parade ground for an hour and then practising left hand and right hand turns for another hour. On Wednesday they were considered ready to go out on the road. After nearly an hour following the Royal Signals sergeant instructor along the highways and byways of Worcestershire, there was, of course, little traffic on the road because of the petrol rationing, the noisy two wheeled crocodile found itself led into an open space at the rear of which was a long wooden building with a big sign on the front, 'Sadie's Café'. "Now," said the sergeant, "you've got twenty minutes. Sadie makes the best bacon sandwich in the West Country. Don't ask me, or her for that matter, where she gets the bacon from, but for one and three pence you'll get a bacon sandwich and a mug of hot sweet tea like you've never had before." And so they did, stopping here every day for the next two weeks while they completed their motorcycle and fifteen hundred weight truck driving courses. The sergeant didn't tell them he got his bacon sandwich and tea for nothing for bringing them there, but it made a marvellous break and David, for one, never ever lost the memory of the flavour of those delicious bacon sandwiches, nor ever tasted better.

After the fourth or fifth visit, Charlie Crew decided he would talk to Sadie. Sadie was probably in her mid thirties, she had masses of raven black hair, a very large bosom made to seem even larger by the fact that she was quite slim on the hips, and blessed with a very clear, if somewhat fleshy, complexion. She wore a dress which was rather low cut and which, as a consequence, showed a not inconsiderable and extremely delightful from the lads' point of view, amount of cleavage. Charlie approached her and without preamble said in his clear upper crust voice, "Sadie, I've never tasted bacon sandwiches like these ever in my life. On the understanding you will make me one every day, would you consider marrying me?"

Sadie let out a peal of laughter and then said, "What's your name, I ought to know the name of whoever's proposing to me."

"I'm Charlie," he replied, "bachelor of this parish, well not exactly of this parish but a bachelor nevertheless."

"Charlie, I'm flattered, but we have two problems. One, I'm old enough to be your mother and two, my husband is a sergeant in the Marines and he might well object."

Charlie turned to David. "You see dear old boy, I've failed again," and turning to Sadie said, "Well, I shall just have to worship you from afar just as I do his wife, though I'm sure I shall never get over two such disappointments in such a short time."

The next day David said to him, "You've got more bacon in your sandwich than we have you rotter."

"Sex appeal old boy, sex appeal. Some of us have it, some of us don't – Sadie obviously fancies me even though she's married and this is her uncomplicated way of showing it. When I get de-mobbed I shall come back here and see if her husband survived, damned if I don't."

"Always assuming you yourself survive don't forget," said David.

"Yes, of course, there's always that to be considered I suppose." He thought for a moment and continued, "In which case, we'd better enjoy these bacon sandwiches whilst we can, don't you think?" and took a big mouthful of sandwich running with H.P. sauce to emphasise his point.

When they got back to camp that afternoon, they were greeted with the news that they were all better off than they were when they left that morning by the astounding sum of sixpence per day. There was considerable discussion as to whether the nation could really afford such magnanimity to the common soldiery, the general feeling being that it was better than a kick up the you know what.

Three days later the bombardment of the south of England began – the 'softening up' that Jack had feared. The first recipients were the naval bases at Dover, Portland, and Weymouth, obviously designed to put ships out of action, which would be used to prevent the coming invasion. The next day it was the turn of Portsmouth and RAF airfields in Kent and Sussex. It was this attack, which started what was to become known as the Battle of Britain. Six hundred planes attacked on that day alone and then Southampton and the airfield were attacked again. David became very worried for the safety of the family at Sandbury, being as it was only a stones throw from Sandbury aerodrome and only a few minutes flying distance from Biggin Hill. After sitting by the telephone that evening for over an hour waiting to be put through, there was no answer from the bungalow, he therefore booked a call through to Chandlers Lodge and then had to wait for over an hour for that connection to finally be made. His mother told him that Pat had been with them during the evening and had just left. They were all alright; there had been some anti-aircraft fire from the aerodrome that day but no bombing, if there was, they would all make for the

Anderson shelter. He therefore had to be satisfied with that, his mother adding she would tell Pat he had phoned.

Day after day, raid after raid took place mainly in the Home Counties but also up the east coast as far as Tyneside and along the south coast to Devon. Sandbury didn't escape. The airfield was bombed two days in succession, some bombs falling wide and landing to the north of the town doing little damage except to an electricity substation which inconvenienced part of the population for thirty six hours until it was repaired. The middle of the month showed a let up for two or three days, because the weather was bad, but by the 24th they were back again with Dover, Ramsgate and Manston being on the receiving end, Sandbury too being subjected to a sustained attack on two separate occasions. The Germans, however, were not having it all their own way. In the two weeks so far, they had had over seven hundred planes shot down according to the Ministry of Information figures, and even as Jack said, if those figures were exaggerated they couldn't go on losing aircraft at that rate.

The cadets were due their first forty-eight hour pass in a little over a week. Totally unaffected as they were by the battle in the south and east, they had enjoyed their opening spell at OCTU. When David and Charlie were talking about 'the 48' as it was generally described, David said that by the time he got to Kent from Worcester and then spent most of Sunday travelling back, it would be more like 'a 24'. Charlie said, "Well look old sport, why don't you get your gorgeous wife to come here and both of you stay with us at Ramsford Grange. We can all have a jolly weekend together! If she travels up on the early train on Friday we can meet her in Worcester after lunch and then we'll get Captain Morgan our agent, to drop her back to the station on Monday."

"Are you sure that would be alright – I mean ration and accommodation wise?"

"You dear old chump, food is no problem and since I think we have over forty bedrooms we're not likely to be short of a bed. Actually there are huge four-posters in the two main guestrooms so you'll have bags of room to frolic around. Then we can swim in the big lake, though I suppose with your missus there we shall have to wear cossies."

"Will your father and grandfather be there?"

"I'm not sure about father; he's got some sort of hush hush job at the War Office and comes home at all sorts of different times. However, grandfather will be there, he'll pump you rotten to find out if I'm any good at what we're doing, I think he's firmly convinced I'm only suitable for being a porter on a G.W.R. branch line station somewhere, or a lance corporal in the Pay Corps."

"I'm inclined to agree with him there, though I doubt you'd ever make lance corporal."

"You stinker, I'll pay you back for that."

The arrangements were therefore all made. Pat was thrilled to bits that she was going to stay with a real live Earl. She chose two items from Country Style's new autumn range for day wear, and a particularly fetching black and silver dress to augment her evening collection, although she had been told that the family did not now 'dress' for dinner. As she said to Ruth "No long frocks – that's a blessing." She did however, select two rather revealing swimming costumes left from the summer stock, costumes which she and Mrs Draper had concluded had remained unsold to the somewhat conservative Sandbury clientele as they were a 'trifle revealing'.

Captain Morgan picked David and Charlie up at the camp and then took them on to the station to meet Pat. They had half an hour or so to wait so he left them there saying he would take the shooting brake on to the feed merchants to collect some urgently needed supplies, this being the sound excuse to enable him to come to Worcester in the first place. When the train pulled in, David went on to the platform to meet Pat, Charlie discreetly waiting at the barrier. After much hugging and kissing, David picked up Pat's case and they made their way to the exit. Here they saw Charlie prostrated over the railings seemingly in a faint.

"Charlie you ass, what are you doing?"

Charlie ignored David totally and spoke to Pat. "I saw you from afar," he said, "and my legs would no longer support me. Why has life dealt me such a bitter blow that I did not meet you before he did?"

"But Charlie, I understood your affection was given to a lady called Sadie, or some such name. Didn't she find the way to your heart through your stomach, or so I've been told?"

"Foul mendacity! I was just caught momentarily on the rebound as you might say."

The banter was interrupted by Captain Morgan reappearing and having been introduced to Pat, leading them out to the station wagon. The journey to Ramsford took about three quarters of an hour through beautiful countryside, the weather was gorgeous, Pat held David's arm and squeezed it to her, she was deliriously happy. Back at Sandbury, the people were in their shelters as the airfield was bombed again and Biggin Hill received it's worst attack of the war so far. There could hardly have been two greater extremes on the same day.

David was a little apprehensive at the thought of making conversation with one of the senior members of the aristocracy but as soon as they were introduced, the Earl being instantly captivated by Pat, he soon found he was at ease. He called him 'My Lord' at the first instance of address, and afterwards just 'Sir' as he would had he been talking to the brigadier or Colonel Tim. As Charlie had forecast, they had been allocated one of the four posters. It was enormous. The carved mahogany posts were at least twelve inches in diameter, the pelmets and curtaining were of the finest brocade and the bed itself was, as David later described on the telephone to the family, "as big as a football pitch."

After dinner, at which they were served grouse 'sent down from my cousin in Scotland' according to the Earl, they walked the mile long drive down into the village, where they had a great time in the saloon bar of the Ramsford Arms until throwing out time at ten o'clock. They were walking back up the drive, arm in arm, singing their heads off when behind them they heard the sound of a car and then were able to pick out the slits of its blacked out headlamps approaching. They stood to one side to allow it to pass. When it reached them, it pulled up. It was an army staff car, from the window of which a head appeared. "Charlie, what the hell are you doing here?"

"Oh, hello Pater, I'm on leave for the weekend. This is my roommate David and his wife Pat, who are staying with us."

"Oh, how d'you do? I'll see you in the morning no doubt. Drive on." And with those few abrupt words he disappeared up the drive.

"That was short and sweet," said David.

"Take no notice of the guv'nor," replied Charlie, "you'll find him friendly enough once you get to know him, though I must say since he's had this job at the Horse Guards, he's been even more brusque than he was after my mother left."

Both Pat and David would have liked to ask about his mother's leaving but were too polite, however Charlie, having paused a short while continued, "She buggered off to Kenya you know with a Yankee millionaire. Oh, I do beg your pardon Pat for swearing like that."

Pat took his arm in hers again. "Think nothing of it Charlie. I know exactly how you feel, my mother buggered off to Malaya with a planter when I was six."

Charlie put his arm round her waist. "Pat, you're gorgeous," he said "how the deuce can I get rid of this heap of rubbish so that I can have you for my own. They say arsenic's pretty painless and quick too. I should think the head gardener may have some tucked away somewhere. I'll have a word with him in the morning." They all linked arms together again until they reached the Big House, and let themselves in. "Well now my beautiful ones, I shall expect to see you at breakfast prompt at nine o'clock – mustn't keep grandfather waiting as he gets a bit shirty – even my father toes the line there. Good night, sleep tight etcetera."

Pat took his hand and kissed his cheek. "Charlie, it's been such fun meeting you," she said, "and thank you so much for inviting us." She kissed his cheek a second time.

"I shall never wash there again," he proclaimed dramatically, holding his fingers to his cheek.

"You'll have to in three or four years when you have to start shaving," declared David.

"By then, I shall have snuffed it with unrequited love so it won't matter," and with head theatrically bowed, he wandered off leaving them to mount the stairs, hand in hand, to that enticing four poster awaiting them.

The Earl was obviously taken with Pat, addressing a considerable amount of conversation to her both at breakfast on Saturday and again at lunch. She commented on the beautiful flowers at the lunch table and confessed she was very ignorant of their names. She could not have broached a better subject. His Lordship was an enthusiastic gardener; his first loves being chrysanthemums and orchids.

"Orchids," exclaimed Pat, "how exotic! Do you grow them outdoors or only in glasshouses?"

"If your husband will excuse us, I will take you to see them after lunch."

"David and I are going to the village to watch the cricket match," said Charlie, "we're going to ride down. So Pat, when you've seen the orchid house, and I can tell you it's worth seeing, why don't you ride down after us, I'll have Compton get you a horse ready and then after the cricket we can have a ride round some of the estate."

Pat spent nearly two fascinating hours in the gardens, most of that time in the orchid house. The Earl was a mine of information about flowering times, origin of the plants and so on, many of which had been brought back by his father from far flung parts of the world in the days of Queen Victoria and from which he had many new varieties. When, at last, he said he'd better let her go to join the boys otherwise they would be worried that she had got lost or something, Pat said, "Why don't you come with me and watch the cricket for a while then we can all come back together."

"I'm not exactly renowned as a cricket enthusiast," was the reply, "the villagers will think the sky's falling in if I turn up!"

"I'm sure they'll be as delighted to see you as I would be to be with you." Pat had sensed that this man, whose wife had died many years ago and who now saw little of his son or grandson, must be a very lonely old man. She could imagine his isolation in that huge house brought up as he had been to have innumerable servants, gardeners, grooms and estate workers, all respectful of him but none of them ever imagining he or she could be a friend to him. Even the agent, Captain Morgan, who was nearer to him than anyone else in the district, acting as adviser, confidant and estate manager, could not call himself a friend. Rank does have its disadvantages thought Pat.

"Do you know, I think I'll take you up on that my dear. By jove, I shall be tickled pink to see Charlie's face when we ride up. I'll go and get some decent boots on and see you at the stables in ten minutes. By the way, what do you think of Charlie?"

"I think he is one of the very nicest boys I've ever met," she replied, with such conviction it was plain she was being quite sincere. "What is more, David says that although he's still wet behind the ears – oh my goodness you will forgive my talking like that of your grandson?"

"Of course, of course, we all know he's wet behind the ears my dear, so don't apologise."

"Well, David says that he's got steel in his backbone that you don't notice until you really get to know him. By the way, did you know David was at Calais?"

"No, by God, I didn't. That rascal Charlie hasn't said a word. But they were all killed or captured weren't they? Unless of course he was wounded and came back on a hospital ship."

"He got a boat and he and his section rowed back across the Channel."

"What? By jove, we'll get it all out of him over dinner tonight, so don't say a word in the meantime please my dear Pat. See you in ten minutes.

Charlie's face, as predicted by his grandfather, certainly was a picture when they arrived, not only from the surprise of seeing this rather reclusive old gentleman suddenly appearing among the villagers, but also from the prospect of being able to share an afternoon's enjoyment with someone whom he loved and admired and had seen so little of for the past ten years. The club secretary, having spotted the new arrivals, bustled around finding them deck chairs, Charlie tied the horses to a post and rail fence behind the pavilion and quickly returned to be asked by Pat, "Where's David?" Charlie pointed out to the middle of the pitch.

"Out there," he replied, "we've both been co-opted into the village team. With chaps away in the forces, they're a bit short at the moment."

"They must be desperate to want you two," teased Pat, "but you've no whites or anything."

"They don't worry about trifles like that. They've found us some boots, David's just gone in number five and I'm number seven. We're not doing very well I'm afraid."

Neither David nor Charlie were very great cricketers. They scored a few runs each, made very creditable efforts in the field where their fitness and speed helped to keep the opponents runs down, but in the end, Ramsford lost by three wickets. The Earl congratulated both captains on a most enjoyable afternoon's cricket and the four left to ride the long way round the estate back to the Grange. As they passed the big lake, the Earl led them down to the water's edge along from which was a high bank overhung with trees. He motioned for them to be absolutely quiet. In a few minutes they were rewarded with the flash of the dying sunlight on the brilliant blue feathers of a kingfisher skimming across the lake to its home on the bank. They saw it only for a few seconds but the memory of its beauty lasted with David all his life.

When they got back to the Grange, and Compton had taken the horses, they all went up to bath and change for dinner. "We're very short of time," said David, "so I'd better come in with you, then I can scrub your back and you can scrub mine" – for some unaccountable reason the bath seemed to take longer jointly than it would have done severally as a lawyer might have put it. When they were seated at dinner, Lord Ramsford having appeared briefly and apologised for the fact he would not be joining them due to a prior engagement, the Earl said, "What a jolly afternoon it was – it's a long time since I enjoyed myself so much. But now, Charlie, why have you not told me about David being at Calais?" David flashed a look of mock fury at Pat, the fact the Earl knew about it, could only have come from one source, Charlie's look of surprise was comical to behold, and for the first time since David first met him at OCTU, he appeared to be completely tongue-tied.

"But grandfather," he at last managed to get out, "I don't know anything about Calais, least of all about David being there."

"In which case Master David, we require to have from you a full account of your exploits day by day, hour by hour, and since you probably know the whole story Pat, if he glosses over anything or leaves anything out, you chime in – what?"

"Well, we know the full story because General Earnshaw made David's men get together in hospital and get it all on paper for him."

"Do you mean Freddie Earnshaw? Do you know him?"

"Yes, he and his wife are very good friends of both our families."

"Well, bless my soul, it's a small world. I knew his father and he too when he was a young officer. Right David, the floor's yours, tell us all about it."

David gave a day by day account, glossing over his destruction of the tank and then becoming so upset over the death of Jeremy and the consequent tragedy of poor Rose being left a widow, that he had to stop. Pat held his arm tight and she too had tears in her eyes. She looked across the table at Charlie and he was openly blubbing, as he would have put it.

"So sad, so sad," said the Earl quietly and then more firmly "well, go on from there David." David told of the French general and the march, getting the boat and the journey across the Channel.

Pat noticed that the two manservants who were waiting on were soaking up very word. "It'll be round the village by tomorrow," she said to herself.

At the end of the story the Earl said, "What a fabulous narrative, now tell me Pat, has he omitted anything?"

"Yes," replied Pat to another furious glare from David, "he's omitted to tell you that he didn't just blow up a tank, he ran across open ground, climbed up on to the tank, lifted the lid and dropped grenades in."

"Only one grenade," chimed in David, "there wouldn't have been time for more."

"And," Pat continued, "he omitted to tell you that he was awarded the Distinguished Conduct Medal for that, and he and all the men were Mentioned in Despatches for the escape."

The Earl and Charlie both sat back in their chairs digesting all this information. At last Charlie said quietly, "You've never said word about this, you never wear your medal ribbon, if I was a bit bigger I'd give you a thorough bashing."

"If you say a word back at camp I'll see that, with your grandfather's permission, you get a thorough bashing – right?"

"Oh you certainly have my permission there," laughed the Earl, "but don't the powers that be there know of your service record and decorations?"

"Oh yes Sir, but as I was a sergeant and had seen some active service and had got a medal, it seemed to me that that might, if it were broadcast, seem to be trying to gain an advantage from the very start. After all, most of the cadets are quite young soldiers, when you become a cadet, no matter what your rank was before, you are then all equal, and that's how it should be. Anyway, I asked permission from my company commander to be allowed not to wear the ribbon and oak leaf and he said we were both probably breaking King's Regulations but he'd turn a blind eye except on passing out parade when I would have to wear them," and as an afterthought, "always assuming I pass of course."

There was a pause for a few moments until David said, "Sir, could I turn the tables on you?"

"What do you mean David?"

"Well Sir, I happen to know that you hold both the Distinguished Service Order and the Military Cross, now I wonder if you would be so kind as to tell us, without false modesty or prevarication of any kind, how these became awarded."

The Earl laughed his head off at this. He hadn't enjoyed a dinner like this for years. The joie de vivre of these young people, their fresh, open minds, their obvious high regard for each other and their ability to include him as one of themselves without there being a shred of familiarity was something that happened to him so rarely, if at all.

"Well, first of all, if you are a battalion commander, as I was at the beginning of the Great War, the D.S.O. comes up with the rations after you've been there a while, provided you survive of course. The M.C. is different. I got that leading a bayonet charge up a kopje in South Africa. We did a dawn attack, were enfiladed and lost half the company – I was a captain then. All the officers in the company were killed or wounded so I gathered the remaining fifty or sixty men together and we charged the crest. We took it, it was very misty and the Boers were running back like mad. It was then I realised we were on a false crest, there was another crest a hundred and fifty yards away where the Boers were dug in and plastering us with Mauser fire. I got the men lying down below our crest line to get their breath back and, realising the only thing we could do was to go forward, I yelled 'we're going on up!' By a stroke of luck, the mist settled thickly again for a few minutes so I told the bugler to sound the charge and we went up at them firing as we went. And that's how I got my M.C. We took a few prisoners, an unusual occurrence I might add because the Boers had no intention of fighting to the last man. When they could see they were beaten, they ran like the devil down the other side of the kopje, jumped on their horses and were away to fight another day as you might say. It wasn't until later in the War that we began to use mounted infantry so that we were as mobile as they were."

"Grandfather, why is it you've never told me all this?"

"Because you didn't damned well ask me."

"Well, I certainly shall from now on, you can bet your last fiver on that."

The rest of the weekend went so quickly. Pat and David were just a little late down for breakfast on Sunday morning, the Earl and Charlie being already seated. David apologised for their tardiness, the apologies being brushed aside by the Earl with, "By jove David, if I had a wife as delightful as yours, I'd be late every morning."

David laughed, Pat blushed and Charlie looked open-mouthed saying to himself, "God, what's got into the old boy?"

Lord Ramsford joined them for lunch. He was in his early forties, a serious sort of man but with an extremely courteous way of speaking. He smiled little, but when he did smile it made his fine, aristocratic features very attractive. Pat found herself thinking why would women want to run away from such charming and good looking men as Lord Ramsford and her own father. But they did.

"Penny for them Pat," said the Earl.

"Oh sorry, I was miles away. I was wondering how they're getting on at Sandbury," she fibbed. "There were mass bombings of the airfields in Kent yesterday according to the news."

"Pat drives a Rotary Club canteen vehicle around our aerodrome," said David, "you will go to shelter won't you when the warning goes?" He laid his hand on hers and looked into her eyes.

"Yes of course my love. In any case, when the alert is on, all the troops are stood to and no civilian movement is allowed, so Lady Agatha and I have to shelter."

"Lady Agatha?" queried the Earl.

"Yes, Lady Agatha's husband is brigadier Halton; she is the daughter of the Duke of Oxleas, although he, I believe, died some time ago."

The Earl and his son looked at each other. "The less said about him the better," said the Earl. "I know Lady Agatha, she's a very, very grand person, the salt of the earth, you couldn't have a better friend than she is. As for her father..." he left the sentence unfinished.

David mused to himself, "This aristocracy lark seems to be one big club, they all seem to know, or know of, each other. It's a bit like Mountfield."

"Now, what time are you going back?" enquired Charlie's father of the two young men.

"We've to be in by ten," replied Charlie.

"In that case, I shall be leaving at eight so I can drop you off if you'd like me to."

"Lord, we shall never live it down," said Charlie, "our being delivered back to camp in a one star general's staff car."

"I could always drop you a mile from the camp so that you can walk the rest of the way."

"Don't worry, Sir," David chimed in, "we can always say we thumbed a lift."

"Who on earth would give a lift to as disreputable a pair as you on a Sunday evening," said Pat, "certainly not a brigadier. Now you might get a lift on a coal lorry if there was one about."

"Father, we shall be grateful for the lift, if only for the fact that that will give us an extra hour here over our having to go by the local train, and then David and I can think up ways of repaying Pat for that last remark."

When the time came to go, Pat and the Earl came out to the entrance steps to see them off. Pat and David had already said their goodbyes in their room when David went up to get his haversack, they kissed again before he got into the car, Pat hugged Charlie and kissed his cheek, and then shook hands with the brigadier before he climbed in with the driver. As the car drove off into the gathering dusk, Pat linked her arm with the Earl and they walked back slowly up the steps in silence. When they re-entered the main hallway, the Earl broke the silence. "It always seems so empty when they've gone, I'm so glad you're going to be with me for a little while," he paused for a moment or two and continued, "when captain Morgan takes you to Worcester in the morning would you mind if I came to see you off?"

"Mind? – I'd be very flattered – I'd love you to come and see me off, I really would."

They talked until nearly midnight, Pat gradually turning the conversation to his early life, how he met the Countess and so on.

"Do you know Pat, in my young days marriages at our station in life were more or less arranged. I don't mean you didn't see your prospective bride until the wedding day or anything silly like that but the parents had a sort of short list you could choose from with the one that suited them in capitals at the top! I did as I was expected and married their first choice. I quite liked Lavinia, and she fortunately quite liked me, but by no means could you say we were madly and passionately in love. We had terrible disappointments in the first years. Lavinia lost three babies in a row, all girls. She was so incredibly brave both physically and mentally, that my admiration for her grew and grew until I knew that I was truly in love with her. In those days it was common practice for male members of the aristocracy, and for that matter, a number of the females as well, to play fast and loose. After all, King Edward VII made it almost a social necessity, but I can truly say I never did. After losing the three girls, I said we must stop, it could be her next she had had such a bad time and that I could not face losing her. She insisted we try once more, she knew it was important to me to have an heir, my only brother was as queer as a four pound note so there was no way the line would continue there. We tried again and she produced a fine strong healthy boy, so our happiness was complete as they say in 'The People's Friend' but not without her health suffering along the way. However, we were never parted for more than a day or two except for the first two years of the Great War, until she died in the big flu epidemic in the early twenties, which carried off more millions worldwide than even the Great War had done." He paused for a minute or so and then continued, "Love's a funny thing isn't it? Some couples start with it in an instant and keep it all their lives, some start with it in an instant and gradually lose it until they end up hating each other, others start off on an almost platonic basis and end up deeply in love – what a funny old lot we are, aren't we?"

There was silence for a while, the Earl thinking of Lavinia, Pat thinking of her David. She continued, "And now you have Charlie to carry on the line," and then added, "you know, of course, he has proposed to a lady already." The Earl shot up in his chair.

"He's what?" he exclaimed.

"Yes, apparently during their motorcycle lessons they always stopped at a café out near Brockhampton owned by a voluptuous lady name Sadie. Sadie makes simply divine bacon sandwiches, if such a repast can be described as divine, and Charlie asked her to marry him on the understanding that she made one for him every day. She replied,

I understand, that flattered though she was, her husband, a sergeant in the Marines, would probably object to the idea."

The Earl laughed and laughed. "Thank God there's nothing queer about our Charlie," he said, "I have to tell you with that piping voice of his, I began to have my fears when he was sixteen or seventeen," he paused again, "the only problem with him is we have all our eggs in one basket which is never a good thing at the best of times and in wartime, it's a downright disastrous situation."

There was another short silence broken by the Earl looking at the clock over the mantelpiece and exclaiming, "Good Lord, it's nearly midnight. Come on young lady, you mustn't miss your beauty sleep. I'll walk you to your room." They walked into the hall and up the magnificent curved stairway, Pat lightly holding her escort's arm. They were still chatting when they reached her door. "I shall have a sore throat in the morning," he said to her. "I haven't talked so much in years. I believe the boys have a seventy-two in a few weeks time, will you consider coming to stay again? I would so much like it."

"I would like it too. I'll talk to David about it and speak to you on the telephone." She reached up and kissed him on the cheek. "Thank you for a memorable weekend," she said.

Chapter Fifteen

On the Wednesday after their return to camp, David was told to go to the company commanders' office. He was rather anxious at this summons since on both the Monday and Tuesday there had been a series of mass attacks on Kentish airfields, which left him most concerned for the safety of his wife, family and friends in Sandbury. He imagined all sorts of bad news as he hurried across the parade ground to the admin block, and presented himself to the staff sergeant in the company office. "I have to see the company commander, staff – Cadet Chandler."

"Oh, so you're Cadet Chandler are you? I've heard one or two stories about you." He genially waved his hand towards a chair. "Take a pew. The OC's busy for a couple of minutes then you can go in. I believe you were in the Rifles at Winchester?"

"Yes, that's right staff, but only for a short while."

"But you would have met my brother-in-law R.S.M. Forster?"

"Oh yes indeed – does this mean that Mrs Forster is your sister?"

"Yes, she certainly is."

"She really is absolutely charming. She and Mr Forster met all my family at Aldershot and we had lunch together."

"At the Victoria," added the staff sergeant. I heard all about it. Anyway you'll be seeing him again in the not too distant future I expect."

"If I pass," said David.

"Well, all I can tell you at this early stage is that if you don't, few will, but don't repeat that alright? Right, it looks as though you can go in now."

David stood up and knocked at the OC's door. "Come," was the stentorian command.

David marched in, saluted and said, "You wanted to see me Sir."

The concern must have been showing on his face because instantly recognising it, the major said, "It's alright, you're not in any trouble so don't look so worried."

"It wasn't that Sir, it's just that there's been a lot of bombing around my home these last two days – I was rather anxious – I thought you might have bad news."

"Quite the reverse – I have some very good news for you." He then went on to say that he had read the citations for his D.C.M. and Mention, but what had not been apparent from them was the fact that

166

the French general he had saved and got back to England was a top V.I.P. As a result, General De Gaulle and his Committee acknowledged the fact that the information General Strich had been able to get to London had been absolutely invaluable to the Free French, particularly regarding forces in the French Empire all over the world who might well be persuaded to break from Vichy and join them. They therefore desired to make Corporal Chandler a member of the Legion of Honour. When this award was made for gallantry in wartime, it was accompanied by the award of the Croix de Guerre and in David's case, it would be awarded 'avec Palme'; the highest grade, as it was being awarded by the army commander. "So you see, you have to be in London a week on Friday to be decorated by General Koenig, I understand General De Gaulle is in Africa at the moment. You can go off after lunch on Thursday and come back on Sunday night. Staff Sergeant Williams will have all your documentation ready."

David remained very quiet, his mind in a whirl. The O.C. sensed he was troubled about something when most young men would have been bubbling with excitement at the news. "What's the matter lad – something bothering you?"

"Well Sir, it all seems so much at once. I've got a D.C.M. and a Mention, now I get two of the highest awards in the French Army, and really I've done so little. After all, I was only over there five minutes. When I think of my father and millions like him who were in the trenches week after week, month after month, performing all sorts of unrewarded feats of bravery and enduring the cold and the mud and the lice, I just feel something of a fraud, I shall just be embarrassed at facing him and my father-in-law, I really shall."

"Where will your father be now?"

"He'll be at his factory."

"Telephone number?"

David gave the number. "Staff Sergeant will you get me a priority call to this number please." He gave the number. They sat in silence and in five minutes the telephone rang. "Hello, is that Mr Chandler? This is Major Noakes, your son David's company commander... No, he hasn't been up to anything, quite the reverse in fact. He's been given two medals by the Free French Committee for his rescue of General Strich, but he feels embarrassed about it because he reckons you did ten times as much as he has. He's an idiot? Your father says you're an idiot – here have a word with him."

David took the phone and told his father the full story. Fred, as ever, broke the problem down into sections. "D.C.M. – you blew up a tank. Mention – you led half a dozen men from certain captivity to fight again. French awards – you saved the life of a general and provided vital intelligence to General De Gaulle that he would not otherwise have had. Whether those separate incidents happened over five days or five years doesn't matter – they happened and they happened because of your bravery and initiative and should be rewarded – and that's how all of us feel – right?"

"Thanks Dad, I'll phone you when I get all the details," and he rang off.

"Sir, I'm deeply grateful to you for bridging that gap."

"Think nothing of it. When you become an officer you will speedily realise you are not there just to be saluted. The welfare of the men under your command is probably the most important of your duties."

David had a momentary vision of Sergeant Harris saying more or less the same thing when he and Jeremy first went to the Selection Board and of Mr Austen agreeing. Now Mr Austen was dead and Lord knows what has happened to Sergeant Harris.

"Right then, go and get your bumph from the staff sergeant and come and see me before you go next Thursday."

"Thank you Sir," David saluted, turned about and marched out.

When he got back to his room, Charlie was anxiously awaiting him. David's face was still quite sombre resulting in Charlie saying, "David, is everything alright? – There's no trouble at Sandbury is there? – Is Pat OK?"

"Everything's OK at Sandbury."

"Then what the merry hell is wrong, you look as though you've dropped a sovereign and found the proverbial tanner."

"I've been awarded two more medals – but not a word outside this room – understood?"

"Cross my heart, dear old sport, but come on, tell me all about it, don't stand there like a spare whatsit at a wedding."

"The French have made me a member of the Legion of Honour and given me the Croix de Guerre for bringing back General Strich and his apparently supremely important briefcase. I keep thinking while I'm getting medals I've left Jeremy there buried in the soft earth and my sister will see me covered in French decorations while her husband is wrapped in a blanket covered in French soil. It's so monstrously unfair."

Charlie put his arm across David's shoulders. Gone was his flippant Eton language, gone was the schoolboy humour, he spoke quietly, sincerely and yet firmly, intuitively understanding the deep sadness within his friend which he could see was always there even if

David rarely allowed it to surface as he had done now.

"Jeremy would be the very last person to deny that you fully deserve this recognition of what you did. You put your life on the block wearing that German uniform, and as far as the Free French are concerned, their numbers will be vastly increased as a result of the knowledge you got to London, I heard my father tell grandfather. So my friend, you will wear your medals with pride – that's an order!!"

"Thanks Charlie."

That evening David phoned Pat who was so excited he could hardly get a word in edgeways. When he did, he said, "I have a problem. According to the information I've received here, I can invite four people to the ceremony which would be you, Mum and Dad and Rose, which leaves out your father, Megan, Anni and so on."

"Darling David, there is no problem. We can all go, including Harry who comes on leave the day before the ceremony. General Strich has invited as his guests, my Dad and Moira, along with Harry and Megan."

"That means Annie and Ernie are left out."

"No it doesn't. This is the exciting bit that you obviously haven't heard about. All your lads are invited each to receive a 'Commendation Parchment' signed by General De Gaulle. Each of them can bring two guests and Kenny Barclay has invited Anni and Ernie. So we shall all be there – isn't it exciting? And, Kenny comes on leave in a fortnight and John and the twins keep asking 'when is Kenny coming, when is Kenny coming?' I've told Susie all about it and she's as excited as we are." At length, she stopped her deluge of words and took breath.

"Now tell me about the raids."

"We've been in and out of the shelters yesterday and today. We have a detachment of the Pioneer Corps on the airfield now – oh my goodness, this isn't careless talk is it?"

"I should hardly think it would be classified as top secret."

"Well a lot of them are Germans and Austrians who have volunteered for service and have been released from internment. One private, Lady Agatha and I spoke to today on our canteen round, used to be a violinist in the Vienna Symphony Orchestra and here he was using a pick and shovel to fill in bomb craters. He said his hands would soon recover; in the meantime they had far more important things to do than play the violin. I really felt like crying, and so strangely enough did Lady Agatha so she's not such an old war horse as she makes herself out to be."

David went to bed that night with his head spinning. The medals, the bombing, Germans filling in holes made by other Germans and then the ever recurring picture of Jeremy wrapped in an army blanket and having the soft black earth of Calais thrown in on top of him until he became hidden from view for ever. "Oh God," he moaned quietly. Charlie heard and kept silent, but he stayed awake for a long time in case his friend should need him.

The heavy raids continued all that week. On the Thursday, Sandbury was bombed again and Thursday night saw the biggest London bombing so far. For seven and a half hours the capital was ceaselessly attacked, this bombardment was continued on Friday night and again on Saturday night for over ten hours. Buckingham Palace was hit; dozens of churches, thousands of houses, acres and acres of dock installations were destroyed. David rang daily, although the wait was sometimes two hours before he could get through and sometimes he couldn't get through at all. On Sunday afternoon his connection was made to the Bungalow in less than an hour however to a Pat who was obviously very upset.

"David, I have some bad news for you. Mrs Treharne is with me," Mrs Treharne was the lady from whom they bought 'The Bungalow' and from whom they had inherited Susie. "Her daughter and son-in-law were killed in the bombing at Hampstead on Thursday night. They were in the house when a landmine, dropped by a parachute, exploded on the other side of the road and blew the whole street to pieces. Mrs Treharne was in the shelter and apart from being shaken was unhurt. She telephoned me from the reception centre and my father went and collected her and brought her here. She's only got the clothes she stands up in, isn't it awful? She's still very shaky; after all she's not young anymore."

"What about the grandchildren?"

"They were evacuated to Wales, they're safe but what must they be suffering poor little souls," she started to cry quietly.

"There, there love, let me have a word with Mrs Treharne, then I'll come back to you. Will it be OK if she stays with you for a while?"

"Yes of course as long as she likes."

When Pat had called Mrs Treharne and passed the receiver over, David expressed his sadness to her and asked where the grandchildren were. She told him they were at a place called New Radnor near Llandridnod Wells. David thought that was about forty miles from Worcester and he would investigate if he could get there to see them and make sure they were alright 'as soon as this medal business was over.'

"Oh David, I do congratulate you so upon receiving these awards.

I feel very proud to know you so how proud must Pat feel!!"

"It really is most kind of you Mrs Treharne. Now, you must stay on at The Bungalow on as permanent a basis as you like. You will be company for Pat and you can keep that lump of tortoiseshell trouble in order. Pat and her father will help sort out all the formalities you're going to have to face now and over the next few months, and when things quieten down we can talk about getting the children back. In any event, I shall be home next weekend and we can talk about it in more detail then, for the time being you must rest and recover from your awful ordeal," he paused for a moment "and as my brother Harry would doubtless say, there's a lot of weeding to do in that back garden."

Mrs Treharne gave a little laugh. "Thank you David, you've made me laugh. I didn't think I would ever laugh again. God bless you, goodnight." After saying his goodnights to Pat, David went back to their room where Charlie was sitting, waiting impatiently to hear the news from Sandbury. In a very short period of time Charlie was being brought face to face with the realities of life – and death – and even though he was not directly connected with Jeremy, David's family, Mrs Treharne and her family, the bombing or the war that created David's medals, the knowledge of all these things at close hand had a profound effect on him. Put simply, he was growing up very rapidly.

The week passed quickly and on Thursday lunchtime David again presented himself to Major Noakes, who wished him good luck and told him not to get in the way of any Jerry bombs. David laughed and said he would do his best, but it really wasn't a laughing matter. London had been battered every night so far this week, raids lasting ten hours and longer, and still the people remained utterly defiant. On Wednesday September 11th Winston Churchill had made a speech saying he expected the invasion to be launched during the next week, the general feeling was 'let them come – the few the Navy let through we'll kill on the beaches.' Never were the people as united as they were when the blitz raged over London and the other cities, and when the threat of invasion hung over the south and east. The Home Guard was on permanent alert for airborne troop landings, hundreds of thousands of eyes that knew every tree, bush and building in their area, a large proportion of them being old and seasoned soldiers made certain there could be no surprise attack from the air, and if there was, would be the first on the spot to try to contain it. The people were adamant – there would be no surrender!

David got to Paddington at a little after 5.30 and made his way to

Victoria. As they moved steadily out through the South London suburbs he heard the obscene wailing of the air raid warning and shortly after that the sound of gunfire to the east. He looked out through the window, and through the cables of innumerable barrage balloons, but could see nothing. As they approached Bromley South guns started to open up much nearer to them and it was then he heard the first scream of a bomb, a sound he had got to know so well at Calais. It was followed by a second, then a third, all three exploding a few hundred yards from the track. Still the train moved steadily on. David marvelled at the unwavering dedication of the driver, doing his job as immovably as if he were passing through a particularly bad hailstorm. At last they reached the long tunnel through the Downs and when they emerged at the southern end, they appeared to have left the bombing behind, but London again suffered another night of merciless pounding. When David at last reached Chandlers Lodge and had eaten with the family, Mrs Treharne included, they all went out on to the front lawn to look north to London where the red glow of the innumerable fires in the City and the docks could clearly be seen reflected from the clouds. From time to time a German bomber could be heard flying back home, its evil work done until it took part in the next onslaught. Jack made what was to prove to be a most perceptive remark when he said, "I cannot understand why Goering has stopped bombing the airfields to concentrate on London. For Hitler's invasion to succeed he must control the air, therefore he must eliminate the airfields. In yesterday afternoons and the night raids on London he lost ninety-three aircraft according to the Ministry of Information. Even he cannot afford to lose vital aircraft at that rate at this time."

"What you are saying then," replied Fred, "is that London's sacrifice will prevent our being invaded."

"I think that is highly probable," said Jack. And so, many years later when experts were able to analyse the Battle of Britain and the blitz with the help of captured Luftwaffe and German central government papers relating to those times, it was clearly seen that Goering convinced Hitler he could bomb Britain into submission. When he found he was wrong, it was too late, and he had too few machines left to be certain of a successful attack on the British mainland. Hitler cancelled the invasion plans.

The next morning the families travelled up to the Free French Headquarters in the west end of London in one of the few periods of 'All Clear' the capital had enjoyed over the last few days. When they reached the suburbs they passed several places where bombs had fallen and where heavy rescue teams were working to hopefully find people in the rubble. The local air raid warden would have the numbers of people normally staying at each house in his or her sector so that in the event of a direct hit there would be an indication of who should be there. David turned to his father, "They're the ones who should be getting the medals," he said quietly.

"They're doing their job; if they go beyond that I've no doubt they'll be rewarded too, so stop belittling yourself." David accepted the reproof and said no more.

They were all most courteously received at General De Gaulle's headquarters, being escorted into a large room with the inevitable black criss-cross tape over the windows. In the garden, about six feet from the windows was a large sandbagged emplacement to above window height, rigidly reinforced with upright and horizontal steel channels. 'That could take quite a blast', thought David as he looked around. Suddenly the young officer who was conducting them stiffened to attention and saluted. They turned and saw General Strich approaching them. He was in his Number One dress uniform wearing all his campaign medals and awards, evidence of a lifetime of service to his country. He greeted the ladies first, kissing each one on both cheeks, then shook hands with the men, Harry standing rigidly to attention, and then he turned to David, put his hands on to his upper arms, looked smilingly into his face and then hugged him, kissing him on both cheeks. "This is the man who saved my life," he said in rapid French to the escorting subaltern who held out his arm to David and shook hands firmly. "We then have a lot to thank you for," he said.

"It wasn't just me," said David, "here are the men that carried him, and I might add, nearly dropped him a couple of times." Through the door had appeared the four riflemen and the ex-riflemen who, such a short time ago had, with David, carried out the audacious rescue of the general, he already shaking hands with each of them. Barclay, Beasley and Piercey were all now together in a service battalion in Nottingham, Smith 24 was at the depot and Riley, now recovered from his wounds was due to start a factory job in Darlington the following week.

"Do we call him Sir yet?" asked Piercey.

"Of course not, cadets are the lowest form of army life, didn't you know," was the rejoinder from Beasley.

"Well, I can see you lot haven't changed," laughed David, "we'll get a chance to talk later," the officer in charge of the parade having asked in French and English if recipients and their guests would kindly take their seats.

Most of the recipients of awards were French. The presiding officer was general Koenig who was obviously well briefed since when David's name was called and he stood to attention in front of him, the general said "Ah, but I see you are no longer a corporal – have they taken your stripes away?"

"Yes Sir. I'm afraid so. I am now merely a cadet."

"Well Mr Officer Cadet Chandler, I will tell you that I was a cadet once so I know what they put you through. I have no doubt you will become a first class officer." With that, he beckoned for the decorations, pinned them on, kissed David on each cheek, and as David took a pace back and saluted, he returned the salute with a smile and, "Bonne chance."

As the ceremony finished they heard the sirens giving the first of what were to be three daylight raids on London that day. They were ushered downstairs into a large cellar, which had been prepared as an air raid shelter. Wall bunks were to be seen on three of the walls, all discreetly covered by hanging curtains. The centre of the room was provided with a massive table upon which was laid out a large selection of cold foods, quiches, salads and so on to which General Strich led his party. "We decided to have a buffet style lunch down here precisely because we were afraid there might be an alert," he said. He spent some time during the lunch talking to each of the family in turn, particularly to Rose and Ruth. He noticed Harry's medal ribbon and congratulated him on it. He too was obviously well informed since he said to Harry, "I understand a number of lives you saved by getting them to the beaches were in fact French soldiers."

"Yes Sir, there was quite a number of French and some Belgians as well."

"Well, on behalf of all of them, thank you very much. They'll always remember you you know, not your name of course, but the story of the English sergeant on the German motor bike who saved them from captivity, will be told time and again to their children and grandchildren."

When the ceremony was over, the 'All Clear' sounded, and at about two thirty they said all their goodbyes and got taxis to Victoria. Before leaving however, a bevy of photographers surrounded them asking those decorated to wear or display their awards since the air raid warning had prevented them taking pictures at the end of the ceremony. David had his picture taken by several photographers with his five men and with the impressive figure of the general in the centre. "I shall see you all get copies," said the general and shook hands again with his saviours before bidding them each farewell and good luck.

As they arrived at Victoria the sirens sounded the alert once again. "I think we'd better get into a shelter," said Fred, "I don't think we'd better risk waiting on Victoria Station," to which sentiments all agreed. There was a large surface shelter just outside the station forecourt, which rapidly became crowded as the noise of gunfire was heard in the distance. Soon it became obvious that the action was in fact going to be very close indeed to where they were sheltering as they plainly heard the bombs screaming down around them. David held Pat and Rose tight as the whole building trembled with the concussion. They stopped counting at twelve, and as quickly as the violence had started, so it ceased and after another twenty minutes the 'All Clear' sounded again.

They left the shelter to hear everyone saying, "Buckingham Palace has been hit again." Six of the bombs they had counted had straddled the Palace causing considerable damage. With the palace being only a couple of hundred yards away or so, they had certainly shared with their King and Queen, who too were in the Palace shelter at the time, the doubtful privilege of being on the receiving end of Hermann Goering's nasty handiwork.

At the Bungalow Pat and David enjoyed a long lie-in the next morning, discreetly undisturbed by the diplomatic Mrs Treharne, then they all lunched at Chandlers Lodge. Around one o'clock the telephone rang which Fred answered. After a while he came back to the others and said to David in a somewhat serious voice, "There's a gentleman on the phone who wants a word with you." David, puzzled, went through into the hall, Fred closing the door behind him, and then turning to the others broke into a grin. "Going to London yesterday has just cost him a few bob," he said to the complete bewilderment of all present.

"Will you explain yourself Fred Chandler before I do you damage," said Ruth, but in the meantime David had returned to face the quizzical looks directed at him.

"That was Mr Forster at the Depot," he explained for the benefit of those who didn't know or know of Mr Forster that he was the R.S.M. who had met and lunched with his mother and father at Aldershot. He continued, "There is a tradition in the sergeant's mess at the depot that if any member gets his picture in the papers for whatever reason he has to pay for a round of drinks for the whole mess. Well, apparently photographs taken yesterday have appeared today in both the Express and the Sketch, possibly others. Now he reckons I'm still an honorary member of the mess as I'm not yet an officer, therefore he's putting the round, which will be drunk on Monday evening, on my tab to be settled when I go back to Winchester. I reckon his reasoning is skating on pretty thin ice, but I told him it would be a pleasure to buy the round and that my father would lend me the money to pay for it – so that's how we left it."

"You cheeky devil," said Fred, "now where's today's Mail. Let's see if there's anything in there, if not, one of us will have to scoot up to Smith's and buy some of the others. Oh, and by the way love (to Ruth) Mr & Mrs Forster are coming on leave to Tonbridge and would like to come and see us towards the end of next week, that alright with you?"

"Yes, of course, we did talk about it at Aldershot; it will be very nice to have them."

The rest of the weekend went very quickly. They found more photos tucked away in the Sunday Dispatch and even the Sunday Pictorial had managed to show a picture of the group. "The trouble is," said David, "all the people at OCTU will know now, that was the last thing I wanted." On Sunday morning he rang the railway travel office at Paddington. There had been further heavy bombing on Friday and Saturday night and he was concerned as to whether the main line trains would have been affected in any way.

The R.T.O. said, "Everything's all over the place. My advice to you is to get here as early as you can, the way things are on the tracks out of London you may have to go via Edinburgh!" David therefore most reluctantly tore himself away from the Bungalow, from Susie and Mrs Treharne with whom he had had a long talk and had told her she must stay until the end of the war, and beyond if she wanted to, and then a long lingering farewell to Pat at Sandbury station in company with a number of other service men having to make earlier departures for their units than they would normally need to do. Timetables at all main line stations were in a state of chaos with railway staff performing miracles of improvisation, permanent way men performing miracles of repair and reconstruction and footplate men working all hours to keep the trains moving, no matter how slowly, as well as having to cope with the difficulties of travelling unaccustomed roads when being diverted. David was on his way by soon after two o'clock, albeit a different route at first to the one he would normally have travelled. That afternoon and through the night the bombers came back again, over four hundred attacking London. This time, however, they got the biggest hiding of the war so far. One hundred and eighty five German aircraft were shot down in the twenty-four hours, but Buckingham Palace was hit yet again and an unexploded bomb threatened to demolish St Paul's Cathedral until a Royal Engineers bomb disposal unit successfully defused it and took it away to Shoeburyness to explode it.

It took six hours to reach Worcester, and when David at last climbed wearily out of the train, he saw the welcome figure of Charlie waving from beyond the exit barrier. "What are you doing here? - How did you know which train I would be on?"

"Well you see dear old boy, we officer cadets are famed for our initiative, so, one, I phoned the R.T.O. and enquired approximately at what time the London trains would be arriving. He said that the first was expected at about eight o'clock and the second at about midnight. I thought the blighters bound to stay locked in his beloved's arms as long as possible so I bet he'll be on the midnight one, in which case he won't get a taxi and will have to hoof it back to camp. So, number two, I then organised with grandfather that we could call on the car hire firm here, he has an account with them to turn out when required. All I have to do now is put tuppence in that little black box in the telephone booth and within five minutes our carriage will await."

"Charlie, you are going up in my estimation in leaps and bounds, but what would you have done with yourself if I hadn't arrived until midnight? Worcester isn't exactly a mecca of entertainment on a Sunday night in wartime, or probably any other time for that matter."

"I would have just waited dear boy, he also serves etcetera."

"Well anyway, thanks very much, it really was very thoughtful of you. And by the way, Pat sends her love and is coming down for our seventy-two."

Charlie grabbed the back of a station bench. "How can I wait that long?" he proclaimed dramatically "how can I wait that long?"

Chapter Sixteen

The next four weeks passed quickly for the Cadets, their days, and many nights too, mapped out so that from early morning onwards they were constantly moving from one place of instruction to another, constantly having to change their dress, sometimes as many as five or six times a day to suit different types of lesson, drill, P.T., weapon training, lectures, field craft, unarmed combat, route marches and so on, and then at night keeping their 'Officers' Note Books' up to date with all the facts they had been given during the day. The plain fact was they had got to assimilate the same amount of information and expertise in three months that a Sandhurst cadet before the war was given eighteen months to achieve. No wonder they all became lean and fit and ready for bed each night. There were the inevitable unfortunates who, for one reason or another, couldn't keep up the pace. They were quietly removed and RTU'd, where they would become NCOs in most cases in a short time, thus realising the level of performance of which they were capable.

During those few weeks, London was attacked night after night. In the month of September, nearly seven thousand civilians were killed in London and nearly eleven thousand seriously injured, but still the capital remained utterly defiant. Sandbury too suffered its first casualties when a bomb hit a first aid centre killing the doctor on duty along with four nursing auxiliaries. A number of people in neighbouring houses were injured and considerable damage was done to property. It was, of course, a pinprick compared to London's suffering but horrific to the victims and their friends and families nevertheless.

Fred had organised fire watch teams at the factory. Shelters had been built to house the workers, but when an alert was in progress, three teams of two men took positions in sandbagged enclosures at strategic places on the roof. Ladders and walkways were constructed so that if an incendiary bomb, which only weighed a few pounds but which could do enormous damage in a very short space of time, lodged in the roof, it could be reached and attacked very quickly with sand and smothered. Being charged with phosphorous it would, of course, not be possible to use water on it. Tens of thousands of ordinary men and women throughout the country sat out on factory and office roofs during those terrible days and nights, unsung heroes facing unknown dangers, each determined to 'do their bit', dealing with thousands of firebombs before they could take hold and in the process saving millions of square feet of factory space so that it could continue playing its part in the prosecution of the war.

In the attack on London, the Great Hall at Eltham Palace was hit by incendiaries on the 17th September, the next night three hundred bombers hit the City and heavy raids were made on Liverpool. On the 26th, London was attacked for the twentieth successive night, but the capital found some consolation in the announcement that Berlin had been bombed continuously for five hours the previous night.

On the 28th September, a Saturday, Jack came round in the morning to Chandlers Lodge. "Have you heard," he said, "they lost one hundred and thirty seven planes during the daylight raids yesterday – they just cannot keep this up, no one could. It's not just planes, it's trained aircrew they're losing, you can't train a pilot in five minutes, nor a navigator for that matter." As he spoke the telephone rang, the caller asking if Mr Hooper was there, he had telephoned his home and had been told he might be at Chandlers Lodge. Ruth, who had first answered, called Jack and left him to take the call. After a few minutes Jack returned to the kitchen visibly upset.

"Jack dear, what's the matter?" asked Ruth, holding his arm with both her hands.

"They blew my offices to bits last night and Ericson and Freeman who were fire watching were killed. They were both in their sixties and started as boys with my father, they were like family." He paused for a few moments, "I knew we should have moved out of London. I put it to the staff six months ago but they all wanted to stay, they all lived within travelling distance, they didn't want to have to relocate somewhere else. I should have insisted, I should have insisted."

"There's nothing to blame yourself about Jack dear. It's a hard thing to say but those men could have been killed at their homes, or travelling to work or anywhere else for that matter. It's so terribly sad for their families; will you be able to contact them?"

"Yes, they both have telephones; we paid for all our essential people to have them installed. I'll go back home and book calls."

"What about all your records?" asked Fred.

"Well there we did have a bit of foresight," Jack replied, "I had everything copied that we would need and had it stored at Paddock Wood. That was in the first months of this year. All new correspondence of any value and the daily business was duplicated and posted there every night, so we can start business there literally on Monday if I can get the staff there. I chose Paddock Wood because it's not far from here, it's not likely to be bombed and it's easy to get to from Victoria. The person who telephoned me has now telephoned all section managers and they, in turn, will contact staff by telegram. It will be interesting to see how many manage to get there on Monday morning. Now I must go and talk to Mrs Ericson and Mrs Freeman. God, what a ghastly business."

It was not only the mainland that suffered. On the 17th September the 'City of Benares' carrying child evacuees to Canada, was sunk by a U Boat and seventy-seven children were killed. The losses of the Allies so far amounted to a monstrous total of eight hundred and thirty four ships. As a result of the bombing of London Docks, all work was transferred to the Clyde, which itself; along with Liverpool and other main ports was suffering at the receiving end of Hitler's hardware. Another port, which should have been added to the growing list of targets, was Gibraltar. In July, the Royal Navy had put a number of Vichy French capital ships out of action to prevent their falling into German hands. On 24th September Vichy retaliated by bombing Gibraltar. However, the Petain government might issue orders to the pilots to bomb, but the pilots, in the main, deliberately dropped their bombs into the sea and went back home. A small number were dropped on the Rock but in most cases they failed to explode and were found, on examination, to have had their fuses tampered with. It was at this time also that Vichy France made a law compelling Jews to carry special identity cards, which was, of course, the precursor of the ultimate obscenity of the train rides to the gas chambers.

A week or so before the seventy-two David and Charlie were sitting in their room writing up their notes late in the evening. Charlie ceased writing for a short while and then turned to David saying, "David my dear old mucker –"

"Mucker? Where on earth did you get that word from – certainly not from Eton I'll be bound."

"Well, no not exactly old sport, in fact I heard one of the maintenance squaddies saying to another that he was out with his mucker Bill so and so last night. Apparently they picked up a couple of the local talent, but I regret to tell you I didn't hear the outcome of the operation, I cannot therefore further satisfy your prurient curiosity. Anyhow, I thought this word must mean someone you 'muck-in' with so I thought I'd try it out since I have the dubious privilege of mucking in with you."

"You're nuts."

"Probably. David, do you think your sister Rose might like to come to Ramsford with Pat next week?"

David sat back. "You know that she is, as they say in the Good Book, with child?"

"Yes, of course, but I presume she would be fit to travel."

"Good Lord yes, she's as fit as a flea, but what made you think of her?"

"Well I though it might make a change for her and at the same time make us a foursome."

"I say this in all seriousness Charlie, most blokes of your age would be, if anything, a bit embarrassed at chaperoning a girl in the family way. You have to remember too that she is a widow and still very sad at heart so wouldn't be like your normal boisterous eighteen-year-old. On the other hand, I'd love for her to come. I don't see enough of her on my leaves. But what about your grandfather?"

"Well look old sport, firstly I'm not a totally insensitive twit so I wouldn't lark around like a two-year-old, secondly grandfather would enjoy her company as enormously as he does Pat's, so he'd be delighted to have us all there. Why don't you pop out and ask her – there shouldn't be much of a delay at this time of night. And if she doesn't feel like making the trip tell her I understand and give her my kindest regards."

When David rang it was Rose who answered. David quickly put Charlie's proposal to her in reply to which she asked David if he could hang on for a minute or two while she had a quick word with her mother. Getting the Thursday, Friday and Monday off would be no problem as she had worked two weekends to cover other staff during the holiday period and could therefore arrange that. She came back to the telephone and said, "Mummy thinks it will be a very nice break for me so I'd love to come, although you realise I can't do anything terribly athletic in my condition!!"

"Don't worry," said David, "just a spot of hunting, cross country cycling and so on – nothing strenuous."

"Oh David you are a head-case! But David, don't you think Charlie might feel a bit awkward with my having a decided bump – after all he's very young, and I don't suppose they had many mothers-to-be at Eton."

"Don't worry about Charlie, he's not as addle brained as he sometimes makes himself out to be, as a few people here, including to their surprise a couple of the instructors, have discovered."

"Alright then, thank him very much, I deeply appreciate his kindness and look forward to meeting him and his grandfather. I'll have a long chat with Pat tomorrow about what to wear and so on. Oh, and Mum said what about rations, incidentally do you know our butter ration has gone down to two ounces a week? Dad insists he'll never survive."

"Don't worry about rations, they don't seem to have too much of a problem there."

When the time came for their journey, Pat and Rose were seen off by Ruth, Fred and Anni from Sandbury Station. As they waited, Jack and Colonel Tim appeared on to the platform.

"Look who I bumped into," said Jack. "I told the colonel you were off to the wilds of the West Country so he said he must come and give you a send-off. A sort of soldier's farewell," he boomed.

Tim grinned broadly. "I hope you both have a lovely peaceful time," he said. Sandbury and other Kent and Sussex airfields had been subjected to hit-and-run raids several times so far in this week, a state of affairs which did, in fact, continue all through the weekend to come, the Saturday also recording the two hundredth raid on London.

With kisses all round, the two girls boarded the train. There were no problems in town other than the usual queue for a taxi and soon they were winding their way out of London, passing bombsite after bombsite. "When you think that those sites mean personal tragedy to countless numbers of people, it's really awful isn't it that one evil man could cause all this?" said Rose. Pat held her hand and they sat for a while in silence.

Captain Morgan and the lads met them at Worcester, Charlie giving Pat a decorous kiss on the cheek and shaking hands with Rose saying, "Welcome to Worcestershire, the most beautiful county in England."

Rose immediately replied. "Next to Kent of course."

"Ah, but I've never visited Kent."

"Then you must come and see it – it's incomparable."

"Oh but then I couldn't, you have a lot of bombs there and I'm a frightful coward."

"If you two can stop your argy-bargy," David broke in, "perhaps we could all get in the car – I'm dying for a cup of tea." He was, however, most pleased that Charlie had started off on the right foot with

Rose, there was obviously not going to be what might be euphemistically called a pregnant pause.

He smiled at the thought, which Pat spotted and said, "And what are you grinning at may I ask?"

"Oh nothing much."

"People get put away for grinning at nothing much," and snuggled closer to him, trying not to make it look too obvious.

The Earl came out on the steps to welcome them – he had obviously been watching for the car to come up the long drive. He welcomed Pat with a kiss on each cheek and then, on being introduced to Rose, took her hand in both of his and said, "Welcome to Ramsford Mrs Cartwright. I have been told of your sad loss, I know how devastating it is to lose a loved one, but I do hope we can all give you a happy and peaceful weekend." He paused, "Mind you my dear, on reflection, there's generally not a lot of peace here when Charlie's around but we'll try and keep him in order." With that he linked her arm with his and holding Pat with his other arm, the three walked up the steps through the massive double doors into the entrance hall, followed by David and Charlie.

They had a splendid meal that evening during which they sampled some superb claret laid down by the Earl some years before. The conversation never faltered once, Charlie and Rose got on like a couple who had known each other since they were children and gently ribbed each other accordingly, much to the amusement of the others. "Now tomorrow evening I've organised an expedition for us all," announced the Earl. "I do hope I've done the right thing and what I've done will be to your liking. As a matter of fact, I'm beginning to have cold feet in case it isn't."

"Now come on grandfather, tell us what it is, it's not like you to waffle on," interrupted Charlie.

"Well, the London Symphony Orchestra is giving a troop concert in Worcester Cathedral – I've got the programme here which you can see in a minute. I've arranged a reserved compartment to take us into Worcester on the local. The concert starts at six-thirty and ends at about nine o'clock, it's early apparently because truck loads of troops from many miles around will be coming in and they then have to travel back. After the concert, I've booked supper in a private room at the Station Hotel; the food there incidentally is absolutely first class. Then we get the last local back here at 11.20. Now, how does that sound to you all?"

There was immediate and universal appreciation of the outing.

"What a wonderful idea" said Pat.

"What a wonderful experience it will be," was Rose's comment, "to hear such beautiful music in such a magnificent setting." And so it proved to be. Among other items on the programme, the Cathedral organ took part in Handel's organ concerto, and the final work was Beethoven's Ninth Symphony with the cathedral choir augmented by the choir from Hereford Cathedral and a local choral society, itself reinforced by soldiers and airmen from nearby camps and airfields maintaining their hobby though far from their own fraternities.

"Do you know," said the Earl, as they ate their supper, "the orchestra had only this one afternoon to rehearse with the choirs, the soloists and the organist."

"They were all superb," David enthused. "I know I speak for all of us when I say it was a unique, thrilling and exciting evening which will stay with us all our days – thank you Sir very much."

There was immediate applause from the others, followed by, "and the grub's not bad either grandfather," from Charlie, followed by a playful boxing of the ears by Rose.

On the Saturday afternoon the Earl took the girls to the orchid house. "I have a little surprise for you both," he said as he led them to a small glasshouse with a workbench in it. On the bench were two pots each containing an orchid, each plant just beginning to produce flowers. One was pale yellow with blue spots fanning out to the rim whilst the other had a deep red centre shading out through pink to white. They were exquisite. The Earl proceeded to tell them a little about the plants. An orchid seed pod can contain something like two million seeds in a form almost like dust, but the seeds themselves, unlike the seeds of most other plants, have no integral food store, they therefore just die by the wayside having nothing to live on. However, if they fall on what is called micorisal fungus they will feed on the glucose produced by the fungus, germinate and grow. This can take several months. It is possible, he went on, that the new plants can be produced on nutrient plates, but a very great deal of skill, patience and devotion to detail is needed to produce new strains, whichever way it is achieved.

The girls were absolutely fascinated by these and a wealth of other facts presented by their guide so that when the Earl stopped in his tracks saying, "My goodness, I hope I haven't bored you to tears – I do get carried away when I get an audience, especially one as attractive as you two undoubtedly are," they each took one of his arms and told him how much they had enjoyed his telling them about these beautiful and interesting flowers. "Well now," he continued, "the little surprise I mentioned. These two plants I have hybridised are unique. They are of the Cypripedium variety and I am naming them Cypripedium Pat Chandler and Cypripedium Rose Cartwright and will register them as such. As soon as I have some of their progeny you shall have them, who knows, you may become orchid experts in your own right in due course!"

When, with the Earl, they rejoined the others, they excitedly told them of their new immortality. They were far more delighted about the orchids than the Earl had thought possible, he had hoped they would be pleased but it was obvious that the pleasure he had given them far outweighed anything he had anticipated – they were thrilled to bits! When the hubbub died down Charlie asked, "Grandfather, would you name one of your plants after me?"

"I've got that organised Charlie. I've got a new strain of rhubarb coming along that I thought I'd name after you – or was it the stuff they put on the rhubarb. I can't remember now." Amid laughter, they all walked into the drawing room for tea.

The next morning they all went to church in the village, being seated in the Earl's private pews. "They don't get used much these days," he whispered as an aside to Pat. The villagers cast sidelong glances at the Earl's companions, particularly the pregnant one walking with Charlie. Eyebrows were raised; speculation in the village afterwards was fuelled by the sight of Rose linking arms with Charlie as they walked to the estate wagon parked a little way along the road. The rest of the day passed, it seemed in minutes, however there was no lift back to camp for the two cadets on this occasion, they had to catch the local to Worcester where transport would be provided for all cadets returning from their seventy-two.

Before they left, while David and Pat were saying their goodbyes in their room and the Earl was organising a car to take the young men to the station, Charlie said to Rose, "I say Rose, do you think I could write to you occasionally?" And then hurriedly "Just as a pen pal you understand, nothing mushy or anything soppy like that – just as a pal as it were," he was getting quite flustered. "You see, I really have no one to write to except father and grandfather, I have no real pals at Eton and I don't know any girls worth writing to."

"Charlie, I'd be delighted if you would. I really mean that. I'd love to know how you're getting on and about all your popsies as you call them including Sadie! And again, you can keep me informed of all the dark doings of that brother of mine!"

"Rose, I tell you this in all seriousness, no one shall ever hear me say a word against David. You'll never know how much he's helped me. I was scared stiff when I went to OCTU. He not only guided me along the right lines but, on occasion when we were forced marching, he physically helped me, carrying my rifle and all that sort of thing so that I didn't drop out, helping me over obstacles on the assault course and so on, all without making it obvious. And not only me either. No, he's a very special bloke – he's my mucker didn't you know?" he continued in his usual cheerful way.

"Your mucker – what on earth is a mucker?" she asked. He told her his version of the origins of the word, to her considerable amusement, concluding, "So you see – he's my mucker."

It was time for them to go. The girls had elected not to go to the station with them so having waved them goodbye from the steps, then went inside to wait for the nine o'clock news, to hear that there had been further raids on airfields in Kent that day. At the suggestion of their host they telephoned Chandlers Lodge to hear that all was well, apart from some gunfire towards Maidstone they neither saw nor heard anything although the alert was sounded twice. Another item on the news was received with some ferocity by the Earl. It was announced that the penalty for looting was to be increased from three to twelve months. "Only twelve months?" he exclaimed. "They should damned well shoot them, that's what they should do."

"And I bet both our fathers are saying exactly the same thing at this very moment," Pat agreed. "How evil can people be to steal under these circumstances, what a wicked thing to do."

The next morning the Earl accompanied them to the station as he had Pat on the previous visit. As they pulled up on the forecourt, a porter opened the car doors and as the Earl alighted said, "Good morning my Lord."

"Oh, Northbourne, how nice to see you, how are your parents?"

"Very well m'Lord, and Lord Ramsford and Mr Charlie?"

"They're very well," he turned to the two girls. "Northbourne's parents worked at The Grange all their lives and now live in one of the retirement houses in the village." He turned again to Northbourne, "Now, will you take my ladies' cases," surreptitiously palming him half a crown, "and find them non-smoker seats together on the London train?"

"Yes my Lord, of course, they'll be at the forward part of the platform m'ladies," and with that he picked up the two suitcases and went ahead to the departure gate.

"M'ladies ey?" joked Pat "are we being admitted to the aristocracy?"

"My dears, you would both more than grace any society you were in, up to and including royalty," asserted the Earl, taking an arm of each and walking towards the platform.

They chatted on for some twenty minutes before the mighty 'King George V' slowly passed them in a cloud of hissing steam. Northbourne indicated from a window where their seats were, the Earl held the girls in turn and kissed each one saying, "Please come again when you can manage it, it's been delightful having you here."

With Pat saying "We will," and Rose saying

"Now take care of our orchids," they climbed into the corridor and reached their compartment. Northbourne wished them, "a safe journey m'ladies." To which they replied

"Thank you Mr Northbourne."

The other occupants of the compartment wondered who the 'ladies' were and why they should know the porter's name.

The Earl came to the window and as the train pulled away, he waved to them walking along with the train a little way until it started to pick up speed. They sat back in their seats silent for a few moments until Rose said, "He'll be very lonely tonight without all of us won't he?"

"We'll telephone him to let him know we got home safely," Pat replied.

Chapter Seventeen

David and Charlie, along with the other cadets, were worked even harder when, on the 14th of October, they recommenced their course to the extent that with several night ops and working through the weekends, they hardly knew at any time which day it was. Back in Kent the attacks on airfields had reduced to just occasional hit-and-run raids, although a heavy assault on London on November 8th resulted in the Tower of London being hit, the Church of St Clement Danes being destroyed as also the Reform and Carlton Clubs, but on the same night, a force of bombers flew sixteen hundred miles non stop from England to bomb the Fiat factory in Turin and the Pirelli works in Milan. At last, the Italians were to receive calling cards from the R.A.F. to let them know there was a war on, if they hadn't already realised it from the thrashing their army was receiving in being driven out of Greece.

On Wednesday 13th November, Pat and Lady Agatha met as usual at the Rotary canteen at 9am to get their mobile unit loaded up for the morning run. They usually left at about 9.30 and then made their way around the perimeter of the airfield from gun site to dispersal point, from picquet post to the main guardrooms, from searchlight batteries to listening posts. It was a cold, bright day. At each stopping point, they were enthusiastically welcomed by the men and women manning their various stations, for them it was a welcome interruption to the tedium of cleaning and polishing their sundry items of equipment which was really all they had to do in between the frenetic periods of being attacked by the Luftwaffe. It is said that a soldiers' life, and in this case an airman's as well, is ninety-five per cent boredom and five percent terror. In the last two months or so that balance had evened up somewhat, but now it was beginning to resume its previous proportions.

It was to universal surprise therefore that a minute or two after Pat and Lady Agatha had pulled up at a Bofors gun emplacement, their last stop but one on their morning's round, the wail of the siren broke the still November morning. Immediately the men ran to their posts, the two ladies jumped down from their serving counter, ran round and lowered the canopy and bolted it into place in the side of the vehicle, and quickly climbed into the cab. Their nearest shelter was about four hundred yards away, but as there didn't appear to be any enemy activity anywhere nearby they were not unduly concerned. Nevertheless, Pat put her foot down to coax what speed she could out of a vehicle that was built for industry rather than performance. As they were half way to the shelter, they heard the Bofors gun they had just left open up, and looking through the driver's side window, they both saw to their horror a single fighter flying at very low level hurtling straight towards them. As they saw the fighter so the fighter pilot saw them. Any vehicle on an airfield is a target and in the instance of seeing its target, the pilot fired a long burst from its machine guns. Mid way through the burst he hit the van, the bullets striking Pat and her companion across the chest. They were killed instantly, the vehicle swerved off the perimeter road and ran down into the ditch at the edge and turned over on its side. When one of the station ambulances roared up a few minutes later they found the body of Pat folded in the lifeless arms of Lady Agatha.

Two hours later David was leaving the dining room with Charlie when an orderly from the unit H.Q. approached them and said to David "Cadet, you're to report to the CO straight away."

Instantly Charlie started ribbing him with, "I know, the frogs have decided you haven't got enough medals yet so they've organised you a couple more."

David just answered, "I'll see you back at the room," and walked away to H.Q. He had a most peculiar feeling in the pit of his stomach that something was very wrong. He started to walk more quickly and then said to himself, "Slow down you lunatic, it's probably something to do with the Passing Out parade next week, perhaps I've won the Belt of Honour for the best Cadet – unlikely – that chap Ritchie from the Green Howards is quite brilliant – it's bound to be him." By the time he was knocking on the C.O.'s door and having been bidden enter, he marched in and saluted. It was then he noticed the padré standing to one side and looking very seriously at him.

There was a chair in front of the C.O.'s desk towards which the colonel waved his hand, "Sit down Chandler," he said in a low, kindly voice. David's stomach started turning again as the colonel continued, "I have some very bad news for you David. I have been requested to inform you that your wife was killed in an air attack this morning at Sandbury Aerodrome."

David slouched forward, put his elbows on his knees and his head in his hands and stared sightlessly at the floor. The padré moved around the desk and gripped his shoulder. The two officers remained quiet, until David slowly recovered his composure a little to say, "Have you any details Sir?"

"Only that they were driving their canteen vehicle which was attacked by an enemy fighter plane. They both died instantly I am told."

"Both? Then Lady Agatha was killed as well? Oh my God, the brigadier will be desolate; they were utterly devoted to each other."

There was silence again for a short while, broken by the colonel saying, "Now David, you are to go on compassionate leave immediately. I'll have a P.U. to take you to the station. As regards Passing Out parade next week you're not to worry about that. I can tell you now that you've passed, in fact, short of something ridiculous happening we knew you would pass a month ago. You'll be gazetted on Friday 22nd so from then on you wear your second lieutenants uniform. From that Friday you have a further seven days leave after which you present yourself back at Winchester on Sunday evening 1st December. If for any reason you are unable to do that and require further compassionate leave, just telephone the adjutant there and he will organise it. Now, have you got all that?"

David nodded, "Yes, thank you Sir." He slowly rose, began to make his way to the door, stopped, turned to the colonel, saluted smartly, and added, "I would like to thank all the instructors for all they've done Sir," turned about and marched out. David's life may suddenly have been shattered but he was still a soldier and would remain at heart a soldier for the rest of his days.

When he reached his room, Charlie was waiting eagerly for the news, but on seeing David's face he instantly saw the pain and sorrow written on it. "David, what's happened, what's the problem?"

"They've just told me that Pat has been killed," he said in a dreadful monotone.

"Oh my God no, not Pat, not Pat, oh no, please not Pat," cried Charlie, as he sat back on his bed, his eyes beginning to stream with tears, "not your beautiful Pat." He began to sob, but quickly pulled himself together. "Oh David, I am so sorry, I should be trying to console you instead of behaving like this. How did it happen, do you know?"

David repeated in the same low voice all that the colonel had told him, and went on, "Can you do me a favour Charlie? Will you go into Gieves at Worcester and ask them to send my uniform, greatcoat and so on to Chandlers Lodge; I've had the final fitting so I know it's OK, but have a quick look at it first to make sure it's alright, buttons the right way up and so on." He paused for a moment, "Will you tell your grandfather, he was fond of Pat?"

Charlie helped David to get all his clothes, books and personal effects packed, carefully wrapping Pat's photograph which he had fallen in love with when David first arrived and put it reverently in the valise. In the meantime the P.U. arrived. They stacked the kit bag, valise and holdall in the back of the motor, the driver saying, "I'll give you a hand on to the train with this lot Sir." It was the first time he'd been called 'Sir' by anyone in the army, it sounded odd.

The journey home was a complete blank. He remembered afterwards getting a porter at Paddington to trolley his kit to a taxi, and another at Victoria to put it on the train to Sandbury. He remembered telephoning his father from Victoria to say which train he would be on, but the remainder of the journey was a total and absolute blank. Receiving all the tearful condolences of the family and having to meet Jack, as shattered as he was himself, proved a nightmare, it was not something which would be over in a few hours or a few days either, it was for ever – for ever without his Pat. In a moment of the deepest despair he realised how easy it would be to join her, and it was with this thought that he pulled himself up short. He said to Jack, "Can I go and see her?"

"I'll take you," said Jack.

They went together to the Chapel of Rest to which both Pat and Lady Agatha had been taken from the hospital mortuary. David looked at his beloved for long, long minutes, still beautiful even in death, and then turned and went back to Jack. In a firm and controlled voice he said, "We shall have to start making arrangements tomorrow."

Jack put his arm around David's shoulders as they walked out to the car together saying, "Yes old son, that we shall."

"In these circumstances does there have to be an inquest?" asked David.

"I understand that isn't required," replied Jack, "apparently if a doctor and in this case there was both an R.A.F. medical officer plus our own doctor in attendance, if a doctor was present at the incident or shortly afterwards, he could then sign the Death Certificate. It would be different if someone was found 'apparently' killed by enemy action, then they would have to have an inquest. I suppose when you think of it, inquests would be out of the question during the heavy bombing in the East End or at Coventry recently when hundreds were killed in one night."

David was silent for some time. "Just to think that what we are suffering is being endured by thousands of others. Complete families being wiped out except for perhaps their young children who were evacuated, and who will never see their parents again. In Germany, before the war, I met a young German whose father had been killed in the Great War. He said to me that perhaps one day he would be able to avenge his father's death. We all thought that was an awful thing to say. Now I understand how he felt, whether it's right or wrong that's how I feel and shall go on feeling."

"I think the only answer I can make to that old lad is from the Bible. How does it go? Something like, 'they have sown the wind and shall reap the whirlwind. I have a funny feeling that although it looks unlikely at this very moment, Germany will, one day, reap the worst whirlwind the world has ever known." But even Jack, with all his knowledge and vision, could not have conceived the dimensions of that whirlwind.

The following day the brigadier came to see David and Jack. The substance of his discussion was that since he and Lady Agatha had no permanent home, no family and few friends other than his immediate military colleagues, he wondered if David would consider there being a combined funeral and for the two 'girls' to be laid to rest side by side in Sandbury churchyard. David looked at Jack who nodded his acquiescence. It was decided therefore that the funerals would take place at eleven o'clock on Thursday the 21st, in one week's time.

That evening a telephone call came for Rose. It was Charlie. He wanted to know how David was but didn't like to bother him personally at such a time. He had a long talk with Rose, telling her how distressed his grandfather was at the news, and then went on to say that they would both like to come and pay their respects at the funeral. Rose said she knew David and both families would appreciate it very much, adding, "But can you get away?" Charlie then told her there was nothing going on on both Wednesday and Thursday, but he would have to be back on Thursday night for the Passing Out parade on Friday. He had, he added, now been told he had passed, much to his astonishment.

The weekend passed and the days dragged by. David stayed at Chandlers Lodge, he couldn't face living at the Bungalow, although he visited Mrs Treharne and saw Susie from time to time. He arranged with Mrs Treharne that she should stay there permanently and that he would bear all the costs. If she felt too lonely she could perhaps have one of the Land Army Girls lodge with her, they were being sent to the farms in increasing numbers and looking for accommodation in many cases. On the other hand, she could always visit Chandlers Lodge when she needed a chat – he would leave it to her.

On Wednesday, Megan's parents arrived and stayed with her, Rita and Buffy came up on the train and were lodged at the Hollies, Charlie and his grandfather stayed at the Earl's club in town overnight and Harry arrived having been granted seventy-two hours compassionate leave. The morning of the funeral was clear and cold and by ten thirty the old Church was filling with a congregation as diverse as it had ever witnessed in its eight hundred year history. In addition to the townspeople – customers, friends, Rotary members, colleagues from the canteen run, Bessie and George and Mr and Mrs Bolton from Mountfield, there was row upon row of service people from the airfield headed by the station wing commander and several of his officers. There were airmen, gunners, infantrymen who guarded the perimeter, W.A.A.F.'s and A.T.S. girls, all of whom had been so grateful to Pat and Lady Agatha for visiting their outposts so regularly. The front half dozen rows on one side of the aisle were filled with the brigadiers' colleagues and his superior officers, one being, of course, the general with Lady Earnshaw. The Canadians headed by Colonel Tim were there as also were representatives from the Home Guard, their company commander being Jack Hooper.

The melancholy tolling of the single bell ceased as the two coffins were carried through the huge double doors and down the wide aisle side by side. David, the brigadier and Jack walked together behind them followed by the remainder of the families. The R.A.F. padré gave a eulogy of the services Pat and Lady Agatha had performed in maintaining the morale and well being of all the men and women on the outposts of the airfield. The parish priest, Cannon Rosser, who had married Pat and David only such a short time before, gave a moving address stressing the friendship between Pat and Lady Agatha and their common desire to serve their country for which they had given their lives. They sang Pat's favourite hymn 'Immortal, Invisible,' after which the immediate families and close friends followed the two coffins to the graveside set in a new extension to the churchyard, an extension which would, in due course, be the last resting place not only of several civilians killed in later raids, but also of allied service men, two German air crews who had been shot down, and later still a small number of Italian prisoners of war who had been brought in to work on the farms locally and had died from one cause or another.

With a last look through tear-blurred eyes at the brass name plate 'Pat Chandler, born 1920, died 1940', David turned away, his arms firmly held by Rose and his mother, to climb into the cars to take them the four hundred yards to the Angel, where a buffet lunch was being laid on by John Tarrant. Fred had taken David to one side the previous evening to warn him about this part of the sad day's events. "It is customary after a funeral to provide refreshment for people who have made journeys," he explained to David, "what you have to remember is that whilst they will all be terribly sad at the loss you and Jack and the brigadier have suffered, they will, of course, be meeting a lot of old friends and relatives they haven't seen possibly for some time and you will notice that they will be smiling at each other – even laughing perhaps. It would be quite natural for you to resent this saying 'this is not a party' particularly when you feel sick inside and know that for you, life can never be the same again. Just remember they are not being flippant or insensitive, everybody feels a deep loss, acting normally is a way of consoling themselves just as they will try to console you."

David had thanked his father and therefore was prepared for the sight of numbers of people seeming to act in a normal way during what, to him, was the ultimate tragedy. Despite this, he did feel resentment, which he realised was totally illogical. All the family and numerous friends did their best to give words of comfort. They were well meaning, there was no doubt about that he thought, but nothing could move this sick feeling of despair in the pit of his stomach, the feeling of near panic at the thought of being without his Pat for all his days. Then raising his eyes, the anguish showing on his face, he found himself looking into the strong, weather-beaten face of the brigadier.

"They say it goes off a little after a while David," he said, "in both our cases I fancy it's going to be a very big while indeed."

"Yes Sir, I think you're right, infact I know you're right. But you know, I was so deep in my own misery it didn't occur to me that you would be feeling exactly the same. I think that's terrible. Lady Agatha was really loved by my family – did you know that? And Pat told us once that the squaddies, who didn't know who she was of course, all used to call her 'love', and that she got such pleasure out of their friendly banter."

"Well, we two will literally have to soldier on," he paused for a moment and then continued "David, will you write to me occasionally? I would be keenly interested to know how you're getting on. Your mother has said I can come and stay at Chandlers Lodge whenever I'm on leave – I'm so deeply grateful to her for that, I've no firm base of my own now Agatha's gone."

"I'll write Sir, I promise."

Gradually people started drifting away, each coming to say goodbye to the brigadier and David in turn. When the brigadier turned away to say goodbye to some fellow officers, Harry joined David, gripping his elbow without making it obvious. "Coping alright old son?" he asked quietly.

"Just about."

"I think you've done bloody well."

"I suppose it's what they call putting on a brave face. I can tell you I don't feel very brave inside. I feel as sick as a dog. God knows how I'll cope when they've all gone."

"We'll all still be here old son, don't you worry," Harry assured him as others came over to bid their farewells.

The rest of the day was a blur as was the next day. On Saturday, David steeled himself to go to the Bungalow where he sat for an hour or so with Susie on his lap talking to Mrs Treharne who he now saw more clearly to be, as he was, a fellow victim of Hitler's evil ambitions. Towards the end of his visit, he broached the subject of Pat's clothes, jewellery, books and so on still in the wardrobes, dressing table and elsewhere. He told Mrs Treharne he couldn't face moving them at the moment. She reassured him that everything would be left where it was; she would make sure every item would be looked after properly until such time as he came to a decision, no matter how long that might be.

On Sunday, Ruth said to him at breakfast, "David dear, can we see you in your new uniform?" This request produced his first fleeting smile since he received the initial sickening news of Pat's death.

Rose quickly followed up with, "Oh yes please, put it on David," so with the combined bidding of two people he would have been totally incapable of denying anything anyway, he finished his breakfast and made his way to his room where the four boxes stood, still sealed, and untouched. It took him a while to unpack them, carefully removing the masses of tissue paper Gieves had used to prevent the precious goods from creasing, and laying each item out on the bed until he found hangers on which to put the service dress, greatcoat and Burberry. He unpacked one of the shirts, silently expressing a word he would not have wanted his mother to hear as he stuck into his thumb one of the fifteen pins he had to remove before he could even think of wearing it.

"One of these days," he said to himself, "I will write a letter to Mister Van Heusen about these blasted pins- what the devil do they need fifteen pins for just to make a shirt to look nice in a box."

Having unpacked it all and neatly folded the tissue paper, he stripped off his civvies and replaced them with the service dress uniform, complete with black buttons, black Sam Browne and black shoes. Gieves had sewn his medal ribbons on the left breast, first the crimson and navy D.C.M. followed by the Oak Leaf, next was the bright red of the Legion d'Honneur and lastly the green with thin red stripes of the Croix de Guerre. In addition they had included a further bar complete with securing pin for fixing to his battle dress, and finally 'with the compliments of the Manager and Staff' a set of miniatures to wear with Mess Dress (if he ever got one), or on a dinner jacket for special occasions. Looking at himself in the wardrobe mirror he thought "Well – clothes certainly maketh the man, I've never looked so posh in all my life!" As he stood there examining himself there was a knock on the door followed immediately by the unbidden entrance of Harry.

"You've been so long they all thought you'd got lost" he said and, jumping to attention, continued "Oh, I do beg your pardon Sir, I was looking for a scruffy urchin called David Chandler – you haven't seen him about I suppose Sir, have you Sir?"

David moved quickly to punch him in the ribs. Equally quickly Harry swayed to one side and in seconds they were having one of their old sparring sessions, interrupted by Ruth, Rose and Megan standing in the doorway saying, "What on earth are they up to?" When the commotion died down, Ruth said, "Now stand still and let us have a look at you," followed by, "well, I must say, they've made a superb job of the uniform."

This was followed by a further voice from the doorway saying, "Pity it hasn't got proper buttons on it though." Fred had followed the others up, slowly, so as to make out he wasn't as excited about a mere uniform as the others but inwardly thrilled at his son being an officer in such a fine regiment, even if it did wear black buttons! "Anyway, you've all got to come down, Ernie and Anni, Moira and Jack have arrived and want to see the budding field marshall."

They all trooped down to the kitchen where David was duly inspected by the newcomers. After a while he excused himself saying, "I'll go up and get into something comfortable."

"God, he sounds like Mae West," quipped Harry. All laughed. It was the first family laugh in ten days. They were slowly recovering.

When David returned, Ernie asked for quiet saying, "Anni has something to tell you."

Anni began, "I know you will all be pleased to know," and then hesitated with a catch in her voice as she began to cry a little "that my father is coming home."

Ruth immediately went and put her arms around her. "Tell us all about it," she urged.

"He volunteered for the Pioneer Corps," she continued "but he was one year too old. He then volunteered for hospital work as a porter but while this was being considered, he was called to a tribunal who unanimously agreed to his release. He will have to report to the local police each week but can start his business again – he will be home at the end of next week." The tears started again as she said, "Ernie and I and father will never forget how good and kind you have all been..."

Ruth held her close and said, "You're all family."

That evening Ruth was very quiet for a while until Fred said, "You alright love?"

"I would like you to do me a great favour," she said.

"Anything but money," came the jocular reply, "although even there I could possibly run to a fiver."

"No, I'm serious. Before Harry goes back tomorrow night I would like you and the two boys to have a photograph taken together in your uniforms – I mean a proper studio photograph not a snapshot. Will you do that for me?"

"Well you know I'm not much of a one for having my photo taken but since you seem so keen on it, I'll fix it for tomorrow lunch time. If you contact Harry and tell David when he comes in, I'll meet them at the Studio and meet you and Megan and Jack if he can make it for lunch at the Angel afterwards. If Rose and Anni can make it, they're welcome too; John Tarrant won't be too busy being Monday."

It was the first occasion that David had walked out as an officer. As he turned into the High Street he was suddenly confronted by a Canadian sergeant and two squaddies, standing by a fifteen hundred weight truck. Immediately the sergeant called, "Parade – shun," and saluted David.

In returning the salute David said, "Good morning Sergeant," and began to walk on past, at which the sergeant said "Sir..." David halted.

"Yes Sergeant."

"Sir, forgive my curiosity, but I'm not familiar with your last two ribbons, would you tell me what they are?"

David explained the significance of the ribbons, the private soldiers having come closer to examine them.

"If it's not a rude question Sir, how did you get them, I mean being French and all?"

David gave a very brief account of how he and his men got the French general to safety ending in, "And then we got a boat and rowed back to England."

"<u>Rowed</u> back to England?" exclaimed one of the squaddies, "Jesus Christ that takes some doing."

David grinned. "Well, I must be off. Good luck all of you." He walked on up the High Street quite oblivious of several admiring glances from young ladies, and some not so young, who he passed on his way to meet his father and brother.

The photography session went well. Fred had changed at the factory into his Home Guard uniform – complete with two pips up. "As you're the senior officer you go in the middle," Harry suggested to his father, "although if he wants the best looking one in the middle it will, of course, have to be me." Afterwards they joined the rest of the family at the Angel and had a leisurely lunch until Harry and Megan had to leave so that Harry could catch his four o'clock train. Although David could still feel the dull ache inside, he found that gradually he was getting back some semblance of sociability towards the outside world. He was sensible enough of people's problems to know that he was not alone. As a result of the bombing, thousands of others were suffering for the same reason he was which, whilst the thought did nothing to make it better for him, at least it helped to put his personal tragedy into perspective. Further, it made him more acutely aware of how poor Rose must have felt a few months ago. He winced at the thought, looked up and saw Rose looking at him. As he caught her eye she smiled. He smiled back.

Chapter Eighteen

David decided that instead of reporting to Winchester on the following Sunday, he would travel on Saturday which would give him the opportunity to use Sunday to get himself organised. Buffy telephoned during the week to tell him that he should come and visit them as much as possible during his stay at the depot, since they all knew he would probably be posted away to a service battalion after a few weeks. This David gladly promised to do – "Oh, and bring your chum with you as well if he'd care to come," Buffy had added they having met Charlie and his father at the funeral and had been told the two lads would be together at least until they received their postings.

Arriving at Winchester mid afternoon, he got a porter to trolley all his kit to a taxi. At the officers' mess, the duty batman put it into his room, which was to be his home for the next few weeks. I'll get your batman over to unpack for you Sir; he knows you were coming this afternoon so he won't have left barracks."
"What's his name?"
"O'Riordan Sir, a real bog trotter, been in the regiment twenty odd years, hates everybody because he can't get into a service battalion as he's graded with bad feet, but can keep a kit better than any other batman at the depot, including the C.O.'s," and as an afterthought, "when he's sober that is."
"Well thank you very much – what's your name by the way?"
"Kenney, Sir."
"Right Kenney, thanks very much, and thanks for the low down on O'Riordan," Kenney grinned and left David looking, with keen anticipation, to meeting his first, if not for long, batman. O'Riordan arrived about twenty minutes later and with a broad Irish accent said, "I'm to look after you while you're here Sir." He was swaying just a little, indicating he had not travelled too far away from the NAAFI bar during the lunch hour. He continued, "Second lieutenant's come and go, but I go on for ever. Have you been in long Sir?" David was wearing his battle dress upon which he had not fixed his medals bar, he was still very self conscious about showing off despite his father's admonition.
"Oh – just a little while."
"Well Sir, if you want to know any of the ropes, I'll be more than pleased to help."
"I'll remember that O'Riordan. By the way, what's your Christian

name?"

"Patrick Sir, they all call me Paddy."

"Then I shall call you Paddy in these four walls – O'Riordan's such a mouthful."

"Right Sir, Paddy it is."

He began to unpack David's large valise, which in addition to housing his camp bed and bedding, also contained his Service Dress neatly covered with khaki tissue paper. Taking a hanger from the wardrobe he picked up the tunic, shook the paper free ready to slip the tunic on to the hanger and came face to face with the row of medal ribbons. He was silent for a minute and then turned to David who was busy putting out personal items on to the dressing table. "Sir," he said, "you've been having me on."

"How's that Paddy?"

Paddy pointed to the medals.

"You didn't get those buggers in the NAAFI – you said you'd been in just a little while."

"Well, four years is a little while compared to you isn't it?"

Paddy turned to continue his tasks, "I'll learn to keep my bloody gob shut one of these days," David could hear him saying as he deftly smoothed down the contents of the valise, suitcase and kit bag and stacked them away.

"Right Sir, that's that lot done. What time in the morning do you want your tea, and what clothes will you be wanting?"

"Well let's say tea at eight o'clock and, as its Sunday, I'll wear my civvies – sports coat and flannels, check shirt and tie."

"Right Sir, eight o'clock it is," he turned to leave and as he reached the door he said in his broad brogue, "I'm glad I got you Sir."

To which David replied, "and I'm glad I got you Paddy."

The other second lieutenants arrived from their various OCTU's during Sunday. David had lunch and went back to his room to put his feet up and read the Sunday paper. A knock on the door disturbed him as he was halfway through the sports page and in walked Charlie. They were each delighted to see the other but after the first effusive greetings, Charlie's face lost its smile as he said "Are you alright now dear old sport, I mean, I know you'll never be really alright, but..." he was lost for words.

"I know what you're asking Charlie. Yes, I am alright. I won't say I've come to terms with what happened, as the saying goes, but yes, I'm alright."

"Good. Grandfather sends his very kindest regards. I saw some of the lads we three had the night with at the village pub, they all sent their regards to you and were dreadfully shocked about Pat."

"People certainly have been very kind." David paused, "Now have you settled in? What sort of batman have you got? Have you met any of the others?"

"The answers to that cross examination – you'd do well in the Gestapo – are that yes I have settled in, I appear to have a batman whose total vocabulary consists of 'Yes Sir' and 'No Sir' and yes I have met two or three of the other newcomers who seem pretty drippy to me. We'll probably meet all of them at teatime I imagine – they'll all be here by then. So how about you getting off your fat backside and walking around the barracks with me to show me the lie of the land."

They walked around the depot, in the course of their perambulations passing the sergeant's mess. This reminded David that he still had to take up his tab for having his photograph in the papers after receiving his French medals, but mentally observed that even if he had forgotten, R.S.M. Forster would be after him on the morrow without any doubt.

At tea, they met up with the remainder of the new subalterns and introduced themselves. There were nine altogether in the new intake. A notice on the mess board had informed them that they were to meet at the adjutant's office at 9.30 on Monday, dress battledress, to receive details of their further training and duties, and for interview with the C.O. David studied each in turn but came to no hard and fast judgements. He had long ago come to the conclusion that the old saying about appearances being often deceptive was absolutely true – look at Schultz at Calais and for that matter look at Charlie!

At 9.25 the next morning they all had assembled in the corridor outside the adjutant's office. At precisely 9.30 they were invited in and told to be seated. The adjutant explained they would be under his charge, which in the main, he delegated to Mr Forster, the R.S.M., who was standing beside him dressed as immaculately as any R.S.M. anywhere in the British Army or probably any other army come to that. He would give them a sound training in drill as performed by riflemen; he would go through guard mounting procedures with them, company and battalion drill procedures, what to look for from their own men on drill parades and so on. They would receive a lecture from the mess President on mess etiquette, another from the M.O. on the bodily care of their soldiers, from the padré on their spiritual care and another from the senior subaltern on the duties of orderly officer, followed by each in turn spending a day with the orderly officer of the day understanding his duties. In between, they would take instruction from the P.T. C.S.M., visit the butts for rifle and pistol practice and testing. When they completed these and other items to the satisfaction of those supervising them they would be sent to service battalions. He ended with "Any questions?"

Inevitably it was Charlie who piped up "what do we do in our spare time Sir?"

"First of all you don't call me Sir – only major and upwards are Sir. Secondly if Mr Forster has his way you'll want to do nothing but sleep so if any of you have any ideas of licentious nights out in the fleshpots of Winchester, I suggest you think again."

They each in turn were then interviewed by the C.O. who, shaking hands, welcomed them to the regiment. When David marched in, the colonel having welcomed him said he was most sorry to hear of the loss of his young wife ending with, "If you want to talk to anyone, at any time David, both the adjutant and I are here, please remember that."

"Thank you Sir, I am very grateful," and with these words he saluted and marched out.

The first week flew past. In the main David took the work easily in his stride. At a convenient time after the first drill session, Mr Forster told David how sad he and his wife were to hear the news of Pat, and as expected, later in the day said, "Don't forget the three pounds ten you owe the mess president."

To which David cheekily replied, "Do I make the cheque out to the R.S.M.'s Benevolent Fund?"

The inevitable answer to that, well out of earshot of anyone else was, "cheeky bugger."

During the second week Charlie, lounging on David's bed said, "I wonder what they'll do with us over Christmas and the New Year?"

"I can tell you the answer to that without any hesitation," explained David. "There are nine days of Christmas from Christmas Eve up until and including New Year's Day. There are nine brand new, innocent, dead keen young second lieutenant's clamouring to be in charge as orderly officer for the first time, and I bet you a hundred to one not one of them will be disappointed."

And neither were they, although when they were not on duty they were given four days off during that period. Charlie's lot fell on Boxing Day, David's on New Year's Eve. As a result, David was home for Christmas and Charlie was at Ramsford for the New Year.

It was a quiet Christmas at Chandlers Lodge compared with previous years. Whilst at home David made several journeys to Pat's grave and stayed each time just a little while. He was never alone. Whenever he went there he found other visitors, young and old, visiting the grave of their relatives and past friends and invariably there was a sympathetic if muted salutation between him and folk he had never seen or spoken to before. It was as if they were both seeking comfort and giving comfort by the simple act of passing the time of day in that sad and hallowed place.

A very happy occasion for the family was the arrival two days before Christmas of Karl from the internment camp. He looked a little thinner, a little greyer, but after tearful reunions with each member in turn, and having regained his composure, his face was a study in contentment in being reunited with all these wonderful people who had befriended him and his daughter.

On Christmas Day, Charlie telephoned wishing them all the compliments of the season, and in the process having a long chat with Rose. David returned to Winchester on the Friday and on Sunday visited Rita and Buffy – it had been a terribly sad Christmas for them too, their first since Jeremy was killed.

David did his first orderly officer duty on New Year's Eve. He had an orderly sergeant with him of the old school who guided him from time to time. One of the duties of the orderly officer is to visit the men during the mealtimes to deal with any complaints about the food. New second lieutenants are always considered fair game by the men in the mess hall as they pass from table to table, but as David was an old hand at the sort of banter coming from the men, he gave a good deal better than he received.

At breakfast parade. "Any complaints on this table?"
"Sir, I got no bacon with my breakfast."
"I see. What's your name?"
"Finkelstein Sir."
"So why then Finkelstein, do you want bacon?"

"To give it to my mate Sir."

"That's against King's Regulations. So if I get you bacon you either get charged with contravening King's Regs, or charged with making up a frivolous complaint or being reported to the divisional rabbi. Which do you think it ought to be Sergeant Miller?"

"I reckon all three Sir."

"Right. Now do you still complain about the bacon – or rather lack of it?"

"I reckon not Sir," with a grin.

They passed on to the next table. "Any complaints?"

And so it went on during the day. Mounting the quarter guard, inspecting the cookhouse, inspecting the latrines, visiting the mess hall at dinnertime, turning out the guard during the day and then during the night, it was all part of the orderly officer's job of being the battalion officer to be contacted in the event of any unusual occurrence taking place and therefore being himself confined to barracks for the twenty four hours he was on duty. He turned out the guard, along with Sergeant Miller, at two o'clock in the morning on New Year's Day, and then swiftly dismissed them back into the warmth of the guardroom. He remembered only too well the times when he had been in command of the quarter guard and been made to stand to attention outside the guardroom for a quarter of an hour in the biting wind up at Colchester whilst the orderly officer played silly buggers inspecting each man in turn as if he were going on duty at Buckingham Palace. When the guard was dismissed back to the guardroom, the guard sergeant asked David and Sergeant Miller if they'd like a mug of tea. They readily accepted the offer and followed the guard sergeant into the spacious guard room.

"Anything unusual tonight?" enquired David.

"There were a few who would never have made it on their own legs," grinned the sergeant "but being New Year's Eve as long as they kept quiet I let them get away with it. I tell you one thing though Sir, I give you ten to one your bloke, O'Riordan won't be showing up with your morning tea this morning, I've never seen anyone so plastered and still standing up."

The three laughed together, David saying, "If it wasn't for the fact that I'm not a betting man I'd have a pound with you on that – he'll be there, his hand may be shaking a bit, but he'll be there."

And promptly at 6.30 he was there. "A Happy New Year to you Sir." his articulation a little slower and a little more Irish than usual, but otherwise as steady as a rock.

"Did you have a good time last night?" enquired David

mischievously.

"I did that Sir, though to be honest, I don't remember much after eleven o'clock except kissing some right old harridans in the Three Brewers when the chimes went. They wanted me and my mate Driscoll to go home with them, but I told them we'd got to be in by one o'clock. I don't remember much else. What will you be wearing today Sir?"

His orderly officer spell finishing at ten o'clock he ate a late breakfast, went back to his room to a blazing coal fire that Paddy had lit for him, changed into civvies, and sat back in his armchair to catch up on yesterday's papers – there were no papers on New Year's Day of course. At lunch time he telephoned the family, having been told to reverse the charges as everyone wanted to talk to him in turn. It was obvious that everybody steered well clear of the traditional 'Happy New Year,' knowing full well that happiness was a commodity it would take some considerable time for him to be able to enjoy again, nevertheless, they all wished him well, even Kenny Barclay who had been with them over Christmas and had insisted on calling him 'Sir – Well, I always called him corporal before didn't I?' – said, "Try and get to our battalion Sir, we could do with someone like you there." Although he was on the line for three quarters of an hour the time flew past and when he rang off he went back to his room strangely drained, laid back on his bed and fell fast asleep not waking up until it had got dark.

By the end of the week they were looking forward to news of their various postings. On Saturday afternoon David and Charlie decided to put on their civvies and take a stroll into the city, David wanted to go to a bookshop and Charlie needed to collect some films he had left for developing before he went on leave. They parted company and agreed to meet up at 'The Buttery,' a small tea shop just off the High Street renowned for its homemade farmhouse cake. David arrived first. The teashop was fairly crowded, and at a table against the wall he saw Mrs Forster with her small son on her lap. He crossed to say hello and she immediately invited him to join her. The little boy looked at David wide-eyed, David smiled back and, to his surprise, the little lad held out his arms to be picked up and saying loudly "Dad, Dad, Dad." David hesitated only for a moment and then he took him from Mrs Forster and stood him up on his lap.

"I don't know which one of us is going to get the bad name, Mrs Forster, his calling me Dad."

"Please call me Marianne, all the rest of your family does, and as for the Dad bit, he calls everyone Dad, so you're quite safe," she laughingly replied.

It was at this point that Charlie arrived to see a pretty woman laughing with David, with David holding a young child and to cap it all with the child calling David 'Dad' with the full power of its not inconsiderable lungs.

Approaching David from behind he said, "Has someone not been telling me everything?"

David turned his head, "Oh, Charlie, sit yourself down. Marianne, this is Charlie Crew." They shook hands. He continued, "This lady is the wife of a very close friend of yours, and this is Mark, their son."

In the meantime Mark had been regarding Charlie with intense curiosity, suddenly throwing his arms out saying "Dad, Dad, Dad," to a startled Charlie who, nevertheless, took him from David and sat him on his lap.

"This is a first for me dear old boy," he said to the youngster "I do hope I don't drop you."

From behind him came the words, "If you do I'll get you posted to John O'Groats for the duration."

"Just to avoid any further confusion," said David, "Mr & Mrs Forster are friends of my parents. This is the first time I had met Mark, and if ever I saw a budding rifleman it's him – don't you think?"

"No he jolly well isn't going to be anything of the sort," exclaimed his mother; "he's going to have a respectable job."

"What do you mean by respectable?" asked Charlie. "I mean will he be a stockbroker? – They're the biggest crowd of crooks in the land. Will he be a doctor? – They're renowned for burying all their mistakes without any comeback. Will he be a parson? – Holier than thou to everybody yet lusting after choirboys all the time. The list is endless. No, I reckon the honest trade of rifleman is as good as any and better than most."

"But how can you tell when you yourself have only been a rifleman for five minutes?" came Marianne's rejoinder.

David and the R.S.M. kept silent; both amused by the genial repartee. Charlie always seems to fit into any sort of company and to be able to tease without causing rancour of any kind, David mused. He was patently such a nice chap that no offence could be taken at anything he said. He continued, "Now there, dear Mrs Forster, you do have a point of sorts. However, my lack of service has been compensated by my having over the past few weeks endured such a concentrated course of indoctrination in the whys and wherefores of being a rifleman by the most fearsome R.S.M. this side of hell's gates, that I feel I shall never at heart be anything but a rifleman for the rest of my days." There was general laughter at this. He continued, "I say hell's gates because as you probably know, all R.S.M.'s elect to go there. They're used by Old Nick to terrify the defaulters – I mean, there would be no point in their going to the other place because by the very nature of things, there wouldn't be any defaulters there for them to have fun with would there?"

"Charlie, you're a priceless ass," said David.

"Here blooming here," added the R.S.M. "As far as I'm concerned, our Mark is going to marry an heiress and keep us all in luxury for the rest of our days. Now, where's that tea?"

They enjoyed their tea together, payment of the bill for which being insisted upon by Mr Forster, with the joking aside, "I earn more than you do," and having shaken hands all round, David and Charlie made their way down towards King Alfred's statue.

"He seems almost genial in his civvies," observed Charlie.

"Don't let that fool you," maintained David, "when he's back in uniform he moves in a different world, surrounded by tradition, love of the regiment, the Army Act, King's Regulations and above all, his duty, which comes before everything."

"By jove dear old sport, you're becoming quite the jolly old philosopher aren't you? What brought all that on?"

"I don't know. I suppose it's because I admire him for being an absolute professional. I know I shall never reach that standard."

"Yes, but you may one day be a major or something and he'll have to salute you and call you Sir, and all that guff as he does now on parade."

"That may be true. But we'll both know he's the professional, he's the backbone of the regiment. They could replace me with a stroke of the pen but they would find it extremely difficult to replace him."

On the following Monday, they were told at breakfast to go to the adjutant's office at 1100 hours to discuss postings. This, they assumed, meant that they would be given a choice of which of the service battalions they would like to join, depending on the vacancy situation in that particular battalion.

"Right, sit down gentlemen," said the adjutant as they filed into his office. "Now, I'll just rough over what's available. First and second battalions are in Palestine and Egypt respectively so you can't go there as they only take full lieutenants. The third battalion is in Northern Ireland – three vacancies – fourth at Catterick – three vacancies – fifth at Nottingham – one vacancy and sixth in Norfolk – two vacancies – guarding airfields at the moment – so… sort it out among yourselves."

As quick as a flash Charlie said, "Could David and I go to the sixth?"

"Chandler and Crew – 6th – righto."

After sorting out the remainder, the adjutant told them their papers would all be ready by Thursday morning after which they could take the weekend off and present themselves to their new units on Tuesday 14th, in the case of Northern Ireland, Wednesday 15th. They were to telephone the adjutant of their particular battalion, their E.T.A. at the station indicated on their papers who would arrange for transport to meet them. As they left the meeting David said, "You jumped in there with both feet didn't you? How did you know I'd want to go to Norfolk, and for that matter, how did you know I'd want to be lumbered with you?"

"Well, dear old sport, that's where the old grey matter suddenly started in to top gear. Norfolk I thought – nearer to London and therefore Kent than any of the others. Secondly it's flat; therefore no route marches up and down one in four hills like Yorkshire and Northern Ireland. Thirdly, we'll be on company detachments on various airfields not in one large battalion lump, which will make life easier. Lastly, as regards being lumbered, you know you can't manage without me. Have I answered all your questions?"

"As I said once before – you'll have to go into politics after the war you crafty blighter."

As they walked on back to their quarters David said, "Looks as though we've got a couple of days leave which I certainly didn't expect, so we'll have to arrange to meet somewhere if we're going up from London together," and as an afterthought, "your grandfather will be pleased to see you again."

"Unfortunately he went to Scotland yesterday for three weeks, so he won't be there."

"Then why don't you come home with me, there's plenty of room at Chandlers Lodge now that the Australians have moved out – I'll confirm it with Mum now if you like."

Charlie needed no second bidding, Ruth was delighted that they would see David again for a few days and would be most pleased for Charlie to stay, adding, "But from what I hear about the grandeur of his home, he'll find it a bit of a come down living at Chandlers Lodge.

"Oh no he jolly well won't," emphatically came the reply, "there isn't a better place on earth like Chandlers Lodge, big or small."

Ruth laughed but was thrilled beyond measure at David's reply, obviously so spontaneous and sincere.

At lunchtime Charlie said to David "I wonder if we could buy a small token to give to the R.S.M. before we go?"

"Do you mean contained in a mauve bottle? – And who do you mean we?"

"I mean the nine of us. He's taught us more in these weeks than all the rest put together. I thought a silver cigarette box – I saw one in the city, what do you think?"

They talked to the others who readily agreed, all chipped in their share of the purchase price and Charlie took himself off into the High Street to buy the box and to have it inscribed. It was collected the next afternoon, and at four o'clock all nine went to the R.S.M.'s office. It had been decided that as Brindlesby-Gore was the oldest of the nine he should make the presentation. He knocked, was bidden enter at which they all filed in to the astonishment of Mr Forster, whose first words were, "Christ, I thought I'd got rid of you lot."

Brindlesby-Gore opened the proceedings by apologising for arriving unannounced stating that the cadre had collected to make a small presentation to the R.S.M. in appreciation of all he had done to make them into riflemen. He handed over the package, which the R.S.M. unwrapped. It really was a very fine looking, well-crafted piece of silver, which greeted his eyes. He lifted the lid and as he did so Brindlesby-Gore said, "We have listed our names inside so that when we all become generals you can say 'I started those buggers off'."

"Well, all I can say is that I am very flattered indeed gentlemen and I shall treasure this all my days."

There was a pause, broken by Charlie saying, "We also thought that you ought to have some fags to go in it so we've brought you these," and out of his pocket he withdrew a packet of ten Woodbines, much bent and crumpled, and handed them over to roars of laughter from the others who had no idea Charlie was going to spring this one.

"You always were a cheeky bugger, but I shan't smoke them, they'll always stay in one corner of the box. Now sod off the lot of you. I've got work to do," and with that they all shook hands with expressions of 'good luck to each of you,,' leaving Regimental Sergeant Major Clifford Forster D.C.M., M.M. to sit at his desk re-opening his box, re-reading the names inscribed therein and wondering deep inside him not how many would become generals but how many would survive even the next couple of years. They were to be platoon commanders, the average life of a platoon commander in action was measured in weeks not months, and there was plenty of action ahead that was for sure. For the first time since the war began, he felt that sitting behind his desk in his cosy office, he was leaving others to do the dirty work – he didn't like the feeling.

Chapter Nineteen

Ruth sat at the kitchen table gazing sightlessly at the Aga and sipping a cup of tea. It was 7.30am on the Thursday David and Charlie were arriving. She had got Fred off to the factory; Rose was still in bed, having left her job at the hospital to prepare for her baby, as also had Anni left from her office at the Co-op. A variety of thoughts were chasing through Ruth's mind, David would be arriving with Charlie – not with Jeremy as he had so many times before and at that thought she gave a little sob. David would be staying at Chandlers Lodge and not at The Bungalow with his beloved Pat, that too saddened her. A year ago it was all so different. Then she thought of the two babies coming along soon and her heart lightened a little. It will be wonderful to have babies in the house again – oh I do pray that all goes well for the two girls she said to herself, momentarily clasping her hands together and closing her eyes.

"Well this won't do," she said out loud, "must get tidied up before Mrs Cloke arrives."

"I've told you before it's the first sign of madness you know Mummy dear when you start talking to yourself." It was Rose from the doorway, "And anyway why do you have to tidy up before the cleaning lady arrives – shouldn't that be one of her jobs?"

"You can't have people arriving to an untidy house," replied Ruth "even if it is the cleaning lady." Rose laughed and asked the state of the teapot and on being told there was plenty there sat and poured herself a cup. A minute or so later Ruth rejoined her, asking in quick succession what would she like for her breakfast, did she have a quiet night with the little one kicking around, wasn't it going to be nice having David home again for a few days so unexpectedly and his going to be stationed fairly near in Norfolk. Rose smiled back at her mother. She knew the reason for this uninterrupted flow; she was always like this when David or Harry were coming home, her excitement heightened by the remembrance of the fear she had felt for those weeks when she knew not whether they were alive or dead. As she took breath they heard the approach of a car on the gravel outside followed by a rat-a-tat-tat on the knocker. "Who can that be I wonder at this time in the morning?" was Ruth's inevitable question to the world in general. Rose heard the front door opened and Ruth say, "Good morning Major, how are you, my goodness you're an early bird. Please come in out of the cold."

"It's my usual quest Mrs Chandler. Can you put a couple of Royal Marine officers up for a month or two whilst they work with the Canadians here – Colonel McEwan's lot who you know quite well?"

"Well, yes of course, we'd be delighted. When do they arrive?"

"Tomorrow afternoon if that's alright."

"Well yes, but they would have to share a room just for the weekend – my son arrives home on leave with a friend today until Tuesday."

"That's no problem – I'll bring a couple of hammocks, they can swing from the rafters being Marines don't you think? Anyway they're both majors, Johnson and Sopwith respectively, knowing how kind you and your family are they're a very lucky couple."

"It's very nice of you to say that major but there is one difference, or at least will be shortly, in our domestic arrangements. We shall be having a new baby in the house soon – I hope that won't cause them any inconvenience."

"Good Lord no and congratulations to you all. If a couple of majors in the Marines can't cope with a new baby they ought to pack it in and start a market garden – what?" And with this final geniality, he shook hands and departed to his car.

Ruth rejoined Rose. "I expect you heard all that," she presumed.

"Mummy, I never cease to be amazed at you. You have a baby shortly to arrive at the house, you have a son and his upper-crust friend coming today to stay for a few days and then you're suddenly landed with two totally unknown Marines out of the blue arriving tomorrow, yet you don't turn a hair. Most women would be running up the wall."

"Well you see dear, it's all in the years of training I've had from your father – never knowing what's going to happen next."

"Does that include the training you had in Chester recently I wonder," enquired Rose. "By the way, when will you be going back again?"

"Next week if I had the chance – but keep that to yourself."

With Mrs Cloke arriving Ruth bustled off with her to get the rooms and beds ready leaving Rose looking at the place in front of the Aga where she had so clearly seen Jeremy all those months ago. The biting misery had left her now most of the time. Whilst she sat here alone in the quietness of the house interrupted only by the occasional cushioned bump of moving furniture from upstairs, she felt quietly happy in the knowledge that Jeremy was watching over her and that soon she would be holding him again in her arms in the body of their baby. It was a warm comforting feeling.

David and Charlie arrived mid afternoon in a taxi so laden with the enormous amount of kit they had now accumulated they could hardly squeeze themselves into the normally capacious Humber. Since most of it would not be needed until they left again, it was stored at the rear of the hall by the stairway, making sure, as David said to his friend not to block the door under the stairs or his father would have something to say. It was only later that Charlie learnt the full significance of that warning. That evening everyone called to see the two arrivals. Most of them had been able to meet Charlie and his grandfather briefly at the funeral, and after a little initial constraint conversation flowed freely, helped in no small way by the contribution from under the stairs, the purpose of not blocking the doorway now becoming clear in Charlie's eyes. Jack and Moira, Anni and Karl (intensely interested in meeting a member of the aristocracy!), Megan and of course Rose were all there and as the evening progressed, Jim appeared along with Alec and Rebecca. At ten fifteen Ernie arrived with his usual, "All under control guv'nor," indicating he had now handed over the factory to the night shift foreman and it was nearly midnight before they all split up and went their various ways.

As David and Charlie sat with Ruth whilst they finished their Whitbread's and Ruth sipped her cocoa, Fred and Rose having both gone off to bed, Charlie said, "I'm deeply grateful to you Mrs Chandler for having me, and do you know, I've never ever had a family evening like tonight ever in all my life." Ruth squeezed his hand across the table. He continued, "I only wish Pat had been here," and started silently to weep, saying "Oh, I'm sorry David, I shouldn't have said that; I'm so sorry."

Ruth quickly got up and went round to him kneeling down and putting her arms around him. "We all feel the same Charlie dear, really we do, so don't be upset."

He gradually composed himself, saying to David "I'll try not to let you down again."

"You haven't let me down one little bit old son, you've just shown what a damned nice bloke you are."

Everything happened the next morning!! David had gone on his own to the churchyard leaving Charlie reading the papers when the telephone rang. Rose answered – it was Harry.

"Hello my precious," was his cheery greeting, "how's the little one?" But not waiting for an answer he ran on. "All our units are moving to London today to help clear bomb damage. I'm going to be at Deptford. I've got a thirty-six-hour pass for Saturday afternoon and Sunday. Can you tell Megan – I can't get hold of her?"

"Yes of course, by the way, David's home for the weekend."

"Oh good, see you soon, lots of love," and he rang off.

No sooner had Rose relayed this information to Ruth and Charlie and was getting prepared to find Megan, the telephone rang again. It was Canon Rosser from the church.

"Oh Mrs Cartwright, I understand David is home. You will know the canteen in which Pat and Lady Agatha so sadly lost their lives, has been refurbished by your father's factory. We propose having it here after mattins on Sunday to dedicate a plaque put on it by Rotary in their name, and to bless its future work. The brigadier is fully in agreement, can you ask David for his accord?"

"Yes of course Canon Rosser. David is at the churchyard at this very moment. You could have a word with him yourself perhaps if you catch him."

"I'll nip out now and do that. Thank you my dear."

This news relayed again, Rose returned to the telephone only to have it ring the second she went to pick it up.

"By jove, that was quick work – were you sitting on the phone?"

Laughingly Rose said, "Well almost – but who is it?"

"It's Ray Osbourne here – I was the Royal Engineers johnny with Harry in France."

"Of course, of course. Are you well again now?"

"Fighting fit thanks, on a new job, bomb disposal."

"Oh my Lord, do be careful."

"That my dear is my guiding maxim, you can rest assured. However, I telephoned to ask is there any likelihood of Harry being home. I've got a weekend free in Chatham and thought I'd pop down to you on Sunday if he was going to be around. I can't seem to get hold of Megan."

"In the first place you would be welcome here at any time whether Harry was here or not," said Rose. "In the second place he will be here on Sunday," and she went on to tell him of Harry's unexpected pass, David's leave and the dedication on Sunday morning if he would care to attend. "There will be all sorts of military hierarchy," she continued, "so you might like to wear your service dress, although with this weather greatcoats I would think will be the order of the day."

"By jove, you sound very knowledgeable about regimental matters."

"It's living cheek by jowl with all this rough soldiery – I pick up the lingo as Harry would say."

After a few further pleasantries Rose rang off and again went off to relay the news to her mother. No sooner was this done when they heard another motor vehicle crunching on the drive, the door knocker put to use, and the voice of Charlie saying, "Thank you very much – where do I sign?" By the time Ruth and Rose came down into the hall, they found Charlie man-handling a largish wooden box into the kitchen. Ruth quickly found a pair of pliers for Charlie to cut the wires securing it and a large screwdriver to lever up the lid. Inside the lid there was a letter contained in a waterproof bag which simply said,

'Dear Mrs Chandler,

Since you have probably got the two hungriest young blighters in the kingdom under your roof at the moment, I thought the enclosed might help out.

Yours most sincerely

Osbourne'

They removed protective material from the top of the box to find inside a dozen brace of grouse, three hares and a small haunch of venison, which they quickly unpacked and hung on hooks from the ceiling of the large walk-in larder next to the kitchen.

"I shall write back straight away and thank your grandfather, he really is very kind," declared Ruth, and then the thought struck her – how do you start off a letter to an Earl? – Well Jack will know she assured herself, he's bound to know. And then a second thought struck her – who's going to pluck the grouse?

As though she had spoken her thoughts aloud Mrs Cloke said, "Would you like my Trev and Julie to de-feather those for you? They're dab hands at it and their little fingers are ideal for the job." Trev and Julie were Mrs Cloke's children, aged nine and seven respectively and born and bred in the country.

"That would be a big help," Ruth replied "but we'll pay them for doing it. Let's say sixpence each bird and you keep two brace to make a nice meal for yourselves – how would that do?"

Mrs Cloke was delighted with the arrangement – so too was Ruth, plucking small birds was a job she had never had any taste for, nor for that matter any proficiency in, as she would readily admit.

Rose left her mother and Mrs Cloke packing the birds carefully into two large carrier bags for Mrs Cloke to strap on to her bicycle carrier, and made her way to the telephone to try and get hold of Megan. Again, as she reached it the bell went. "The thing's alive this morning," she exclaimed as she picked up the receiver.

It was Buffy. "Just looking for the current situation report on my grandchild my love." Rose had a long chat with him, among other things telling him of the proposed dedication on Sunday. She then talked with her mother-in-law at length – all baby talk of course, or as Harry would say 'all piddle and biscuits!'

At length, Rita said she'd better go or father would dock her housekeeping to pay the telephone bill and then added, "Oh, wait a minute, he'd like a quick word."

"We would much like to come up for the Sunday service Rose dear – do you think someone could put us up on Saturday night?"

"Uncle Jack is sure to have room – I'll phone him and then ring you back."

Rose carried out her chores of getting hold of Megan with the good news, contacting Jack at Paddock Wood and getting a welcome compliance with the arrangements for the Cartwright's in the form of a typical Jack statement – "Saturday? Of course – stay as long as they like!" and finally calling Buffy again to pass on the news. By now, it was nearly one o'clock as she made her way to the kitchen to join the others, feeling somewhat tired as a result of all the organising she had been doing. No sooner had she sat down at the table and started talking to David and Charlie, when there was a crunch of wheels outside and a further summons from the front door knocker.

David got up to answer the door just as Ruth came downstairs and they met in the hall. On opening the door they were confronted by two very burly, rugged looking characters, one of whom said, "Mrs Chandler? I'm Major Johnson and this is Major Sopwith – I believe you were expecting us – leastways I hope to goodness you were." He smiled a smile that changed his much battered features from the sort of character one would not like to meet in a dark lane to one of considerable geniality – somewhat like Victor MacGlagen as Ruth endeavoured to describe him to Megan later.

"Can we help you with your kit Sir?" asked David as Charlie joined them. Both were in civvies, which prompted the major to say, "Civilians don't call us Sir, I therefore assume you are in His Majesty's Forces." Ruth quickly made the introductions.

"Oh, so you're in the Rifles are you?" and continued by addressing his remarks to Major Sopwith, "Aren't they the idiots who run everywhere instead of walking like reasonable people? In any event, we're living in your house so I suggest we cut this 'Sir' business out – I'm Ken and this is Ivan."

Together they moved the kit into the hall and repaired to the kitchen. "We've got marrowbone soup and fish pie for lunch if that is to your taste," Ruth informed the newcomers, "we normally have dinner at seven but can usually alter that either way to suit your commitments."

"Please – you are not to alter anything to suit us Mrs Chandler, nothing whatsoever. If we can't meet your arrangements for any reason then that's our bad luck and we'll do the re-arranging."

"Ivan has spoken," pronounced Ken with another of his genial smiles, "and when Ivan speaks, the world listens!"

Over lunch they explained what they were going to do at Sandbury, commencing with "There's nothing secret about this caper since half the county will be watching I daresay before we've finished." They were specialists in the operation of assault landing craft and were here to teach the Canadians how to use them. The plan was to use the Medway just south of Rochester, so for the foreseeable future hundreds of Canadians were going to have the doubtful pleasure of being soaked to the waist – or more if they fell over – on a cold January morning. David wondered whether these exercises were the prelude to anything more serious proposed for the Canadians but wisely kept his own council.

During a break in the discussion about the assault craft exercises, Ivan fired a question, which left everyone silent for the moment and left Ivan himself utterly mortified at the answer.

"And your husband Rose – is he in the Rifles as well?"

Rose raised her eyes and said in a calm controlled voice, "No Ivan, he was, but he was killed at Calais."

"Oh my God, please forgive me for asking you such an abrupt question, I really am most deeply sorry."

"You weren't to know Ivan, there is nothing to forgive. We have had a sad year. In November David's wife died in an attack on the airfield here, she was driving a canteen vehicle with her friend, Lady Halton when they were fired on by a Messerschmitt."

Rose's recital of these facts was made in a firm, factual voice, a voice devoid of drama, but intense in its poignancy for all that.

"Oh how awful," replied Ivan, followed by, "I can only say that you all have our most sincere sympathy."

The meal finished, the formality of handing over ration cards having been completed, Ken announced they had to report to a Colonel McEwan – did they know him? They were speedily told they knew him well, he was a frequent visitor to the house and his unit was out on the Maidstone road, directions to which being more fully described by David, since as there were no signposts to anywhere anymore, (they had, of course, all been removed before the invasion threat), unless you had an Ordnance Survey map with a map reference of your destination, it was extremely difficult to get from point A to point B with any degree of certainty. It was possible, of course, and often necessary to ask one's way, the problem then being that you ran the risk of suspicion of being a fifth columnist, this particularly so during the invasion scare.

The next morning was bright and cold. After breakfast Charlie cornered David in the hallway and hesitantly said, "David, dear boy, would you mind awfully if I took some flowers to Pat?" David, afterwards, remembered he said 'To Pat' and not 'To Pat's grave'.

"No of course not, it's a very kind thought."

Rose, coming out of the kitchen, heard the last words and said, "What's a kind thought?"

"Charlie is going to take some flowers to Pat," repeated David.

"Could I come with you, I could show you the way?"

"I would be most grateful if you would, although it's quite a little walk, are you sure..." It was obvious the direction in which his thoughts were taking him.

"Now look here Charlie Crew, since when did you become an expert in pregnancy?"

"Well you see my dear young mother to be, I was rather concerned that if you got tired – or worse – I might have to give you a piggy back or a fireman's lift or something which would be most difficult under the circumstances. I could borrow a wheelbarrow from someone though I suppose. Failing that I would probably make a first class midwife once I got the hang of things."

Rose squeezed his arm, "I'll go and get my coat on," she said.

They each bought a small posy in Sandbury. Charlie wrote 'with love to Pat from all her friends at Ramsford', Rose put simply 'with love from Rose'. As they approached the grave they saw the stooped figure of the brigadier bending over Lady Agatha's grave and waited a short distance away until he turned to leave. He didn't notice them at first, being so consumed with his own thoughts and then, realising who they were, he raised his hat in greeting. "Rose, how are you my dear, how nice to see you. Oh, and its Mr Crew isn't it? I remember meeting you at the funeral. We shall be meeting again tomorrow I trust?"

Rose replied for them both.

"Yes, we shall be there Brigadier. I wonder if you would care to join us for Sunday lunch after the service that is if you're not going to be tied up elsewhere?"

"I have an idea one or two people would like to see me tied up at the moment – literally – but that's another story." He smiled his slow smile – he's such a handsome man thought Rose. He continued, "I would be delighted to join you, I was going to lunch at The Angel. However, we do have to mention the little question of rations don't we? The days of taking something out of the larder are long gone and your mother might have problems with an extra mouth to feed."

"As it happens, there is no problem, thanks to Charlie's grandfather. Knowing what a hog Charlie is, he sent us a big box of grouse and other goodies so that he didn't eat us out of house and home."

"You can see Sir, she has the advantage of me at present as I can't put her over my knee, but rest assured I'm saving it all up in my tiny brain."

The brigadier chuckled at their gay banter.

"Well I must let you go, I gratefully accept your invitation and will see you tomorrow."

They stood by Pat's grave in silence for a while having put their posies beside the flowers already there. Charlie broke the silence by saying to Rose, "Rose dear, I'm not much of an expert at this prayer lark, but do you mind if I say one now?"

"Of course not."

He bowed his head.

"Dear Lord, look after our dear sister Pat for us, and at the same time keep a watch on Rose and her new baby for Jeremy. Amen."

They walked back out of the churchyard towards home without conversation for a while, Rose lightly holding Charlie's arm. After a while she stopped, turned to him and kissed him on the cheek. "Thank you so much for your prayer Charlie." Charlie remained silent and they walked on home, each full of their own thoughts, Charlie somewhat confused as to his feelings for Rose, he liked her enormously but had enough sense to know that, as yet, he had no stronger feelings than that. Rose's thoughts were entirely of Jeremy and the coming baby. She was very happy that she had such good friends as Charlie, and Tim McEwan but it would not have crossed her mind for an instant that either of them would consider her romantically. Her world was wrapped around her family and her baby. No doubt that would change in time but that is how it stood at the moment.

When they got home, Buffy and Rita had arrived and true to form, had brought a goodly haul of rabbits and pheasants, a couple of hares and above all, two boiling fowls which had for some months ceased providing eggs for their master's breakfast table and therefore had, as Buffy said, 'to face the inevitable chop'. The two marines were there, sitting around the kitchen table with the others enjoying the family atmosphere, when Rose announced to her mother that the brigadier was coming to lunch tomorrow. Ruth showed no surprise merely remarking that one more will make little difference, but the two majors looked at each other with raised eyebrows.

"You don't entertain field marshalls by any chance Mrs Chandler do you?" asked Ivan.

"No, but we often have a lieutenant general pop in for coffee," she quipped. "Mr Churchill comes over for a drink when he's down at Chartwell of course and the Lord lieutenant is a constant visitor."

The two majors could not quite make up their minds as to whether she was stringing them along or not, she had made her reply with such a completely straight face. When she smiled, Ken said, "You had us believing you there you know."

"Well one part was true, we do have a general who comes to see us along with his wife. In fact he commands the corps of which Tim McEwan is a part. He really is a lovely man."

"I have to disillusion you Mrs Chandler," quipped Ivan, "there is absolutely no such thing as a lovely general. There might be such a being as a lovely wife of a general, though I've yet to see one, but a lovely general – such a character has not yet been invented."

"Well, when he comes we'll tell him what you said," joked Rose "I reckon it will be at least the Tower for you, I mean they don't give majors jankers do they?"

Sunday dawned cold and sunny. The church was full for mattins, regular worshippers, men and women from the airfield, Rotarians of all denominations, senior officers from the same corps as the brigadier's and not least, of course, the Chandlers family and friends. When mattins was over, they all filed out to the large open space at the front of the Church gate where the mobile canteen stood, already surrounded by a considerable crowd of townsfolk and service men and women who had not been to church. The canon made his way to the front of a roped off square facing the uplifted serving canopy on the side of the vehicle, followed by the families and other invited friends of the two women who had so tragically lost their lives. There was a hush as the canon's strong voice rang out into the cold January air.

"Oh Lord, we are gathered here to remember the sacrifice of our dear sisters, Pat Chandler and Lady Agatha Halton, killed by enemy action whilst on duty in this vehicle. Their names are engraved on a plaque displayed within this canteen so that future users will know of them. When we have overcome our adversaries and this vehicle is no longer needed, the plaque will be removed to be repositioned in our church as a constant reminder of the selfless courage of these two ladies."

He paused, moved forward closer to the canteen and continued.

"Oh Lord, we dedicate this vehicle in Thy Name to continue to give service and comfort to our armed forces. Bless the people who so unselfishly give their time to carry out this work and keep them safe.

In the name of The Father, The Son and The Holy Spirit. Amen."

The 'Amen' was echoed by the large assembly and after a few moments people began to drift away. The canon talked to David and the brigadier who thanked him for both a moving sermon, with the text based on sacrifice, and for the dedication of the vehicle. As they moved together to join Fred and Ruth and the others, the brigadier put his arm around David's shoulders and said oh so sadly, "It's all very comforting David my boy, but it doesn't bring them back does it?"

"No Sir it doesn't," he could think of nothing else to say in answer.

Chandlers Lodge was bursting at the seams that day. In addition to Buffy and Rita, all the family were there which naturally included Anni, Ernie and Karl. Tim, Jim, Alec and Deborah came in the afternoon, Ray Osbourne came with Harry and Megan, the two marines were there and at four o'clock Jack and Moira arrived and with them they brought the general and Lady Earnshaw. Witnessing these last arrivals Rose sidled up to the two marines and said, "Well now, what's it worth to keep quiet?"

By this time the general, having been welcomed by Ruth and Fred, was being led over by Colonel Tim to meet the rugged pair.

"Quick now, what's it worth before you go to the Tower?" ribbed Rose again.

"General, these gentlemen are Majors Johnson and Sopwith who I believe you know about."

"Yes indeed I do. How do you do and welcome to Sandbury. You've certainly landed on your feet being with the Chandlers. And Rose dear, how are you? Silly thing to ask – you look utterly lovely as always." He took her hand, bent over and kissed her on the cheek. "Now gentlemen, mustn't talk shop today, but is everything organised?"

"Yes Sir," said Ken, "Colonel McEwan has everything tied up to a 'T'."

"Jolly good – well I'll see more of you by the river I've no doubt." He moved away.

"Now that," said Rose "is one you owe me! Those dungeons are very cold at this time of the year. Now admit it – don't you think he's lovely?"

She was speaking with her back to most of the people in the room and had, therefore, not noticed that Lady Earnshaw was making her way toward their little group until she saw the two majors automatically stiffen to something approaching attention as they would for the drawing near of a person of importance. As she said 'Don't you think he's lovely,' Lady Earnshaw said, "Who's lovely Rose dear? Let me meet him!"

"You already have," replied Rose "I was talking about the general."

Lady Earnshaw turned and regarded her husband, talking animatedly to Fred and Karl a few paces away. "Well now I am, of course, prejudiced. I think he's lovely, but I have to confess that few others would, particularly among the military, in fact I go so far as to guess that they have vastly different sobriquets with which to describe him. In any event, Rose dear, please introduce me to your friends."

Rose made the necessary introductions. The two majors describing to her what they were here to do, how friendly everyone had been to them, and in particular how welcoming the Chandlers had been and how comfortable they had made them.

"Mind you," continued Ivan, "we have a little trouble with this young lady from time to time," indicating Rose.

Lady Earnshaw put her arm around Rose's waist and said, "I don't believe it. I think she's utterly gorgeous."

"With that sentiment," replied Ivan, "I thoroughly agree."

They all laughed, but Ivan wondered afterwards whether they had noticed that he had made the remark just a little too seriously for it to be a conversational flippancy. As Lady Earnshaw moved away, Ivan admitted "Rose, I have to hand it to you; there is such a being as a lovely wife of a general. Even on such short acquaintance I have to say that she is one of the nicest and most refined people I have ever met."

"Much too good for a general," Ken butted in.

"Yes, much too good for a general," Ivan agreed.

The weekend quickly passed and it was time for David and Charlie, on Tuesday morning, to make their way to their first posting as officers. Having loaded up the station taxi again and said goodbye to all the family, having given strict instructions to Rose and Anni to take the greatest care of themselves, and having told his mother and Ernie to telegraph him immediately there was news, they drove off to the station. Sitting quietly in the back seat with luggage piled all around him Charlie, at length, touched David's shoulder and said, "Aren't they all lovely people – it was the most marvellous weekend of my whole life."

Chapter Twenty

As David was travelling to Norfolk for his first posting, Lieutenant Dieter von Hassellbek stood on the docks at Calais looking towards Dover. It was Tuesday 14th January 1941. This was the first time he had been able to visit the town since he took part in the invasion of France the previous May, having had a variety of occupational postings in Normandy, Brittany and further south in Bordeaux. He had, however, heard of the defence of Calais by, as he subsequently found out, the Rifles and their French allies. He also heard they were all killed or captured, and knowing that it was very likely his friends David and Jeremy would have been there, he had long harboured a desire to visit the battlefield to see if he could get a lead as to whether they survived the slaughter. He had had a few days leave in Paris and decided on impulse to take the train to Calais.

Dieter was consumed by a mixture of feelings. He had no animosity toward Britain and the British, nor the French for that matter. On the other hand he was a true patriot, but even this was confusing since although he had no idea of the extent of the persecution of the Jews – 'The Final Solution' – he could not understand why it was necessary. Communists yes. Like most middle class Germans he had a profound fear of communism, and fear generates hate. Yet Soviet Russia was, if not an ally of Germany, certainly not an enemy. The Russians were supplying enormous quantities of war materials to Germany, as well as grain and much needed oil, but in Dieter's mind if he should be fighting anyone it should be the Soviets. They, after all, had the paramount intention of making the whole world subservient to communism, they even sang about it in their national anthem. It still remained that after the partition of Poland, Germany and Russia were next door neighbours – the Red Army had not got far to go to pick the plum of Greater Germany. Over my dead body he thought. Again, where does Japan fit in? Germany and Italy had a ten-year mutual assistance pact with Japan signed in September giving Germany and Italy the leadership of a New Order in Europe and respecting the leadership of Japan of a New Order in Eastern Asia. They had pledged mutual assistance if any of them were attacked, so if Russia attacked Germany, Japan would attack Russia – or would they? Japan's eyes were facing south, Malaya, Indonesia, Australia even; there was no doubt about that. Not only that their hands were pretty full in China.

As he stood there in the hazy January sunlight he thought of those wonderful holidays before the war with David and Jeremy, Pat and Rose and, of course, Anni whose mother died in Dachau. He wondered sadly whether the families had survived the awful bombing which, according to the news, had virtually obliterated the major English cities and left the countryside a wasteland. Why didn't their government sign an armistice after Dunkirk so that Europe together could face the red menace from the east? With most of their manufacturing facilities in ruins and most of their weaponry lost in France, it was surely pointless for them to carry on such an unequal struggle. The Wehrmacht, as far as he could see, was invincible. The Luftwaffe so commanded the air that they could bomb with impunity. The U-boats were sinking British ships at such a rate that soon there would be no merchant navy left and the people of Britain would starve to death. He contemplated all these factors with such sadness. There was, after all, no disgrace in being beaten in war by a superior enemy, why couldn't the British Parliament realise that Germany bore no ill will to the British, end the killing of thousands of innocents and join the crusade against Bolshevism which he felt certain was inevitable, whatever the present treaty arrangements with the Soviet Union were.

He, like David, had undergone experiences he would never have dreamt of since they were all cycling through the beautiful English countryside together. He graduated second in his year at the military academy at Potsdam and elected to join the Panzer Grenadiers. He loved the army life, the discipline, tradition and comradeship, particularly as he found himself in the regiment, which, as far as possible, kept itself out of politics and in which there was a certain disdain, kept strictly under control, of the Nazi hierarchy. They were professionals and although Dieter enjoyed himself as all young officers will, and should, he continued to study after leaving the Academy in two directions. Firstly as his ancillary subject, each cadet was encouraged to take up a subject of his choice. He had decided to learn Russian. He already spoke good French at school and whilst visiting relatives in Switzerland, he was almost fluent in English, so in discussion with his father they had concluded that Russian could be very useful to him both now and after the war. How wise that decision proved to be! Secondly he studied all there was to be found on armoured warfare. He read the history of tank warfare in the Great War, the use of tanks in Spain by the Soviets, the Italians and the Wehrmacht. He got books from England by Major General Fuller and Captain

Liddell-Hart, from France by a Colonel de Gaulle and as much information as he could through the good offices of the military attaché's in London, Paris, Rome and Moscow. One evening after dinner he was reading an article in English by Liddell-Hart on the ability of armoured formations to attack France through the Ardennes, considered by most military pundits in Germany, and even more so in France, as impossible. As he read he was joined by his colonel. He immediately sprang to attention, was told to sit down and asked what it was he was so absorbed in. Dieter offered the colonel the article and quickly summarised its contents.

"So you speak good English?" asked the colonel, continuing, "and French?"

"Yes Sir and some Russian as well, which I'm gradually improving."

"Shouldn't you be in intelligence in that case?"

"Definitely not Sir, I want to be a real soldier," said somewhat vehemently "that is Sir, no disrespect to the intelligence people of course."

The colonel smiled. "No of course not, although there would appear to be too many so called intelligence people around these days, many of them, it strikes me, singularly lacking in the commodity they profess to embrace." He started to leave. Dieter so rarely had the opportunity to speak to the colonel on close terms, he decided to broach a subject to which he had been giving deep thought over the past two or three months.

"Sir," he said, "could I keep you for a further minute or two?" The colonel paused and re-took his seat.

"Carry on."

"In brief Sir, we in the armoured divisions are, of course, very mobile. With the exception of a few self-propelled guns, most of our artillery is horse drawn or towed by slow tractors. Therefore in a speedy advance we would leave our artillery well behind. It occurred to me that if we had a Luftwaffe radio control up with the spearhead units, housed in say a specially adapted armoured half track troop carrier, they could call on Stuka dive bombers to take the place of the artillery as well as to attack enemy tanks." Dieter paused – did it sound a crackpot idea to the colonel – coming from the army the Luftwaffe could probably be against it anyway – was he, being a very junior officer, being presumptuous in suggesting such a scheme? All these thoughts were going through his mind as the colonel sat for a minute digesting what he had expounded.

"I can see considerable merit in what you're proposing. Write a full report on your ideas, include how close the Stuka base would need to be, mention that as they can actually see us, which artillery cannot, they could operate much closer to our most forward units. Include your ideas on recognition factors – you will obviously have given that some thought. Give some thought to target identification – coloured smoke or similar. When you've got it prepared, bring it to me personally and I will study it and move it forward – oh, and don't forget Stuka's will need protection – they're quite slow."

"I will do that Sir, thank you Sir."
"Good night von Hassellbek."
"Good night Sir."

Dieter sat back in his armchair, his head a melange of thoughts. Far from being scornful of his ideas the colonel was obviously genuinely interested, which was certainly the first hurdle overcome. It would be an achievement on his part if the scheme was adopted, but knowing how slowly the army moved on any innovation, he had no wild expectations of its happening the day after he made his presentation to the colonel!!

Two weeks later, Dieter took his carefully prepared project to the C.O.'s office. A week after that he was told to present himself to the colonel at 12 noon dressed in service uniform. When he was taken in to the colonel by the adjutant, he found himself in the presence not only of his commanding officer but also of a general who he immediately recognised as General Guderian. The general opened the proceedings with, "I have been shown your proposals von Hassellbek. They show a lively mind, and a keen appreciation of one of the dangers of the 'lightning war'. Can you think of another?"

"The danger of flank attack on extended forward thrusts Sir?" stated as a question.

"Excellent. Now I'll not waste time. I am going to take up your suggestion and see if we can't get some units on the ground for the summer manoeuvres. I understand from Colonel von Herzberg that you speak a number of languages. Why don't you go into intelligence, you obviously have an enquiring mind?"

The colonel broke in, "I asked him that Herr General, he replied he wanted to be a real soldier!" They both laughed heartily.

"Well good luck von Hassellbek – I have a feeling we shall meet again."

At the beginning of July, extensive manoeuvres were held in

North Germany, at the end of which instead of being sent on leave, which was the normal practice, Dieter's regiment was moved in small groups by rail and by transporter to a large tented area in woodlands, east of Furstenwalde some thirty kilometres from the Polish frontier at Frankfurt-am-Oder to become part of the German Eighth Army. All tanks and soft skinned vehicles were rapidly serviced, full war strength armament was supplied or fitted, emergency rations delivered and a full censorship of all mail, officers included, was instituted. On 20th August there was much movement, shouting of orders, a great deal of tidying up as happens in any unit when someone very important is visiting. To Dieter's surprise it was the Fuhrer himself, accompanied by two field marshalls, a bevy of generals, and tucked away at the back, the insignificant figure of Dr Joseph Goebbels, the man who had spoken at Augsburg, on one of the occasions when David visited the von Hassellbeks in Ulm. The Fuhrer passed within two metres of Dieter, talking animatedly to one of the generals, but turning to acknowledge the troops as he passed. When he reached Dieter he looked straight into the young soldiers' eyes, returning Dieter's salute with a smile. Dieter was struck immediately by the vital magnetism in those hypnotic blue eyes. He understood in those few seconds the power this man wielded over those close to him and the spell he was able to cast over the masses who listened to him, and it frightened him; but he couldn't tell why.

On Wednesday 30th August even tighter restrictions were instituted. No movement was allowed either into or out of the regimental area. All unnecessary personal baggage was put into a central store. Regimental commanders were called to Divisional HQ and returned with sealed envelopes and even more tightly sealed lips. At 8am on Thursday 31st August the officers were called to regimental headquarters and told that as a result of frequent violations of the German frontier by the Poles, culminating in the unprovoked attack on the German radio station at Glewitz, along with the infamous treatment of ethnic Germans in the Polish territories taken from Germany by the Treaty of Versailles, the Fuhrer could no longer stand aside and accept this situation. At dawn therefore, the next day Friday September 1st the Poles would commence to receive the lesson they deserved. Dieter learned that his regiment was to be the spearhead to cover the left flank of the Tenth Army whose task was to make the main thrust to Warsaw from the south west. He was rather disappointed at this – he would have much preferred to be spearheading the Tenth Army itself and be where the action was, but he need not have worried, he would see plenty of action in the next three weeks.

September 1st dawned fine and clear. The air above them seemed full of aircraft of all types, dive bombers, fighters, light bombers all heading towards known Polish airfields to attack machines on the ground. Of the nine hundred first line aircraft in the Polish Air Force, over half were destroyed in the first hours without even taking off. It was approaching midday before the regiment moved off, moving south east in a loop to bring them parallel with the Tenth Army. There was some resistance, but mainly ineffectual as what was left after being swiftly dealt with by the Stukas directed by the Luftwaffe teams on the ground, was speedily mopped up.

On September 4th at the officer's evening meeting to receive orders for the following day, the colonel, grim faced, informed them that Britain and France had declared war on Germany the previous day as a direct result of their invasion of Poland. There was jubilation on a few of the younger faces, but in the main the news was received with grave unsmiling features.

"It is now going to be a long war," said one reservist officer, a veteran of the 1914 war. "Let us just hope that America stays out this time."

"Oh, they'll stay out," replied the colonel, "they're more isolationist now than they've ever been. Now, let us pass on to more immediate matters."

On a number of occasions in the first few days when heavier resistance was met from strong points, the armour by-passed it, leaving it to be dealt with by supporting infantry later. It was essential that Dieter's regiment kept station with the main thrust some thirty kilometres to the south, which meant also that when they pushed too far they had to harbour and await orders to move on.

It was on one such occasion they had to harbour all night in an area of open woodland, the tanks spread around the perimeter of the wood with the soft skinned vehicles in the centre. As soon as it became dark, sentries posted and all lights and fires extinguished, the men got down to sleep. Dieter stretched his groundsheet alongside one of his tank tracks, rolled himself in his blanket and was soon asleep. He was awakened by the shouting of the sentries, rifles being fired, a machine gun from one of the tanks being loosed off over to his right, but most of all, by the thunder of hooves on the hard ground in front of the wood. He pulled his Luger from its holster, cocked it, and ran to the front of the tank shouting for his crew to mount. Reaching the front of his vehicle he saw in the moonlight a trooper coming straight at him full gallop, sabre raised ready to cut him down. As the sabre swung down, Dieter in a reflex action, which saved his being decapitated, fell to the ground. As it was, the razor sharp steel edge caught his right epaulet neatly severing it at the shoulder and leaving it flapping from its securing button. He turned to shoot the trooper but he and his mount had raced on into the interior of the wood and with what appeared to be hundreds of his comrades, was wreaking havoc in the soft skin areas, the night air being rent with the agonising screams of men being mutilated by their ferocious attackers.

Shots being fired from those being attacked were cracking over Dieter's head and hitting his and neighbouring tanks. He swiftly decided, therefore, his safest place was inside with his crew. Having checked all were present, he gave the order for the machine gunner to load and await further orders.

At the firing of a green Very light the cavalry turned outwards and charged at full gallop out of the wood. This time, without the benefit of surprise, they were hit by merciless machine gun fire from the tanks as they left, the horses suffering even more than the men. The carnage would have been even worse had the moon not clouded over when they were in the clear ground, as it was, their losses were heavy.

The regiment had not come off scot-free by any means. Some thirty soldiers in the soft skin area had been cut down, and as many again suffered severe injuries. As they left, the troopers had hurled phosphorous grenades into vehicles, one, carrying reserve ammunition, exploding and setting fire to several other trucks. It taught them all a lesson. The Poles might be poorly armed, have little or no air cover, have very little armour, but if they lacked in equipment they certainly did not lack in courage.

Dieter wore his epaulet dangling from the button all through the rest of the campaign as a talisman, although he woke up on numerous occasions in the following nights sweating at the thought of how close that sword had been to ending his days.

The next few days saw the Eighth Army pushing forward steadily just south of the Bzura River, with the Tenth Army away to their right. It was on 9th September that General Kutrzeba commanding the Polish army around Posnan, decided on a bold move to sweep south through the Eight Army and hit the Tenth Army on its vulnerable flanks, thereby stopping the head long dash to Warsaw.

For nine days the Eighth Army, relatively weak compared to the other four armies, battled against a fanatical enemy but on the 18th, reinforced by a corps detached from the Tenth Army and another from the Fourth Army sweeping down from the north, the fighting ceased leaving thousands of Poles and Germans killed and wounded and the enormous total of 170,000 Poles taken prisoner. This was the biggest, and most ferocious action of the campaign and Dieter who, a few days before had been disappointed at not being where the action was, now had seen what war was all about when the opponents were almost equally balanced.

The Poles had armour and used it well. Dieter's regiment, engaged in a pitched battle with a tenacious foe, lost a number of their lighter tanks; as a result, half a dozen leaderless units tacked themselves on to Dieter's pennant during the battle. It was shortly after midday on 14th September that Dieter leading his now increased flock in open formation, carefully moved to the crest of a small ridge only to find hulled down some 400 metres away, a number of Polish tanks but, more importantly, three anti-tank guns, one of which loosed off at him the minute he breasted the slope. It had fired solid shot, the projectile hitting the side of the turret shattering the radio aerial housing. Dieter therefore could no longer talk to his tank commanders, could not stop them from breasting the same slope and receiving the same treatment, nor could he direct any future activity against the enemy opposing them.

Without a second thought he opened the cupola, and fired a red Very light to halt the advance. The appearance outside of the top half of his body, was greeted by a hail of machine gun fire hitting the ground and ricocheting off the steel armour, it was a miracle he escaped death. His driver, in the meantime, had slammed the engine into reverse and when below the crest line, swung round.

From then on for the next hour Dieter controlled his mini-battle by using hand signals. He directed his tanks on a flanking move, using such cover as he could find to get round behind the Poles. In doing this, they brushed with a number of infantry units dug in, but ignoring them spun round in a big half circle until Dieter judged he was in a position to attack the hulled down armour in its most vulnerable position, the sides and rear. On numerous occasions he was shot at by the infantry as he stood in his turret but he seemed to have a charmed life.

The remainder of the battle took only minutes. As they came down on to the rear of the Poles, firing their main armament as they advanced, the anti-tank gunners were annihilated by the secondary armament machine guns. Seeing this, the Polish armour backed out of its hulled down positions in an endeavour to escape, but found itself sideways on to the three tanks Dieter had directed around to his left. The Poles were doomed. Solid shot rained in to them until two caught fire, the remaining five then opened their hatches and piled out with hands raised.

For the loss of one tank and his own vehicle damaged they had destroyed seven of the enemy. For this action he was awarded the Order of the Iron Cross, Class II, a counterpart of the old original Prussian Iron Cross, which had been re-introduced by Hitler on 1st September 1939, Dieter being one of the first to win it. It was, however, some weeks before it was presented to him by none other than General Guderian who remarked, "There, von Hassellbek, I said we would meet again and I wager this will not be the last time either!"

Dieter had one regrettable feeling about the medal itself. In the centre of the cross was implanted the inevitable swastika, a symbol of those people he and his family, with the exception of his sister Inge, disliked, despised and above all secretly feared having, as they did, the power of life and death over everyone. As a soldier he had been unable to opt out of swearing the personal oath of loyalty to Adolf Hitler, which every member of the German forces was required to do. He had wrestled with his conscience regarding this matter, trusting in the end that someone, or something, else would solve the dilemma for him. This apart, he felt proud at having distinguished himself and had faced his foe without flinching.

After the battle had been won at the River Bzura, Dieter's unit pushed on to catch up with the Tenth Army at the outskirts of Warsaw. The city was held with such fanaticism that eventually the two armies, having lost over sixty tanks to well dug-in and brilliantly led defenders, were given the order to withdraw and hand over to the Luftwaffe. On the 27th September, after a mass bombing campaign augmented by the use of heavy guns brought across from the western front, Warsaw was left with hardly a building not damaged or destroyed. The city capitulated. General von Blaskowitz, an officer and gentleman of the 'Old School', in acknowledging the incredible bravery of the defenders, allowed the officers to keep their swords and the troops to go into captivity for only as long as it took to 'dispose of the necessary formalities'. But this was not the 'Old School' any more; this was the 'New School' where the S.S. and Gestapo scum knew nothing of honour or tradition. Once General von Blaskowitz returned to Germany a few days later einsatzgruppen were set up under Theodor Eicke whose orders were 'incarcerate or annihilate every enemy of Nazism'.

Thousands of officers were shot, tens of thousands of soldiers put to slave labour, then they turned their fury upon the Jews, the aristocracy, academics and deviants. No one will ever know how many died, in concert with a similar programme being carried out by their Russian allies on the eastern half of the country, which they had now occupied.

Immediately the campaign ended, Dieter's unit was withdrawn and found itself as a mobile reserve stationed near Wiesbaden behind the Siegfried Line. At Christmas 1939 he was given leave for ten days and went home to Ulm. Neither he nor his family discussed the war, except that his father, like Dieter himself, was deeply suspicious of having the communists right on their doorstep. His view was that if the French and British attacked when they were fully mobilised, and in his mind they surely would, the best of the German divisions would be needed on the western front, which would provide a temptation too great to resist for the Russians. Frau von Hassellbek's view was, "Enough of such depressing talk – it's Christmas."

On Christmas Eve, Dieter's cousin Rosa and her mother arrived from Munich to spend the holiday with them. Dieter was very fond indeed of his cousin, and had been ever since their holiday in England with David and his family. Since joining the army, Dieter's leaves had been few and far between, so they had seen little of each other during the past couple of years although they had corresponded regularly. Rosa, in turn, had been very busy at University in Munich where she was studying medicine – a five-year course with two years to go before qualifying. She had had many propositions from fellow students and tutors, some subtle, some more than explicit, but despite the fact she had all the urges of a normal twenty-one-year-old she was single minded about her feelings for Dieter and laughed off invitations for casual liaisons in which the majority of the students openly indulged.

On the day after Christmas they walked together on the very side of the Danube along which Dieter and David had ridden their bicycles during those happy days before the war. Dieter slipped his arm around Rosa's waist, she laid her head on his shoulder, it was impossible to believe that only a few weeks before he had been involved in the slaughter of his fellow human beings, when all around them were the cool, crisp, frosty woodlands with the silent peaceful Danube flowing by just as it had been for thousands of years. Rosa looked up at him. "You're quiet?" – it was more a question that a statement of fact.

"You know I love you Rosa don't you?"

"We've both known how we feel for a long time."

"Do you think your mother would allow us to marry? I mean, my being a soldier and our being cousins and your still being at university has all got to be taken into account. And you wouldn't see me for months at a time and I might get wounded and be a liability to everybody...." his voice petered out as he thought twice about his intended conclusion of the sentence which would have been, 'or I might get killed'.

"Dieter von Hassellbek – Iron Cross Second Class, are you proposing to me? It certainly sounds like it. I therefore require you to take my hand, go on one knee and do the job properly before I say yes."

"So you are going to say yes," he teased.

"You, Dieter von Hassellbek must wait and see."

He went down on one knee, took her hand and said "Rosa dear, will you marry me?"

The last word was just leaving his lips as she went down on her knees before him, took his head in her hands and kissed him long and passionately, at last replying, "That means yes, as soon as possible darling, darling Dieter."

They walked on air back to the house. When they arrived, the family were in the main drawing room. The two young lovers stood just inside the doorway with Dieter's arm around Rosa's waist as their parents looked expectantly at them sensing that something exceptional was afoot. Dieter spoke.

"I have asked Rosa to marry me. We would like your blessing."

Rosa's mother was the first to jump to her feet and move towards them. All she said was, "I am so happy for you both." She was swiftly followed by Dieter's parents, and then as always happens on these and similar occasions, everybody started talking at once. Rosa's father had died some years before as a result of wounds he had received in the Great War, so it was decided that the wedding would be at Ulm, the date to be finally decided by Dieter being able to get leave, but provisionally set for Easter. Rosa would, of course, continue with her university studies.

Dieter returned to his unit and having requested an interview with his colonel, was given permission to take leave for seven days at Easter, always provided military considerations allowed. They spent their honeymoon in a small hotel on the Swiss border, and within an hour of their returning to Ulm the telephone rang and Dieter's Company Commander was on the line informing him he must return 'immediately

– not tomorrow – immediately'.

Thus began Dieter's second experience of the art of warfare, in which he took part in what was to become a masterpiece of military strategy. Terence said two thousand years ago that 'Fortune aids the brave.' The plan to attack through the Ardennes against any enemy superior in numbers, possessed of an equal number of tanks, some much heavier than the German Panzers, and above all with the enemy dug in to well prepared positions, was brave in the extreme. Staff colleges before the war would have considered such a plan suicidal. If you attack a defended position it is always considered you require two to two and half times the forces possessed by the enemy, to attack with equal forces is asking for trouble. But attack they did, their greatest fear being they would be held at the Meuse, since the French would have all the bridges ready to be blown. Dieter found himself in General Guderian's Corps at Sedan, taking part in another major battle, but cross the Meuse they did and once they had brushed aside French cavalry, they commenced their headlong dash towards the English Channel. Exhilarated as they were by their almost uninterrupted successes not even the more level headed thinking men among them harboured any guilt about the morality of having started this great adventure by violating the neutrality of Luxembourg, Belgium and in the north the Netherlands, with all of whom the German government were at least, on paper, on friendly terms. Neither did they know of the German intention, should they be held in the north, to invade Switzerland in order to hit the soft underbelly of France in the south – Operation Tannenbaum. In the event, the violation of Switzerland was not required; the blitzkrieg in the low countries and the Ardennes succeeded beyond all measure.

Apart from heavy fighting outside Abbeville, Dieter's war was one of encirclement and taking prisoners, thousands upon thousands, and then chasing south to try and capture those heading for Le Havre, Cherbourg, St Malo and other smaller ports further down the coast. It was a succession of short sharp engagements against a demoralised foe who often turned and fought valiantly but who, in the end, was overwhelmed by superior forces superbly led. It was a tradition in the Panzer Divisions that the commanding general always was in the spearhead of the attack, having radio communication with his chief staff officer some distance back to whom he would issue orders as to the further disposition of his forces as the battle situation changed. It was because of this method of operation that Dieter again found himself held up on a road side by side with General Guderian who yelled at him above the noise of the engines, "We meet again von Hassellbek – I said we would – this is a bit different to Bzura is it not?"

Dieter grinned broadly and saluted as the general moved forward. If ever I become a general he said to himself, I would like to be exactly like him.

So the campaign petered out. It was undoubtedly a glorious victory. For the next few months they led an easy life in various beautiful chateaux, brief leaves in Paris where on one occasion he was joined by Rosa for a whole week. Now it was January and his unit was, once more, on the move but this time the rumour was they were going back to Poland for 'exercises,' then perhaps we'll get some home leave after that he told himself. But it was going to be a long while before he got his next home leave and terrible things were to happen in the meantime.

Chapter Twenty One

It snowed heavily on the journey through East Anglia, the train being nearly an hour late arriving at Norwich Thorpe. They were met by a cheerful cockney driver with, "Blimey, I thought they'd lost you Sir," to David as he saluted smartly. He went on to say he had to take them to battalion HQ in a small village west of Norwich, and then on to the airfield upon which they would be stationed.

"Where will that be?" queried David.

"Dunno Sir, till they tell me."

The snow had stopped as they drove up Prince of Wales Road, past the castle and then out of the city, arriving eventually at a nissen-hutted camp passing a sentry who sprang to attention and saluted as they drove through. Leaving their kit on the truck they were directed to the adjutant's office, who welcomed them warmly saying, "We've got to go into the C.O. straight away – he's tight for time with your train being late."

They were ushered to the C.O.'s office and having saluted was asked, "Right, which one's which?"

"I'm Chandler Sir, this is Crew."

"Well as you will have read on the door, I'm Brindlesby-Gore – and the adjutant here is Tony Flamborough." He had hardly finished these introductions when Charlie interrupted. David would have kicked him if he had been able – didn't he learn his lesson when they were first at OCTU?

"Sir, we had a Brindlesby-Gore with us at Winchester."

The colonel smiled, obviously not taking offence at being interrupted, unlike the D.L.I. man at Worcester.

"Yes, he is my younger brother." He paused for a moment and continued, speaking just that fraction too casually, "er, how did he get on?"

"He was very good Sir, apart from David here, he was the best of our bunch." David could have kicked him a second time, but by now, Charlie had got the bit between his teeth.

"Mind you Sir, he was a bit po-faced at times. We put that down to the fact that firstly he was a bit older than us and secondly had been a barrister. I mean, it's common knowledge that all barristers are po-faced, it makes everything in a case sound worse than it is, then they can charge bigger fees."

Both the colonel and the adjutant were ginning widely at this.

"Well, down to business. We are sending you both to D Coy at Highmere. The aerodrome there is a peacetime one unlike the other three we are guarding, so you'll live in a comfortable mess with the R.A.F. bods. The awkward bit is you're a mile and a half away from the company HQ and men's quarters so you'll be issued with a bicycle each to get to and from your platoons. The O.C. is Major Ponsonby, second in command Captain Flavell. They know you're coming this afternoon but won't have your papers for a day or so as we have work to do on them here. I would add we only received them from Winchester today so have had no time to go through them yet. I visit you all on Thursday evenings for dinner, along with Tony here, when we have a general chinwag and pass on the news from the other companies on the other aerodromes. If I can't make it then Major Webber, second in command and on leave at the moment, will come and see you. Right then, get off to Highmere and I'll see you on Thursday evening."

As they saluted and turned about, the adjutant called out, "Wait in my office will you?" and as they closed the door behind them he turned to the colonel and said, "They look a very good pair Sir."

"Yes, I agree... po-faced – oh I shall love to tell him that." The two laughed again as the colonel continued, "As long as Ponsonby doesn't spoil them."

"What are you going to do about him Sir?"

"Nothing as yet, I reckon if I give him and Flavell enough rope, they'll both hang themselves in due course."

"I liked Crew's loyalty to Chandler – I thought it was quite spontaneous about his being the best on the course."

"I'm going to Winchester in a couple of weeks, if I get the chance I'll have a quick word with Mr Forster – he'll give us a straight opinion with no bullshit."

"I'll get them away then Sir, your Humber's ready when you are, though with all this snow around it might be well to take your toothbrush, you might get snowed in at Brampton!"

"That'll be no hardship. Freddie Groombridge always has a good stock of decent claret in his mess," and as he went through the doorway the adjutant heard him saying, "Po-faced – oh my goodness!"

When the adjutant rejoined the two chums he gave them further instructions and ended cryptically, "And if you have any serious problems, remember I'm here to help." They thanked him and went out to the truck.

As they drove to Highmere David said in a low voice, "I wonder what he meant by the serious problems bit. Normally your first port of call if you had a problem would be to your company commander."

They arrived at the airfield just as it was dark and walked into the company office. The company clerk looked up from his desk, pointed with his thumb to a door and said, "He's in there," and bent his head over his desk again.

David was suddenly quite angry, not so much that the rifleman's manner was bordering on insolence, but more because of the fact that the rifleman was not acting like a rifleman and was therefore insulting his regiment. David walked over to the desk.
"What's your name?"
"Roberts."
"Well let me tell you three things Rifleman Roberts. When Mr Crew or I come into this office you stand up. When you talk to Mr Crew or myself you address us as Sir, and when you refer to the company commander you refer to him as the major - do you understand that? Because if you don't you will find your feet will not touch the ground. Have I made myself clear?"
Roberts in the meantime had pushed his chair back and stood up, visibly shaken.
"Right now, start again."
"The major's in there Sir, waiting for you."
"Thank you Roberts, now carry on."

David knocked on the major's door; a belligerent voice from within bellowed, "Come." The two new platoon commanders to-be looked at each other with eyebrows raised, marched in, halted and saluted.
"Second Lieutenants Chandler and Crew Sir, I'm Chandler."
"You are over an hour bloody late."
"I apologise Sir, our train was delayed by the snow."
"Well I can't wait around any longer now. Have you got your papers with you?"
"No Sir, I understand the adjutant will be sending them on," continued David.
Ponsonby was a heavily built man; mid to late thirties David judged, heavily jowled with the flush of a man whose connection with a bottle was probably more than just mere friendship.
"That means they'll be a bloody week," he growled. "You,"

(pointing to David), "which school were you at?"

"Cantelbury Sir."

"Oh yes, one of the minor ones isn't it?"

David did not answer. He was already feeling that they had made the wrong choice in electing for the Sixth Battalion. Ponsonby continued.

"And what does your father do?"

"He has an engineering factory in Kent, Sir; they're mainly in war work."

"I see, another bloody war profiteer eh?"

David still kept quiet although the thought flashed across his mind as to what would happen if he thumped major red-necked bloody Ponsonby. The ignorant sod could be as rude as he liked to him, but he was treading on dangerous ground in insulting his father. "And you," to Charlie, "which school were you at?"

"Well actually Sir, I just went to the village council school," said Charlie, his face as innocent as a newborn babe's.

"A council school – and what the hell does your father do for Christ's sake?"

"He owns the village butcher's shop," still as innocent as before.

David could hardly stop himself from exploding.

"Bloody hell, what's the regiment coming to – a butcher's son in the mess, the Army must be damned hard up that's all I can say." He continued, "Be here nine sharp tomorrow morning." They saluted and marched out.

Their cockney driver opened the doors for them and they clambered in to the make the last part of their journey to the R.A.F. mess on the other side of the airfield. They were both silent until David started rumbling with laughter.

"You silly sod, what are you going to do when he finds out?"

"A bloated twit like that won't say a word when he knows pater's a brig and anyway, he does own the butcher's shop and the pub, and the post office."

The driver butted in. "Sir, can I say something out of turn?"

They looked at each other. David replied, "Well, alright, as long as it's not too scurrilous."

"Everybody in the battalion from the C.O. down knows that that Major Ponsonby is a right prat, and his sidekick Captain Flavell is nearly as bad, and D Company is a shower."

"Well I'll pretend we didn't hear that, but thanks all the same," and continuing to Charlie he said, "this is another fine mess you've got me in Stanley," giving a passable imitation of the great Oliver Hardy.

"We'll sort the bastards out dear old sport, with your brains and my charm we'll sort the bastards out. By the way no one's mentioned the other platoon commander – I wonder what he's like?" They would not be long in finding out.

They were cordially welcomed by the mess president, a regular R.A.F. officer, who gave them a mass of information regarding dinner night, when all available R.A.F. officers were obliged to attend – "and no battle dress," he added – and to which function the Pongos were cordially invited.

"Pongos?" queried Charlie "what the hell's a Pongo?"

The squadron leader laughed, "That's all you brown jobs," he replied. He went on to give them a résumé of the officer's facilities for buying drinks in the mess and arrangements for officers to get into Norwich, and finally calling a mess steward who told them their room numbers. "Your batmen have been here a couple of days and will have had your kit out of the truck by now, so I'll say cheerio and see you for dinner this evening."

They thanked him warmly and followed the steward to their rooms. Charlie dropped off first a few rooms away from David. When David walked into his room he had the surprise of his life. There, unpacking his valise was the burly frame of none other than Paddy O'Riordan.

"What the hell are you doing here?" exclaimed David going over to Paddy and shaking hands.

"Well Sir, I badgered the R.S.M. at Winchester to get me regraded and told him I wanted to come and look after you. He pulled a few strings, I think, and here I am —though I will tell you that he said to me – O'Riordan you look after him with your bloody life, you understand? Or I'll swing for you I promise. Then I asked him to let my pal Driscoll come and look after Mr Crew, which he did, so I can promise you there's nothing either of you gentlemen is going to go without if Driscoll and me know anything about it."

David sat on the edge of his bed and roared his head off. All he could say was, "I'm damned if I know – as my brother would say, this beats cock fighting." He hesitated for a moment and continued, "But you do realise Paddy you'll have to be on route marches and company exercises and so on with me? A batman in a service battalion has to act as runner and do all sorts of other jobs for his officer when we're out on training."

"Don't you worry Sir, I'll be right beside you all the time, and so will Driscoll with Mr Crew, R.S.M. Forster laid it in to him like he did to me. Now Sir, what will you be wearing tonight and tomorrow?"

"Best battledress and shoes tonight, second best and boots tomorrow."

They talked on as Paddy unpacked. He had already put his ear to the ground and was a mine of information about the general state of affairs in D Company. Putting it mildly it was a shambles. They had had three sergeant majors in six months, each requesting a move elsewhere. The major was hardly ever at the camp after eleven in the morning, traipsing all over the country and beyond to race meetings and point to points wherever he could find them. "Where he gets the petrol from is anybody's guess," added Paddy. Captain Flavell spent most of his time in Norwich where, apparently, he kept a floozie in a flat just off the Haymarket. Major Ponsonby was stinking rich, his family owning half the coal mines in south Wales. Captain Flavell was the younger son of a Lord Sherrington with estates up in Yorkshire. Most of the organisation of the guards on the airfield was done by Roberts, the orderly room clerk who wasn't beyond altering an inconvenient duty for half a crown or so. All in all morale was very low.

"Paddy, how have you found out all this in a couple of days, and who is the other platoon commander and where is he?"

Paddy continued by explaining that he knew one or two of the old sweats who had been drafted into the battalion and a couple of pints in the R.A.F. NAAFI – "By God, these R.A.F. blokes know how to look after themselves," was Paddy's considered opinion – a couple of pints in the R.A.F. NAAFI soon produced the whole story. As for Mr Burton, the other platoon commander, he would be leaving soon. He was a nervous wreck as a result of the continual bullying by Major Ponsonby, the fact that he was continually duty officer and was, therefore, out night after night, and thirdly having wife trouble at home."

"How did you find that out?"

"His batman told me Sir, it'll go no further."

"Well, to say this place presents a bit of a challenge seems to be the understatement of the age."

"It is that Sir, but I reckon you're the one to do it."

"Well I don't know about that – I'm only the boy around the place at the moment."

"You and Mr Crew will sort the bastards out Sir, that I'm sure."

"It's funny you should say that, that's exactly what Mr Crew said, though quite how we're going to achieve that result I'm blowed if I know. By the way, where are you billeted?"

"It's funny you ask that, Sir, and when I tell you you'll never believe it. It's every soldiers dream – we're in the WAAFs quarters!! Well not exactly in their quarters you understand Sir, but in a little annexe next door so every time we go back to our rooms we see half dressed WAAFs through the windows. It's very uplifting as you might say, Sir, so it is."

The laughter following this was interrupted by a light tapping on the door. Paddy opened it, immediately stood to attention saying, "Good evening Sir," and then turning to David said, "Mr Burton Sir."

"Come in Burton, come in. Now Paddy, will you go along to Mr Crew and ask him to come along if he will be so kind."

"I will that Sir and I'll be back in half an hour to see you off to dinner."

"Thank you Paddy."

Burton was about twenty-four or thereabouts David thought as he gave him a rapid inspection. Medium height, medium build, badly needing a haircut, he had something of a hang-dog look behind the half smile.

"I am David Chandler, oh, and this is Charlie Crew," as Charlie came into the room, "what's your Christian name?"

"I'm James, they call me Jim."

"Well Jim give us the low down on the most desirable posting in the British Army, apart from the presence of one Ponsonby, apparently," quipped Charlie.

"So you've heard about him already have you?" replied Jim Burton dejectedly. "He really is the absolute terminus, and Flavell is as bad. Nothing is ever right for either of them. They ridicule you in front of the men, they play off the platoon sergeants against the officers, as a result as soon as the platoon commanders get their second pip they apply for a draught and off they go. The only saving grace is that they both get off the aerodrome as fast as they can each day and rarely come to the mess in the evening, except on Thursday's when the C.O. comes."

"The C.O. seems a pretty bright spark – hasn't he noticed any of this?" asked David.

"Well, being a detached community as it were they can get away with murder, but I suspect both the C.O. and the adjutant have a pretty good idea. On the other hand when the C.O.'s here they are both on their best behaviour, as they are during the occasional C.O.'s inspection. We don't get inspected very much as we are so committed to all the guard duties and patrols we have to do. This means there's only part of a platoon ever available at any one time."

"What about the platoon sergeants?"

"They've all been in for some while and like all old soldiers just keep their heads down and wait for better days. I think all three would be pretty good if they had the right leadership and were able to do their jobs in a proper manner."

David looked at his watch, "I don't know about you two but my stomach thinks my throat's cut – lets get some dinner. Five minutes back here and we'll go in together – agreed?"

They had an extremely good meal during which a number of the R.A.F. officers came over and made the two newcomers welcome.

"I think I may well begin to enjoy this place," was Charlie's considered opinion eyeing a little group of WAAF officers at another table, one of whom was particularly pretty and vivacious.

Jim, perceiving the direction Charlie's eyes were taking observed with a smile, "Nothing below squadron leader tempts them I'm afraid Charlie." It was the first time they had seen a smile on his face.

"That, my dear old sport, I consider to be a challenge. See me in a week's time!"

At five to nine the next morning the two new platoon commanders presented themselves at the company office, having made the journey from their quarters on the bicycles provided for them. At their entry Rifleman Roberts sprang to attention. David said, "Good morning," and Roberts sat down again. Inwardly smiling, David said to himself, "Well we've shaken at least one bastard up already."

Nine o'clock prompt became twenty minutes to ten before Ponsonby arrived, clearly hung-over. Since he had to take company orders at ten o'clock, which is dealing with the men on disciplinary charges of various sorts, he had very little time with his platoon commanders. His instructions therefore were, "You'd better get to your platoons and sort them out. Chandler, you take One platoon, Crew, Three platoon, and you Burton can carry on ballsing up Two platoon as usual." They saluted and walked out.

Jim Burton showed the newcomers which huts were which; David's being the nearest to the company office.

"There's a NAAFI van which comes at about eleven, when all the men have a break," Jim informed them, "how about you two coming into my platoon office for a general chinwag – I'll organise the tea and wads?" This agreed, David walked into his hut. As he entered, a corporal standing just inside the door called the men inside to attention and saluted. David returned the salute and then told the men to stand easy.

"Where is everybody Corporal?"

"Sergeant Ayres is guard commander, some of the men are on guard, three on report, three on leave and three sick."

Crikey, what a start thought David. Of a platoon of thirty-six he had barely twenty men.

"Alright, everyone up this end," he called, and they all moved down between the rows of double bunks positioned against each wall. He introduced himself, told them he would see each man in turn and assured them that if they had any problems or complaints he was there to help them if he possibly could or find somebody else who could if he couldn't. In return he expected 100% effort from every single man, immaculate turnout, immaculate weapons, total loyalty to the regiment, to their comrades and to himself. He ended by saying, "I know that continually being on guard is a morale sopping situation. It's as boring as hell, but it's got to be done. When you're not on guard, I will try and make your training and recreational periods as lively as I can to offset the monotony of guard duty. That's all for now." The corporal called them to attention and saluted, David said, "Carry on," and then asked the corporal to come into the platoon office with him.

He found Corporal Corrigan to be a first class man. He was, he judged, in his late twenties, big for a rifleman, over six feet tall and heavily built, showing the marks of having had his face attended to inside a boxing ring at some time in the past, but to compliment his somewhat brutal appearance he had a modest, unassuming method of address. David thought to himself, "He doesn't have to make a lot of noise or throw his weight around; few people would step out of line with him in the first place."

The next day Ponsonby was more civil and they met Captain Flavell for the first time. They assumed the civility on the part of the major was because of the forthcoming dinner with the C.O. Flavell was the archetypal dissolute looking son of the landed gentry. As Charlie remarked later, "He's a dead ringer for Reilly-Ffoull in Jane's strip in the Mirror."

"I would have thought you only read the Times?" Jim had replied.

"Oh I do old sport; I was reading David's paper when I spotted 'Jane'."

The meeting with the colonel and the adjutant went off quietly, Ponsonby even telling the colonel the new officers were settling in well. The next day, however, the major was back to his previous bad tempered self, having made up for time lost in the bar caused by the colonel's visit the previous evening by doubling his input in the time left when the colonel had gone.

During the following week David got into the routine of being duty officer every third day. His query to Jim as to why Flavell didn't take an occasional turn of this chore was answered by, "You're joking of course – his bed in Norwich is much too comfortable." David decided not to pursue the subject further but he did ask how it was that the major could indulge his love of the races and point to points and be away most days and shouldn't Flavell be on the airfield at least at nights in case anything startling happened?"

"They think they're a law unto themselves, but one day they'll drop a clanger," was Jim's considered opinion on these points. The clanger was to be dropped much earlier than anyone had expected. The following Tuesday, David was duty officer, sleeping fully dressed, as all duty officers did, in a small room next to the company office. At three o'clock on the Wednesday morning the telephone shrilled, startling him awake.

"D Company office."

"Is that you David?" – it was the adjutant, "there's a red alert. The Home Guard have reported parachutists dropping between Cromer and Aylsham and east of you in the Brundall district on the road to Acle. Stand to and report every half hour."

"Message understood."

David went immediately into action. He woke the duty orderly, who in turn rushed half dressed into the next room to get the bugler to sound the alarm. He used the field telephone to alert the main guard at the bomb dump. He telephoned the officers' mess but they had already been signalled, and had passed the message on to the army officers, both Rifles and Royal Artillery, the latter would be manning the Bofors guns and searchlights. Everything being organised, David awaited the arrival of Major Ponsonby and Captain Flavell. After five minutes or so Charlie arrived, very out of breath, after pedalling like mad against a strong wind.

"Have you seen the major and Flavell?" asked David.

"Not a sight dear old boy," replied Charlie, "I'll dash off to my platoon posts – Jim has gone straight to the bomb dump defences."

"Right – I'll stay here and man the command post until one of them arrives – will you tell my platoon sergeant where I am and that I'll join him as soon as I can?"

"Will do – see you later," and he rushed off.

The C.S.M. appeared, still only half dressed and shivering with cold.

"All ammunition and grenades issued Sir," he reported, followed by, "No major or captain Sir?"

David was just trying to provide a diplomatic answer when the telephone shrilled out again.

"D Company."

"David – is Major Ponsonby there?" David hesitated just a fraction too long for the adjutant at the other end of the line.

"David, don't bugger about, where are Ponsonby and Flavell?"

"To be honest I don't know – all officers were informed at the mess, Charlie and Jim are both in position."

"Right, you stay where you are and take over for now, the C.O. and Major Webber are on their way over."

The C.S.M. looked at him enquiringly.

"The C.O. and 2.I.C. are on the way here, better get the rest of your clothes on Mister Townley," said David with a grin, "though what the hell they're going to say when they find me in charge God alone knows."

"If you ask me Sir, they might be quite pleased at the turn of events," hinted the C.S.M. You didn't have eighteen years in the same job without learning a thing or two.

A quarter of an hour later, the colonel and his second in command arrived. To his question as to the whereabouts of Ponsonby and Flavell, David could only give the same answer as he had given to the adjutant.

"Right Michael," to the 2.I.C. "you stay here and take command if you will, David you come with me."

They went out to the staff car, "Take me to Major Ponsonby's room."

David gave directions and then sped round the perimeter road to the senior officers' quarters where Ponsonby was housed. The C.O. walked straight into the room where he found the major still half dressed from what he had worn the previous evening, slumped out face down on his bed absolutely dead drunk. A figure appeared behind them in the doorway and stood rigidly to attention.

247

"Who are you?" asked the C.O.

"Pickering Sir, I'm the major's batman. I tried to wake him up, I even lifted him up but he hit me across the mouth and went back on his bed again." Pickering's mouth was still trickling with blood and there were blood stains on his shirt.

"Where's Captain Flavell?"

"He'll be in Norwich with his woman Sir, he takes his batman with him."

"Do you know the address of this woman Pickering?"

"No Sir, I can't help you there."

"Alright lad, get off to the M.I. room and get that mouth seen to and then report to Major Webber at D Company office – alright?"

"Yes Sir."

"You've had a rotten time Pickering; we'll do something to make it up to you."

"Thank you Sir."

"See if you can find a bucket David."

David went out into the corridor and soon found a broom cupboard in which there was an enamel bowl. He took it back to the C.O.

"Fill it up and douse him with it," he was told. David, with a considerable amount of internal satisfaction, did precisely that. Ponsonby came to, coughing and spluttering.

"What the bloody hell are you playing at?" he yelled, seeing only David through his fuddled gaze.

"Stand up," barked the C.O. Ponsonby looked round myopically as the command made its way slowly through his bovine brain. He attempted to stand but fell back again across the bed.

"Sit him up."

David reached under the major's armpits, swivelled him round, pulled him up the bed and let him fall back against the head board, causing his head to crack against the wall in the process, with a recurrence of the inner satisfaction he had previously experienced. "That's one for Jim," he said to himself.

"Major Ponsonby, you are under close arrest. You will not leave this room except for meals until I send for you. Do you understand?" Ponsonby nodded. The colonel continued, "Because you are drunk I will write this order and leave it here on your table." He took a sheet of paper from his message pad and repeated the order in writing. He continued, "Where is Captain Flavell?" Ponsonby shook his head. "Did you authorise him to sleep away from his duties?" Again Ponsonby shook his head. "Is that no?"

Ponsonby replied, "No I didn't."

They left Ponsonby lying on his wet bed and went back to the car. As they drove back to company headquarters the colonel was quiet for a while, finally breaking his silence to say, "I never ever dreamt it possible that a field officer in the Rifles could behave like that. I've seen even generals drunk before, but to hit your servant across the mouth..." He was lost for words for the moment, but then continued, "Get to you post now David, I'd be grateful if not too much of this got out. I shall be giving them both the boot this afternoon, assuming this present alert is over, and I shall need you to be there should I have to have your corroboration as to what we saw and so on. Tony will be contacting you during the morning." The car stopped, David got out, saluted and doubled off to his platoon headquarters.

At nine o'clock on the Wednesday morning, they were stood down. It transpired that the parachutists spotted were in fact the crews of three German bombers each of which had been hit on a raid on Liverpool and which had tried to limp home across East Anglia. By coincidence, two of them gave up south of Cromer, twelve men from the two planes bailing out, and the third one did likewise near Brundall. All were rounded up by the local Home Guard units along with military police detachments sent from Britannia Barracks in Norwich. It was a false alarm, but proved to be a good exercise in the ability of the various services to answer an emergency when called upon so to do.

Major Webber stayed on at D Company office. At ten minutes to ten, Captain Flavell breezed in and was somewhat taken aback by the sight of his superior officer sitting, obviously unshaven, in Ponsonby's chair. He suddenly had funny feelings in his spine as he half-heartedly saluted and said, "Hello Sir, what's up?"

Webber sat steely eyed.

"You are under close arrest by the C.O.'s order. Go to your room. Stay there. Do not contact any other person until you are sent for. Understood?"

"But why Sir," he whined, "what have I done?"

"I've nothing to add. Get out!" Flavell turned and slouched out. Major Webber was in half a mind to make him come back and salute before he left, but instead let him get away with it.

At ten thirty a message came from the C.O. that the two officers were to pack their kit ready to be loaded on to a fifteen hundred weight to leave at 14.30 hours. Major Webber had a brainwave. He called Jim Burton in.

"Jim, I would like you to take a copy of this message to Captain Flavell and Major Ponsonby to ensure they receive it. Do not, of course, enter into any discussion with them about the matter," he sat for a moment with the vestiges of a twinkle in his eye and continued, "oh and try not to gloat too much."

Later that afternoon the two officers arrived at Colonel Brindlesby-Gore's office, noticing as they arrived the brigadier's staff car outside. They were ushered in, saluted, and were left standing. The brigadier started the proceedings.

"I've heard of your disgraceful behaviour," Flavell started to interrupt.

"Be quiet," roared the brigadier. He was a small man, known in the regiment, though not to his face, as 'Half Pint'. He had a voice as commanding as any sergeant major, was seven stone of nothing but whipcord and leather, and as tough as old boots. "I've heard of your disgraceful behaviour and I intend that you shall be called to account. Tony, will you put Captain Flavell in your office, where he will remain. Do you understand Flavell? Rejoin us then please, Tony."

"Yes Sir, of course."

Ponsonby, left on his own, was beginning to regain some of his normal arrogance.

"May I ask why I've been dragged here Sir?"

"You may not. Neither were you dragged here, so don't compound your outrageous behaviour with insolence to me. Firstly you have been absenting yourself from your post to follow your own pleasures continuously for some weeks that we know about. That is a court martial offence. Secondly, you deserted your post as a result of being drunk during a general alert. That is a court martial offence for which in days gone by you would have been shot. Thirdly, and most seriously, you struck your servant, causing him actual bodily harm. He had to have three stitches inside his mouth because of you. That, too, is a court martial offence. I've no doubt that when Colonel Brindlesby-Gore goes into the paper work he will find many other offences of a lesser nature, including misuse of War Department transport, which will be added to the score. I am giving you a straightforward choice. You can either resign your commission now or you can be court-martialled. If you resign your commission you may well be called up into the ranks again when, and if, your age group is called. I shall ensure you will never be an officer again. The only reason I've given you this option is because I would be most unhappy for the name of your fine regiment to be besmirched by having your crimes made public. Well, what's it to be?"

"Can I have some time to talk to my family solicitor about this?"

"SIR," bellowed the brigadier, "you call me Sir until you become a civilian, then you can call me what you like, and I you – understand?" he continued.

"You may make one telephone call from Captain Flamborough's office. I will give you half an hour at the end of which I shall get the court martial papers drafted. Right Tony, take him away and bring in Flavell. Oh, and from now on you will revert to your substantive rank of captain, I don't want you swanning around the valleys of South Wales calling yourself a major." A very downcast looking Flavell came back with Tony.

"Captain Flavell, I'll be short and sweet with you. As from now you revert to your substantive rank of lieutenant. You will return to your company office and hand over to Captain Laurenson from C Company who is there at the moment. Provided there are no improprieties in the imprest or other accounts you will, first thing tomorrow morning, travel to Colchester where you will be issued with tropical kit. You will join a troopship leaving Southampton over the weekend for West Africa where you will join a unit training soldiers from the Gold Coast. The C.O. of that unit is a very old Sandhurst friend of mine, I have wired him your details, you will have a very strict eye kept on you in the hope that you can redeem yourself. Have you understood all that? I would add that the alternative is a court martial for being absent from your unit at the least, or even desertion for which, without doubt, you would be cashiered. Well, what have you to say?"

"I'll go to Colchester in the morning Sir."

"In which case you can go into Captain Flamborough's office and take one of those pips off immediately."

Tony took Flavell off and returned with Ponsonby. The major's face was an absolute study in apoplexy. The whites of his eyes were almost as red as his face which itself was of a similar hue to one of the countless bottles of claret which had passed his lips over the years. The hatred of his expression was such that neither of his senior officers had any doubt about his decision.

"Well," barked the brigadier.

"My lawyer advises me to resign."

"Tony, take him away and draw up the necessary papers, see that he changes into plain clothes, take him to Thorpe station where he will buy his own ticket to wherever he wants to go. And remember this Ponsonby; we can still prefer the charges against you regarding

Pickering if it were ever necessary."

Ponsonby turned without a further word and walked out. There was silence in the room for a few moments until the brigadier turned to the colonel.

"You know Stuart; you don't come out of this very well. I know you've not been here long but bastards like that can ruin a good company in next to no time, you should have sorted it out."

"I know Sir, I gave him too much rope, I was just hoping he'd hang himself. It won't happen again."

"Make sure it doesn't," and with that gentle rocket, the subject closed.

Chapter Twenty Two

It was twenty-five minutes past one on the morning of Saturday the twenty sixth of January 1941 that Rose went to her mother's room to tell her that she thought she had started. Ruth telephoned Doctor Power, their family doctor and Rotary friend, who said he would come on round – "But don't expect to be a grandmother again in the next ten minutes – these first timers sometimes keep us waiting for days!" In the event, Rose lived up to her reputation for not making life difficult for others by producing a six pound ten ounce boy at a quarter to six in the morning. She had the baby at home. He was to be christened Jeremy Richard Frederick. All had gone remarkably smoothly.

Anni in the meantime was still waiting. When the news from Rose was telephoned to her at seven o'clock she sent a message back, "Tell Rose somebody always has to come second!" But only two days later she too was taken in to hospital in view of a possible slight complication, which might prove to be troublesome. It wasn't and at twelve noon Anni too produced a bonny bouncing boy at seven and a half pounds lustily squalling its head off.

The news as it occurred was telegraphed to David who found himself wetting the babies' heads in the R.A.F. mess on two evenings with Charlie and Jim, along with Mark Laurenson, who the three platoon commanders hoped would be made up to major and take command of D Company. When David telephoned Chandlers Lodge on the evening of the 28th to ensure all was well, he was much amused by his mother recounting the unforgettable sight of two sixteen stone Royal Marine majors tiptoeing around in their army boots whispering, "Mustn't wake the baby up."

The next evening when he telephoned, his mother said, "Ernie's here and would like a word."

After the initial preambles Ernie said, "David, both Anni, her father and I would like to name the baby after you. If it hadn't been for you neither Anni nor her father would be here, and might have been dead by now for all we know, and if it hadn't been for you I wouldn't have been in Sandbury Engineering and met Anni as I did. Will you agree? Oh, and by the way, we would like you to be a godfather."

David paused for a few moments. "I really am overwhelmed. I am delighted and very flattered, I really am, and as for being his godfather,

I'll have to look up the manual of responsibilities, if there is such a thing to find out what it entails. Whatever the duties are I agree, and tell Anni from me she's a very clever girl."

The battalion padré visited D Company once a week to hold a short service and to talk to any of the men who had problems or were seeking advice. After his visit the following day David tackled him about his forthcoming duties as a godfather. The padré, a genial character far removed from the hell-fire and brimstone brigade, put the situation to him that although his prime duty was to ensure the child was brought up in the Christian faith, learnt its catechism and so on, the main responsibility beyond that was to provide a solid reliable firm base the boy could approach at any time in his life for advice and comfort if needed.

"Oh, he'll get that alright," David assured him, then went on to tell him about Jeremy and how he died, and if he had knocked out the tank five minutes earlier Jeremy would still be alive. The padré let him talk on, recognising how deep seated his anguish at the loss of his friend and the tragedy of his sister and unborn child was, and how it had caused such suffering within him over these past months. David then went on to tell him of the loss of his wife just as he was beginning to reconcile himself a little to the death of his friend.

The padré paused and put his hands on David's shoulders looking him straight in the eye. "David, old son, I'm not going to give you all that guff about God moving in a mysterious way. The reasons some have to suffer, as you have, are quite unfathomable. It is a fact that time is a great healer, but there are no short cuts. If I could invent a time machine to help you I would but I can't. I'm a great believer in prayer and I shall pray for you, as I'm sure your parents and relatives do already, that's the spiritual side dealt with. On the physical side, keep busy, keep writing regularly to your friends and family, and whenever you feel like it pick up the blower and get in touch with me and I'll pass on all the latest gen from around the Battalion. That means day or night – understood?"

"Thanks padré, you're a brick."

Back at Sandbury both girls were being inundated with visitors. Buffy and Rita were on the first available train after having received the news, arriving in the late afternoon, bringing with them in addition to their customary gift of rabbits and hares, the beautiful pram they had bought months before when the news of the forthcoming event had first been passed to them. Getting it to Romsey station on the back luggage grid of the taxi there, getting it into the guard's van to Waterloo, on to the taxi at Waterloo, into the guard's van at Victoria and finally on and off the taxi at Sandbury, was accompanied on each occasion by Buffy fussing and telling porters and taxi drivers, "Be careful, make sure it's not scratched, handle it carefully – it's for my grandson you know – mustn't have anything happen to it."

As Rita told the amused audience at Chandlers Lodge, "I think he spent more in tips ensuring its well being than we spent in the fares to get here!"

As soon as Anni was allowed visitors, everyone visited her in turn, including the majors. The matron had been to see her each day. She had been appointed at the New Year but had known Megan for several years; Anni was therefore given a certain amount of V.I.P. treatment. Matron Duffy was somewhat removed from the standard conception of her species in that she was in her late thirties, tall, slim, classically good looking and very Irish. On the evening the majors called she chanced to visit the side ward to say goodbye to Anni who would be leaving the next day, the matron's day off. As she entered, the two vast khaki clad frames arose as one and were duly introduced by Anni. They chattered together for several minutes until matron said she must be leaving, at which there were further handshakes and Ken Johnson hurrying to open the door, moving extremely quickly and lightly for such a big man. As matron passed through he said, "I do hope we meet again."

She looked straight at him with her beautiful blue Irish eyes and replied, "Yes, I hope so too Major."

Having bid farewell to Anni and the beautiful baby, the two walked home through the bitterly cold clear night, looking even more gargantuan in their heavy greatcoats. After a few minutes silence Ken casually asked, "What did you think of the matron?"

"Utterly gorgeous, but far, far too good for you."

"I think I'll give her a ring."

"Do you mean a telephone ring or a diamond ring?"

"She'd probably think twice about consorting with the licentious soldiery, but I must say she is something very very special."

When they got to Chandlers Lodge, Megan and Harry were there. Harry's company was clearing bomb damage rubble from Deptford and dumping it in a disused quarry near Greenhithe in North Kent. Harry had been put in charge of the dumping and levelling in the quarry base, the work being carried out by a platoon of the Pioneer Corps aided by a cheerful corporal of the Royal Engineers from nearby Chatham operating a noisy, smoke-belching steam-roller. As it would have taken as long to get back to Deptford each night as it did to get to Sandbury, Harry had been able to persuade his company commander to let him have a sleeping out pass for the duration of the job. He was not alone in this. Several of the drivers working in Deptford and with homes in East and South East London, went home after their day's work – there was no reason why they shouldn't.

After supplying the two officers with a glass of Whitbread's, and their having given an account of how Anni looked, how beautiful the baby was and so on, Ivan very casually remarked, "Oh, and I think a certain member of the staff has not escaped the notice of a certain person who, so far, has escaped the predatory clutches of the fairer sex."

"Who would you be referring to I wonder," Megan queried.

"Hospitals are very dangerous places," continued Harry, "I went on an errand of mercy to visit my young brother and look how I got trapped. They really ought to ban visiting hours; you're very vulnerable with all that anaesthetic around deadening your senses."

"Come on Ivan," added Ruth, "tell us the whole story."

"Well, we were chatting away to Anni when in walks this vision of authoritative stunnery leaving Ken open mouthed in his obvious admiration of her image and presence. Electric sparks cracked through the air," his voice became more dramatic, "there were only two people in the room, transported from our earthly sphere!

"Oh shut up you twit," Ken butted in.

"But who was it?" asked Megan.

"Your boss – the matron, and I must admit that with your being there and the matron being there, there is no other hospital I would like to be in should I ever need one, so I can't really blame the poor stricken chap."

"Well come on Ken, tell us all about it," asked Ruth. "was it really love at first sight or what?"

"First of all, I will agree I was very taken with the lady in question. Secondly I did say I hope we meet again, and she was kind enough to say that she hoped so too. Thirdly, I noticed after I said 'I hope we meet again,' she was wearing a wedding ring, and I'm not the type who goes after married women. Finally, I shall give her a ring because I'd like to know more about her."

Ruth looked at Megan. "What do you know about her?" she asked.

"I've known her for about ten years. She is a widow. Her husband died of T.B. about five or six years ago. She is highly intelligent, very firm, very fair and a good leader. She has two children, a boy of nine and a girl of seven. They live now in Sandbury – anything else you want to know?"

There was a pause, broken by Ken. "Yes, what's her telephone number."

To general laughter the gathering broke up, leaving Ken with a firm feeling that he was about to embark on an adventure new to him. Before the war as a junior officer in the marines, he had travelled the world on the big ships, never putting roots down anywhere for long. The one or two girls he had met in England and become fond of, soon realised the disadvantages of being attached to someone who might be in Malta or China or somewhere equally far removed at any time, and had settled for more mundane partnerships. He had, therefore, long come to the conclusion he was wedded to the service and when war came and he found himself back in Plymouth, he threw himself into his work to the exclusion of social life, quickly becoming promoted to captain and then major. It was there in the middle of 1940, after a leave at his parents' farm at Glastonbury, that he renewed this acquaintance with Ivan, they having first served together in Singapore three years before. He was instructed to set up an assault boat training cadre with Ivan as his second in command into which project he had thrown himself with enthusiasm, but even he, with all his expertise and knowledge, had no conception of the enormous role this method of attack would play in the coming four years.

The air attacks had slackened during January, mainly due to bad weather. On the 29th, Dover was shelled, bringing a new dimension to the suffering of the people of Kent and the South East. On the first of February, all Home Guard company commanders were promoted to major, Jack Hooper therefore now receiving that rank, and Fred as his second in command now became a captain. Ruth was beginning to be a little worried about Fred. With the long hours he worked at the factory, combined with his Home Guard duties taking up what little spare time he had at weekends along with the occasional evening during the week, he was beginning to look, as she put it, "A bit peaky." One evening, as they sat alone for once, she broached the subject to him by saying, "Fred dear, you won't overdo things will you? You're not indestructible you know and you work so hard. Couldn't you take a few days off and let me look after you or, better still, go and stay with Rita and Buffy?"

"What and leave you with two marines in the house? Not Pygmalion likely," he joked.

"Well, will you go and have a check-up with John Power just to put my mind at rest? I've been very unhappy with that continual cough you've suffered these last two weeks."

"If that's what you want my love – anything for a quiet life. You fix it up with him, preferably during my lunch hour if he can manage it, your wish as you can see, is my command."

And so it was arranged for the fifth of February, although it transpired as he walked to John Power's surgery, his indestructibility was, in fact, severely put to the test. Two days before, the Luftwaffe had been back over Kent, Sandbury on this occasion, although being flown over, not having received any close attention. As he left the factory the mournful wail of the sirens echoed around the town, but Fred decided to push on, it was only a ten-minute walk to the surgery. He had got half way with no cover to hand when he heard the sound of planes and the heavy anti-aircraft battery on the north of the town opening up. This, he said to himself, is definitely no place to be, but having said that he firstly found himself in the midst of a veritable cascade of shrapnel bouncing in showers of sparks off the road in front of and behind him, followed by the scream of a bomb being jettisoned from the plane on the receiving end of the ack-ack fire. He threw himself off the road into the narrow ditch at the side, the ditch itself having a foot or so of very muddy water in it. The bomb hurtled down exploding in the soft earth of the field at the side of the road some fifty or sixty yards away. Apart from being momentarily deafened, leaving his head singing for a while and being covered in fine quality Kentish soil, he was unhurt despite the fact the bomb had landed so close. As he said later, being in the ditch and with the bomb embedding itself in such soft ground, the blast had passed well above him. He had barely had time to collect his thoughts and climb back on to the road, when he heard the unmistakable sound of Ernie's motorbike.

"You alright guv'nor? Jesus Christ, what a mess you're in," and mess was no exaggeration. He was covered in black mud and earth from head to toe, water was dripping out of his sleeves and down his trousers on to his feet, he'd been wearing a trilby which was floating half in and half out of the water and he'd lost one shoe which was somewhere in the bottom of the ditch.

"What are you doing here you lummock, you should be in the shelter," expostulated Fred.

"And leave you to fight the Luftwaffe on your own? Now I couldn't do that could I? Anyway, let's find your shoe and get you home before anything else livens the day up."

When they drove up to Chandlers Lodge dodging the razor sharp pieces of shrapnel in the road; there was no answer to their knock at the front door. Fred having left his keys on his office desk, walked with Ernie round to the back of the house as the 'all clear' started, to be confronted by a startled Ruth, Rose carrying Jeremy, and Mrs Cloke who had all just emerged from the Anderson shelter.

"Before you say anything, I am perfectly alright, I dived into a ditch when the bomb came down, the ditch was a little on the damp side. Now, will you kindly ring John and tell him why I haven't turned up and I'll be there in an hour if that's OK by him, and will you also kindly run me a bath while I get out of these things. Oh and by the way love, what you said about my not being indestructible – I'm beginning to think I am!" Ruth and Rose hugged him, wet though he was.

John Power was not so cheerful. "I'm going to be blunt with you Fred. Your left lung is not as it should be. You're to go to bed immediately and I'll come and see you in a couple of days to see how you're getting on, but you're to stay there for a week at least. If there there's no improvement I'll call a specialist in, and as they say in the Home Guard – that's an order."

"But what about the baby?" asked Fred.

"You're not having a baby are you? By God, we'll make a fortune if you are."

"No you crackpot. We've got a young baby in the house as you well know. I don't want to pass any germs on to him."

"No fear of that as long as you don't cuddle him up or anything daft like that."

So Fred had his first enforced rest in years, Ernie coming in daily to report and receive advice and instructions, the time strictly limited by Ruth to fifteen minutes morning and evening and not a second longer. Other visitors were given five minutes, no more, except for Jack. At the end of the week John declared an improvement and that another week should see him up and about and able to go to the factory for four hours a day – no more until he gave the all clear. Despite Fred's misgivings about his absence, the world didn't stop turning, the factory didn't grind to a halt, the Home Guard still marched more or less in step, and Japan continued to assure the world 'that they did not and would not contemplate any military or political hegemony over territories in South East Asia'. This was followed shortly afterwards by the new Japanese Ambassador to Australia on his arrival in Canberra stating, "Japanese/Australian friendship should be cultivated to the full."

As Jack said, "If you believe all that you'll believe anything."

One advantage Fred experienced as a result of his enforced leisure was that he could actually read the newspapers. Normally all he could manage was a brief look at the headlines relying, in the main, for news from the wireless. The newsreaders now gave their names when they were about to start their programmes, thus the format became 'This is the news and this is Alvar Liddell reading it.' As a result everybody got to know Alvar Liddell's and the other voices and straightaway knew it was the truth, the whole truth and nothing but the truth, since no one with such lovely voices as that would tell fibs or half-truths. Fred now was able to read the complete newspaper for the first time almost in years. Information leaking out of Norway through Sweden shocked him. Himmler had stated publicly that Norway would become an integral part of Greater Germany. At the same time, not so publicly, he was opening concentration camps to house all the Norwegian dissidents and the usual categories that filled the camps in the rest of occupied Europe. He had now abolished professional secrecy. Doctors, lawyers, clergy, post office officials and so on were no longer allowed to refuse to divulge confidential information to the Gestapo, on the pain of being incarcerated. Information passed through Sweden, itself doing a bumper trade with Germany, particularly in iron ore, was that Norway was being plundered of its food by the Nazis. Despite all this despoliation, there were still traitors who formed a Norwegian Nazi Regiment this, Fred found, barely believable until Jack said, "It might well have happened here old boy, it might well have happened here."

News was also released of the first British airborne attack on the enemy. On the tenth of February a small group of the newly formed parachute force, along with a section of Royal Engineers, parachuted into Southern Italy with the intention of blowing up the Tragino aqueduct which carried the main water supply for a province of two million people and two major naval harbours, the forty odd men in the party only partially succeeded in their efforts, but sufficient damage was done to rate it a success. Considerable knowledge of the problems of mounting airborne attacks were gained and above all, the enemy was shown we could still, contrary to their beliefs, pack a punch to be reckoned with.

During the second week of Fred's indisposition, Ernie arrived most unusually at three o'clock in the afternoon, apologising to Ruth but asking if he could have an important chat with the guv'nor.

Uncharacteristically Ruth said, "What do you want to bother him about so urgently?" to which question Ernie hesitated for a few moments before replying that he was very sorry but he was not allowed to tell her. Instantly Ruth apologised for her abrupt question continuing with, "Of course you must see him, I should know that you of all people would not worry him if it wasn't absolutely necessary."

Fred's question was even more to the point.

"What the hell do you want? Has the place burnt down or something?"

"I've got some M.A.P. people at the factory guv'nor." M.A.P. was the Ministry of Aircraft Production.

"What do they want; we're up to date with all the R.A.F. contracts aren't we?"

"Yes, right on the button as always. They've come to see us because they've heard we have a very high quality wood working shop and they want us to build some assemblies for an airplane."

"You're joking – a wooden airplane? – They went out with the ark!" exclaimed Fred.

"Not this one," continued Ernie, "I've seen the drawings and it is the most beautiful aircraft I've ever seen and it's made entirely of wood. They want us to do tail frame assemblies, but they need to know whether we can cope since the first deliveries have to be made in July."

"Can we?"

"Yes."

"Right, go and tell them."

As Fred lay back on the pillows mulling over this short conversation he reflected on how total was his reliance on his right-hand man, how great was the trust he reposed in this good-natured utterly loyal colleague. Then he thought, 'a wooden airplane, what the hell will they dream up next?' But that wooden airplane was the Mosquito, one of the greatest and most versatile aircraft ever built as well as being arguably the most beautiful piece of machinery ever designed, and Sandbury Engineering proudly made their parts for it right up to the end of the war by which time no fewer than thirteen thousand had been built all around the world.

With Ruth's no-nonsense control of her husband's sickroom, his food, his visitors, his medication and, above all, his strict adherence to 'doctor's orders', Fred made rapid progress. By the end of the third week, during which he had been allowed up and to take short walks when the weather was reasonable, he was given the all clear. However this was under the strict understanding he spent only four hours a day at the works for the first week, and not to go mad after that. "If he does," said John to Ruth, "you telephone me straight away. This is going to be a long war and we can't afford people like him cracking up when it can be avoided. After all, he is now turned the sixty mark even if he does feel otherwise."

A week or so after his return, a telephone call from Ruth to the factory informed Fred that a friend was on his way down to see him, and with Ruth promptly putting down her ear piece, he was left mystified as to whom it could be. He had not long to wait when there came a knock on his door and Ray Osbourne, wearing battledress, was shown in. He was made most welcome by Fred, who called Ernie in to say hello, and was especially made a fuss of by Miss Russell, Fred's middle-aged gem of a secretary, so much so that when the tea was brought in Fred remarked, "I notice we've got the special biscuits out today Gladys," and aside to Ray, "only extra special people as judged by Miss Russell here get the best biscuits."

"And only the best biscuits are good enough for heroes," retorted Miss Russell, looking deliberately at the ribbon of the Military Cross on Ray's battledress.

After a short period of tea drinking and an explanation of his presence in Sandbury – "I had a day's leave so I thought I'd take a trip down to see the babies!" – Ray asked whether it would be possible to have a look at the factory.

Fred answered that it would be a pleasure to show him round, although there were two places he was not allowed to take visitors into without prior ministry approval – "But you'll see most of what we do." It would be difficult to judge who enjoyed the conducted tour more, Fred was proud of what they were doing and enjoyed showing it to a professional engineer. Ray was keenly interested in the techniques developed by the company necessitated by having to rapidly solve problems in an atmosphere of urgency caused by the war and meeting delivery schedules. When they got back to the office an hour or so later, Ernie was waiting for them and was joined in the discussion which followed, a discussion which would have a very great affect on Sandbury Engineering in a few years time.

It started by Ray asking, "What will you do when war production ends Mr Chandler?"

"Why, do you think we're going to win then?" joked Fred.

"Without doubt to my mind. But seriously, hundreds of firms, possibly thousands, will find themselves without full order books from the ministries, and will be at a loss as how to cope. I know there will be the inevitable slimming down, and probably you will expect better margins in peace time than you get on government contracts, but even so, I've no doubt you've thought about the problem."

"Yes we certainly have, that is whenever we get five minutes to spare to think! Obviously as war production reduces one hopes that peace production will fill its place. We have our agricultural market, which after all is why we first started. There will be a greater emphasis on mechanisation on farms after the war; there's no doubt about that. Our specialist vehicle market will be developed, and so on. Ernie here, and Jack Hooper, both keep their ears to the ground, so if we're left behind I shall be very surprised. Having said that, you're an engineer as well as being a 'Royal Engineer' – have you got anything in mind?"

"Plastics."

There was a silence following that one definitely spoken word. Ray continued.

"To my mind one of the biggest developments when the war ends will be in the field of plastics. As you know, the first true plastic, Bakelite, was invented as long ago as 1909, but its uses are limited. DuPont invented nylon in 1935, which most people associate with stockings but which can be used for all manner of things."

Ernie interrupted. "Ray, please excuse my ignorance but what exactly are plastics, my mind runs on plasticine when I hear the word mentioned."

"Well, put chemically they consist of numerous synthetic materials obtained mainly from the refinement of petroleum products. They consist of giant molecules called polymers. In practical terms they are seen as granules, which can be heated and formed in various ways. Thermoplastics when heated retain their chemical properties after they are cooled; thermosetting plastics are softened by heating in the same way, but then set hard and cannot be softened again. I.C.I. are one of the leaders in their field, they invented a material called polythene just before the war started, one day everyone will be using it."

"Two questions," interjected Fred, "what is celluloid – is that a plastic? And secondly, how would we fit into all this?"

"Searching the depths of my not particularly brilliant memory," replied Ray, "your first question will only get an approximate answer. Celluloid is a plastic, but is obtained from natural not synthetic products. It was discovered by an American called John Hyatt in the last century. It is, of course, very flammable, much more so than synthetic plastics.

Second question – hundreds of products currently made with metal, bowls, buckets, bottles and thousands of decorative components will be made of plastic as they will be cheaper, lighter and in many cases stronger. Where you might come in is either in the production of the final articles, or alternatively in the manufacture of the precision machinery required to make the end products." He paused. "Or both of course."

There was silence for a few moments. Running through Fred's mind was the fact that the company was doing so well they could readily put some money by to develop a project of this nature. There was no rush; it could be years before the war ended. He broke out of his reverie.

"Ray, could you get on paper all you've told us and as much else as you know and can find out? We'll pay you for your time of course."

"I shall gladly do that, but will be mortally offended if payment is mentioned," replied Ray with a grin.

"Well we can't risk your mortality, so we'll let that one pass for the time being! Anyway, when you've had a chance to set it out we'll have a day together at any time to suit you, along with Mr Hooper and Reg Church, our accountant. In the meantime, I see I shall have to make a couple of visits to the library so that at least I have a slight idea of what you're talking about."

"Me too," Ernie chimed in.

Ray said his goodbyes and walked back to Chandlers Lodge to keep his invitation for afternoon tea with the family. Anni and her father were there, but the main attraction as far as he was concerned was Rose, who he found utterly delightful without, it must be said, making his feelings obvious in any way. Rose, bound up as she was with her lovely new baby, her security within the family and the love of her in-laws had no perception whatsoever that close to her were three men, all admiring her as if from afar. Colonel Tim, for whom it had been more than a year ago love at first sight, Major Ivan and now Captain Ray. And then of course there was Charlie, not in love with her probably, but certainly could be if he thought about it.

Chapter Twenty Three

Things at Highmere improved dramatically during February. Captain Laurenson was promoted to company commander after a couple of weeks, and a Captain Fort-Smith came from the depot as second in command. Two suggestions from David were taken up. Firstly that only one platoon should be involved in guard duties on any one day. As a result of the fact that some duties were for twenty four hours and some for twelve hours, it interrupted the platoon's training over two days, but at least on the third day no one in the platoon was on duty so that the platoon commanders had a complete unit, other than the usual leave and sick parade personnel. The second suggestion was that they appoint a sports officer, and since he had suggested it, he was unanimously voted to fill the post. As he said to the others at dinner that night, "My father always told me never to volunteer – he'll never forgive me!" However, straight away he started a five-a-side football competition in the company, the men playing in plimsolls on an unused concrete dispersal point near the billets. He got the R.A.F. maintenance people to knock them up a couple of sets of goal posts, complete with nets, and then set about organising a knockout competition, each platoon providing five teams and a couple more from company headquarters. By the beginning of March the final two teams were ready to take the field, the C.O. was invited to see the clash and present the 'cup', an inexpensive trophy purchased by David on one of his excursions into Norwich. This rivalry, plus the fact that the men were able to have a kick about whenever they wanted to – weather permitting – did a great deal to lifting the spirits of over a hundred soldiers who had been so demoralised by the Ponsonby regime.

Another improvement affecting the platoon commanders was that the C.S.M. and the new second in command volunteered to do one 'duty officer' each week. The problem with the duty officer chore was that if one of the platoon commanders was on leave, the other two were on duty every other night. Having the two nights in the week taken over by the sergeant major and Captain Fort-Smith certainly eased the load.

They found living in the R.A.F. mess very interesting indeed. David had half expected the pilots to be a pretty brash tally-ho lot, but quite to the contrary, found them to be level-headed professional types using understatement as a way of life. Johnny Mathers, a flight lieutenant who piloted a Wellington was a prime example of this genre returning from Bremen in an aircraft which had been so badly damaged it was held together almost completely by its electrical cables, related to David the next evening that, "The old kite got a bit knocked about."

On another occasion a pilot remarked, "We had a bit of a prang this morning," which David subsequently learnt was the description of a Wellington landing with only one wheel, subsequently spinning round and round like a Catherine wheel when one wing tip hit the deck, gradually losing one section after another until it came to a standstill in a dozen different places. They loved their Wellingtons, describing the geodetic construction of the aircraft as being the brainchild of a genius, as indeed it was, having been designed by Barnes Wallis. The aircraft could be shot to pieces like a colander and would still fly, which fact gave a tremendous feeling of security to those who flew in them.

Often at night when David was on duty out on the airfield, he would look up at the sky and wonder where the chaps were he had been talking to the previous day, what sort of hell they were flying through to reach their targets. Like Mr Forster at Winchester, he had a deep-rooted feeling that other people were doing his dirty work for him, but when he voiced this viewpoint at dinner one evening, Jim Burton spoke to him quite strongly saying, "We can't all be at the sharp end all of the time or, for that matter, all at once," followed by Charlie rounding off with a jocular.

"Don't forget dear old boy, they also serve, etcetera, etcetera." Nevertheless, there was this consciousness they should be doing more.

One evening towards the end of February Paddy asked David if he could have a few words. The batman was getting his officer's service dress laid out for the Wednesday dinner night, a regular function headed by the wing commander at which all officers not on flying or ground duties were expected to attend. "Go ahead Paddy, what's on your mind?"

"Well Sir, on my evening off, and on Saturday evenings, I go to a little pub near the cathedral called The Four Elms. Over the past two or three weeks an Irish fellow has made himself known to me – a civilian you understand. He tells me he's a traveller for an Irish company. He knows the Rifles are on the airfield and a couple of times he's asked me questions – casual like – and I've not wanted to be rude but I've hedged round, you know. Last Friday that big new four engined job came in as you know."

"Yes, the new Halifax."

"That's it Sir. Well I suppose everybody in Norfolk saw it, but he started asking me whether I saw it bombed up – he knows we guard the bomb dump, how he knows it though I don't know. Then he said, "I'd be very interested to know how much it carries," and straight away I said "Why?" and he laughed it off and said that aeroplanes were his hobby and he'd never seen a big bugger like that before. I told him I'd try and find out and we left it at that."

David thought for a moment or two. "There may be nothing in it of course Paddy, but I'll have a word with the adjutant and see what he thinks. You haven't told anyone else have you?"

"Not at all Sir, not at all."

"Right, I'll talk to you about it again tomorrow."

Before going to dinner, David telephoned Tony Flamborough, who immediately said, "We've got to take this seriously – leave it to me."

At eight o'clock the next morning there was a knock on David's door just after he returned from breakfast. Paddy, who was getting his officer's equipment ready for a route march that morning, opened the door to be confronted by a short, stocky, ginger haired civilian of around forty, who walked in saying "You Mr Chandler? And are you O'Riordan?"

David was a little taken aback by the abrupt entry and even more abrupt questions.

"We are, and may I ask who you are?"

"My name is Wilson. Captain Flamborough has given me the gist of the conversation you had with him last night, I need now to go over it in detail with the pair of you."

"But we're on a route march in a few minutes."

"They'll have to go without you, can you contact them?"

"Yes, I can telephone the company office."

"Do it. Don't tell them why. Tell them you have a special job to do for your C.O."

David was getting a little annoyed by the attitude of this aggressive civilian standing there in his room ordering him about.

"Before I do that I want to know who you are and what authority you have to come in here and order me about."

Wilson pulled an identity wallet from an inside pocket. It said he was Chief Inspector Hector Wilson, Special Branch. As he offered it he grinned, "I was just seeing how much you'd tell me before you asked who I was," he said, "you'd be surprised how much even some senior

267

officers tell me when they don't know me from Adam. By the way, any tea going?"

David accepted the explanation with good grace. "Pop in next door Paddy and get Driscoll to get us some tea, there's a good chap and then come on back. I'll phone the office." He was able to do this from the telephone in the passageway outside so that in only two or three minutes all three were settled. First Wilson wanted to know all of Paddy's background, his army service, his family and any special friends male and female. He then asked Paddy the gist of the various conversations he had had with the Irishman, and what name he had given Paddy, where he came from in Ireland and where he stayed in England. Paddy answered all the questions except that he didn't know where this Henry Burke, as he called himself, stayed in England. He had merely told Paddy he moved around all the time staying mainly in B and B's.

"When do you next go to The Four Elms then Paddy?" asked the chief inspector.

"On Saturday evening Sir," replied Paddy.

"Right, this is what we do. You just talk to him as usual. If he doesn't bring up the subject of the Halifax bomb load, and I'm sure he will, then you slip it in to the conversation. You can tell him it will take up to nearly ten tons of bombs so you've been told. Make a joke about it – tell him a squadron of those will put the shits up Hitler – or something of the sort."

"And does it carry ten tons?" asked an incredulous David.

"Christ no, but he won't know that, and a little bit of false information won't do any harm. Anyway, when he leaves you he'll want to get off to pass this information on to his contact. When he goes you stay in the pub till closing time and leave the rest to us – OK?" Paddy nodded.

"Will you let us know what happens?" David enquired.

"I think that's unlikely, but I'll try to give you some idea of the result if I possibly can. Anyway Paddy, you've done a good job no matter what the outcome and it won't go unnoticed, I'm sure."

The next two days dragged for both David and his batman, but when Saturday came Paddy made his way to The Four Elms to find his usual seat at the bar already occupied by Henry Burke – if Henry Burke he really was. The stool was immediately vacated with the salutation "Just keeping it warm for you Paddy – what are you going to have?"

They chatted on for about half an hour or so until Burke said, oh so casually, "Did you find out about that big bugger we were talking about?"

Paddy, in a masterly piece of acting, pretended not to comprehend for a moment or two, and then excitedly said, "Oh, the Halifax, it's certainly a big bugger alright. They tell me they put ten tons on it, a few of them over Berlin will put the shits up old Hitler, that's for sure."

"Jesus Christ," were Burke's first words, followed by, "how the bloody hell does it fly with that lot on it?"

"Well I saw it take off and it went up like a bird. I know one thing; I wouldn't like to be on the receiving end of the bastard."

"Nor me either," agreed Burke, and after a short pause changed the subject. About twenty minutes later he said, "I've got to make it an early night tonight, so drink up my friend and have a drop of short before I go – that's if they haven't run out." They hadn't run out. Burke bought two drops of scotch, swallowed his down, shook hands, "See you soon Paddy," and was off out into the black-out. It was only by a great strength of will that Paddy prevented himself from watching him go in order to see which of the other drinkers would be the one to follow him.

Instead, he fixed his eyes on an advertisement for Guinness on the wall behind the bar and sat and thought, 'I wonder what will happen now. Is he a spy? If so, will he lead the Special Branch men to others, and if so would they be caught and then shot like all spies?' Should this be the case, far from feeling he would have the blood of Henry Burke on his hands; he would as he told himself, "Pull the bloody trigger myself, the bastard."

Closing time came and he made his way to the recreational transport point in the Haymarket to get the R.A.F. truck back to the airfield. On arrival he went straight to David's room to report on the evening's events and was surprised to find not only David but the chief inspector there as well. He greeted Paddy with a firm handshake and said, "Well done Paddy my boy. I can't tell you what's happened but it was all very successful. In addition to Henry Burke – not his real name as no doubt you guessed – we got the one we've been looking for. Now, not a word about this to anybody – drunk or sober – OK?"

"Not a word Sir, not a word."

The following Tuesday David had to visit battalion HQ, and whilst there was told to see the adjutant. This he duly did and was told the C.O. wanted to have a word with him. With the inner thought,

'What the hell have I done wrong now?' he knocked on the C.O.'s door and was bidden enter.

"David, I want to reward O'Riordan in some way for what he did – any brilliant ideas – you know him better than most. We can't give him a medal for obvious reasons – any other ideas?"

"Well Sir, I wondered about this and it occurred to me that that's just what we could do."

"Go on, I'm listening."

"Well Sir, he's never been awarded his eighteen year Regular Service and Good Conduct Medal for the simple reason he's not exactly got a spotless conduct sheet. Most of what is on there is fairly innocuous except for the fact that on one occasion he emptied a bucket of slops over an R.S.M."

"Oh my goodness, now I've heard it all! Tony," he bellowed, "come and hear this."

The adjutant came bustling in. "Tell Tony what you've just told me." David repeated the story. His audience roared with laughter, which, David thought, would have been far from the case if they had been the R.S.M. or, for that matter, trying the offence if it had come before them.

"Why did he do that?" asked Tony.

"He told me it was a mistake, he intended to empty them over the provost sergeant because he called him a useless ignorant bog trotting Fenian, but by the time he had bent down to pick up the bucket, the R.S.M. had got in the way."

"How long ago was this?" queried the colonel, still grinning.

"About twelve years ago, Sir, in India," replied David.

"Well I don't know what you think Tony, but I reckon that what he's done now more than cancels out his previous misdeeds. Have a word with whoever it is you have to have a word with and see if there's any reason why we can't give him his medal."

"I know R.S.M. Forster at Winchester thinks highly of him Sir," said David. "I don't know if that helps."

"I should think it would help no end. Mr Forster doesn't give approval lightly, that's for sure."

And so it came to pass that three weeks later Rifleman O'Riordan was called to company office, told to go and get his best battledress and boots on and go to battalion headquarters in the P.U., which had been sent for him and report to the R.S.M. Before leaving, he sought out David, firstly to tell him what was happening and secondly to elicit his officer's opinion as to the purpose of this visit which required him to be in his best uniform. With David's well-acted, total inability to even begin to guess what was in the wind, he departed in the fatalistic frame of mind held by all old soldiers – 'Well, they can only shoot me'.

When he arrived at the orderly room, he marched into the R.S.M.'s office where he halted in front of the desk rigidly to attention. The R.S.M. stood up, walked round the desk, walked round Paddy, flicking one of his trouser bottoms with his cane properly into place over its gaiter and then said, "Well, O'Riordan, I hear you're a bit of a bloody hero," and continued, "stand easy for Christ's sake, you're not on a fizzer."

The R.S.M. returned to his desk, lifted the telephone and said "Captain Flamborough? O'Riordan's here Sir." He was obviously instructed by the adjutant to take Paddy into the C.O. so reaching for his cap he said, "Right – stand outside the C.O.'s door and when he's ready I'll march you in."

After this it was all a bit of a haze in Paddy's mind. He was marched in, halted, "Salute the officer," and found himself looking into the smiling face of the colonel.

"O'Riordan, we've been most interested in your caper with the Special Branch and more than pleased with the very satisfactory outcome, as we understand it, of the results of your vigilance and intelligent appreciation of the situation. Because of the secrecy of this whole business we are unable to recommend you for an award, but at the suggestion of your officer, Mr Chandler, we have obtained remission of all your past sins and are able to grant you your Regular Service and Good Conduct Medal." He took a maroon coloured box from the desk behind him, opened it, took out the medal and pinned it on Paddy's tunic.

"Thank you Sir – God bless you Sir," was all Paddy could say as the C.O. gripped his hand in a firm handshake.

After a second's pause the R.S.M. barked, "Salute the officer – about turn – quick march," and once again Paddy found himself back in the R.S.M.'s office.

"Sit down, I'll find us a cup of tea," he was genially informed, and thought to himself, 'Jesus Christ – have I died and gone to Heaven? Drinking tea with the R.S.M.? – No bastard will talk to me if this gets around'.

"So, how do you find this Mr Chandler?" he was asked as the R.S.M. came back into the room.

"In my years in the regiment, Sir, I've not met a finer man and I can tell you all his platoon, including Sergeant Corrigan, will bear me out so it's not just he's got me the medal that makes me say that. Since he and Mr Crew came to the Company they tell me it's been a different place to the crap heap it was before, you ask Sergeant Corrigan, he knows what it was like."

"I understand he lost his wife?"

"Yes Sir he did. He doesn't say much but he's awful sad sometimes, what with losing his brother-in-law at Calais and all. Holy Mary, those two things happening so close together could make a man very bitter and twisted, yet he's so courteous in the way he speaks to people, and cheerful with it, my God, he's got some character has that one."

"What's he like to those who step out of line?"

Paddy thought for a moment. "Well Sir, it's funny that. Not many seem to – I've only seen a couple. They only do it once though – he stands no bloody nonsense, and with the service he's had he knows when anyone's coming the old soldier – they don't get very far." He finished his tea. "Well, thank you for the tea Sir."

"Right, congratulations on your medal, not many of us get that you know, be proud of it."

"I am that Sir, I am that," and with that he stiffened to attention, turned about and marched out to the waiting P.U.

When he arrived back at the airfield officer's quarters, the first people he met were David and Charlie who drew up on their bicycles beside the P.U. as he was dropped off. He immediately sprang to attention and saluted the two chums.

"Well, where have you been, chauffeur driven and all," said David mischievously.

"Sir, if you'll pardon my saying so, you know bloody well where I've been and you knew where I was going and why I was going before I went."

"By God," Charlie chimed in, "of all the convoluted statements I've heard in my life that one takes the biscuit. What's he on about?"

"Go on Paddy," said David, "show us what it's all about." Paddy reached into his breast pocket, pulled out the medal box, undid it and showed it to the two officers.

"You didn't know about this until now?" queried Charlie.

"No Sir, but this one did, he was the one who got it for me. I thought I was going to HQ for a bollocking for some reason and I come back with a medal." Charlie held his arm out and shook hands warmly with this veteran soldier.

"You damned well deserve it – even if it was only for having to look after this heap of an apology for a rifleman, you would have deserved it, but for all the years you've served you more than deserve it."

"Thank you Sir, thank you very much Sir," and then back to business, "What will you be wearing tonight Sir?"

"Service dress Paddy – dinner night tonight."

"Service dress it is Sir, I'll go and get it ready."

As Paddy saluted and made his way to David's room, the two chums stood and watched him depart, until Charlie turned, looked David straight in the eyes and said, "There's more to this than meets the eye – what's going on that I am too young to know about? – Mysterious civilians cluttering up the corridors – officers missing route marches – Paddy getting his medal when we all know he has, from time to time, been a very naughty boy. Now come on dear old sport, spill the beans as Mr Cagney said on the NAAFI film show last night, tell your uncle Charlie all about it."

"Charlie, believe me, if I could I would. It is an official secret apparently, but when I'm old and grey I will divulge all the gripping details. It will, I calculate, take at least ninety seconds; there is so much to tell."

"Well, with that I shall, I suppose, have to be content. Now back to more important things. Since we're both off this evening, how about taking the passion wagon into Norwich after dinner night and have a glass of beer in one of the hostelries?"

"That's probably the most intelligent remark you've made today." They parted to get ready for the dinner night.

After dinner, they slipped on their Burberrys and caught the last passion wagon in to the Haymarket. They both preferred wearing their Burberrys rather than their greatcoats. Whilst you were clearly an officer, Burberrys carried no badges of rank, whereas if they wore their greatcoats their one pip on each shoulder indicated they were among the lowest form of life, namely a second lieutenant, an individual not to be taken too seriously, an apprentice, a novice, just a boy around the place. In the Royal Welsh Fusiliers, second lieutenants were known as 'Warts' because of the funny little protuberance on each shoulder. The two chums consoled themselves with the fact that in a couple of months with their six months probation up, they would be full lieutenants. As a full lieutenant you became seriously an officer, the second pip providing an enormous amount of extra self-assurance to the wearer.

It was well after nine o'clock when they walked into the saloon bar of the Castle, which was fairly full considering it was midweek, mainly civilians with just a handful of service people. At the bar, talking to a civilian man and a lady, was a tall, extremely handsome major who, half turning, instantly recognised David, broke off his conversation with his friends, took two paces toward the newcomers, held out his hand and then, to Charlie's astonishment, clasped David in a bear hug.

"David, dear boy, what are you doing here? How lovely to see you. Do come and meet my friends. What are you both drinking? Oh! What a lovely surprise."

The hubbub dying down a little, introductions were made all round. The major was Rueben Isaacs who, known only by a very few people of which David was one, lived in a ménage a deux with David's old peace-time boss and mentor, Peter Phillips. Living together in this fashion was, of course, a criminal offence, such a situation being fraught with the danger not only of being discovered by the long arm of the law but also beset with the menace of being discovered by would be blackmailers and extortionists. Rueben and Peter therefore kept themselves mainly to themselves, never wrote letters to one another for fear of there being intercepted, and were doubly careful when making telephone calls that they could not be overheard. With all this secrecy they had now been together for over six years. In reply to David's asking what on earth he was doing in Norwich, Rueben answered he was carrying out special camouflage surveys of the various airfields, "Not terribly top secret David, everybody knows we've got to camouflage the blasted places, though how you successfully conceal something covering anything up to five square miles or more is, to say the least, a tall order."

When Rueben started to chat with Charlie, who immediately took a liking to this astonishingly good looking, extremely amiable friend of David's, David himself struck up a conversation with the two civilians. The man was in his mid thirties, the woman probably thirtyish, he judged. They had been introduced as 'my friends Reggie and Pamela Sherbourne – Pamela is doing her utmost to keep the theatre here alive and kicking, Reggie ploughs up half of Norfolk I should think, so you'll have something in common since your family makes agricultural equipment.'

The conversation between them commenced with the two men pursuing this common interest, until David, wishing not to exclude the lady from the discussion said, "And are you involved in the ploughing of half of Norfolk Mrs Sherbourne?" There was an immediate tinkling laugh from, what David was beginning to recognise as being, an extremely attractive and vivacious young woman.

"To answer your question David, firstly I am only involved in what you might call the admin side of the business. Secondly I am not a Mrs – Reggie is my brother," she laughingly continued, "I see you wear a wedding ring – have you any children?" Rueben and Charlie overhearing her question instantly stopped talking. David caught with his guard down, fought to say something but no words came.

Pamela realising she had precipitated some sort of crisis, put her hand to her mouth and was just about to ask had she said something wrong, when David recovered himself sufficiently to say, "I'm dreadfully sorry Miss Sherbourne, you rather caught me on the wrong foot. You see my wife was killed in an air attack last November. She was much loved by all of us," he added, indicating Charlie and Reuben.

"Oh my dear. Oh I am so sorry to have been so abrupt."

"You weren't at all, you couldn't possibly have known, please don't distress yourself," David replied, the reassurances coming in quick succession in an endeavour to check her agitation.

"Would it hurt you greatly to tell me what happened?" she asked, her hand lying lightly on his arm. David told her of the events of that day on the airfield at Sandbury, the others listening in silence.

"How dreadful," she said, "how very dreadful."

The short silence which followed was broken abruptly by the landlord, standing close to them at the bar, bellowing in his best sergeant major style voice, "Last orders please."

At which Charlie quipped, "He'd do well in our lot as a Drill sergeant." Although it was not exactly the joke of the year, they all laughed and it had the effect of putting the atmosphere between them back on a similar plane to that obtained before the sad subject of Pat arose.

They finished their drinks during which time Reuben asked, "How are you all fixed on Saturday – dinner on me at The Roebuck?"

David replied that barring accidents, he and Charlie would be OK (he was using 'OK' quite a lot lately), since he was on duty on Sunday and Charlie, the duty officer on Friday. The Sherbourne's had nothing planned, so it was arranged they would meet at six o'clock for a drink before dinner – dinner in the provincial cities at that time being served early compared to pre-war days.

The two chums strolled back to the Haymarket in silence until, at last, Charlie said, "Rather a pretty girl what?"

"She's too old for you."

"I wasn't thinking of me."

Chapter Twenty Four

It was Sunday evening 30th March. It had always been the practice at Chandlers Lodge to have the main meal midday, tea at about five o'clock, after which visitors would arrive for the evening and they would end up enjoying a cold supper. Since the war, the rationing had severely restricted what could be offered for supper. No longer could a one and a half pound block of mature cheddar be placed on the table when the ration for the family of three for a whole week was only twelve ounces. However, with considerable ingenuity, Ruth made pâtés and brawn from unrationed scraps, so there was always something tasty to end the day with, even if it did mean they had margarine with their bread, a situation about which Fred complained constantly, bitterly and totally without any sympathy from the rest of the family. There were always people who could get goods from 'under the counter' but both Fred and Ruth were firm in their outlook regarding this nefarious business, so much so that Fred had made it clear to all foremen and charge hands at the factory, that if any black market deals were discovered taking place in the works he would have no hesitation in bringing in the police and discharging the offenders. As a result, Sandbury Engineering remained relatively free of being a clearing house for goods off the ration, unlike many other business premises.

Along with the family were Jack and Moira, Anni, Ernie and Karl, with baby David tucked up cosily in the big pram in the sitting room. The two marines were also there, but Megan was on duty that night, the twins being looked after, as usual, by Nanny at the Hollies. The topics of discussion ranged from the new 'Lend/Lease' programme, which had just been confirmed and which Jack stated was another nail in Hitler's coffin. With the unlimited backing of the industrial strength of the United States behind them the Empire and its allies would never want for arms and equipment. Another item of news released the previous day was that substantial reinforcements had arrived in Malaya from Britain, India and Australia.

"I don't think that will dissuade the Japs in any way," was again Jack's opinion, "when they're ready – they'll go."

But the most immediate concern of them all was the problem posed during the past two weeks with trouble being caused in the town by certain elements in the Canadian Battalion, commanded by their friend Colonel Tim, who had been stationed in the camp out on the Maidstone road for over a year now. Ivan described the reason for this as being purely and simply inaction. They were taught to be aggressive fighting men and all they were doing, apart from endless exercises, route marches and the like, was sitting on their backsides. They had come to Europe to fight. They had been made very welcome locally, they, in turn, had been civil, courteous and well behaved, but now the frustration and boredom was beginning to be shown by a small unruly section of the force, ending in punch-ups in the pubs with airmen and other troops from the airfield, and on two occasions with the local constabulary. Colonel Tim had immediately tackled the situation by doubling the regimental police presence in the town, but the previous night a wooden bench in the town centre had been thrown through a plate glass window, as a result the whole battalion was confined to camp until further notice.

"Sandbury is not the only place it's happening," Ivan informed them. "I understand that at Godstone a crowd from the Canadian Battalion there threw the local bobby in the duck pond. It only takes a few idiots with too much booze inside them to cause absolute mayhem. Perhaps they'll find a job for them soon."

During the evening David made his usual Sunday evening phone call, telling his mother about his meeting Reuben and how he and Charlie had had dinner with him and two of Reuben's friends the previous evening. He ended his call with, "Oh and by the way, I'm coming on ten days leave in two weeks, so get the bed aired."

"Is Charlie coming as well?"

"No, unfortunately. As we're placed at the moment only one of us can be away at any one time, so he's going next week, and I go when he comes back."

"It will be lovely having you home again – I'd better warn Susie – we mustn't spring a surprise like that on her!"

David arrived on leave on Monday 14th April, having first been cautioned by Major Laurenson to keep in contact with Chandlers Lodge should he go elsewhere for any reason. The Germans had invaded Yugoslavia and Greece on the sixth of April without any declaration of war and there was a strong rumour floating around that the battalion was to be uprooted and sent to the Middle East. "I know we've all heard it before David, but be on the safe side," the major had said.

Having changed into civvies, the first thing he did was to visit

Pat's grave. It was early evening and getting toward dusk. The churchyard was deserted and so very peaceful as David stood by the headstone and thought of all the wonderfully happy times he had shared with this darling girl. Strangely, he felt at peace, not sad, or even grief stricken, as one might have expected, it was as though he had not lost his love, she was still with him. And then he glanced at Lady Halton's headstone and was glad she was with her friend Pat, a second thought being he must see the brigadier during his leave. He wandered home, being welcomed at his arrival by his mother with, "Everything alright dear?" – just a simple question but asking vastly more than the three words would normally convey.

"All OK mum, thank you – I must see the brigadier while I'm home.

"We'll invite him for a drink and supper one evening."

"Thank you, that would be ideal."

The leave passed pleasantly and all too quickly. He spent long hours with Rose and her baby and with Anni and Karl and baby David. On the Sunday they had the double christening and a host of guests in the evening to celebrate the event. Buffy and Rita and the Lloyds came up for the weekend, the general and Lady Earnshaw came, as also did Colonel Tim, Jim and Alec and his wife Rebecca. It was the first occasion upon which the two marines had been part of a full-scale Chandlers Lodge party, and whilst there was an underlying sadness that Jeremy was not there, it was not allowed to reduce the pleasure that everyone was to enjoy in having the two newcomers to the family. Anni, her husband, father and son were family and always would be. However, the main talking point of the evening was the appearance at the christening, and afterwards at the house, of Major Ken Johnson, Royal Marines, accompanied by none other than Matron Kathleen Duffy, a superbly elegant figure in a classical dark green baratkea suit who turned all eyes. Ruth had already told David that Ken seemed very smitten, this evening it was patently obvious that it was not a one way attachment, Kathleen held his arm constantly and frequently her beautiful blue eyes looked smilingly at him. Seeing this, David wistfully realised how much he missed this one-ness, the gentle touches and fleeting smiles between two people that he had so enjoyed, pleasurable incidents that made an ordinary evening, extraordinary. His musing was interrupted by the voice of the brigadier.

"Well David my boy, how is life in the Rifles these days?"

"To be truthful Sir, very boring in the main, although we do get some relief with the aircraft taking off and returning. We army people on the airfield do feel a bit left out of it all with these aircrews going out and doing battle time and again, but there you are, someone's got to guard them and their airplanes I suppose."

The brigadier thought for a moment. "I know how you feel. When I first went on the staff and started being instrumental in getting other people to do things, people I didn't even know in the main, I felt like a manager rather than a leader. I had been used to being a leader ever since I left Sandhurst, it was very strange pushing bits of paper and knowing you were having far more influence on the conduct of affairs than you ever did as the chap up at the sharp end. What I'm trying to say I suppose is that when you study it, we've all got a job to do and doing it conscientiously and well is what counts. God, I'm beginning to sound like a second rate politician trying to persuade the workers to work even harder! Anyway, I wouldn't worry too much if I were you, I've heard a whisper, not a state secret I might add, that the R.A.F. are going to have to guard their own airfields soon, the army has other plans for all those battalions doing two on and four off day and night. Now, to change the subject, aren't those two babies the most beautiful you've ever seen?"

"They certainly are, prejudiced though I may be, they certainly are, and they behaved wonderfully at the christening. Apparently when I was christened I behaved abominably, screamed the place down at one end and disgraced myself at the other just as the vicar took me in his arms – I've never lived it down." Ruth, watching carefully in case the pair became too grave was relieved to see them laughing together. Time does heal she thought, even if never completely.

On Monday morning the telephone rang, answered by Rose who was passing through the hall at the time. It was Major Laurenson, David's company commander. Rose told him David had gone out but would be back soon – could she get him to return the call?

"No, not to worry, I'll telephone again at midday. I can get a priority call through very much more quickly than you would be able."

"Major – you're not going to tear him away from us are you?"

"No, far from it, giving him an extra day as it happens."

"You know what they say – beware of Greeks bearing gifts – what has he got to do to get an extra day?" This question was put to the major in the vivacious laughing manner of the old Rose, which began to quite captivate the thirty-year-old bachelor at the other end of the line. As a result, the conversation lengthened into questions about the christenings, which David had told him about, a real concern about how David was bearing up at home, the loss of his wife being more immediate there perhaps than when he was tied up in his work, and finally a few words about Rose's sad loss. He then went on, "You know, you ought to come up to Norwich for a weekend – have a break – we could all have dinner together."

"You wouldn't go slumming with a mere second lieutenant would you?"

"He'll be a full lieutenant by then, and anyway with someone as captivating as you in the party, I wouldn't even notice he was there."

"Major Laurenson, you are chatting me up."

"Of course – but I was hoping you wouldn't notice. Oh, and by the way, I understand you have some Royal Marines in your house. I should warn you, they're a notoriously dreadful lot, but then I expect your parents keep you locked away from them most of the time. If they don't, they should."

"I'll tell them what you said when they come in." The light-hearted conversation continued for some time, Rose asking which part of the country the major came from and what he did for a living when not soldiering. She was asked to please stop calling him major, his name was Mark. He told her he came from Shrewsbury where his father was the principal in a long established legal business, and he laughingly told her finally he had never had a proper job, he was a career soldier – "But not a Blimp I hasten to add, but then I expect David has already told you something about me."

"What David has told me about you would get him cashiered I wouldn't doubt," she teased, and in the ensuing shared amusement heard the door open to admit David. "Oh Mark, David's just come in. I'll say goodbye and pass the phone to him, bye bye now, maybe we'll meet in the not too distant future."

With that she passed the receiver to David, who, putting his hand over the mouthpiece, said, "Who the devil's Mark?"

"Your boss I'm afraid, but don't worry you're not being called back."

"Thank God for that. Hello Sir, what's up?"

"You have to go for an interview in London on Wednesday David. I don't know what it's all about. I'll give you all the details in a moment but because of your having to go during your leave you can come back here on Friday instead of Thursday. Now, the place you have to go to is The Combined Forces Entertainment and Education Service – got that?"

"Yes Sir, I'm writing it down."

"Right. The address is 39C Roper Street, off Baker Street, W1. You have to report to a Major Swift at 11am, can you manage that?"

"Yes Sir, of course. What's the dress Sir?"

"They suggested civilian clothes, or if you haven't any available – lots of people have grown out of their civilian clothes since the army made men of them and they've no coupons to buy new, if none are available, ordinary battledress."

"What's it all about Sir?"

"Haven't the foggiest notion, perhaps they're going to turn you into a chorus boy for Ensa."

"They'd better not try."

"Well, whatever it is, I'll ring you on Wednesday evening to find out how you got on. You'd better watch out though David, they tell me these entertainment mobs are full of poofters – keep your hand on your ha'penny."

"I will that Sir, as O'Riordan would say."

"Speak to you later then – oh and give my regards to your delightful sister."

David replaced the receiver. "What did he say?" questioned Rose.

"He reckons you're delightful – I didn't put the squeak in for you by telling him otherwise."

Rose promptly punched him in the ribs. "Tell me what he said," she repeated holding his ear.

"What who said?" came the enquiry from Ruth who had just emerged from the kitchen.

"David has had a call from his company commander."

"Oh you haven't got to go back yet have you dear?" said a concerned Ruth.

"If you two females will give me a chance I will tell you what it was all about," expostulated David, and continued, "I have to go for an interview to a unit called The Combined Forces Entertainment Service in London. As a result, I get an extra day's leave and go back on Friday instead of Thursday."

"But what on earth do you know about Forces Entertainment?" queried Ruth.

"Absolutely nothing, but if they think I'm being parted from my job in the Rifles they've got another think coming. That," (spoken very decisively), "is a fact."

The two marines were away for the next three days, which prevented David from having a word with them as to their opinion regarding his interview. He thought of telephoning the brigadier, but on second thoughts felt that asking about such a trifling matter would be presumptuous. Had he known, the brigadier would have been delighted to talk to him at any time, no matter how insignificant the subject might be.

Wednesday came and David caught the nine o'clock out of Sandbury to be in town in good time. Arriving at Victoria he hopped a bus for Baker Street —having to watch the pennies when he worked in Victoria Street before the war, automatically made him think of buses before taxis. He was half an hour early so he had a cup of tea and a soft bun in a café on the corner of Roper Street, not because he was hungry, but to pass the time, wondering what the next couple of hours had in store for him. But he would never have guessed in his wildest dreams what the outcome of those hours would be.

At ten minutes to eleven, he approached the doorway of 39C Roper Street. Roper Street was a small cul-de-sac housing typical Victorian middle class type buildings, mostly three or four floors with a basement area for the kitchen and tiny windows set in the roof where the skivvies of bygone days would have their rooms. Some of the houses were still privately owned, some had business or professional plates beside their doors, 39C was the last building on the left opposite which was a boarded up bomb site. The road ended in a high brick wall shielding it from whatever was beyond. There were two plates beside the doorway; one indicating 'The Combined Forces Entertainment Service'. a second had the legend 'Discharged Officers Resettlement Organisation'. David's first thought was perhaps they were going to give him his ticket, but since he hadn't won the war for them yet his second thoughts were that this was unlikely. He pushed open the heavy front door and walked into a small hallway at the centre of which was a reception desk manned by an attractive A.T.S. sergeant.

"I have to see Major Swift," he smiled at the sergeant. "My name is Chandler."

No answering smile came from the receptionist, checking his name on her clipboard. "Mr Chandler, City Rifles, is that correct?"

If I was a bloody major I bet I would have got a smile thought David. "Yes, that's correct."

"Have you got your identity card and discs?"

David produced his officers' identity card and fumbled in his shirt to pull out the identity discs. For the sergeant to see the discs he had to bend forward and she had to stand up.

"I've never seen identity discs on a gold chain before," she said, and then actually smiled.

She thinks I'm a blooming plutocrat, thought David.

"It was a present," he said, not elaborating further. The chain was, of course, a gift from General Strich, a reminder of their conversation in the dugout at Calais. It had been given to David after the general had stayed at Sandbury for his convalescence. It had caused interest at times during P.T. periods with his platoon back at the airfield when, of course, his wearing just a singlet made it immediately visible. He recalled that one day the joker in the platoon had approached him and said quite seriously, "You know Sir; if we go into action every man in the platoon will follow you anywhere." David was too old in the military tooth to accept a statement like that without a degree of suspicion.

"What makes you say that Reynolds?"

"Well Sir, you're bound to be the first to stop one and then there'll be a hell of a fight who gets your chain."

David grinned at the recollection. The sergeant looked up from her checklist.

"Will you please go down the right hand staircase," she said, pointing further down the hallway, "and go to Room 21 along that corridor."

David voiced his thanks and headed for the staircase. It was a metal, spiral stairway, which descended to a much lower point that would have been the case for an ordinary basement level. This led him to suspect that this was not part of the original house but had been constructed afterwards. When he finally reached the bottom and looked along the corridor, the ceiling of which was little more than seven feet high and very obviously solid concrete did he conclude his original belief to be correct – this place looked as good as bomb-proof. One thought quickly followed another. Why would an entertainment organisation require a bomb-proof office? Why would it house so many people as to require at least twenty-one rooms – possibly more? The corridor stretched for quite a distance in front of him. He brushed the thoughts aside and headed for Room 21, odd numbers on the left, even on the right. Despite the number of rooms there was no activity in the corridor. Odd, he thought, probably all in the canteen having their elevenses. He knocked on the door of Room 21 and was bade enter by a firm sounding female voice which he discovered to be another A.T.S. sergeant, not quite as attractive as her front desk colleague but nevertheless alright on a dark night, as his brother Harry would have concluded.

"I have to see Major Swift," David announced.

"Yes, that's right Mr Chandler," came the reply, "will you please have a seat, you will not be kept long." She indicated an easy chair against the wall. Seating himself David looked around the small office. It told him nothing, it was as plain as a pikestaff, just a desk, side table with typewriter, filing cabinet, wall mirror and the sort of cupboard, which housed stationery. A hat stand with an A.T.S. raincoat and cap completed the furnishings. Sparse it was, not improved by the fact that the electric bulbs, there were two pendants hanging a few inches from the ceiling, had no shades, reflecting the hard light from the white paint, which made David consider that after working all day in this light you'd be in need of a few aspirin.

The sergeant disappeared through a connecting door into the adjoining office and within a minute reappeared, saying, "Please come through Mr Chandler." David thought, dark night or not I prefer her to snooty upstairs, but these thoughts were swiftly dispelled when to his utter astonishment the tweed jacketed figure that rose from behind a modest desk with hand outstretched to greet him was none other than Charlie's father, Brigadier Lord Ramsford.

"Come in David, come and sit down."

"But Sir, I understood I was to see a major Swift."

"One of my pseudonyms I'm afraid – I'll explain all in due course, but first of all I have to get you to read and sign this," he handed David a single sheet of paper headed, 'Official Secrets Act.' David read the paper carefully, which in essence obliged him not to divulge any information in respect of the present interview or of future events in connection with it for a period of thirty years or until so authorised by His Majesty's Government. David signed, but having done so, smiled at the brigadier and said, "Do all people in Forces Entertainment have to do this Sir?" Lord Ramsford smiled back, took the paper and witnessed it, handed it to the sergeant, who also witnessed it 'J.E.C. Swift Major.' As she was standing beside David whilst she completed this task, he clearly saw the signature, which she made no attempt to hide. Catching her eye David smiled, gave a little shrug, received an answering smile and was left to wondering why brigadiers hid away in concrete basements and why A.T.S. majors dressed up as sergeants. All very odd he thought, and oddest of all, what the hell was he doing here. He was soon to find out.

"I'll come straight to the point David. I want you to do a job for me for a period of three months after which you can rejoin your battalion should you so desire. The job is in France." He waited while this latter disclosure sunk in. David remained silent. "I will tell you what it's all about, but first of all I want you to know that if you decide you would prefer not to take part there will be no recriminations whatsoever, you will go back to your unit on Friday and this interview will never have happened. Is that clearly understood?"

"Yes Sir."

"Right then, I'll outline the situation. There is a considerable build-up going on at the moment of the French Resistance. Unfortunately, as far as we are concerned, there are two French Resistance movements, the De Gaulle faction and the communist faction. Although the communist faction is at present fairly quiescent because of its antagonism to the treaty between the Soviet Union and Germany, there is no love lost between their members and the De Gaullists; as a result we are piggy in the middle. I suspect that since we occupy that unenviable position we are not getting all the information from either side that we should be getting.

Now to my second point. Near Le Mans there is an army group headquarters. There are more generals there than there are in any one other place in the whole of France, except possibly for one or two bordellos in Paris," he added with a grin. "We have, in conjunction with some very fine colleagues in the French telephone service, been able to establish a listening post in order to tap the lines from the two senior officers' messes. It is our intention to eavesdrop on them when they are not suspecting it, trusting they will give away snippets of information when perhaps they've had one or two over the odds, which they would be unlikely to do from their offices where they would be more security conscious and would use code for anything secret. You will have two German speaking French assistants, you will work in shifts, and the other two will record anything they think is of importance for you to vet. Now, how does it sound so far?"

"It sounds very exciting and interesting Sir, but all sorts of things come to mind, primarily what do I tell my family – I obviously can't be in touch with them at all? And what do I tell Charlie and the others at Highmere?"

"You tell them you are going on a mission; you will not be able to contact them for a few weeks. As regards your family, a named person, presumably your mother, will be telephoned every so often to let her know you are fit and well. From what I hear of your family they are very intelligent, level headed people who will accept the situation."

"Right Sir, in that case I'd like to have a crack at it. What would be the next step?"

"You will report here on Friday in plain clothes and will be taken to a place in Sussex where you will have two week's intensive training, including brushing up your French – I understand your German is pretty well perfect anyway. You will be given a full briefing regarding the known generals at Le Mans and their responsibilities, and various other things such as operating the radio you will take with you and the code systems. Your servant is a man called O'Riordan I believe. He will bring all your kit from Norfolk and will look after you in Sussex and then will do other jobs until you return. Finally you will assume the rank of temporary captain as from today, you must have some status, particularly with the communists. You will be flown in and out – we have quite a bus service going there these days. Right then," he pressed a button on his desk at which the 'Sergeant' reappeared. "You can see David off the premises Jessica if you'd be so kind, and I'll see you in Sussex next week to see how things are going."

Jessica duly took David to the front entrance, passing snooty on the way, who, in fact, gave him a smile. That, thought David, was because she must have heard he was now a captain. They shook hands, before she opened the door.

"Goodbye," said David, "by the way, do I call you Ma'am or major or sergeant or what?"

"You call me Jessica – I shall be coming with you to Sussex incidentally although I'm not on your project. So it's not goodbye, it's au revoir until Friday."

He walked out into Roper Street, along to Baker Street, his head a melange of thoughts swimming around, with the ultimate one being 'Holy bloody smoke, what have I let myself in for?' He remembered his father's oft repeated advice 'Never volunteer', he'll kill me he thought and then reconciled himself with the further thought that despite his admonition his father, over the years, had volunteered time and again, the latest occasion being for the Home Guard at a time when every thinking person fully expected to be defending his country against the invader. He walked on down to Oxford Street, turned towards Marble Arch and suddenly felt peckish. It was just after one o'clock. Finding himself outside the Marble Arch Lyons Corner House, he decided to have a snack lunch before going on to Victoria on the bus. He had to queue for a while before being shown to a table by a pleasant faced 'Nippie', the name given to all the waitresses in the Corner Houses. He decided that soup followed by a Cornish pasty with vegetables would save him from starvation until he reached Chandlers Lodge, and sat back to wait for the repast, at the same time regarding the others eating, or waiting to eat, in the crowded restaurant.

After ten minutes or so the 'Nippie' returned with his soup and a roll with a small pat of margarine. She smiled at David and apologised for the delay in his being served. David assuring her he was in no hurry. Then, for what reason he was never able afterwards to explain he asked, "What is your name?"

Looking at him, she saw he was not being at all presumptuous, and replied, "We're not allowed to be familiar with customers Sir, but it's Maria, Maria Schultz." David's hand which was just reaching for his roll, stopped in mid-air. Immediately the vision of Cedric the Brave flooded back into his memory and the vision of Cedric's truck being blown half way up a wall only seconds after David and he had bid hearty cheerio's to each other. Cedric – poor Cedric. He must have gone pale as the young waitress asked, "Are you alright Sir?"

"Yes, yes, I'm alright, it's just that I lost a comrade named Schultz at Calais. It's an unusual name to hear in England, it rather shocked me for a moment."

Looking up at her he saw that she too had gone deathly pale after hearing his explanation. He stood up, took her elbow and seated her in his chair. "Was he known to you?" he asked gently.

"He was my brother – Cedric," she replied.

"Is everything alright here?" came a firm but not unfriendly voice from behind David. Maria immediately regained her self-control and said, "This gentleman was with Cedric at Calais Mr Stratton."

Mr Stratton was the floor manager, and in the manner of a man who has seen most of the extraordinary things that can happen in a restaurant, swiftly took charge of the situation. "Miss Schultz, conduct the gentleman to my table and bring him fresh soup please."

"Yes Mr Stratton."

Maria led the way across the floor to an alcove where there was a table laid for one out of view of the other users of the restaurant. She invited David to sit down. By the time he had seated himself the manager re-joined them.

"Cedric used to work in the Brasserie downstairs," began Mr Stratton; "he was much liked by us all. By the way, what is your name?"

"My name is Chandler."

"Corporal Chandler?" immediately queried Maria.

"I was then," said David, "how did you know that?"

"In Cedric's last letter he mentioned how sad he was that a Corporal Cartwright had been killed, but his mate, Corporal Chandler, Corporal Cartwright's mate that is, was still battling on. He said you were the most smashing blokes he'd ever met. I remember clearly he said, "If I could be as good a soldier as those two, I'd be very proud."

They were all silent for a moment, until David said, "Look Maria, I'll give you my telephone number at home. I shall be there today and tomorrow. Please telephone me, and perhaps you will get your father to talk to me as well."

Maria replied she would like to do that when she got home this evening and had spoken to her father. David acknowledged he would be there to take the call. He finished his lunch, shook hands with Mr Stratton who refused to present him with a bill, and then held out his hand to Maria. Impulsively, she took the hand, kissed it and then putting her arm around David's neck, kissed him on the cheek.

"What have I done to deserve this?" he asked laughingly.

"Because you were a friend of my brother, and because you are very brave – Cedric said so."

A little self-consciously David looked at Mr Stratton who just raised his eyebrows and smiled. "Take good care of yourself Mr Chandler and come and see us again won't you? By the way, you say at Calais you were a corporal, may I ask what you are now so that we know how to address you?"

Thinking quickly, David replied, "Well, as from now I'm a captain."

"Well, good luck Captain Chandler, please come again."

David hopped the bus down to Victoria, had to run to catch the Sandbury train and as he sat back in a corner seat, mulled over the things that had happened to him since he left home that morning. Then he was a second lieutenant on a home posting, now he was a captain being sent into enemy territory to meet goodness knows what sorts of dangers. On the way, through one of life's great coincidences, he met a relative of a man he had much admired and had witnessed being blown to bits. It was a hell of a lot to take in within such a short space of time.

When he reached home, Ruth immediately bustled around to make tea whilst Rose gently moved the pram out of the kitchen into the hallway whispering, "I've only just got him off to sleep, if he knows you're here he'll only wake up again."

David smiled to himself thinking that a three month old baby would have to be pretty forward to recognise his uncle, and wondered where all mothers got these funny ideas from. Rose returned, "Right Master David, now tell mum and me how you're going to entertain the forces, more that is than you probably do now."

"Well first of all I must tell you that I have had to sign the Official Secrets Act which means that I can tell you very little. I'm not pulling your legs, I really am being quite serious." His mother and sister looked at him, realised he was not joking and immediately concern registered on both their faces.

"Does this mean you're going away?" asked Ruth.

"Yes, I am on a mission for a few weeks and whilst I am on it I shall not be able to contact you, or you me. However, someone will telephone you every two weeks to let you know I am fit and well. They will just announce themselves as 'a friend of David's' and..." – Ruth broke in.

"Supposing you are not fit and well? Will they tell us that I wonder?"

"Don't you worry mum, I shall be alright and well looked after."

"And is that all we can know?" Rose's voice showed the anxiety she was feeling for her brother.

"I'm afraid so. When the job's done I'll tell you all about it."

"What do we tell other people, all the family in particular?" queried Ruth.

"Just what I've told you. I'm being sent on a special job for a few weeks."

Ruth took his hand across the table. "We shall, of course, be worrying about you all the time. You will take care and do nothing foolhardy, won't you?"

"You can rely on that absolutely," he reassured her.

Having got over that first hurdle, David told them he was going to put his feet up for an hour before his father and the two majors came home, he suddenly felt very tired. He went into the drawing room, passing little Jeremy fast asleep in his pram on the way, slipped his shoes off and stretched out on the settee. He was asleep in minutes. At five o'clock he was awakened by someone entering the room and looking up, saw his father coming towards him. He looked at his watch.

"Hello dad, you're early, who's going to clock you out?"

"Your mother phoned."

"So you know the news then? Well I can't tell you much more than I told them. I'll be going off from here on Friday and will be away about three months – I've told mum and Rose a few weeks – it sounded better. I can tell you I'm not on a raid or anything dramatic like that so there's no great cause for concern."

"Well you just take care of yourself whatever it is – understand?"

David smiled in agreement. "I shall certainly do that you can be sure."

Just before seven o'clock that evening, the telephone rang, answered by Rose. A somewhat guttural voice at the other end asked if he could speak to Captain Chandler. Thinking it was someone wanting to talk to her father on Home Guard business she called to him and with a hand over the mouthpiece said, "Somebody for you Dad, sounds like a foreigner."

"Hello, Chandler here."

"Ah, Captain Chandler, this is Heinrich Schultz, you met my daughter today."

"I'm sorry Mr Schultz, there must be some mistake, I've been in my factory all day."

"You are not David Chandler who was with my son at Calais?"

"Oh Lord, now I begin to see the light. David is my son. I'll get him for you." He called to David who was in the kitchen telling him there was a Mr Schultz wanting to speak to him. David hurried into the hall.

"Mr Schultz, how pleased I am to be able to speak to you."

"Well Captain Chandler, my daughter has told me how she met you today – I think it was a miracle. She also told me that you were only here for today and tomorrow. I know I should not ask this but does this mean you are going to do battle again somewhere? If so, please know my family will be remembering you in our prayers. Now please tell me about Cedric, I would particularly like to know whether he suffered at the end, we have worried so much about that."

David, in a low serious voice, told Mr Schultz the whole story of A Company's universal admiration of his son's dogged bravery, devotion to duty and complete lack of consideration for his personal safety. He continued, "When I asked him why he still drove on through all the shellfire, all he said to me was, 'Well you see, it's my job!' The men christened him Cedric the Brave you know. Night after night, morning after morning, he came to us. When we were more or less snug in the bottom of our slit trenches when all manner of stuff was being hurled at us, he would drive his truck through it all. He was fearless."

There was a pause at the other end. "Tell me captain."

"Oh please call me David."

"Tell me David, how did he die?"

"He had made his evening delivery to us and we had loaded him up for his return journey. He called out a cheery goodbye to us and drove off. When he'd got a few hundred yards, a salvo of shells came in; one making a direct hit on the truck. He was killed instantly. He is buried next to my brother-in-law Corporal Cartwright."

There was another pause. "All the family will be very grateful to you for letting us know all this. I thank God for his crossing your path with my Maria today. Good luck to you David, wherever you are going. Will you now have a few words with Maria?"

When Maria came on the line, she thanked David for all he had said to her father. She told him she could see the pride on his face through the sadness, she knew that the message David had given him would make all the difference in his life. She then hesitated before asking, "David, when you are next in London will you please come and see me again, I would like that so much."

"It will probably be some little while," he replied, "but yes, I shall be delighted to come in and see you. Perhaps I could meet you after you finish work so that we can have a chat, but it will be months rather than days I'm afraid."

"I don't care how long. I shall look forward to seeing you again. Goodbye now, please take care."

He rang off, thinking to himself irreverently that everybody appears to be very solicitous of his welfare lately, a situation which increased in its intensity during the evening as all the rest of the 'family' called in to wish him well and to 'take care'.

When he returned to the kitchen from taking Mr Schultz call, Rose looked at him and said, "That gentleman asked for Captain Chandler – I thought he meant dad?" the phrase put as a question.

"Well, I forgot to tell you. They made me up to captain this morning – apparently it goes with the job." Everyone looked at him blankly.

"David, are you pulling our legs?" asked his mother.

"No, God's honour mum, I'm Captain Chandler now – same as dad. But it won't go to my head like it does to some people. I shall still be my old unassuming modest self, just as I was as a corporal, so don't move to a bigger house will you?"

Chapter Twenty Five

On Friday 25th April 1941, David presented himself in civilian clothes to Roper Street as previously instructed. There had been somewhat lingering farewells from all at Sandbury, Jack Hooper giving him a bear hug that nearly squeezed the breath from him, and even his father seemed more serious than his normal pensive self. He himself had butterflies in his stomach as the train moved on towards Victoria, which he brushed away with the thought that what he was about to do was a bit more positive than guarding blooming airfields. When he reached Roper Street he was again checked in by an A.T.S. sergeant in the front hallway, but this time by a barrel shaped no-nonsense lady wearing the General Service Medal from the Great War, a complete contrast to snooty of two days ago. He was again directed down the iron stairway to be met at the bottom by Jessica, dressed in neat tweeds and looking very trim. She could have bought those in Country Style he thought, and then winced at the thought of his Pat who was no longer there, but rarely far from his thoughts.

"Hello David, we're in for a bit of a wait I'm afraid – come this way." She led the way down the corridor almost to the end, opening a door into a comfortably furnished pleasantly lit sitting room. "Have a seat for a while, the usual conveniences are through there and I'll get some coffee sent along straight away."

David chose an armchair back against the wall facing the doorway, picking up a copy of the Daily Telegraph off a side table on the way. He had hardly started to read when a young A.T.S. corporal arrived with a tray of coffee and biscuits, which she put down on a table beside him. He thanked her, but she said nothing in reply, just smiled and left. For the next hour he read his paper, wondering from time to time, whether he had been forgotten.

There were several items of interest in the Telegraph. With Yugoslavia having capitulated the previous week, the position in the Balkans looked ominously like that in Belgium a year ago. Our troops in Greece were being driven back. Churchill had told the Axis powers that if either of them bombed Athens or Cairo we would blast Rome to bits. So far little aerial damage had been inflicted on the Greek mainland, though some of the islands had been attacked.

British troops in Iraq were preparing to face up to the possibility of fighting the Nazi sympathiser Rashid Ali's government troops. As these were supported by the Vichy French forces in neighbouring Syria, this could be, and eventually did become, the first occasion that we would be fighting our former allies. War makes some strange bedfellows as has often been said, but none more strange than the occasions upon which the French Foreign Legion were involved both here and in North Africa later. There were English and German Legionnaires along with French officers fighting the British and Free French. There were Vichy French troops fighting De Gaulle. There were Syrian Arabs fighting with Iraqis, the majority of whom were pro-British with a Nazi leader. It was all very confusing.

The back page covered the forthcoming Cup Final – Preston North End against Arsenal – good old Arsenal said David to himself, they'll win ten nil! But they didn't – they drew the first game at Wembley and Arsenal lost one nil in the replay at Blackburn!

Soon after noon Jessica returned. "Sorry to keep you hanging about. I'm afraid in this business an awful lot of time is spent in just waiting – days sometimes, so it's just as well you get a bit of practice now." Without further enlightenment as to the cause of his having to cool his heels, she departed, leaving David to think to himself that he was warm, he was comfortable, he was fed and he was being paid – why should he worry about being kept waiting? At ten to one Jessica reappeared with the invitation, "Come and have some lunch." They went into the corridor along to another room where there were several tables with starched clothes on, one table being laid up for two people to which she led him. They had a simple lunch, served by the young corporal who had brought him the coffee, comprising oxtail soup, meat pie with vegetables, and ending with apple pie and custard.

"I thoroughly enjoyed that," was David's verdict at the end of the meal.

"Just like mother makes eh?" replied Jessica

"Now there I have to disagree with you. Nice though it was, nobody cooks like my mother – she's a genius."

During the meal David had studiously avoided asking any questions about the general set-up and what the plans were for him, keeping the conversation to items he had read in the paper. However, when they had finished their coffee, Jessica told him she was sorry but he still had some waiting around to do, they were not leaving for Sussex until seven that evening and went on, "But as I said before, the waiting will be good practice for you." David was to remember her words on several occasions in the coming weeks when a number of places in which he had to wait were far less comfortable and secure than those he at present occupied.

When he got back to the sitting room he studied the small number of books stacked on a bookshelf in the corner of the room. Tucked away at the end of one of the shelves he came across the English version of 'The Good Soldier Schweik' and immediately a wide grin spread across his face when he recollected the time, many years ago now, when he read of the antics of the man who somehow always managed to survive chaos, bungling, and sometimes unadulterated anarchy, at the bottom of the pile in the German army. He had then read it in German, now sinking back into his chair; he started to read this edition with total absorption. At about half-past four the corporal brought him tea and a further plate of biscuits, but still remained silent. 'As Paddy would say' thought David, 'she knows how to keep her gob shut'.

At six o'clock Jessica reappeared, "We're going to have a quick bite," she informed him "and then we shall be on our way." They retraced their steps to the dining room where they were fed cold ham and chips, each finishing with biscuits, and a chunk of cheddar as big as the complete weeks ration for the whole Chandler family back at Sandbury.

They had just finished their coffee when the brigadier appeared, dressed in tweeds as before. "Sorry you've had to hang around David, but the car's ready now so off you go and I'll see you early next week."

They each got their belongings together, but instead of ascending the iron staircase, Jessica led David to the far end of the corridor, into a small room little larger than a cupboard, on one wall of which was a lift door opening into a fairly sizeable lift. Having ascended to 'G' a door opened on the opposite side of the entry door on to a covered yard in which stood a black Austin 16 – civilian plates noted David – with its back to them. The chauffeur opened the boot and quickly packed their things into it, he then held a rear door open for Jessica while David went to the opposite rear door and climbed in beside her. The driver flashed his lights at which two khaki clad figures ran out of a hut, peered outside through spy holes in the gate, and then quickly opened them for the car to exit into what was another side street which, in turn, led back into Baker Street. David found it extremely difficult not to comment, probably facetiously he thought afterwards, on all the cloak and dagger goings-on, but wisely kept his peace. He would learn one day that absolute attention to detail was the only means of staying alive in this business, hence the well-rehearsed procedure for leaving 39C Roper Street without being observed.

As they drove towards Marble Arch, Jessica told David, "You can talk freely in front of Mr Bellamy – he is a W.O.I. in the Intelligence Corps."

Again David had the facetious thought that regimental sergeant majors, which is what a W.O.I. was, weren't normally associated with the requirements of the Intelligence Corps, but he thought better of it. All he said was, "Nice to meet you Mr Bellamy," to which he received just a salutary nod of the head in reply, followed by silence for the rest of the journey.

They drove out through Brixton and Streatham, and as it got dark, David lost his bearings completely when Mr Bellamy cut across country on two occasions. At nine o'clock David was fairly bursting to 'water the horses' as Jack Hooper would have said, but was saved from what might have been a minor embarrassment in having to ask for a stop by Jessica saying, "Pull up at The Cricketers Mr Bellamy, we'll have a quick one there, I'm dying for a pee."

David giggled at this saying, "You and me both," and then thought she obviously knows the way pretty well. In about five minutes they drew up on the forecourt of a pub in the middle of a small village and went into the saloon bar, Mr Bellamy staying with the car. In reply to David's question as to what she would like to drink she said she would have a sherry, medium dry if they have it. They had, and David ordered two on the premise that if he had a beer he would be wanting to go again in the near future, he had no idea how much further they had to go and he was already wise enough in the workings of this outfit not to ask.

It was nearly 9.30 before the car swung into a narrow byroad and David eventually saw in the dim light of the slits from the blacked out headlamps the approach of a large pair of wrought iron gates. A War Department policeman emerged from the gatehouse to meet the car as it arrived whilst a second came out and stood ready to open the gates. Everything being satisfactory they passed through and drove up a long drive to a sizeable mansion barely visible in the dark of the night and against the background of trees. As they approached, a soldier and an A.T.S. girl emerged from the house to meet them. David got out of the car as the soldier approached.

"Did you have a good journey Sir?" said the unmistakable voice of Paddy O'Riordan.

"Paddy, how good to see you," replied David, grabbing Paddy's arm and shaking his hand warmly.

Jessica joined them. "Good evening Paddy," she said, "will you take Captain Chandler's things to his room whilst we get a bit of supper."

"Yes ma'am, certainly ma'am."

David had the certain feeling these two had already met, which meant Paddy had been here at least a couple of days. "God, I'm even thinking like an undercover man already," he told himself.

They had some cold beef and pickles and some trifle which had, apparently, been left over from dinner, taken in a small side room off the main entrance hall, at the conclusion of which Jessica told him that she would take him to his room and that he should present himself in the main hall in plain clothes at 8 o'clock the next morning, when she would introduce him to the Commandant. They would then have breakfast after which she would show him around and at 10 o'clock he would start on his instruction.

David had been very circumspect so far, not asking questions, not querying anything that was happening to him, not asking where he was or what the instruction he was to receive was all about, but his curiosity got the better of him when Jessica told him he would be making a start in the morning.

"Jessica, before you take me off to my room, is it in order for you to tell me exactly what you are and where you fit in here? You are obviously not an A.T.S. sergeant, you work closely with a brigadier, and I only know he's a brigadier because his son is a great pal of mine and I've stayed at their home with the Earl, his grandfather." He had spoken quite seriously up until now but ended in a jocular frame, "It's all very confusing to a simple soul like me."

Jessica put her hands on his forearm across the table and looked directly into his eyes. "For reasons you will fully understand later, it is essential you don't know who I am nor what I do. Jessica is not my real name; any more than the pseudonym you will be given will be your real name. By these means we hope to keep secure from each other in the event of one of us being caught."

"You mean in the event of my being caught," replied David. "After all, you already know who I am."

"Someone has to know – unfortunately – but the fewer the better."

"I understand," he paused, "but does this mean you're going over as well?"

"That is not something I can answer."

"I'm sorry Jessica, I shouldn't have asked you all that. I shall be awake all night though trying to imagine what your real name is!" She squeezed his arm.

They got up and walked out into the hall and up the magnificent stairway, the treads of which were boarded over for protection from the hobnailed boots of the rough soldiery to whom the mansion had been loaned for the duration. On the second landing she approached a magnificent oak door and said, "Well here you are – eight o'clock main entrance hall – see you there," turned and walked to a door two rooms away, opened it, turned and looked at David still looking after her, gave a little wave and was gone. He walked into the room to find Paddy sitting in an easy chair.

"There you are Sir, I've got everything tidied away. Now, what's the programme in the morning Sir?"

"Not so fast, not so fast," replied David. "I want to know how you got here and if you know what the hell's going on, knowing as I do, if you don't know, nobody does."

Paddy told his story. The adjutant himself had arrived at Highmere on Tuesday night and got the orderly corporal to find him. "It was about nine o'clock and Driscoll and me had had one or two in the NAAFI, but I was fairly sober you understand."

"I understand," David said with a half grin and an inward chuckle.

Apparently the adjutant had told him to get all his own and Mr Chandler's kit together, "and I mean 'all'," he said, "and have it ready to load on a civilian shooting brake which would arrive at 0830 Thursday morning – yesterday that is." He was then to be prepared to be on detachment for three weeks and was given an A.P.O. number where people could write to him. He was brought to the hall, made to sign the Official Secrets form, told he was not to endeavour under penalty of imprisonment to find out information to which he was not entitled, and that was that.

"I put two and bloody two together Sir, and I came up with the answer that you're on some bloody operation or other and that hopefully I shall be coming with you."

"All I can tell you Paddy is that I'm afraid you won't." Paddy looked as crestfallen as David had ever seen him.

"Then I'll say some prayers for you Sir. I don't say many, come to that I don't say any very often, so perhaps they'll work all the better."

"Thanks Paddy. Now, in the morning, tea at 7.15, civvies, brothel creepers," (brothel creepers were his crepe soled shoes – he judged they would be better to walk around the mansion in rather than the brogues) "and as soon as I know more about what you are to do while I'm off I'll let you know."

Paddy said his goodnights and went off leaving David again to try and imagine what the morrow would bring, and where would he be, and what would he be doing in another month's time. As he climbed into bed, he remembered Cedric looking down into his slit trench and saying 'Exciting isn't it?' and wondering if at this moment he was excited, scared, curious or just plain fatalistic. Thinking of Cedric led him to thought of Maria. Just an ordinary girl, he thought, pretty but not glamorous, a nice trim figure but not voluptuous, she had a kind gentle manner, softly spoken and sincere. Due to the circumstances in which they had met, he had no means of knowing whether she was amusing or whether she totally lacked a sense of humour. Well, when this caper was over he would see her and find out. He had quite taken to her, and then he had the amusing thought – a captain in the Rifles taking a waitress out? What the hell would Ponsonby have said about that? This led to thinking of Charlie's extracting the urine out of Ponsonby, at which he chuckled to himself. Charlie, poor old Charlie, how is he going to manage for three months without me to wipe his nose for him? He chuckled again and soon was asleep.

They breakfasted well, before which Jessica announced a slight change of plans. The commandant could not see David until nine o'clock, so they would tour the inside of the establishment after breakfast, then see the commandant, and after that have a quick look around outside. As soon as they had met, Jessica told him:

"Normally the commandant would see you first and tell you your code name, by which name you will be known to everybody. Your batman has already been told not to mention your name to anyone. Anyway, apparently the commandant was held up at the airfield this morning, that's why he's late, I have therefore been instructed to give you your nom de guerre by which you will be known to all here and in France. It is Cooteman – I don't know where he got that from."

"I do, Colonel Coote-Manningham was the founder, with Colonel Stewart, of the first corps of Riflemen during the Napoleonic Wars. By jove, he must have gone to a lot of trouble to delve into regimental history and find that one."

"As you will see over the next couple of weeks, attention to the finest detail is the watchword here. Your name, therefore, will constantly remind you of that requirement."

As they made their rounds, they met several people to whom David was introduced – 'This is Cooteman' – until when, at last, they reached the commandant's office he was already beginning to think of himself as Cooteman. The places he was shown were as diverse as could be. There were several small classrooms, what appeared to be a chemistry or physics lab, a very well equipped gymnasium, a swimming bath, wireless room, cinema, and a drawing office where two men and a young woman working at their boards nodded and said hello as he was introduced.

Jessica knocked on the commandant's door, which was opened by a middle-aged civilian lady, introduced to David as Mary who asked them to come straight through to the inner office. David had been trying to build a picture in his mind as to what the commandant would look like, half suspecting he would be either a suave Ronald Coleman type or a rugged older version of Jack Hawkins. In the event he was more than surprised to find the man who greeted him, dressed in the uniform of an RAF wing commander, was small, thin, sparsely tonsured and wearing old style pince-nez spectacles. As he gripped David's hand in welcome however, David got his first intimation that there was more to this man than met the eye. The grip was firm, the look penetrating, the movements quick and decisive.

"Please be seated," he asked, and continued, "well Cooteman, I do apologise for being late, we had a little trouble last night." He did not elaborate on this statement. "Jessica is your mentor for a few days, anything you need, anything you want to know, see her, she has authority to the highest level here. By now you will have understood the reasons for the apparent secrecy at this establishment. In covert operations what you don't know, and even more important, who you don't know, can't be dragged from you should you be caught. Secondly making this sort of detail a religion in your own life reduces your being caught to an absolute minimum. You will learn that unfortunately the security factor of some of the people over there you have to deal with is pretty minimal, but you will be given instruction as to how to cope with this as far as you are able. We've only got two weeks to assess you, train you and provide you with all the information you will need to do the extremely important task you have been set. If at the end of the two weeks we consider that you are not ready, we shall have to return you to your unit. I tell you that because I'm obliged to – I personally think, having read your record and the reports on you through your career so far, it will be most unlikely such an event will occur." He lifted a file from his desk and gave it to Jessica. "Take him to Robin at ten Jessica please and give this to Mary, will you? Thank you my dear." At that he stood up, all five feet five inches of him and concluded, "I shall see you every couple of days – keep at it."

"Yes Sir, thank you Sir."

"No Sir's here, you call me commandant."

They left the office and made their way out of the building to a large rear quadrangle which housed a number of garages, some of which were open, showing a variety of civilian and service vehicles. Beyond the quadrangle there was a sports field containing a football pitch and a running track, and against the background of a very thick clump of trees, David saw a twenty-five-yard firing range. It crossed his mind that although this unit was very well provided for in the way of space, facilities and equipment he hadn't, as yet, seen more than a dozen or so people. Very puzzling.

At ten o'clock they attended the admin office where he was introduced to Robin, who looked and probably was an ex-diplomat. He told David he had arranged his course for him and then launched into a fast and furious description of what was to happen in perfect German. Gradually the monologue developed into a two way conversation, David being a little slow at first, but gradually regaining all his old fluency.

After twenty minutes of this exchange Robin said to Jessica, "Well, his German is pretty well faultless," and to David, "Now, we've got to teach you the Swiss accent and peculiarities, because the background you have to adopt is that of a Swiss engineer, a specialist in corrosion technology in France to work for the Todt organisation. I understand you did, in fact, work on one or two corrosion projects with Mr Phillips before the war – is that not so?"

"Er, yes, that is so." He was bursting to ask how and whether he knew Mr Phillips.

"Right then, we have a Swiss book on corrosion which you can mug up in your spare time. This cover is obviously only to be used should you ever be stopped. Your passport and entry visa and letter from the Todt people will carry you through any ordinary check, but if you were interrogated in any depth, the product knowledge could make all the difference to making you look bona fide. Now the next thing is to brush up your French so that you can talk reasonably intelligently to the

Resistance people. We have a sort of language laboratory which you will attend for two hours each day, concentrating entirely on spoken French, learning the slang and so on. You will have one hour per day for at least four days in the cinema where you will be shown, and in some cases, hear the generals we anticipate being at Le Mans. There will be an intensive course on German Army general staff structure, divisional and army pennants and so on, all of which must be memorised as you can carry no aide-memoirs of any of these matters. You will learn to use the radio, but it is unlikely you will be called upon to carry out this task as we have a specially trained cipher man there to transmit your messages. Your main problem, which will be described to you in much fuller detail later, is getting the message to the transmitter, since he has to move constantly to avoid being traced by the Gestapo detector vans. You will, incidentally, take him a new and better radio when you go. Right, well I think that's all for now. You've got twenty minutes before your first French lesson at eleven o'clock. I suggest Jessica takes you to the canteen for a quick coffee."

David stood up and said, "Thank you..." he was just going to say 'Sir' – after nearly five years in the army it was almost second nature – but he recovered himself and ended with "...Robin." As they walked quickly to the canteen David remarked to Jessica, "What the hell do I do in my spare time?"

The days passed quickly. David was worked from 8am until 1pm, then 2pm to 5pm. Dinner at 6.30. Final session 8-9.30. Exhausted he just fell into bed each night. On the second day he asked Paddy what he did with himself all day.

"Well Sir, they knew I'd been in the M.T. section for several years so as from tomorrow they're going to get me overhauling all the vehicles, cars, motor bikes, vans, lorries, even a bren gun carrier they've got here, civilian and W.D. I tell you Sir, it's an eye opener. They tell me that when you've gone I have fourteen days leave and then come back and carry on until you return. It seems I'm the only regular here except for half a dozen A.T.S girls who look after the permanent staff."

"Have you got your feet under the table in that direction yet?"

"Well Sir, you know me better than that, though I must say there's a nice piece of homework in the kitchen I could fancy. Still, it's early days yet."

"I thought there might be somehow, so take care, wilier birds even than you have been caught in the snare before today."

"I'll remember every word you've said Sir."

On the Saturday afternoon Robin told him he was doing well enough to take a day off on Sunday. "There's a Morris 10 with a full tank in the garage you can borrow – will get you to Sandbury and back with no trouble I should think." He passed a quarter inch Ordnance Survey map on the table. David was astonished and delighted.

"But I thought…" he started to say.

"This isn't a concentration camp old boy. If we couldn't trust you out on your own you wouldn't have been here in the first place."

"To be truthful I just hadn't thought about it at all. I just assumed that once I was here that was it."

"Well, give my regards to your family. By the way, you know Brigadier Halton I believe."

"Yes I do." (But how the hell does he know that?)

"If you should bump into him give him my regards, we are good friends from way back."

David decided to make an early start the next morning. The first his family knew of his presence was the black Austin 10 crunching up the drive soon after eight o'clock. Rose looking out of the window called to her mother, "There's a black car coming to the front, who on earth can that be?"

"Well it wouldn't be the billeting officer, he always comes in an army car, and Jack's car is maroon."

They both hurried to see who their caller was at such an hour, opened the door and were confronted by the least likely person in the world they would have expected to find on their doorstep that morning. After the initial excitement and a cooked breakfast using the last of the week's eggs, during which David had to tell them he was only there for a few hours, the car had been loaned to him, and the course he was on was quite interesting. Apart from that he said the job he was on would be starting soon, and then he'd see them all in a few weeks. They were all intelligent enough not to probe further.

"We're going to church at half-past ten for the eleven o'clock service," said Ruth, "would you like to come?"

"Yes, very much," he replied, "but I'll go a bit earlier and see you there. I want to go to Pat first."

"Alright dear, we put fresh flowers there yesterday from the garden. We'll save a place for you in our usual pew."

David walked to the churchyard and as he had done so many times before, stood by Pat's grave and reminisced in his mind all the wonderful times they had shared together from the time he first saw her as a young girl, elegant even then, riding her bike. He smiled as he thought how he had passed her several times before he plucked up the courage to speak to her and how neither of them had ever looked seriously at anyone else ever since that day. As he stood there, lost to the world, a familiar voice at his elbow said, "Are you absent without leave?" He turned and smiled at the brigadier.

"Not exactly Sir, but while we're on our own a chap called Robin asked me to give you his kindest regards."

"So that's where you are," – the brigadier's voice had turned from the jocular to the very serious. "I'll be thinking of you David. Tell Robin from me," returning to the jocular, "I'll have his guts for garters if he doesn't look after you properly, that's a threat!!" And he added, "We were at school together you know."

"I'll tell him Sir – but if I do, am I likely to be cashiered?"

"Civilians can't cashier you, not even important ones." They said no more on the subject.

After the service they all went back to lunch, including the brigadier. Anni, Ernie, Karl and baby David were already there but the marines were away on an exercise on some lake or other in mid-Wales, so David was informed. It looked possible that they would be losing Ivan and Ken soon, which as Ruth said, was very sad. They had both become part of the home, as did Alex and Jim before them. Not so much the Australians though but that wasn't their fault. Then these inconsiderate generals whisk them away, with a look of mock censure at the brigadier.

"C'est la guerre Ruth, C'est la guerre – blame Hitler. On the other hand you wouldn't have had the pleasure of knowing them if it hadn't been for Hitler, so perhaps you ought to drop him a line and thank him." This riposte caused general amusement, but David noted that his mother and the brigadier appeared to be on Christian name terms. Who would have thought back at Mountfield such a relatively short time ago they would be entertaining a general for lunch on first name terms? He smiled to himself, and then remembered how Pat had caught him smiling to himself on one occasion. What are you smiling at? She had said. Nothing was the reply. People get put away for smiling at nothing she had told him, snuggling up a little closer.

"Wake David up," he heard Rose saying.

"Oh sorry, did you say something. Come to think of it that would not be unusual, you are usually saying something," came the quick rejoinder from David.

"Punch his ribs brigadier please," asked Rose.

"Sorry my dear, against King's Regulations. It clearly says brigadiers must not thump captains – at least when anyone is looking."

"I was asking, dear brother; at what hour do you have to depart this evening?"

David addressed the brigadier, "Sir, why is it that as soon as you get home they all want to know when you're going back?"

Rose butted in. "In your case the reason for that must be obvious." David winked at Anni, sitting next to Rose.

"Thump her ribs," he asked.

"Can't thump nursing mothers," replied Anni.

By no stretch of the imagination could you call this badinage the epitome of dinner table conversation thought the brigadier, but how enjoyable it was to someone like him who had seen so little of family life since his dear wife was killed, furthermore how preferable it was to some of the pompous bores he had to listen to at the senior officers' mess. Just as in years gone by, the Chandlers had brought Jack Hooper out of a state of despair into normality, so now, without their consciously doing it, the same was being achieved with the brigadier.

After Sunday lunch they all sat around talking about the war situation. Fred came from the factory soon after four o'clock – there was no work there on Sunday nights, the only time in the week when the place was more or less silent except for the maintenance men working on essential tasks and earning double time and bonus into the bargain. They could earn nearly five pounds working through Sunday night, that was the equivalent of a week's wages for an ordinary bench hand, but few had the skills or the stamina for the tasks involved, consequently there was no queue at the factory gate of people looking for one of the jobs.

They had tea and soon it was time for David to say his farewells and climb back into the Austin. It had been a lovely day, a totally unexpected, wonderful surprise for the family. He wondered when he would see them all again. He wondered if he would see them all again and then brushed that thought aside as being in the same class as defeatism, and that would never do.

On Monday, Lord Ramsford arrived and joined David during his coffee break. He said he was pleased with David's progress and grateful to him for his application to the tasks he had had to undertake.

"Is it in order to ask when I can expect to be on my way Sir?"

asked David.

"Yes of course, but the truth is I cannot answer you with any degree of certainty. Sometimes we can tell you to the minute, sometimes you have to wait around for days. There are so many variables, weather here, weather over there, availability of the return passengers, whether the landing sites are clear or not, suddenly imposed curfews, all sorts of things can throw spanners in the works. I shall see you on Friday or Saturday to finally brief you, by then we should know positively."

"Thank you Sir."

On Wednesday they checked all the civilian clothes he would be either wearing or taking, making sure that no telltale labels could give him away should he be stopped for questioning. To add authenticity, a Swiss label was sewn on to his sports jacket after they had made sure none of the selvages on the cloth had a British name, which of course meant removing some of the lining and then resewing it. His shoes were an absolute giveaway, sporting a 'British is Best' imprint on the inside of the upper. They were speedily replaced.

"We do all this here David," explained Robin, "but when you get to the airfield you will be stripped and every single garment will be examined again to make sure nothing has been missed or you haven't left an unpaid gas bill in your pocket accidentally."

That night David was lying in his bed in the light of the bedside lamp finishing off 'The Good Soldier Schweik', which he had 'borrowed' from Roper Street. It was close to midnight when there was a tap on the door. David called, "Come in," and to his surprise Jessica came in to the dimly lit room, closing the door behind her. She was dressed in a green dressing gown over pale green pyjamas and wore a pair of moccasin type slippers, which moved noiselessly over the large square of carpet with which the room was furnished. Approaching the bed David saw her face clearly for the first time, no longer the serene, competent, confident Jessica of Roper Street, but a Jessica showing great strain, almost fear.

"What's the matter Jessica?" said David, starting to sit up.

"Please David; may I come in with you for a little while?"

"Of course, of course, what has happened?"

She slipped into the bed; it was only a single bed so that David had to move hard up against the wall to let her in, but as he did so he slipped his arm around her shoulders and held her closely to him. She was trembling uncontrollably, he kept silent. At length her agitation decreased and she whispered, "I'm so sorry to have bothered you like this."

David held her closer, "Now, what's the matter, what's happened?"

"I'm away tomorrow. Usually the night before I go I sleep like a top. I have an early night and nothing wakes me. Tonight I've had such a terribly life-like dream. The Gestapo were chasing me and set dogs on me which were tearing me to pieces – it was so real."

"I know I shouldn't ask you this, but you said that usually you sleep like a top. Does this mean that you've been over before?"

"Yes, this is my fourth operation."

"God, no wonder you had a nightmare."

"I feel much better now, thank you for not getting the wrong idea." David held her close against him and they stayed silent for probably half an hour as she became more and more peaceful. At length she turned her face to him and in hushed tones murmured, "David, I am twenty-eight-years old and I'm still a virgin. When I come back do you think we could meet again like this so that I can thank you properly? I would tonight but it's not possible. Probably that's one of the reasons I'm a bit low." She hurried on, "When I first saw you at Roper Street I was immediately attracted to you." She held him closer and put her head onto his chest so that he could not see her face. "I would like my first experience of real intimacy to be with you."

There was another long silence until David lifted her chin, kissed her gently and replied simply. "I would like that honour very much." They kissed again before she said she must now go.

"Before you go, know that I shall be thinking of you all the while," David assured her.

"And I you. Goodbye now. I'll come and meet you when you come back. I shall be here before you return."

But she never did come back. A member of the group she joined took blood money from the Gestapo and betrayed her and two of his comrades. After a perfunctory examination her two comrades were shot. She was shot the following day attempting to escape. The bulk of the payment the Judas received was spent in the company of a whore, who promptly ditched him when the money ran out. His wife found out about this and told her brother, who was also a member of the organisation. Along with the surviving members of the group they took the miserable wretch to a farm some fifteen kilometres from their village, threw him bound hand and foot into a cess pit which accepted the drainings from dozens of pig sties, and held him under with long handled hay forks. They considered it was a fitting way such ordure should end its days.

Chapter Twenty Six

On Saturday 10th May David was called for a briefing from Lord Ramsford. The main thrust of the information the brigadier was looking for and hoping to obtain from the eavesdropping David was to carry out, was first and foremost intelligence relating to the suspected invasion of Russia by the Wehrmacht.

"We have information from our people in Poland of large troop movements there, but no definite information as to their purpose. What we want to know is if and when the attack is to take place, where the main assault will be and, if possible, who the commanders are. Now I know that's a tall order, but if you can find out part of what's going on it will help. Secondly the government is most anxious to make a register of senior German officers who oppose Hitler. You will get no indication of direct opposition that's for sure, but you will certainly get occasional covert remarks which might give you a lead."

After a lengthy discussion on procedures, security and other matters the brigadier ended with, "Only use the radio for urgent messages, but keep a day-to-day diary of exchanges of relevant conversations you overhear, even if you don't consider them greatly of use, and send them back on the bus service marked 'Robin.' We shall then analyse them." He ended abruptly – "You will be away on Monday night, Robin will give you all the details. Good luck David, I'll see you in a few weeks, and don't forget, keep out of trouble, you're not there to fight." He then added, "Not that the poor blighters have anything much to fight with at present so you should be safe enough on that score." He stood up, shook David's hand warmly and said, "Take care." Another one telling me to take care, thought David, as if I'm going to do anything else but!

On Sunday afternoon he got his final briefing from Robin. He would be taking off from Tangmere at 11pm the next day flying due south, landing near the small town of Alencon. He would be accommodated overnight at a safe house on the outskirts of Alencon, the next morning travelling by train in the company of a young woman from the safe house who would conduct him to another safe house in Le Mans. There he would be contacted by 'Gérard' who would acquaint him further regarding the operation. "Remember always travel first class and be well dressed, you will be less likely to be stopped and searched. The girl, incidentally, will act as if she was a particularly good friend of yours, but don't get any ideas or you'll have Gérard slitting your throat!"

It was the custom for agents to be invited in uniform if they were serving officers, to dinner with the C.O. at Tangmere before they changed into the civilian clothes they would be wearing in France. As a result, Paddy was sent in a p.u. with David's civvies and would bring back his uniform after the mandatory strip search before he boarded the aircraft. There were four flights going out that night, one of them carrying a French colonel who, meeting David in the anteroom of the mess before dinner, came over and embraced him.

"I will not ask how you came by those honours," he said, pointing at the two French medal ribbons, "I will only say you must have performed an outstanding service to my country for which I salute you."

"Thank you Sir, you are most kind."

At the end of the meal the wing commander rose quietly and sincerely wished their guests Godspeed and a safe return, after which David was taken to a dressing room where he was surprised to see Robin stretched out in any easy chair talking to Paddy. "Thought I'd come and see you off," he said.

"Now Sir, you've to take everything off and change into these clothes. I've pressed them up well so you should look reasonable, like they told me."

Robin continued with further instructions. "Here's your suitcase with spare clothes, Swiss razor and shaving soap etc and in this smaller case is the radio. They'll take that from you when you land; we can't risk your carrying it on the train. In this wallet, 'Made in Germany' incidentally, is your passport, visa, letters of introduction and so on, and a reasonable amount of French and Swiss money. In the base of the suitcase there is a substantial sum of French Francs in case you need it for any purpose. Gérard will tell you where you can get further sums in case of emergencies, we can't see that happening but you never know. All fit then? Right, we'll go and meet your pilot – your carriage awaits."

"I must have a 'Jimmy Riddle' first."

"I guessed you would – everybody does!" They both laughed at what was, in the final analysis, not exactly a laughing matter.

When David returned, Paddy held out his hand, "God bless you Sir, I wish I was coming with you."

"Do you know what Paddy? So do I."

They shook hands firmly and Robin led the way to the hangar where the aircraft was waiting. Robin introduced David to the pilot who was to fly the Lysander, affectionately known by all as 'the Lizzie' into France in a couple of hours' time. He pointed out the flight path on his map to David, showing how they would be going more or less due south with a small detour to miss Caen where there were some rather nasty ack-ack batteries. The pilot was a staff sergeant who looked terribly young even to David, who himself was not exactly ancient at the age of twenty-three.

"We'll cross the French coast just east of Arromanches. I'll fly in as low as I can to try and catch them by surprise, but we're bound to get a bit of flak there – nothing to worry about though."

David wished his feelings were as optimistic as the staff sergeant's, his stomach beginning to do a tango at the thought of being shot at again.

As they stood there looking at the Lizzie, David noted the auxiliary fuel tank slung under the belly.

"Mind if I have a look at that?" he asked.

"Be my guest," replied the pilot, "but I must say that's the first time anyone's asked to do that – it's not exactly a stunningly attractive part of the airplane."

David grinned, looked at the serial number and reference code stamped near the filler cap and read, "Type 22Z 1764 940 SE."

"What's so interesting then about that?" asked the pilot, watching David read the classification.

"My father made that tank," he answered.

"In that case, if it doesn't work I shall remember not to come and pick you up," the pilot laughingly told him. "In fact, what happens is we use that tank first and then dump it, so every flight I make means a few bob more for your father I suppose," ribbing David gently.

"I'll tell him you're on commission."

After some twenty minutes an L.A.C. came to the group. "We've got to roll you out now staff." A corporal and three others appeared, switched the hangar lights off, opened the main door and rolled the Lizzie out. "See you in about half an hour," David was cheerily told.

That half hour dragged to about forty minutes before the L.A.C. came back and reported, "We're ready now Sir."

David shook hands with Robin. "Now don't forget to listen out for the BBC announcements. You know what the various messages mean by heart, so listen out even if you're not expecting anything. Goodbye, good luck, see you in about three months."

The L.A.C. led David out to the ladder at the side of the rear cockpit. David climbed in, was handed his two cases, helped into his harness by the L.A.C. who also showed him where his flying helmet with the communication line to the pilot was situated. The helmet having been put on, the L.A.C. tapped him on the shoulder, gave him the thumbs up, leaned back, slid the cockpit cover forward and secured it, climbed down, took away the ladder and stood clear of the aircraft.

"Next stop France," David said to himself as slowly the Lysander made it's way out on to the field revving up hard as it went. "I wonder how he does that without it taking off," David said to himself. "I shouldn't think they'd have a clutch, perhaps he's got his foot on the brake." He made a mental note to find out once he got the chance. Slowly the short squat plane with its high level wings turned into the wind, rushed forward and in an incredibly short space of time was airborne. David had been told that Lizzie's could take off and land on a cricket pitch, and although that was rather stretching a point, it didn't seem far from the truth to him as he began to experience his first flight. They ceased climbing after a while and levelled off. There was a crackling in his headphones as the cheery voice said, "All OK back there?"

"Yes thank you – but this is my first flight so I hope I don't disgrace you."

"You'll have no trouble, there's little wind tonight. If you were sick of course you would have to slide the cockpit cover open, then I fly upside down so that the gulls can have it." David marvelled at the sangfroid of this young airman. He imagined that when he met people on leave and elsewhere and they asked him what he flew, he would just answer "Oh, just a Lizzie." They would probably never find out he flew this Lizzie into moonlit fields deep in France time and again landing by the light of a few torches, never knowing whether he was flying into a hornet's nest or not, running the flak gauntlet each time he crossed and recrossed the coast. There was none of the glamour of flying a Spitfire or a Stirling. I reckon he's a bloody hero, he thought. A bit like old Cedric in some ways. Thinking of Cedric made him think of Maria, and he smiled. Yes, he would like to see Maria again. I wonder what she would think if she knew I was several thousand feet up above the English Channel at this moment, he thought, that's if she ever thinks of me at all.

But she was thinking of him, and had hardly stopped thinking of him since she kissed his cheek a month ago.

He saw the dark mass of the coast line approaching and as he had been warned, several streams of tracer soon started drifting up towards him. Initially it was well off target, but suddenly a stream hurtled towards the tiny aircraft causing David to duck as it crackled above him. His headphone crackled again.

"You alright Sir?"

"You're joking of course – I'm glad I've got my brown underpants on." There was a laugh from the pilot.

"It doesn't last long. We'll get a few more bursts," – as he spoke another stream of lights flew up on their left. David knew that for every tracer he could see there were probably between ten or twenty rounds of most unpleasant hardware spaced between. He would be not unhappy at all to be somewhere else at this moment. In a couple of minutes, which seemed like hours, they had flown over the coastline and were heading inland.

"Not long now Sir. I may have to stooge around to find the landing site, so if you can keep watch over the port side – that's the left side to you – I'll watch out on the right. If you see torches giving three long and one short flash, that's our lot."

After another ten minutes David heard the engine throttling back and started to watch out as he had been instructed. It was then it struck him that his machine had got to land with no landing lights on a rough field at approaching a hundred miles an hour initially. As a result of these thoughts his stomach started another tango. His trepidation was interrupted by the pilot calling, "Over on the right." David looked out and saw the flashing torch, and when an answering flash went back from the young staff sergeant, the plane banked and turned and headed for its landing place. As it did so, David saw torches held in a letter 'L,' the pilot to land along the upright of the 'L' and turn 90 degrees and stop along the foot. As they started to run in David received his final instructions. "Hang up your helmet when I've finished Sir, get your cases ready to hand out and get out as quickly as you can so that my return passengers can get aboard."

"Passengers?"

"Yes, I'm taking two back tonight. It's a bit of a squeeze. Damned good job they're not both your size. Good luck Sir, see you again."

"I sincerely hope so, and many thanks. I shan't forget my first flight for a while I can tell you."

As David took off his flying hat and hung it up, he could see they were swishing in towards the straight row of torches on a stretch of open ground bordered on three sides by woodland. Deftly the staff sergeant put the Lizzie down on to the lumpy field, turned her to the left and stopped, keeping the engine revving slightly. Instantly half a dozen men ran to the plane, put a short ladder against it, took the two cases, helped David down and then helped the two returnees in. They both looked like women David thought, though they were well muffled up making it difficult to be sure. Two bundles were handed up; a bottle of champagne was passed up to the pilot, the ladder cleared away and the men all stood clear. Within four minutes the Lizzie was taking off again leaving a welcoming silence with those on the ground.

"Come quickly Cooteman, we must get away from here," said a voice at his elbow. He was handed his case and followed the others to a nearby wood and then along a narrow track through the wood for half an hour before emerging at the rear of a cluster of farm buildings. In the farmyard was a battered Renault truck with a covered in back into which the men climbed, indicating that David should join them. With the back sheets pulled over and secured, the truck started off through by-roads to the safe house at Alencon some ten kilometres away. On the outskirts of Alencon they turned into what David subsequently found to be a builder's yard. The gates being closed behind them, the men dispersed silently into the night leaving David with the man who had first spoken to him at the landing site.

"Come Cooteman, you will be staying here for two days, before you go on to Le Mans."

They went through a small door into the rear of the building, along a passageway, which led into the kitchen. His guide then removed his balaclava and jerkin and introduced himself as Guy, and the middle-aged couple who awaited them as 'our farmer friends – it's as well you do not know their names'. On the table they had laid out ham and cheese and some crispy homemade bread, indicating the two arrivals to be seated and eat up. David marvelled at the quiet courage of these people, knowing as they did what would happen to them if the Gestapo or even the French special police discovered their activities. It would only take a carelessly dropped word in a café or market to give away their complicity with the Resistance to the sharp ears of the security men; it was as well that as few people as possible knew their names.

The next two days passed very slowly, David remembering what Jessica had said about 'waiting around'. He had been told not to wander outside, they were fairly near a main road and casual callers were not unknown. On Thursday evening Guy appeared and said the truck would call for David at 8 o'clock the next morning with a young lady called 'Georgette' who would take him to the railway station and then on to Le Mans. This is it, thought David, I've got to go out there and face people, even Germans. The tango started all over again. The journey was, however, reasonably uneventful. They had first class tickets and steering clear of the compartments labelled 'Nur fur Wehrmacht' they found an empty compartment, where at the second stop they were joined by a cleric who immediately broke into a voluble conversation with David who in turn answered by asking if the reverend gentleman could speak more slowly as he was Swiss and his French was not as good as it should be. The priest murmured his apologies and promptly stopped talking altogether – it was David's first experience of the suspicion held by the populace at large of anything that was not immediately explicable. The cleric was travelling with a person who did not speak good French, he probably, therefore, being Swiss spoke German. In that case, it would be possible that he was not Swiss at all, but German, and if he was pretending to be Swiss he could be Gestapo. If he was Gestapo then the less said the better.

When they alighted at Le Mans, David helped Georgette on to the platform and was rewarded with a little kiss on the cheek as she took his arm and walked toward the exit, she looking up at him talking and smiling as they approached the barrier, to all the world like a young couple in love – which in France as David mused afterwards, would reduce any suspicion there might be to nil. They boarded a bus to the centre of the town and got off at the Hotel de Paris. From there Georgette crossed the road, went into a bookshop by the front entrance and after a few seconds pause, out of a rear entrance into a narrow side street. A few paces further she entered a bar, went through the bar and out of the rear door into yet another side street and then through a large door opposite into the courtyard of a house. David had been put through the drill in England as to the precautions one had to take to approach a safe house, how to vary the approaches, how always, if possible, to have an escape route from the approaches. Attention to detail – detail is everything he had been told; now he was seeing it in action.

Georgette knocked twice on the large rear door of the house, paused for a couple of seconds and then gave three further knocks. Immediately the door was opened and they moved quickly in to the somewhat gloomy interior. As soon as the door was closed and bolted behind them Georgette flew into the arms of the stocky dark haired man who had admitted them. "So" thought David, "this must be Gérard – he of the throat cutting propensity".

Gérard turned, "Welcome Cooteman," he said, shaking hands with a massive fist instantly reminding David of Jack Hooper, his father-in-law, who had hands like dinner plates. "We shall have some lunch and then I will show you what we are going to do and introduce you to your two assistants." They went up to the second floor to a bedroom which looked out through shutters over a fairly busy road along which half a dozen young German soldiers were walking, talking loudly and ribbing each other as young soldiers do in any army.

"This is your room Cooteman; I will show you the escape route from your corridor out of the back of the building and over the next roof later on. Let's hope we never need to use it."

Detail, David thought again, all this detail.

Gérard spoke good English, but David's training caused him to resist asking how and where he had become so proficient. After lunch Gérard announced they would now go down to the listening post. This was located in the cellar at the end of a passage behind two heavily built doors each fitted with substantial bolts on the operators' side. He wondered about this but when they entered the cellar, a room about twelve feet square, Gérard pointed to a stack of wine crates. "Behind those is an exit to the next two cellars along the street. Should there be a raid you bolt the doors and go out that way and out into the street behind."

The equipment in the cellar was quite basic. Just three sets of headphones at a well-lighted bench against one wall. Gérard explained "Our colleagues in the telephone service have been able to tap into the wires from the three main senior officers' messes and have run them here. They worked right under the noses of the German security people, and openly in the streets as if it were an everyday job. They had vans everywhere and because it was all so obvious not a single Boche suspected anything!"

As he spoke the door opened and in came Georgette with two young lads.

"These are your helpers," announced Gérard. "This is Jean-Paul, this is Jacques. They are both seventeen-years-old and in the top grade at the high school here, with German as their special subject. I believe you are to get out a rota as soon as you can establish when the need is greatest, so I'll leave that to you to work out."

David shook hands with the lads. They both looked very young indeed and yet here they were, prepared to risk their lives for their country, at a time when it would appear to the world the Germans were invincible.

"When do we start?" asked David.

"It is all ready now," replied Gérard; "it was finished yesterday. So – we switch on the main here, the white lights above each set of headphones show that the lines are operating, and underneath there is a green light which will come on when the line is in use. You can note the timing of the calls – it may be important perhaps – from the clock on the wall, but remember the clock has to be wound up, we could not risk an electric clock, the supply gets interrupted from time to time as you will soon find out. That too is why we have these stand-by candle lamps. The telephone incidentally still works even if there is a cut-off in the electricity supply."

As they spoke one of the green lights went on. Gérard indicated to David to take the headset, he then experiencing the strange feeling of listening in to a senior German officer talking to a tailor in Le Mans about some breeches he was having made. The call finished, David explained to the others the gist of the conversations; the only important part of it being that the general called himself General Freiber, so that name would be the first item on the list of what David had noted in his mind, as being 'seemingly useless information', although as had been pointed out to him in Sussex 'what may seem useless to you may well be invaluable to us – we put the jigsaw together – you provide some of the pieces'.

During the rest of the afternoon and evening they checked the calls made. It soon became apparent that the heaviest traffic took place between six o'clock and seven and then from eight-thirty until ten, the gap being the result of the conquerors stuffing themselves with the best of French food. The two young friends were very angry about this. As Jean Paul said, "They take the best we produce and the French people have to pay the German government the full cost of the occupying troops."

Jacques added "Not only that, we have to pay the costs of their keeping all of our soldiers in their prison camps as well." They explained that these ruinous terms had been written into the armistice agreement when France fell. It was Germany settling part of an old score against France for the Treaty of Versailles, which brought the Germans to their knees after the Great War in 1919.

The next few days continued as before. A number of conversations were noted but nothing of any great import overheard as far as they could tell. On the 23rd they were told to bundle their notes for despatch over the weekend. It was an odd feeling for the three eavesdroppers to know that the next person or persons to read their carefully written notes would be a British intelligence officer back in England. When Gérard came to the cellar on Friday 23rd to collect the bundle, David asked if he could go to church the next day.

"Are you a Catholic?" asked Gérard.

"No, but I could go to a Catholic Church if the priest doesn't object."

"The curé of a small church near here is one of us – I could take you there tomorrow."

"Thank you. My brother-in-law who was also my best friend was killed a year ago tomorrow at Calais, I would like to go to pay my respects and to pray for my sister and her baby."

"We'll go privately after the early morning Mass."

"Thank you Gérard."

The days dragged on, although the evenings were sometimes quite interesting. Several of the officers had liaisons with local French women; some of the conversations therefore being somewhat unfit for the ears of the seventeen-year-olds. They'll certainly grow up fast working here thought David, but each took it all in his stride. One or two of the Germans could speak fluent, if heavily accented French; as a result the two lads were invaluable in providing the translations, which would have defeated David. On the other hand, David often had to take over when a German was speaking to another German particularly on technical matters. So far there had been no mention of any invasion of Russia, although several references had been made regarding certain commanders going to the east. All was logged, all bits of the jigsaw David told his helpers.

During the next two weeks they developed a routine using the experience they were obtaining to adequately cover the times when there was most traffic. During the day little happened, David therefore stood by whilst the lads still attended school. It was essential that no suspicion should fall on his two helpers by their having continual absences from class, but soon it would be the school summer holiday period when they would be able to take a turn during the day to give David some relief. It was late in the evening of May 29th that their first major success was logged. David had just sent Jean Paul home and was waiting the usual ten minutes before despatching Jacques. It was just after ten-thirty and curfew was at eleven o'clock, when the green light came on above one of the headpieces. David took it up telling Jacques he could go now, turned and bent over the bench to record the message. A deep guttural voice, seemed to be thickened by the amount of drink its owner had consumed during the evening was saying, "Rudie, you old bugger, what are you doing here – I thought you were on Barbarossa."

"I am, but when I was given the order to join my division I was on leave so I've had to come back here to get all my gear. I'm off again first thing so I thought I'd ring and say goodbye – that's if you were not too pissed to speak to me?"

"Me, pissed? You know a drop never touches my lips."

"I know that you old sod, it goes straight down your throat. Anyway, how's that tart of yours in Rennes? I hope you haven't put her in the family way yet. I should hate to read orders saying General Schiele had been relieved of his command for absenting himself too often to dip his wick." There was a roar of laughter from the other end.

General Schiele, noted David. I wonder who the other one is, and is Barbarossa the code word for the invasion of Russia? The conversation continued along the same lines until General Schiele declared, "I hope you've got your snow shoes with you."

"Not likely, we shall be in Moscow by the time the snow comes. I'm tucked in behind Fast Heinz (Guderian's nick-name) and that bugger doesn't hang about. And do you know what? We kick off on the very hour and day of my birthday – 4.00am on 22nd June – how's that for a lucky omen. The Ivans won't know what's hit them – bash down the door the Fuhrer said and the whole ramshackle house will fall down, and he's right. We've got orders to eliminate every possible enemy of National Socialism, that gives us plenty of scope."

"You don't mean killing civilians? I know they're a sub-human lot but that's way against the Geneva Convention."

"They don't subscribe to the Geneva Convention and anyway, as far as I can see there won't be a Jew or a communist left when the Einsatzgruppen behind me are finished. I've never seen such a foul lot in all my life, half of them, even the officers, are criminals convicted for murder and such like and released to volunteer for Himmler's private army. They don't even come under the jurisdiction of General Kolb, the corps commander but report straight to Himmler. I tell you there's going to be mass murder over a nearly three thousand kilometre front from Finland to the Black Sea, that we shall never be able to hide from the rest of the world."

"Who cares about the rest of the world."

"Well certainly the National Socialists don't but I'm a solider, and they never taught you and me when we were cadets together to go around killing civilians without cause."

"All I can say my dear old friend is, face your front, what other people do behind you is not under your control."

"Yes, but in time we shall all be tarred with the same brush, you mark my words. Anyway, apart from that I'm looking forward to running the reds into the ground. We shall do what we should have done in 1917, gone all the way to Vladivostock, although I will agree that would have been easier said than done. Anyway old friend, look after all the French girls for me until I return, I'll bring you back a Fabergé egg for a souvenir."

"Goodbye my dear old Brauer," at last I've got his name said David out loud, "take good care of yourself and if there's anything you want that I can beg, borrow or steal just send me a wire and it's yours."

David sat back looking at the hastily scribbled pile of notes he had made. As he finished Gérard appeared.

"Gérard look at his, I've got the code name, the time and date of the invasion of Russia. We must get this sent to London tonight. I'll send it in a condensed form and we'll get the full transcript off in the next Lizzie."

Gérard looked very serious. "It may take me a little while to find out where the radio is tonight, and then it won't be easy to get to the operator with the curfew in force. Anyway, give me the message and I'll get it to him somehow."

David quickly wrote.

"Subject: Invasion of Russia. Information from a divisional Commander (General Schiele) taking part confirms Russia will be invaded on a 3000km front at 4.00am on 22nd June. Full report following Cooteman."

By 11.45pm Gérard established the operator was about a mile away across the city. Using a combination of back alleys, public parks and twice across rooftops he reached him at 12.20am. The message was coded, despatched, and subsequently received in Whitehall from the listening post in Sussex at 12.40. It was rushed to Mr Churchill who had just gone to bed in the basement of the command building in Whitehall. He studied it and at 1.05am telephoned Lord Ramsford asking him if Cooteman could be fully relied upon, and for that matter who the hell was Cooteman. On being reassured that the information was totally trustworthy at 1.20 he telephoned the Soviet Embassy on the scrambler and told the ambassador the full details of the forthcoming invasion of his country. The ambassador was deeply grateful and at 1.50am the coded message was radioed to Moscow. At 2.10 Stalin was awakened and given the information, declared it to be Anglo-American propaganda, therefore absolute nonsense and promptly went back to sleep. Since Stalin had declared the message nonsense nothing further was done, as a result the Germans eventually walked into Russia with little opposition to begin the biggest invasion the world has even seen or is ever likely to see. Stalin's reaction was the single biggest example of making the wrong decision of any leader during the war.

Chapter Twenty Seven

Harry's bomb-site clearing job lasted from January until the end of April. On Monday 28th April he told the family this would be their last week. It had been like having a civilian job, getting his motorbike out at eight o'clock and riding off to work, coming home at tea time into the welcoming arms of his wife and young family. The Pioneer Corps men, a number of them conscientious objectors, along with the RASC lads, had made a good job of clearing up Deptford, though sad to say future raids, to say nothing of the doodlebugs and rockets, would knock the borough about even more over the coming years. On the bright side a number of the men, including some of the German and Austrian ex-internees had made some good and lasting friends among the local people.

On the 2nd May Harry sadly told Megan that he would be going back to Bulford the next day, "Though when the C.O. sees the state of our vehicles he'll have a baby," Harry observed.

Megan was silent for a few seconds, and then declared with a bubbling laugh, "He won't be the only one."

The penny failed to drop for the moment, but when it did he grabbed his Megan and started dancing her around the kitchen. With the initial excitement abating he said, "Are you sure? When will it be?"

Megan hugged him close. "Of course I'm sure, I'm a nurse aren't I? You will be a daddy again in November – God willing."

"Well I suppose there's no arguing with that. Does anyone else know?"

"Only Doctor Roberts at the hospital – I'll tell the rest of the family over the weekend."

"Oh no you won't – we'll go round and tell them tonight, after all I had something to do with it, didn't I? Or have you been giving the glad eye to that milkman again while I've been slaving away for my King and country? Now," he added seriously, "you are not to do any daft things – promise? If some silly whatsit is falling out of bed you just let him fall – promise?"

"I promise." Harry was, of course, referring to her first pregnancy during which she lost her baby trying to prevent an elderly patient from sliding over the side of his bedstead.

The family, of course, were thrilled to bits at the news – Fred remarking, "Another blooming Christmas present to find, I suppose."

"How do you know it will be only one?" teased Megan. "I might have twins again. Twins run in my family."

There was a pause in the jubilation, interrupted by Anni saying, "I wonder where David is tonight?"

"Don't you worry about our David," replied Harry, "he can look after himself you can be sure. Look what he did at Calais. He's not only got the brains, he's got his father's cunning as well, so he's bound to be alright."

There was general amusement at this, Ruth thinking, "thank goodness for Harry, he can always change an awkward moment."

When Harry arrived at Bulford he received a shock, which wiped the smile off his usually cheerful countenance. Bumping into the R.S.M. after he'd seen his trucks parked and his men in their quarters, he was told, "You're going on embarkation leave next weekend for overseas."

"Where we heading for Sir – the Isle of Man?"

"You'll know soon enough. Be on orders Monday morning, the C.O. wants to see you."

Harry thought he would delay passing on the news to Megan of his impending posting until he had seen the C.O. He was beginning to get that funny feeling he was going to soon be losing his winter pallor very rapidly where he was going. The question was would it be Egypt, India or the Far East? Well, it would have to wait until tomorrow. On the other hand it could be Iceland, that's not so far away, I'd get home from there once in a while he thought.

He was left in no doubt on the Monday. The C.O. congratulated him on a job well done in London, but as Harry suspected, complained bitterly about the state of the vehicles. "Now the point is Sergeant Chandler, a new company is being formed to be sent overseas. You have been appointed the company sergeant major, with the rank to take effect from today. You will join the new company immediately at Larkhill; you will go on fourteen days embarkation leave as from Friday 9th of May.

The unit will move out at the end of June. Any questions?"

"Well, no Sir, thank you Sir, except where are we going?"

"You'll be briefed on that when you get to Larkhill. I'm extremely sorry to lose you but if it's any consolation the powers that be instructed me to send the best we had and there's never been much doubt about that, eh Mr Rosen?" (To the R.S.M.).

"You're right there Sir."

"So off you go then, get your gear together and we'll organise to take you over to major Deveson. You two are not going to have much time to knock a new unit into shape but if anyone can do it you can. So good luck, Mr Chandler," the C.O. stood up and shook hands with Harry.

"Attention, salute the officer, about turn, quick march," and Harry was out on the C.O.'s veranda again.

"We're going to miss you Harry."

So it's Harry now is it, now I'm a company sergeant major, thought the newly promoted warrant officer class two.

"Well, that's life in the army Sir, isn't it? But then they say a change is a good as rest."

Arriving at Larkhill, Harry reported to Major Deveson who turned out to be a genial, rotund, fortyish officer of the old school brought up, as Harry was to soon find out, to leave the running of his company to his sergeant major. As company commander, he interpreted his orders from higher authority; issued guide lines to his junior officers, but the admin and discipline of around two hundred men he made the responsibility of the C.S.M. This did not mean he sat back and did nothing. Inside his velvet glove there was an unexpectedly iron fist, as a number of young officers, and some not so young N.C.O.'s had discovered to their cost in the past. Harry took an instant liking to him.

"You've come to me very well recommended Mr Chandler," he had said.

"That's because no one has found me out yet Sir," Harry had replied.

They both grinned; they were on the same wavelength.

"May I ask where we're going Sir?"

"Singapore."

"Well, I suppose it could be worse."

But both the major and Harry would one day find out that it could never in their wildest dreams have been worse.

That evening the new C.S.M. telephoned Megan on duty at the hospital. He decided it would be best if he put the bad news to her without beating about the bush. Megan was the most level-headed woman he knew, comparable only with his mother – they were two of a kind. He got through in a few minutes and without preamble told her he'd got some unpleasant news.

"They're sending you away again," – a statement of fact not a question.

"Yes."

"Overseas."

"Yes." There was a long pause during which Harry could visualise his wife trying to overcome the sickening hurt of her being parted again.

"I've got fourteen days leave from Friday so we'll talk all about it then. Oh and by the way, they've made me a C.S.M. so you now have to call me 'Mister'." The old Harry was creeping back.

"Harry, I'm so proud, so will your Mum and Dad be, and everyone. But we'll miss you so very very terribly." She was nearly crying.

"And I'll miss you love. But we'll have two lovely weeks together and then you'll have the little one to look forward to, the time will soon pass." They both knew that that would be far from the case, but perhaps there was a little comfort in having said it.

When Harry rang off Megan immediately rang Chandlers Lodge with the news. Pride at Harry's promotion mingled with sadness at his going abroad again and fear for his safety left conflicting emotions in the family, but Ruth and Rose who spoke to Megan did their best to comfort her, both having experienced this same sad situation in the past.

Ruth and Rose rejoined Fred and Jack Hooper, who had called in just as the telephone rang. Sad faced they told them the news. Jack, in reply, said he had come over to tell them he'd got bad news as well. Moira who was working on a top secret project, was going to have to go to America for six months from the end of May and had just telephoned him from her office – she was on duty in Whitehall that night.

"Bad news always comes in threes," quoted Ruth "I wonder what will come next?" As she spoke a car was heard driving up to the doorway subsequently depositing Ivan and Ken and an enormous amount of baggage on the front step.

Having been warmly welcomed after their spell in Wales, Ivan said, "We've got some bad news for you I'm afraid Ruth – well that is bad news from our point of view."

"Don't tell me, don't tell me – I've just said bad news comes in threes – you're going away and leaving us – is that right?"

"Yes, we're very sorry to say that it is. But tell me," his face concerned "the other bad news, the babies are alright aren't they? There's nothing wrong with any of the children?"

"No, all is well there, but Harry is being sent overseas again and

Moira is being sent to America for six months. And now you're going. Oh, I do hate this war."

Rose, with a twinkle in her eye, looked across at Ivan and enquired, "How do you think Kathleen Duffy is going to manage without a certain handyman to come round each evening to mend the fuses?" The others looked on in amusement.

"Oh, I expect there will be a queue of soldiers and airmen waiting to step into the size elevens that have beaten a path to her front door just recently," replied Ivan.

"No they jolly well won't," retorted Ken, "I didn't do a course in laying minefields without learning a thing or two. Anyway," he continued mischievously, "how you do you know I shan't be taking her with me?"

"Not where you're going old son, that's one thing very certain. I'm sure the thought of sleeping under canvas in the company of the licentious soldiery would not appeal to her all that much." Ivan joked "You see Ruth, we're going off to a summer camp on the coast of West Wales to do more of the job we've been doing here. We've learnt a lot here with the Canadians; they've been the guinea pigs. All the mistakes we've made we hope we have now ironed out so that we can do exercises on a much bigger scale all through the good weather, the theory being that the better the men are trained the better chance they have of survival when the real thing happens. Anyway, we shall be leaving on Monday. Tim McEwan is throwing a party on Saturday night in his mess to which naturally you will all be invited, service exigencies and air raids permitting of course, but you'll hear more about that in a day or so."

The evening broke up and on Wednesday they all received their invitations. Nanny was an absolute brick, readily volunteering to have all the children for the evening, which would enable Rose and Anni to enjoy their first real night out for months. On Thursday evening, after dinner, Ken was sitting in the kitchen on his own when Ruth came in with some logs for the sitting room fire – it was quite chilly although early May. Instantly he jumped to his feet, "I would have got those for you Ruth, let me carry them in." She relinquished her load into his huge arms and followed him into the sitting room.

"Ruth, while we're on our own can I ask you a favour?"

"As Fred would say, anything but money."

"I have a leave coming up at the end of May for two weeks. I would like to spend most of it here in Sandbury for obvious reasons. Do you think you could put me up? I will of course insist on paying you. I can't stay at Kathleen's house and compromise her, but I would of course be spending time there. She will be getting a week off and I'll be taking her and the kids about as much as I can. I need a firm base to operate from as it were."

He paused for a few moments and continued.

"It is my intention to ask her to marry me. We have this religion problem. I don't know how we're going to overcome that yet. Our padré is such a dyed in the wool anti-papist I can't go to him for advice, so that dilemma is yet to be solved. Anyway, first things first."

"First things first Ken my dear, you can stay here whenever you want, and as for payment I'll clip your ear, big as you are, if it's mentioned again. Secondly, why not have a chat with Canon Rosser, I don't know what he can offer in the way of advice but he's a thoroughly decent, liberal sort of chap. He will know the local R.C. priest as well – they both belong to various organisations of the town. Of course I don't know how committed a Catholic Kathleen is, but my guess is she will be quite strong in her faith, she's that kind of person, so it may be that you will have to come to the inevitable compromise. Firstly you marry in the Catholic Church and bring any children up as Catholics – surely that's not as horrendous as it sounds – or secondly you marry in a registry office as Anni and Ernie did. Mind you Anni was a lapsed Catholic, which I suppose makes a difference."

"Well, whichever way it goes, I intend to marry the girl even if I have to drag her kicking and screaming to a synagogue!!"

"Somehow I don't think that will be necessary. It is wartime; the priest is bound to be as understanding and helpful as he possibly can be. But what about your family? Will they think marrying a Catholic will put you beyond the pale?"

"My father might be a bit sticky. He's a church warden down in Glastonbury and you don't get much more sectarian than that. My mother and my sister, she's younger than I am, wouldn't care two hoots. I'm taking Kathleen to see them during my leave, so I shall have a clearer picture after that."

Ruth was quiet for a few moments. "You know, we do mess our lives about with what are really only trivialities don't we? Love is what counts, nothing else should interfere with that."

The party was an enormous success. Again Tim McEwan asked Rose if she would be so kind as to help him welcome all the guests. "After all, you did such a marvellous job of it before," he had added when he telephoned to ask her. "In addition," he added, "it will at least put a brake on your being mobbed by these young subalterns."

When Ruth and Fred retired to bed after the party Ruth was strangely quiet for a while.

"Something bothering you?" asked Fred.

"I was thinking about Rose. Most people there had partners. She looked so lovely I thought, what a terrible shame it was that she was all alone."

"I think if certain people had their way that could easily alter," surmised Fred.

Ruth spun round. "What on earth do you mean?"

"Well I always understood feminine intuition was such that nothing escaped the womanly sixth sense. Obviously in this case the military eye, namely mine, trained as it is to observe every part of the terrain for movement of any sort, has observed things surprisingly unnoticed by your, up until now, infallible perception."

"I'll throw something at you if you don't stop all that waffle. What on earth, or more to the point, who on earth are you talking about?"

"Well let's take a roll call. First of all let's consider Colonel Tim McEwan. He's been struck on her for months, but appreciating the position she was in said nothing. Tonight he held her arm as often and for as long as he decently could without making it obvious. Number two on the list, Ivan Sopwith. He never looks at Rose without that adoring smile coming into his eyes, holds her hand whenever he helps her from her chair at the dining table, and wrote to her twice a week while he was in Wales. Number three, David's O.C. Major Laurenson, phones her for an hour at a time – must be made of money – and is going to meet her in town next week while he's on leave. It'll be my bet he'll visit her down here as well. Last, but not least, Charlie Crew. Now our Charlie hasn't made any move yet – he's still on 'good friend' terms. But he is very fond of her, writes and phones every week, she's very fond of him, as we all are, and they're of an age. Now you tell me Mrs Chandler, whether the time I have spent in reconnaissance has been wasted or not!"

"I'm flabbergasted – absolutely flabbergasted. Now you tell me then, Mister Military Genius, which do you think will win the day – if any?"

"Well, I'm hoping none of them – yet, anyway. This war hasn't really started yet as far as the army is concerned, and each one of those four could be in the thick of things when it does. The last thing I would want my daughter to be is widowed a second time, so I just hope she stays friends with all of them and emotionally attached to none."

There was a silence between them for a short while, ended by Ruth stating, "You never cease to amaze me – four of them and I didn't give it a thought!"

Harry came on leave in time for the party, which he attended in civvies and to which he was warmly welcomed by Colonel Tim. Megan had been upset when he told her he was bound for Singapore knowing that a posting that far away, even though it was not in the war zone, would not be a five minute affair. "Still, it's better than the desert," she had said, a phrase that echoed and re-echoed in Harry's mind in times to come, when he was suspended between life and death. 'It's better than the desert' became a kind of personal joke with which he could mock himself and keep his spirit from giving up the ghost.

On the 12th May, Rose was to meet Mark Laurenson at his hotel in town where he was to spend a few days of his leave. On the Sunday after the party he telephoned from Norfolk, firstly to say he was definitely coming on leave on the 12th but wondered whether Rose would object because of the bombing, to his staying locally instead of in town. He had the 1939 A.A. book which said there was a good hotel called 'The Angel,' he could book in there if they had vacancies, he could then commute to town should he want to before he went off to Shrewsbury on Friday to spend the rest of his leave with his family. Rose replied that she would have no objection at all and suggested she could make the booking and that he could ring again in an hour or so to confirm all was well. All was well, Rose went back to Ruth and Fred relaxing in the sitting room to be met with, "What was that all about?" from Fred.

"Mark Laurenson has decided to stay a few days in Sandbury instead of in town. The hotel he was to have stayed at was bombed in the big raid on Saturday night. Did you know that not only was The House of Commons destroyed and Westminster Abbey badly damaged, but the British Museum was wrecked as well? Isn't it awful? – Anyway I've booked him in with John Tarrant."

Fred looked at Ruth with the biggest 'I told you so' smirk she had ever seen cross his face. "So you'll be needing a baby-minder for a few days will you?" he enquired in all innocence to Rose.

"Why are you volunteering Daddy dear? Surely you'll be much too busy flogging the work force during the day and playing at soldiers during the evening? Anyway, providing there are no raids, I expect the galloping major will want to spend most of his time in town; after all, he's never met me although we've talked a lot over the telephone. He'll probably be bored to tears after a couple of days with we yokels."

"We'll have a little party on Wednesday evening," said Ruth, "just a few friends and the family. After all, he is David's company commander; we ought to offer him some hospitality."

"What a good idea," replied Fred, "now we can ask Colonel Tim, Ivan of course, I don't suppose Charlie could get down could he? Oh, and a few others. Should be an interesting evening." If Ruth had had anything throwable, and if Rose had not been there to witness it, Fred Chandler would have been on the receiving end of a flying object. As it was, Rose, innocent of the underlying nuance of Fred's words, enthusiastically agreed and raced to answer Mark's second call with the news that all was arranged at the Angel and that when he had settled in perhaps he could telephone Chandlers Lodge. This he agreed to do.

At half-past four on Monday afternoon the telephone rang, Ruth answering it. Mark introduced himself and immediately won her regard by saying, "Mrs Chandler, Rose and I have had numerous telephone conversations as you are aware. I would like you to know that I would like to get to know her better. I am well aware that she is newly widowed and I shall treat her with the greatest courtesy and respect. Sounds a bit old fashioned but I'm sure you know what I mean."

"Yes, I do Mark, and thank you for being so honest with me. Oh, here is Rose, I'll doubtless see you soon, bye bye." She passed the receiver to Rose.

After the customary small talk, which tends to precede all telephone conversations. Mark asked, "Rose, I have a couple of questions to ask."

"Fire away."

"Firstly, can you come and have dinner with me this evening, I understand the food is well above average here and I'll get a taxi to pick you up. Secondly, can you tell me where there is a gent's outfitters nearby – I seem to have come away without spare shirts, unless my batman has packed them into my main suitcase which I've left at Paddington."

"Well firstly I shall be delighted to have dinner with you. What time?"

"Say about seven – they eat early here – I'll get the cab to you for 6.45 and meet you in the reception area."

"That would be lovely. As regards outfitters, if you go out of the hotel and turn left, cross the road, and about two hundred yards along you'll see a Meakers shop. The manager there is Horace Catchpole, a friend of ours, he'll look after you. If you get really stuck I expect my father will have a spare one – what size are you?"

"Sixteen and a half."

"So is he – give me a ring if you get stuck. Oh and Mark, thank you very much for asking me out. By the way, how shall I recognise you?"

"I think it very unlikely there would be two riflemen in the establishment with two heads!! Anyway I shall know you. I've got a photo of you I pinched from David."

Their evening passed quickly and very pleasantly. Each felt they knew the other well as a result of their lengthy telephone calls so that conversation came easily. After dinner they retired to the residents' lounge. During the meal John Tarrant came over, delighted to see Rose out and about, asked after the baby, was introduced to Mark and shook hands warmly. As he walked away Rose said, "You've passed."

"I beg your pardon?" replied a mystified Mark.

"You've passed. If John had decided you were not suitable company for me he would not have shaken hands, he would have just bowed politely and gone on his way."

"Well, let's hope the analysis is as good when I meet your parents, and in particular when I meet your son. Can you tell me when that's likely to be?"

"If you would like to walk me home you can see them tonight, and on Wednesday night we're having a little party so that you can meet the family and some of our friends, David would be very cross if we hadn't arranged that," and then like a shot from a gun, "by the way, where is David?"

Mark was silent for a few moments and then took her hand. "I can tell you truthfully Rose, I honestly do not know. He's on some sort of mission, I know not where or with whom. Nobody is told anything – even the C.O. won't know and it's all entirely to ensure the safety of each individual taking part. I'm sorry I cannot be more help than that."

She squeezed his hand in reply.

"No, it's I who should be sorry. I should not have asked – but I couldn't bear to lose David."

"You won't lose him. He's one of the most resourceful people with whom I've come into contact, so don't worry," he continued holding her hand which she did not take away, and continued

"Well now, if I go and get my cap we can make tracks for the second scrutiny of the evening – wish me luck!"

"Are you interested in what in fact was the first of the evening?"

"Do you mean John Tarrant?"

"No, I mean Rose Cartwright."

"If you must know, I'm too petrified to even hazard a guess – did I pass?"

"One day I will tell you." She laughed impishly.

When they got to Chandlers Lodge; Ruth, Fred and the two majors were sitting in the kitchen. Ruth came into the hall when she heard the front door opening and having been introduced suggested they go into the sitting room.

"The kitchen will be warmer," advised Rose, "that's if you don't mind sitting in the kitchen."

"We have a big old farmhouse at home and we almost live in the kitchen, so lay on MacDuff." Rose led the way and the three occupants rose to greet the new arrival.

"Now major, can we press you to a glass of beer or would you prefer something else?"

Fred was hoping he'd plump for the beer. His last bottle of Scotch was looking decidedly the worse for wear and there would be no hope of a replacement for another week or so. Scotch wasn't rationed but there was very little to be had except on the black market, which Fred steadfastly refused to patronise.

"Beer would be very acceptable Mr Chandler, in fact the fame of your inexhaustible supply from under the stairs has reached even the wilds of Norfolk, mainly I would add from the lips of one Charlie Crew. As a matter of fact, I'm pretty sure he'd be tearing his hair out if he knew I was, at this very moment, about to sample it." There was general laughter at this sally.

As the men were talking Ruth watched Mark carefully. He was entirely different to the two marines. They were burly great six footers, with fists like prize fighters and rugged faces so alike they could have been brothers. Like most pre-war officers, they were exceedingly well spoken but at the same time deep voiced and forceful in their conversation. Ruth was reminded of the army song she had heard David and Harry singing 'My brother – Silvest', she could imagine either of these two colossus 'holding the Lusitania to his chest'. Mark however was a complete contrast. Although he too was around six feet tall, he was quite slimly, and elegantly built she thought. His service dress was immaculately tailored, his hands were those of an artist rather than a blacksmith, his face was finely chiselled, very expressive and readily dissolved into laugh lines as he talked. Rose, watching Ruth watching Mark, leaned over and whispered, "So – how many out of ten?"

Without removing her glance from the subject of Rose's enquiry she whispered back, "Ten."

After half an hour or so Mark said he had better make tracks for the Angel or he would be locked out. Shaking hands all round he said to Fred, "Thank you for the beer Mr Chandler – I now understand why my subalterns are so keen to get to Sandbury!"

Rose saw him to the door. He held out his hand to shake hers, but she took the hand and reached up and kissed him on the cheek. "Thank you for a lovely evening."
"May I telephone you in the morning?"
"Please do, perhaps you could call and see my little boy."
"I would like that very much. Goodnight."

During the rest of the week Mark came to the house on the Tuesday morning and met Jeremy. In the afternoon he had to go to town to see relatives. On Wednesday he asked if he could look at the factory, which Fred was most pleased to arrange and, in the event, conducted him around himself. The party on Wednesday evening went off very well. On Thursday evening he invited Rose, Ruth and Fred to join him for dinner at the Angel, which they did, and on Friday he telephoned at ten in the morning to say he was just leaving and to thank Ruth and Rose for making him so welcome. After this call, mother and daughter repaired to the inevitable kitchen table for a cup of tea. When all the preliminaries were accomplished and the tea safely poured out into their respective cups Ruth asked, "Well?"

Rose delayed answering for a while and then quietly started to cry. Immediately Ruth came round the table and put her arms around her. "Come now," she said, "what's the matter?"

"I just don't know," Rose replied "he is such a nice man, under normal circumstances I would be very very attracted to him, but I can't. I'm not ready. I feel all the time that I am betraying Jeremy. Jeremy was the only man I ever loved. I couldn't imagine being loving to anyone else, let alone having passion for anyone. It's so unfair on him because I don't want to tell him. I know he feels strongly towards me and I don't want to hurt him. Neither do I want to lose his friendship; he is one of the most charming and intelligent people I have ever met. What can I do Mummy – what can I do?"

"You do nothing my love except remain very friendly with him. I can tell you he is a most understanding man. He assured me before we even met that he appreciated your position exactly and would treat you with the greatest courtesy. This, I am sure, he has done and will continue to do. In due course time will help you. From my experience over the years, especially after the last war, I know this to be a fact.

Most people can learn to love more than one man, probably in different ways. There are other people I know here and now, who have the very highest regard for you, which could turn to love given the opportunity. So give it time, give it time. Anyone who really loves you will understand and if he doesn't..." she left the sentence unfinished.

"I think I am upset partly because I did feel attracted to him and that made me feel disloyal to Jeremy. I thought too that Jeremy's mother and father would think badly of me if they knew of my having some feeling for someone else."

"Look, dear, let's have a final word on this subject. Jeremy is secure in your heart and your love for him. His parents love you and little Jeremy and always will. Neither Jeremy nor his parents would want you to spend the rest of your life grieving. When your heart tells you that someone is dear to you, the rest of us will be happy for you, all of us, including Jeremy's parents, you have my word on that."

Rose hugged her mother and the subject was closed.

On Saturday evening Jack came to Chandlers Lodge for dinner. He was missing Moira terribly and as a result was spending more time with the Chandlers. Megan and Harry joined them and after dinner Karl, Anni and Ernie arrived with little David cosily tucked up in the big perambulator. Inevitably the conversation turned to the arrival in Scotland of Rudolph Hess, Hitler's deputy, a few days earlier. The general view was that it represented serious dissension within the Nazi hierarchy. Doctor Goebbels had announced the flight to the German public stating that Hess had, for some time, been suffering from delusions, but the fact remained that Hess was a great personal friend of Hitler – the only man among all the Nazi ministers who he addressed in the familiar 'du'. Ernie Bevin, the Minister for Labour and a former trade union giant plainly stated that Hess was a murderer and should be tried and executed. He had seen to the collection of every index card of trade union officials in Germany and then had had them arrested and sent to camps or murdered.

"So, he was the man who had my mother killed," Annie said quietly.

The following Friday 23rd May, Harry went back to Larkhill. The twins sensed that although they were used to having their Daddy come and go, that something different was happening this time, there was such an atmosphere of sadness in the houses. On Thursday, Jack had taken Harry aside and said, "Harry, this is the last address I had in Muar of Pat's mother. If you get the chance will you call and see how she has fared? I don't know why I want to know when she was so wicked to Pat and me, but I don't like to think of her in penury – if indeed she is."

"I'll do my best," Harry had replied.

With Harry gone, the sadness continued in Chandlers Lodge the next day, it being the first anniversary of Jeremy's death. Rose, with baby Jeremy, and Ruth went to the side chapel at Sandbury Church, where they were joined by Megan and Jack, Canon and Mrs Rosser, Anni and Karl and to their pleasant surprise, Colonel Tim. The short service of remembrance over, they all went back to Chandlers Lodge for lunch. Soon after their return Rose received a telephone call from Rita and Buffy, they too having been to the church where Jeremy was christened and confirmed. They were sad, but over the past three months or so they had come to terms with their loss and were living on the expectation of the happiness their grandson would bring them.

As the lunch ended, the unanswerable was asked by Ruth of the assembled family and friends – "I wonder what David is doing now?" The question was never far from their thoughts.

Chapter Twenty Eight

After three weeks at Le Mans, with the routine well established, David was beginning to feel a little claustrophobic living, as he did, in his bedroom in the small room where they took their meals, or in the cellar. The only outside life he saw was through his bedroom shutters, which he thought to himself could hardly be described as 'vistas broad'. Gérard knew that continued confinement for any operative was dangerous, tending to cause him or her to make thoughtless mistakes. On the last Saturday in May he spoke to David about this and asked him if he needed 'some female company'. He continued, "Several of the girls at the Blue House belong to our organisation, I could arrange for one to visit you," and to David's amusement added, "and she wouldn't charge of course."

"That would be her contribution to the war effort would it?" David joked.

"In all seriousness Cooteman, they do a lot for us. We get all sorts of information from them, which they get from the Boche, which we can sometimes put to very good use. If they were found out they would be shot."

"I'm sorry Gérard, I didn't mean to pull your leg, as we say in England, but no, I don't think I need accept your kind offer, tempting though it is."

Gérard grinned and clapped him on the shoulder. "Chacun á son goût, as we say." He continued by suggesting that on the next day he should, with Georgette, explore the old town of Le Mans, its huge cathedral and quaint streets, say for an hour or so, and the following Sunday take the train to Chartres. It would 'break the monotony of his life'.

"I don't know about the monotony – I shall probably be having kittens all the time," was David's reply, and then observing the total lack of comprehension on Gérard's face of this remark, had to rephrase it.

At eleven o'clock the next morning David found himself walking through the cobbled streets of the old town, past the cathedral from which people, including a number of German soldiers, were emerging after Mass. Georgette constantly held his arm, and looked adoringly up at him from time to time. On one of the cramped pavements they found themselves confronted by two burly soldiers who plainly had no intention of giving way to the young couple. Georgette pulled lightly on David's arm pointing to an old saddlery shop on the opposite side of the narrow street, and they crossed to it, she pointing to an object in the window and discussing it volubly. The boorish behaviour of these two Wehrmacht men was in contrast to their next encounter with the military. Passing a café, with the usual array of tables and parasols outside David suggested they have a drink, but being Sunday the café was crowded inside and out. There was a small table with one empty chair next to a table with four chairs, three of which were occupied by soldiers, leaving the fourth empty. Immediately one of the soldiers stood up, picked up the empty chair at his table and placed it beside the other empty chair, indicating with a slight bow the new arrivals should seat themselves there. His companions joked with him at the gesture saying that Franz was becoming quite a gentleman these days. David thanked him in German – his French might well have been suspect – to which a second soldier said, "You are German?"

"No, I am Swiss," replied David, "my friend is French. Whereabouts are you from?"

"We're all from Rostock, up on the Baltic."

David turned to Georgette and translated the discussion, at which Georgette smiled sweetly at the soldiers as the two sat down, Georgette immediately taking one of David's hands in hers. The waiter arrived in the usual 'flicking the dust off the table type hurry' adopted by men of his profession, anxious to quickly take an order and move on to the next customer. David ordered a Suze for Georgette, a beer for himself and then turned to the soldiers asking, "Can I buy you a cognac?"

Private soldiers of any European army have never been exactly overpaid. These three were no exception, jumping at the chance of a free drink, along with an opportunity to speak to friendly civilians for a change. There were plenty of friendly girls in the brothels, at a price, there were plenty of subservient people in the shops and bars, but there were very few people who, under normal circumstances, were anything other than sullen, unsociable, even hostile at times. They drank David's health, and that of his pretty companion, chatted to him about the fact they were artillerymen, and in the process let slip there weren't many of them there now, most of their regiment had been shipped east.

"And they're bloody welcome to it too," said the youngest. At length they said they had to go, they were on picquet duty that afternoon and it wouldn't do to breathe cognac all over the Sergeant.

"Though no doubt he will have had a few himself by then if I know him," another joked.

David stood up as they made to go. They each bowed to Georgette, each shook hands with David, the eldest of the three saying, "perhaps we shall bump into you again."

"I hope we do," said David, as they put on their side hats, turned and walked away over the cobbles, their heavy boots echoing against the walls of the houses closely built on either side.

David and Georgette sat silently for a while. "What are you thinking Cooteman?"

"The inevitable I suppose. Under different circumstances I could be killing those three instead of shaking hands with them. One of my best friends is a German. If it was his duty to do so I've no doubt he would kill me. I cannot understand the morality of all this except that Hitler must be the most evil man that ever lived to bring all this about, and we therefore have no choice but to do our duty and defeat him."

"We think a little differently. The Boche has invaded us, has ravished our country. In due course they must die, good or bad, honourable or dishonourable, they must die. There is no alternative." Her blue eyes were steely in their resolve and determination. He took her hands in his.

"You are right of course, when you have been occupied by the enemy it puts an entirely different complexion on the situation. You can afford only to be completely single minded. I've learned a good lesson from you this morning."

They finished their drinks, paid the bill and made their way back through the back streets, taking all the usual precautions when approaching the safe house. Gérard met them. "Well, how did it go?"

David replied, "Well, apart from Georgette trying to get off with some German soldiers, it was alright."

Gérard put his arm around his sweetheart's shoulders. "For doing that she would attract a fate far worse than death," he said in mock ferocity.

The next three weeks dragged by as they waited to see whether their single biggest item of intelligence was in fact to be proved true. If Barbarossa did not take place he realised a lot of people, notably himself, would end up with egg on their faces. He fully appreciated that the information he had sent would be put through all levels of secret government departments to the very top – probably Churchill himself. His private thoughts were mixed. The thought of Hitler taking on the ten million strong Red Army he found to be stupid in the extreme.

Surely if he wants to fight the Russians, and as far as I am concerned he is welcome to them thought David, he has got to finish us first, he can't possibly fight on two fronts at once. Then it came to him that if he secured his eastern frontiers – wherever they might eventually be – by concluding an armistice with the Russians he would then be in the position to concentrate on Britain. He rubbed his chin – all this strategy is beyond me, he concluded, I can't see my ever making staff college.

On the early morning news from London on Sunday 22nd June they heard the excited announcement or as excited as the BBC announcer ever got, telling the world that the Nazis had invaded Russia against strong opposition. David's thoughts were – we were right, I wonder if our message helped in any way always supposing it wasn't pigeonholed by one of the links in the chain to Churchill, and finally I wonder where Dieter is now.

News came in during the week of swift advances on all fronts, there seemed to be little organised opposition. Where there was opposition the dry flat lands allowed the panzers to by-pass it; it was land made to measure for tank warfare. The immediate effect in France, and elsewhere on the European mainland for that matter, was the immediate rounding up of all known communists. Up until now as a result of the treaty between the Soviet Union and Nazi Germany, communists, even those left in Germany itself, had been unmolested by the Gestapo. That didn't mean they had escaped observation, far from it. As soon as the tanks moved into Russian-occupied Poland, the Gestapo moved in on what was known as 'the Red Orchestra,' the Russian intelligence organisation throughout Europe, as well as all party members of any distinction. Vichy speedily broke off relations with the Soviets and instigated a round-up of all Russians living in the unoccupied zone, including those naturalised from 1930 onwards.

Gérard was most concerned at these turns of events. Although he was a committed de Gaulist himself, many of the people in his immediate organisation were communist. His worry was that not one of those, arrested by the Gestapo or French secret police, could under torture betray the others. Alternatively there would always be the odd one who would act as informer either for money or to save himself or his family. It was a worrying situation, which had to be dealt with immediately. He was sure the safe house was safe. The only people who positively knew its whereabouts were the five of them who used it and the two telephone engineers who originally made the final connections, these latter being absolutely trustworthy. He discussed the situation with David, who came to the opinion that they were as safe there as anywhere at present, so they sat tight.

July came. They heard from the BBC that victory had been obtained over the Vichy Forces in Syria, after bitter fighting. The tragic picture of French fighting French was something the allies had dreaded; now it had happened. On Thursday evening 3rd July David was on watch when he obtained his second coup. He picked the headphones up when the green light came on to hear a voice saying "Stiebner here." He knew the name. General Stiebner was one of the top quartermasters. "It's Hans Kopp, general, sorry to telephone you at such an hour, but I'm back to the east tomorrow and my general asked if you can do anything to improve our delivery date for winter clothing. It was given to us as September 15th. We need a month to get it up to the forward units, maybe more if they keep moving as they do now, which is driving it up a bit fine. It gets damned cold by mid October in Leningrad."

"I'll do all I can but I can't promise. How are the drives going?"

"Well, Field Marshall von Leeb on the Baltic/Leningrad is a bit slow. Field Marshall von Bock on the centre thrust to Minsk and Moscow is racing away. In southern Poland the drive to Lwow and Kiev is breaking all records and the Bessarabia to Odessa and Crimea dash by von Runstedt is going very well. But the winter clothing is vital."

"But the Nazi Goebbels said it would be all over by Christmas."

"That little runt would say anything to please the Fuhrer. These Nazi crap-heads live in a dream world – how can you possibly capture a country covering a fifth of the world's land surface in a few weeks?"

"Well I'll wish you luck, and I'll do all I can from the central supply unit when I get to Berlin on Monday."

David excitedly wrote out a message to be sent that night detailing the lines of advance, the names of each commander, the ancillary information that the advancing troops had no winter clothing up with them, and that Messrs Stiebner and Kopp had no love for Hitler's henchmen. Again Gérard located the transmitter, got the message to the operator just before curfew started but then had two near confrontations with the municipal police on the way back. The problem with the police was that some were sympathisers, but some were pro-fascist, anyone caught abroad would never know which faction was which until they were told to get under cover quick or alternatively were marched off to the police barracks.

July generally was quiet. Many senior officers appeared to be on leave, there seemed to be, as far as David could tell from the conversations he overheard, no fear whatsoever that there would be any attack from across the channel. Apart from very occasional bombing, being stationed in France was like living in a big civilised holiday resort; the only fear being the good life might suddenly be turned upside down by a transfer to the Russian front. Even there it would be good fun finishing off all those Ivans; it seemed such a totally one-way business from what they heard.

It was four o'clock on the morning of Tuesday 29th July when David was awakened by shooting. He jumped out of bed, pulled the blackout curtain aside, took a quick look from the window but could see nothing, put the curtain back and the small side light on and then quickly got dressed. As he was pulling his shoes on Gérard burst into the room.

"We've got to get out," he said, "they've started searching at the end of the road, we can't tell whether it's only one set of apartments or if it's a general search of the area, but they've met some opposition from people I know nothing about."

While he was explaining he closed down David's suitcase, which was always packed ready and into which David had thrown his toilet bag and travel clock. David looked around the room quickly to see nothing remained and followed Gérard out to the well practised escape route across the roofs and away from the direction from which the shooting had come. In a short while they came to the edge of a flat roof some twenty feet high. Gérard took a skein of thick cord from inside his shirt, attached one end to David's suitcase and lowered it to the ground. As David leaned over the balustrade to watch the progress of the suitcase, fast disappearing into a murky alley at the bottom of the wall, he noticed a large diameter pipe fastened to the balustrade, and fixed away from the wall as far down as he could see by large steel clamps, Gérard pointed to it.

"Put your hands around it and slide your feet down to each set of clamps. Watch me." He went over the balustrade hanging on to the pipe, slid down a few feet and stopped with his feet on the first set of supports. Repeating this four or five feet at a time he was soon down in the darkness at the bottom. As David swung himself out on to the pipe he found himself repeating the famous last words of Sydney Carton in 'The Tale of Two Cities' – 'It is a far, far better thing that I do now etc etc,' and wondered to himself how he could be so undisturbed when normally climbing on to a chair was enough to give him vertigo. Yet here he was twenty feet up in space and in his own assessment of the situation not even needing his brown underpants. He quickly made it to the bottom albeit losing the skin on one set of knuckles on the way, which caused him to swear an Anglo-Saxon four letter word his mother would have been most surprised to hear from him. Gérard led him through two alleyways, through a hole in a fence into an overgrown garden of some sort and then to a door at the rear of a building of some size. Gérard turned the handle of the door and pulled David in to a pitch black passage way closing the door behind them.

"All well?" enquired a voice from along the passage.

As Gérard answered, "yes," a dim overhead light snapped on. David found himself in a low narrow brick corridor having an uneven stone floor and a semicircular roof. It smelt dank and musty. To his surprise the person who had posed the question was the padré to whom he had been taken by Gérard back in May when he was newly arrived. The curé turned and led the way up a flight of stone stairs to a very old and solid oak door, which he opened and through which he led them. David noted that despite its weight and age the door had opened noiselessly. More attention to detail he thought. The door led into a small room with a window high up on the wall. Again David thought whoever was normally housed here got little chance of being distracted by the outside world; you would need more than a chair to stand on to look out of that window. There were two iron framed beds in the room, a washstand, with water in a jug, and a flask of wine, some cheese and bread under a glass cover.

"Get some sleep now," said the priest, "I will visit one of my sick parishioners along that street in the morning and find out what has happened."

David and Gérard washed their hands, which were filthy after scrambling over the roofs and down the pipe. Both feeling peckish they gratefully ate some of the bread and cheese and sampled the wine.

"After the war I shall come here and buy the padré the best meal he's ever had," David promised Gérard. It was probably the feeling of being able to relax after a period of tension that caused them both to enjoy the simple food to the extent they were.

"But first we have to win the war, that could take a long time, and who knows how many will be left at the end of it?"

They got their heads down and just before eight o'clock David awoke to find Gérard already washing. At nine o'clock the priest appeared with a jug of coffee from which, with the food left from their overnight repast, they made their breakfast.

When the priest again returned at just after ten o'clock, he had visited his sick parishioner and by asking others he met in the street he established that the police had raided one of the houses, from the lower part of which they had reason to believe black market operations were being conducted. Having smashed the door down and caught their suspects, two young people in an upper apartment of the house, who were active in the communist party, mistakenly thought the police had come for them, as a result they had tried to get away over the back roof. The police, seeing them running for it, thought they were connected with the black market people and opened fire, killing one and wounding the other. Apparently no other premises in the street were visited, and there was no police presence this morning.

'Nevertheless,' he continued after relating this account of the events, "I suggest you lie up here for a couple of days to make sure all is definitely quiet, you never know what they may be dragging out of the people they've arrested. They may be incriminating others living in the street, and there could be further raids."

They waited three days. It was very boring, David clearly remembering what Jessica had said to him at Roper Street 'You may have to wait around for days sometimes.' He wondered where Jessica was. She should be back in England by now he thought, and his heart gave a little leap at the prospect of seeing her again. At the end of the third day, as soon as it became reasonably dark they made their way through the back streets to the safe house. Georgette was there and waiting, having been away in Alencon when the raid occurred. At eleven o'clock they tuned in to the BBC to monitor the messages being sent, David expecting his recall at any time now. There were close on a dozen seemingly innocuous announcements, which of course German intelligence would be picking up and trying to decipher, or link in with previous messages to establish some sort of pattern. The British, on the other hand, would be mixing genuine messages with bogus ones, these designed to lead the Germans up the garden path and to waste a lot of time in the process. There was nothing for David, but two days later on the Sunday evening after a particularly boring session at the telephone desk; his message came through loud and clear. After half a dozen meaningless phrases he heard

"The weather has cleared in the west."

His heart gave a great leap; this was his notification that seven days from now he would be on a Lizzie back to Blighty. After his first feelings of delight at the thought of going home his mood changed to one of sadness that he would be leaving these good people, with whom he had become such great friends, to unknown dangers stretching far into the future. When, therefore, Gérard arrived an hour later he looked quite different to his normal cheerful self, prompting Gérard to say "Bad news?"

"I've had my recall."

"Surely that's not bad news? I would have thought you would have been jumping for joy."

"It's the thought of leaving you all here that depresses me."

"Don't you worry about us Cooteman. This station has served its purpose for the time being at least. We shall revive it I've no doubt when your leaders decide the invasion is approaching. In the meantime we shall organise our members so that when the arms and explosives are available and can be despatched to us, we shall be able to take the offensive against these people defiling our country." He paused. "Now, down to more immediate plans. On Tuesday we shall move you back to Alencon, I don't quite know how yet, I will confirm that tomorrow. You will stay in the safe house there where you were before and then if everything goes according to plan you will go back on the aircraft at around midnight a week from today. Now, are there any gifts you would like to take back with you?"

"I noticed perfume in the shops when I was out with Georgette. Could I get four small bottles for my family and a bottle of cognac for my father?"

"Four small bottles? Don't tell me you have four wives Cooteman," jested Gérard.

David's face clouded over. "The Germans killed my wife last November," he said, "these will be for my mother and sisters." He did not further explain.

"Cooteman, I am very sorry, I should not have jested like that, it was very unprofessional. Maybe in a little while we can all get together and tell everything there is to know about each other. There is so much sadness behind each one of us." He went on, "But I will get your gifts and send them individually to Alencon for you to take home."

On Monday they made their final log of calls, which along with the previous week's logs were put in an envelope to be taken to Alencon by the courier. Gérard came during the evening and told David of the arrangement for the next day. He was to go by train with Georgette again, there was less likelihood of his being stopped and searched travelling first class with a young lady than there would be going by motor car, where the possibility of meeting road blocks manned by bored and officious police was quite on the cards.

Despite having first class tickets they had to stand in the corridor for the whole of their journey. A contingent of Wehrmacht was being moved from Le Mans up to Le Havre, as a result all the first class seats had been commandeered. As far as David and Georgette were concerned this was fortuitous in that since the whole of the first class area was so crowded with troops, civilians, luggage and soldiers' equipment cluttering up the gangways, it would have been impossible for any police check of identities to take place.

At Alencon they were met by a studious young man, who kissed Georgette on both cheeks, shook hands with David and took charge of his suitcase. Leading them out of a side exit from the station he crossed a narrow road into a small park where he led them to a coffee stall set back against a high wall. He sat them down at a table where they had a full command of the view of the territory they had just covered. He bought three coffees, which they drank even though they tasted like strained horse dung and after ten minutes the young man picked up the suitcase. Instead of going back across the park as David had expected he led the way to the rear of the café where there was a door in the wall which he pulled open and ushered them through. The door opened into another side street where a battered old Citroen was standing. The young man opened the rear door indicating David and Georgette to get in, pushed the suitcase on to their laps, jumped in the front with a driver who neither looked at them nor acknowledged them and they were off.

They took mainly side streets out of Alencon. When eventually they turned on to a main road David read they were on the N12 towards Mayenne. After about half an hour they turned north towards Carrouges, shortly after taking that road, turning off on to a side road which from the state of its overhanging vegetation was little used. In two kilometres he saw a small group of farm buildings ahead, the lane they were travelling appearing to be the only approach. They drove into the farmyard, the Citroen did a swift three point turn and, depositing David and Georgette, was gone, complete with the young man who had met them at the station, with just a hurried 'Bon Voyage' from the young man and nothing at all from the driver. 'Well it takes all sorts', said David to himself.

As the Citroen drove away a lady in her mid-forties David judged, emerged from the farmhouse. Speaking good English with a definite 'upper crust' accent she welcomed the two arrivals, taking them into an extremely comfortable sitting room, offered them coffee – coffee so different to the liquid which had usurped its name in Alencon that David remarked, "This must be the most delicious coffee I have ever tasted."

"Well," came the reply, "we have a small store put by but I have to tell you you must drive the Boche out within two years or there will be none left."

"I shall see to it myself – you have my word!" laughed David. It was however, to be nearer three years before that happy day came, during which time they were each to go through ordeals and experiences they could never before have imagined.

The time spent at the farm was extremely pleasant. The owner had a good library of French, English and Italian books, which David thirstily explored, and of which he had been deprived over the past three months. The three ate together, but conversation was strictly impersonal, although a good deal of discussion took place as to how the Wehrmacht would fare in Russia, Madame asking David's opinion of the different news items coming from French, British and long wave German radio which David translated for them.

Sunday came, 10th August. In the morning Madame had announced that everything was going according to plan. The landing field was some five kilometres away. Three of the farm workers would come at ten o'clock that night and lead David through the surrounding woodland to the take off point; he was scheduled to leave at midnight. They had a fine lunch of chicken, washed down with champagne, with toasts to Victory, Mr Churchill and General de Gaulle. As they stood and completed the toasts, David, looking out over the road to the narrow lane, saw a car approaching.

"Madame," he said, "we have visitors."

Approaching the entrance to the yard they saw a small open topped army car, in which were four German soldiers, the driver and an officer at the front with two soldiers armed with rifles on the rear seat. David immediately took control.

"We'll go out to them Madame. You introduce me as your nephew Carl from Switzerland – I have a Swiss passport if they investigate – and Georgette is my fiancée." They went to the front door as the young officer vaulted from the car and came up the steps two at a time. Saluting Madame he said in passable French that they were searching the neighbourhood for a small Fieseler-Storch spotter plane, which was overdue and may have force landed. Had they seen anything of it?

"No, I cannot help you. My nephew and his fiancée have been with me here all day and we certainly have seen nothing."

"Have you a telephone Madame?"

"Yes, it's here in the hall."

"May I make a call please?"

"Of course – Carl show the officer where the telephone is." At this the young lieutenant grinned. "Carl? That's not a very French name."

David replied in his fluent German, albeit with a Swiss accent.

"No, I am Swiss. I am here on a few days holiday to see my fiancée," and with that he put his arm around Georgette's shoulders, she responding by snuggling up to him.

"Well, all I can say Carl is I wish I were so lucky," with a smile and a slight bow to Georgette.

David led him to the telephone leaving him to make his call, which took only two or three minutes before he returned.

"They've found it," he said, "down near Bagnolles. Honestly these Luftwaffe people aren't safe to be let out on their own!" With another salute to Madame he bounded down the steps into the car and was away leaving the three waving from the steps breathing sighs of relief, which could have been heard a hundred yards away.

At last, darkness came and the three estate workers arrived to lead David on the first stage of his homeward journey. One took his suitcase as David shook hands with Madame and expressed his appreciation of all the hospitality she had shown him, hoping that one day he would be able to repay it to her back in England. He then turned to Georgette and held both her hands.

"I think you are the bravest young woman I have ever met," he said, "please do take good care of yourself."

Georgette released her hands and putting them up around David's neck, pulled his head down, kissed him on both cheeks and then lightly on the lips.

"And you take care too Cooteman. God go with you and keep you safe." David turned and followed his guides, the two women, with their arms around each other watching them until they disappeared into the shadows. Georgette turned to Madame and said, "Mummy, is it possible to be in love with two men at the same time?"

The countess replied "Your head will tell you no my darling but only your heart can tell you for certain."

Chapter Twenty Nine

When they reached the landing field they joined another party of four men and a second passenger who, on being introduced, David discovered to be a woman, code name Sophie. Just before midnight they heard the familiar sound of a Lysander, familiar that is to those gallant French patriots who soon would be moulded into arguably the world's most famous resistance movement. They moved to their allotted stations and the signal having been flashed shone their torches upwards. The Lysander swooped down; the hatch pushed back, the ladder put to the side. Out came a suitcase followed by a somewhat bulky individual who shook hands with David and Sophie waiting at the bottom of the ladder. David shinned up the ladder and wedged himself in to the side of the cockpit as far as he could go. Up came Sophie who scrambled in to sit half on and half off his lap, David's suitcase and Sophie's grip were literally squeezed down on top of them, the cover pushed forward and secured leaving Sophie's neck bent at an impossible angle which after much wriggling, and giggling they managed to make more comfortable. The traditional bottle of champagne was passed up to the pilot, the ladder whipped away, a hefty slap on the side of the aircraft to denote all was clear, the engines roared as the plane taxied to turn into the wind and in a few yards they were airborne. As they left the ground Sophie planted a smacking kiss on David's face only a few inches away. "That's for luck," she shouted.

David smiled and since he had his arm around her gave her a tight squeeze and shouted back, "It's the best bit of luck I've had in a long while!"

They met a little flak on the way back over the coast but were soon clear and winging their way over the channel. The wind had increased considerably since they left France, as was evidenced firstly by the aeroplane giving its impression of a flyweight boxer ducking and diving, and secondly by the white tips of the waves they could clearly see in the moonlight down below. David began to get the feeling that he was soon to part with the excellent lunch Madame had provided for him – I wonder what her name was he thought – but by a tremendous effort of will he managed by taking a long succession of deep breaths, to keep his manly dignity in the presence of his companion. Sophie however was not so lucky. She had been given a farewell party at lunchtime at which the Calvados to which she was extremely partial had been consumed in some quantity. As a result, she now suffered for it, so too did their baggage and the bottom half of David's trousers. When she had recovered a little she shouted her apologies, David reassuring her that if that was the worst thing that was to happen to him in this war he would consider himself lucky.

The moon was still bright when they landed at Tangmere and taxied over to the hangar David had left three months ago. The engine gave a last roar and then petered out. From the hangar a small group of men emerged, some obviously R.A.F. men to look after the Lizzie, others civilians, and one the unmistakable upright figure of Paddy O'Riordan. A ladder was placed against the fuselage, an R.A.F. man pushed open the hatch and lifted out Sophie's grip and David's case handing them down to Paddy. With much giggling Sophie extricated herself from her entanglement with David, the latter worrying she might do him an awful injury in the process, and found herself sitting on the edge of the cockpit with her back to those waiting below.

"Now what do I do?" she asked David.

"Well you could do a backward somersault on to the tarmac," David suggested.

"Alternatively if you stand up in the cockpit and turn round you could get your leg over on to the ladder."

"I've never had my leg over on a ladder before – I wonder what it feels like? All I can say is it's a good thing I've got trousers on. Here goes." And she made a creditable exit with the willing help of the men below.

David then stood up, but almost collapsed back again. His right leg and the cheek of his backside had gone to sleep due to his being cramped up for the past couple of hours. After much stamping he got some use back in the leg, swung over on to the ladder and was back on terra firma in 'Good Old England.' The first to welcome him was Robin, quickly followed by Paddy, who said little but from the warmth of his grip showed how relieved he was to see his officer back. To both of them he said, "Please excuse me for a moment," as he saw Sophie moving towards the pilot who had just climbed down.

Sophie wasted no time in putting her arms around the slender young flier and in implanting a big kiss on each cheek, much to the amusement of the onlookers and the embarrassment of the fresh faced young recipient. Releasing him she said, "Thank you for bringing us safely home."

"And the same here," said David seizing his hand, and marvelling again that this young man not much more than a boy, had the skill and courage to land people in an enemy occupied country and pluck them out again with the sangfroid of a Green Line bus driver.

Paddy was at his elbow. "I've got a P.U. here Sir to take you and Mr Robin back to H.Q. – when you're ready Sir."

"Right Paddy, I'll be with you in a minute." He turned to Sophie. "I do hope I see you again Sophie," he commenced.

"I'll have to get permission from my husband to do that," she laughingly replied. David shrugged.

"Well, you can't win them all I suppose," gave her a hug and then turned and followed Paddy to the P.U.

Whilst they were driving back to H.Q. Robin said,

"David, I have to instruct you that until you are fully debriefed you may not contact anyone outside the H.Q., and even when debriefing is complete – probably five or six days – I am obliged to remind you that you are still subject to the Official Secrets Act. I know that such a reminder is not necessary but I am obliged to give it. Incidentally your mother will be told this morning that you are safely back and will be contacting them all in about a week's time. Now that palaver's over, down to the nitty-gritty. You will have some breakfast when we reach H.Q., which will be ready for you. You can sleep then until midday, and we start debriefing in room five at two o'clock. It's a long and tedious business, which sometimes produces quite astonishing results, making it all worthwhile. Last but by no means least, congratulations on a job superbly carried out."

"Thank you Robin, but I truly feel that I have done very little and performed no great acts of valour in doing it. One thing I do have though is the very greatest admiration for all those people I've been with. If ever there is instigated a 'Hero of the Resistance' award, they'll all deserve one for their sublime courage." He paused for a moment and continued, quite casually, "By the way, have you any news of Rebecca; we had a tentative date on my return."

Robin was quiet for several seconds. "I have to tell you David that we lost her."

"What do you mean – you've lost her?" The words came out harshly, so out of character to David's normal mode of speech that even Paddy gave a momentary glance over his shoulder to see what was up.

"I mean she was betrayed by one of her group and shot by the Germans whilst she was trying to escape," continued Robin, his voice sad and melancholy.

David slumped back into his seat. "The bastards," he said grimly, "the bloody sodding bastards," and after another short pause, "is there any hope of finding out who informed on her?"

"He was found out and has been dealt with."

"Nothing that could be done to him would be bad enough," was David's bitterly expressed opinion. Robin, who had received details of the summary execution of the perpetrator of the foul deed, said nothing more.

It was therefore a very sad David who picked at his breakfast and then turned in to bed, unable to sleep for a long time thinking of Rebecca being brutally killed and the evil swine who had brought her to it. At last he slept, until he was awakened by Paddy with a mug of tea.

The debriefing was carried out by two professional-looking individuals named Robert and Roger. Both in their fifties, both slightly built, balding and bespectacled, both with rapier-like minds searching and probing for hidden meanings in every recorded conversation. They had obviously been through the logs before but now were seeking confirmation from David of the tone of voice, spontaneity of opinion, and so on of the speakers, as far as David could remember. The astonishing thing was that he did remember a large proportion of the exchanges, which pleased his examiners and as he afterward thought about it, astonished him. They had two sessions each day, nine till one in the morning, with a half hour break, and three to six in the afternoon, again with a half hour break. David found it very draining, and slept like a log each night, but by Saturday lunch time they were finished, his two interrogators expressed themselves most grateful to him for his excellent co-operation and superb retention of the detail of his mission and handed him back to Robin. (They're all 'R's' thought David, Robin, Robert, Roger – I wonder when I shall meet Rupert, Roland etc).

Robin went to lunch with David and told him he could now make outside calls if he wished. Tomorrow he would see the commandant who would give him details of leave entitlement and other matters, and thank him for a job very well done.

When lunch was over David made his way to the telephone booths in the front hall. Firstly he rang Chandlers Lodge speaking to his mother, father and Rose. "You'll run out of money for the box if we carry on like this," Rose declared.

"Don't worry;" was the reply, "this is all on the house."

"I would be intrigued to know which house," she answered, "but I don't suppose I ever shall."

After speaking to the family at length, promising them he would let them know shortly when he would be getting leave, and receiving the startling news that Kenny Barclay and Piercey had both been made lance corporals, "God, what's the army coming to," being his reply, he then booked a call to the company office at Norfolk. By a stroke of good fortune Charlie was duty officer, so David was able to ask him how they had possibly managed without him, receiving the reply in excited tones a couple of pitches higher than even Charlie's normal treble, that they hadn't even realised he'd gone for about three weeks! After a long chat, during which Charlie not once referred to where David had been or what he had been doing, they rang off. David saying he would arrange a meeting when he came on leave.

His next call was to be a little more difficult. He wanted to contact Maria, but knew they had no telephone at home. He also was well aware of the fact that the practice of receiving personal calls at work was severely frowned upon in all business premises. He therefore decided a little subterfuge was in order – he would contact Mr Stratton, Maria's immediate boss, who in accordance with his position would be allowed calls from outside. Having booked the call, he had only to wait for a few minutes before the reply came, "Marble Arch Corner House."

"Can I have a few words with Mr Stratton please?"

"Who is it calling?"

"Captain Chandler."

"Hold the line Sir."

The 'Captain' bit was a last second master stroke, he considered.

"Captain Chandler, how nice to hear from you, and how gratifying to know you are safe and well."

"Thank you Mr Stratton. I apologise for the impertinence of troubling you but I wanted to contact Miss Schultz - her address is in my kit at home and I don't think she has a telephone number."

"She has now. Apparently it took the family over a year to get it because of the waiting list, but I have the number here if you would care to note it down." He gave a Chingford number. David thanked him profusely, and then asked if he had been able to escape the bombing, and was shattered by the reply that a month ago he had lost his little five year old granddaughter in a near hit on a school shelter. "There were just a few people sheltering there overnight," he went on, "My daughter was injured but the little girl was killed along with three grown-ups – isn't it appalling?"

"It really is absolutely frightful. I really am so sorry Mr Stratton. Is your son-in-law in this country?"

"No, he's in Singapore with the Essex Regiment. It must have been terrible for him. It was their only child and he idolised her."

David was fighting for something intelligent to say to express his great sadness of the loss to this patently decent man of his little granddaughter, but nothing would come. He was saved by Mr Stratton continuing with, "But then we all have our sorrows to bear, and I daresay there will be many more before this war is over. But now Captain Chandler, put all that to one side, and enjoy the leave with which I presume you will be rewarded, and maybe I should have the pleasure of meeting you again one of these days."

"I shall make a point of it Mr Stratton, and many thanks for your kind help."

David booked his Chingford number with mixed feelings. First of all he had no real reason for telephoning other than he had promised he would contact Maria in a few months. Secondly she might be going out with a sixteen stone stoker for all he knew. Thirdly, like Rose, he wasn't sure how he felt at present. The thought of Pat was constantly with him, the memories of her and the love and passion they had shared were literally only like yesterday, but he had to admit to himself that to have the friendship of someone like Maria would be something worth having, and anyway it was going to be no more than that. At last the call was answered in the deep, unmistakable tones of Mr Schultz, who when David introduced himself, excitedly exclaimed

"Captain Chandler, how wonderful it is to hear from you. Since you went away there have been very few days that we have not asked each other 'I wonder how Captain Chandler is' or 'I wonder what Captain Chandler is doing'. Are you quite well?"

"Fit as a fiddle Mr Schultz, fit as a fiddle."

"For that I am very grateful. Now I will say goodbye and pass you over to Maria. I hope my wife and I meet you one day Captain Chandler, we have more to thank you for than you can ever know."

Maria came on the line. "Thank you so much Captain Chandler."

David interrupted her. "David," he said, "just David."

"Thank you so much David for telephoning, but how did you find the number?"

"I spoke to Mr Stratton, he was most kind. He told me about his little granddaughter – isn't it appalling?" He paused for a moment, "Maria, I am being given leave in a few days. I wondered if we could meet one evening. I know that after looking at food all day the last thing you would want to do would be to go out to eat, so could you perhaps give a little thought as to what you would like to do? I will telephone you when I get home, probably by the end of the week and we can then fix something up – go dancing or something, not that I am any great shakes as a dancer – two left feet and all that – that's if you're not going steady with someone who might object to the extent of punching my head in of course." He paused for breath and heard amused laughter at the other end.

"Well firstly David, I am not 'going steady' as you put it. Secondly I would love to go dancing with you, I have two right feet so we should get along perfectly, and I shall look forward very much to your call. Now, am I allowed to ask what you have been doing these last months?"

"I know it sounds ridiculously melodramatic but I'm afraid I can't tell you that – I assure you I would if I could."

"That's alright David, but do take care."

"Everybody – all my family and so on keep on telling me to 'take care.' As a complete coward I can assure you that 'taking care' is my prime object in life."

"You forget that we know you are far from being a coward, so I say again – please take care."

After a few pleasantries had passed between them David rang off, still wondering whether he was doing the right thing in meeting Maria. After all, it was only nine months since Pat's death – what would other people, particularly his family and Jack Hooper, think about his associating with another woman so soon. I will let it be known to them he said to himself, that Maria is just a friend, no way could she ever take Pat's place in his affections. But then they would know that without his telling them he reasoned, if he protested too much they could very well believe the opposite. Still, first things first, he would meet Maria and tell her about Pat – she knew nothing of his personal history as far as he knew. She may then not want to play second fiddle to someone who existed so strongly in his memory and that would be the end of that. On the other hand, she might be entirely sympathetic and be perfectly prepared to have a platonic relationship for a while letting time provide the answer. On the other hand – God! How many hands have I got, he thought – on the other hand she might find me so boring she'll run as fast as she can back to her sixteen stone stoker!

The interview with the commandant next day, Sunday, was a relaxed affair. First of all he shook David warmly by the hand congratulating him on a job very well done, and which, he said cryptically, gave a very positive reminder to a person in the very highest place of their continued existence. He did not elaborate. The brigadier would be coming down tomorrow and would spend some time with David and then on Wednesday he would go on leave for fourteen days, the brigadier would also inform him where he should report to after his leave. As all of David's kit was with him in Sussex, O'Riordan would drive him home, take the P.U. on to Roper Street, and then himself go on a well deserved leave – "He's been an absolute gem here, fixing everything that has needed fixing for months."

In the back of David's mind was the thought that Paddy knew of this place, obviously knew of Roper Street, and in addition, knew of where David and presumably others were going or had been. Without thinking he said, "Are you recruiting O'Riordan, commandant?"

"Now you know I can't answer that, but he's covered under the Official Secrets Act if that answers your question. Anyway, off you go now and come and see me before you go on leave to say 'Au revoir'."

"Au revoir, commandant? Only au revoir?"

"You never know in this business," he answered with a smile.

David was surprised when he was having breakfast the next morning to be joined by the brigadier dressed in the same tweed jacket with the leather elbow patches and cuff reinforcements he had been wearing when David first met him at Roper Street.

"By jove Sir," said David rising to meet him, "you must have been up early this morning to be here at this time."

"As a matter of fact David I haven't been to bed – I came down late last night to meet some people coming in and they were very much behind schedule, so I'll join you for breakfast if I may." (Crikey – a brigadier asking me if I will allow him to join me for breakfast. Things are looking up he thought!). After breakfast David was asked to come to number one interview room at nine o'clock. The brigadier was waiting for him when he arrived and wasted no time in adding his congratulations to those of Robin and the commandant. He went on, "Now I've had reports that you were confronted on several occasions by German soldiers and officers, that you took the encounters in your stride and were accepted by them as being who you said you were. You've probably been wondering where you are going to be posted next. You are going on leave tomorrow and whilst you are enjoying that, and I sincerely hope you will, I would like you to consider what I am going to put to you now. Firstly, after your leave, you can rejoin your battalion; you will retain your captaincy and Colonel Brindlesby-

Gore will be delighted to have you back. Secondly you can go on to the intelligence staff in London. Thirdly you can stay on in my firm to do another special job early in the new year, before which you will receive four months of intensive training, including how to jump out of an aeroplane. Now, I don't want you to decide straight away, give it a lot of thought, and no matter which direction you decide to take, you will have my full blessing."

David thought deeply for a few moments.

"May I ask some questions Sir?"

"Ask away, although you will know by now you may not necessarily get an answer to them."

"Sir, ever since I was commissioned I've had the ambition to lead my platoon back into Europe. I know these other jobs are frightfully important but I've always seen myself as a regimental officer. The third option you put to me intrigues me. May I know where the operation would be, secondly how long it would last, and thirdly why do I have to learn to parachute – I get dizzy standing on a chair!"

"Let me start at the beginning. You're leading your platoon or company or whatever back into Europe is not going to happen for a while yet. No matter how much the Russians scream for us to invade, and they'll certainly be doing that louder and louder over the next months, we are physically and materially incapable of mounting an attack on Europe, which is rapidly turning itself into a fortress thanks to Mr Todt. I give it at least two years before we're ready. Cynics may say we're giving it as long as we can, hoping the Russians will kill off enough Germans to make the job easier for us on this front. The Nazis on the other hand think they're going to enjoy a walkover against the Red Army – I have my doubts. So you see, you have a year or two in hand.

To get back to your original question. The operation would be in Switzerland and then Germany itself, lasting some four months or so. Lastly you need to parachute, as we shall drop you in France near the Swiss border. I've told you a bit more than I should have done at this stage perhaps, but you've more than proved yourself so I have no worries on that score."

David thought over the brigadier's final utterances. Back to Germany – there's a thought!

"I think I've made my decision already Sir – I'd like to stay on with you for another trip. Incidentally Sir, I shall be seeing Charlie at the end of the week, can I tell him I'm working for you? Oh, and can I take O'Riordan with me on the courses?"

"As regard Charlie, I don't see why not, he won't blab it around.

As regards O'Riordan, by all means take him with you, he may even feel like jumping once he gets to the parachute training centre, and he's cleared under the Official Secrets Act for the other places you will go to. Anyway, enjoy your leave and report to me at Roper Street at the end of it. By that time we shall have established your programme up to the end of the year." He stood up and held out his hand, "Glad you decided in favour of us," giving David one of his rare smiles.

David wandered back to his room thinking as he went 'God Almighty, what have I let myself in for – and as for jumping out of aeroplanes, I must be stark raving bloody mad'. When he reached his quarters he found Paddy packing all his kit.

"What will you travel in tomorrow Sir?"

"Best battledress I think Paddy."

"Right Sir, I'll pack your S.D. in the valise. I believe I'm driving you home Sir and then going on to London?"

"Yes, that's right; you'll be able to meet my family."

"I'd like that very much Sir. Should take us about an hour and a half from here, so if we leave here about ten you'll be home in good time for lunch. They'll all be awful pleased to see your Sir, that they will."

"They'll enjoy meeting you too Paddy, you see if they don't." He started putting some personal things into a holdall. "How do you feel about jumping out of aeroplanes Paddy?"

"Holy Mary, you're not serious Sir, that's a terrible crazy thing to do – they're not getting you on to that lark are they?"

"They are," smiled David "and, furthermore, they said you can have a bash at it if you felt like it. Now I know you're a bit old in the tooth," giving Paddy a sidelong glance to see how he accepted this piece of mischief, "but it might be something to tell your grandchildren about one day."

"Jumping out of bloody aeroplanes could mean you'd never have any children let alone grandchildren I reckon. As for being a bit old in the tooth – I've got plenty of fight in me yet." He pondered over the thought of hurling himself into nothing and continued "But Jesus, it wouldn't half put one over on old Driscoll wouldn't it? And would we get a set of those wings they wear?"

"We would if we passed the course and did all the qualifying jumps."

"Alright Sir, you're on. If you go out before me each time I'll be able to scrape you up if your parachute doesn't open!"

"That's kind of you. And if you pass me at speed while I'm floating down, I'll do the same for you."

The next morning they left at ten and were at Chandlers Lodge just before midday. All the family were there to welcome David back, including Nanny with young John and the twins, Jack Hooper, Anni and young David, and as they arrived Ernie and Fred pulled in driving the works truck. Paddy was introduced all round, finding himself a little overawed by the warmth of his welcome, the size of the house and the apparent social standing of the people to whom he was being introduced. After the pandemonium of the arrival, things quietened down a little allowing Paddy to say, "I'll get your kit in Sir – where do you want it?" That being organised, and Paddy returning downstairs Ruth went into the hall to talk to him.

"Paddy, you will stay and have lunch with us won't you?"

"Well ma'am, it's a bit difficult do you see. He's my officer, we don't normally sit down with the officers."

"Well at Chandlers Lodge you do..." and as she spoke David appeared.

"What do you do at Chandlers Lodge?" he asked "anything that I am old enough to know about?" His mother put her arm round his waist.

"I was persuading Paddy to stay for lunch," she said.

"Of course he stays for lunch – best cooking in the country here Paddy – I guarantee it."

"Well thank you, ma'am and thank you Sir; it'll be an honour to join you so it will."

When Paddy left after lunch, having arranged to return to collect David on Wednesday 3rd September as instructed, David walked out with him to the P.U. and asked him where he was spending his leave.

"Well Sir, you may remember I told you there was a rather nice woman in the kitchen in Sussex I was getting to know." David nodded. "She lives with her parents at Aylesbury, so I'm going there until Friday when she goes back. Then I go to Cork – in civvies of course – Mr Robin has asked me to do one or two things for him while I'm there."

"Has he now? Well I won't be so inexpert as to ask you what those one or two things are, but you take care, do you hear?"

"I'll do that Sir, that you can be sure."

"Oh and one last thing, what's the name of this fortunate young lady on whom you are bestowing your favours?"

"Mary, Sir, Mary Maguire. She's a strict Catholic girl so there's no hanky panky, but she's taken a fancy to me and I find her very comely."

"That's an old fashioned word."

"Ah, but then Sir, I'm a very old fashioned sort of a fellow, so I am."

David clapped him on the shoulder and then shook hands, "See you in a fortnight," he called out as Paddy drove away.

After chatting a while with his mother, Rose and Anni, nursing the babies in turn and remarking how they had grown, he asked if they would excuse him. He left the house, walked to the shops in the town centre and bought a small but beautiful posy to take to Pat. In the silence of the churchyard he stood and looked at Pat's headstone for long minutes, so overcome with heartache that it was a physical pain within him. He thought of the love they had had for each other, the fun they had had together, the excitement and the pleasure. It would never return, never, never. There are times when in a flash life doesn't seem worth living, no amount of consolation or 'thinking straight' can overcome the terrible burden of sadness which can cause a man, totally out of character, to throw the whole lot in and do away with himself. Lost in this black cloud of despair he failed to notice Canon Rosser had come up beside him.

"Hello David," he said quietly, "I saw you from my study window – anything I can do?"

David looked at him sightlessly for a moment.

"Not really padré, other than what you have now done, for which I'm very grateful. When I spoke to the brigadier some while ago he said something like 'they say it gets less hurtful in time', we both agreed that was sheer optimism."

"All the same, it does I assure you. You never lose the pain entirely, but it does recede for longer periods as time goes on. Now, come and have a cup of tea with me and my gaffer, it should be all ready by now," and taking his arm he led the way to the rectory.

That evening after supper David went to his room and got the presents he had brought from France. He was a little concerned that the production of the gifts might lead to a welter of questions regarding their origin, questions around which it might be difficult to hedge without appearing to be needlessly dramatic.

"I've one or two small gifts for you, not very much I'm afraid – I couldn't carry much," he uttered hesitantly. Handing a small box each to Megan, Anni, Rose and Ruth, he gave the larger box to his father adding, "This you're to share with my father-in-law."

They opened the packets quickly with Rose saying, "French

perfume – oh David how lovely." The four stood up all trying to kiss him at once. Fred took a little longer to undo the box containing the cognac and when he had accomplished this operation handed the bottle to Jack to examine.

"So that's where you've been is it?" observed Jack, "Well we shan't ask a thing about it. Thank you very much old son – when your father and I and Ernie as well, have a nip of this we'll think of you and the very brave people you got it from."

"One day I'll tell you just <u>how</u> brave they are," replied David, the only time he referred to his recent undertaking for some considerable period of time.

On Wednesday evening he telephoned Maria to arrange to meet her on Friday evening. She was apparently on early shift this week, finishing at five o'clock. David therefore arranged to meet her at 5.30 at the entrance to the nearby Cumberland Hotel. She arrived spot on time, (as he said to himself), he held out his hand in greeting which she took and then reached up and kissed him lightly on the cheek.

"I thought we could have a drink and a chat for a while," David told her.

"I'd love that," she replied, taking his arm as they went through the reception area to the bar, which was already filling with service people, others who one would have thought would have been old enough and fit enough to be service people, and finally little groups of sleek, well fed men of varying ages who certainly didn't exist on two ounces of butter a week. David pointed to a table for two in the corner and asked if that would be alright. Maria answered in the affirmative and they made their way to it and sat down.

"Well," she said, "let me look at you." She gazed at him searchingly.

"You have lost a little weight," she judged.

"My mother will soon remedy that over the next couple of weeks," he replied.

"David, I really am so very very pleased to see you, but can I ask you a question which I have been a little anxious about? You see you have spoken of your mother on two or three occasions, but I notice you wear a wedding ring…" she faltered, not knowing how to finish the question she was trying to ask.

"I'm glad you've asked about that Maria." He leaned across the table and took her hand as he did so, the waiter appeared.

"Would you care to order Sir?"

After the usual 'what would you like?' they settled on a Mackeson for Maria and a pint of best bitter for David. The waiter having disappeared David took up her hand again and continued.

"I'm so grateful you asked that question. You see, my wife was killed by a German aircraft nine months ago. I intended telling you of this as soon as the opportunity arose. We were sublimely happy together; we had known each other since we were in our teens and never looked at anyone else. I have to tell you I miss her dreadfully. I wanted to see you, and tell you all this so that we could be friends together. When I first saw you I thought you were so charming and such a pleasant person that I would like very much to see you again."

"David, you need say no more. I really do fully understand. There is no reason at all why we cannot be dear friends if that's the way our friendship develops. That would not in any way mean your being disloyal to the memory of your wife. If you want to talk to me about her I would be only too pleased to listen. The only way to overcome these sadnesses is to talk about them – my family has discovered that I can assure you. One thing does occur to me. Will you tell your parents and your wife's parents about me or of any other friends you may have?"

"Yes, I intend to do that immediately I had told you about Pat. As for other friends I don't think I make close friends very easily."

"I'll say one last thing, then we can close the subject if that is agreeable to you. Life has to go on, I speak from experience. Please therefore, dear David, be as happy as you can and do not feel any guilt at all about being happy."

David squeezed her hand, half rose from his seat, leaned across the table and lightly kissed her lips, much to the amusement of two middle-aged, affluent looking couples sitting at the next table.

They sat sipping their drinks, chatting without restraint until David asked, "What shall we do?"

"They do have dancing here, downstairs," Maria told him, "we used to have our Christmas party here. I'm very interested to see your two left feet."

"Well how about our having a bite of supper down there and tripping the light fantastic?"

"That would be marvellous, though I have to tell you that my last tube goes at ten past ten from Marble Arch."

"Right, well if we leave here by a quarter to ten you will be in good time, and I shall be in good time for my last train at Victoria at ten to eleven. Let's just hope that Mr Goering doesn't decide to upset all our plans or I shall be extremely cross!"

They enjoyed their evening together. Maria recounted to David that her father had got a job as a lorry driver when he was released from the prisoner of war camp at the end of 1918, having been given permission to stay in the UK. In 1919 he had married her mother, who he had previously met when being let out to work on a farm near Chigwell. He worked long hours until he had saved enough to buy a small garage repair business at Chingford, building it into a sizeable concern over the years and getting a Bedford truck agency. Then the war came and he lost three of his best mechanics. The business was ticking over quite well now due to repair contracts he was getting from the GPO, the local authority, the Water Board and so on. Both Cedric and she wanted to go into the catering business so they had decided to start at the bottom, and were extremely fortunate in obtaining places at the Lyons Corner House early in 1939 when Cedric was eighteen and she nineteen. Restaurant managers were renowned for being beastly people, particularly to young staff just starting out, but she had been extremely lucky in being placed in Mr Stratton's domain, who was the kindest and courtliest of men, albeit a stickler for the highest professional conduct in respect of service to the customer and duty to the Company. To him J. Lyons and Co were next to God.

And so they chatted, dancing the slow ones, as David put it, "You can't go far wrong with the slow ones," until looking at his watch he said, "good Lord it's twenty to ten, we must make a move." He walked her to the underground, suddenly wondering, 'Should I make another date?' and immediately answered his own question by saying, "I'll phone you tomorrow evening if you're going to be in. Perhaps we can arrange another outing?"

"I shall not move more than a yard from the telephone all evening," she replied, looking up at him in the dim light of the underground station.

He bent and kissed her lightly. "Thank you for a lovely evening" he said.

"It is I who should be thanking you," she replied. He watched her as she disappeared down the escalator, then turned and walked rapidly at rifleman pace to Victoria, realising by the time he reached there that four months of mainly sitting on his backside in front of three sets of earphones had not contributed in any way to his being the fittest captain in the City Rifles. We'll soon change that he told himself.

The next morning Rose received a long telephone call, after which she joined David and Ruth back in the kitchen.

"Well?" quizzed Ruth, "which one was it this time?"

"It was Mark Laurenson. He wondered if David could take me up to Norwich next Friday and stay till Sunday. Charlie's grandfather is coming; Charlie has Friday night, and all day Saturday free. He has booked rooms provisionally for us and would very much like to see David again."

"What utter rot," David countered. "It wouldn't matter to him two hoots if he never saw me again. He's looking for a chaperoned chat up – don't you think so Mum?"

"Yes I do, and what's more, good for him."

She swung into her top organisational Ruth. "Now, David must go to town, get the tickets and reserve the seats. While you're away I can look after the baby. You will have to go and see Mrs Draper and get a couple of new frocks – we'll find the coupons somewhere. And you'll need a new suitcase; your present one looks rather battered. If you have your hair done on Wednesday it should be just right for Friday, but remember Wednesday is early closing. Oh and you must of course insist upon paying your hotel bill, even if Mark has booked it."

"Why's that Mum? It's rather exciting to think the hotel might wonder if I'm a kept woman or not."

"Well no one has asked me if I'm free that weekend, have they? Asked David.

"And are you?" – Enquired Rose and Ruth together.

"Well I could be if, under the circumstances, my expenses were covered. Considering the delicate nature of the expedition you understand. I should not be out of pocket in any way being a poor underpaid member of His Majesty's Forces."

As they were talking Jack and Fred arrived, Jack having been at the factory on what they called their 'mini board meeting,' sorting out minor problems and discussing progress.

"So what's going on?" Fred asked having seen the playful clip around the ear from Rose at David's last remark.

"David and I are going to Norwich next weekend to see Charlie and his grandfather and Mark Laurenson," replied Rose.

"Dad, did you note she left Mark Laurenson's name until last? He obviously is the main character in this dramatic piece yet she left his name until last – don't you find that odd?" David received another clip round the ear.

They chatted on for a few minutes until David, who had been funking the issue a little, announced, "I have one or two things I would like to tell you all about." They looked at him in anticipation.

"Last evening I took Maria Schultz to supper at the Cumberland. I explained to her all about Pat." He was finding difficulty in getting his statement put in a lucid form. "That is I told her how much we were to each other and that it would be a long long while, if ever, before anyone could take her place. But she is such a nice person I would like to be friends with her. She said she was quite happy to accept the situation. She is a very serene person, I feel calm with her – it's difficult to explain, but I wanted you all to know that I'm not being disloyal to Pat, that I could never be."

"I think I'd better be the one to answer this," Jack reasoned, "as I've been in a similar position in some ways in that my wife left me and if it hadn't been for your family in particular being friends with me I could have led a very lonely life. So I say this to you David. Don't have any qualms about meeting and enjoying the company of other women. Although you don't show much of your agony on the surface we can guess what is going on underneath, and if anyone can help to overcome this they will be doubly welcome to us."

There was general agreement from the others.

David replied, "Thank you all very much. I shall bring Maria to see you one day. I'm going to see her parents one evening next week, they want to thank me in person for helping them over the death of Cedric – though what I did I really don't know. Now, I've a couple of other things to tell you about my future movements. I am going to be involved on certain courses until January. One of those is being trained as a parachutist, being accompanied incidentally by Paddy."

Ruth and Rose looked at each other in shocked concern; Fred and Jack just raised eyebrows at each other. He continued, "So I shall get leaves in between each posting and then in January sometime, or whenever the powers that be decide, I shall be going off again for four months so shall not be able to contact you. It's nothing dangerous or anything silly like that, it's just that you won't hear from me. As before, you will get a report every couple of weeks," he paused. "I think that's about all."

Ruth was the first to speak. She looked pale and anxious. "You say it isn't dangerous. Isn't jumping out of an aeroplane dangerous?"

"So is crossing the road in the blackout – it's no more dangerous that that," replied David in a jocular voice that was not mirrored by the feeling he had inside him.

"Well all we can say is as we said before," Fred added, "just you take care and don't do silly things. Not that I think you will for one moment. And we'll be thinking of you when you do go. In the meantime telephone us regularly. Regarding Maria, we'd like to meet her, so bring her home if you can before you go back."

"Right Dad I will."

That evening David telephoned Maria and was answered by her. "Were you sitting on the phone?" he joked.

"Absolutely glued to it all the evening," she replied.

He wasted no time in telling her of his talk with the family. He told her of his proposed visit to Norwich the following weekend. She, in turn, asked if he could meet her at lunchtime the next Wednesday as she had a half-day off and then visit her family to which he readily agreed. She added, "David, could you come in your uniform, it would make them very proud."

"Yes of course. Now the other thing is that my family would like to meet you. My mother suggested that if I met you on Monday evening from work, after we've been to Norwich you could come down here and stay overnight. Then you could go back on Tuesday morning."

"I will be scared to bits."

"No you won't, they're all lovely people."

"I'll broach it to my father and let you know on Wednesday."

David's visit the following Wednesday was an unqualified success. He had been feeling some trepidation at the prospect of talking about their son who he had, after all, seen blown to bits, but they showed him photos of the baby Cedric, the boy Cedric and the young soldier Cedric as if he were still with them. He left at 8.30 to be in reasonable time to get his Victoria train, having first been hugged by both parents, and then receiving a further hug and a kiss from Maria as she saw him off at the front door with the parting words, "You'll never know how much good you've done this evening."

On Friday he and Rose left Sandbury on the ten o'clock, seen off by Fred and Ruth, the latter carrying little Jeremy who smiled and gurgled away merrily. Ruth had wondered what Rose would do should the baby scream its head off at the parting, fortunately he was, as his granny afterwards told all and sundry, 'as good as gold'.

The Norwich train was crowded but as they had reserved seats at least they were comfortable. When they arrived at Thorpe St Andrews, to their great surprise and pleasure they were met by the Earl, with Charlie literally dancing attendance, he was so excited to see them. The weekend passed so quickly. Mark Laurenson joined them for tea at the hotel. They talked and talked until the Earl said he had arranged for a buffet supper in his suite for 7.30. They had supper and afterwards migrated to a table in the corner of the downstairs bar. And then it was time for bed. David noted how attentive Mark was to Rose, not only in ensuring her chair was properly held for her whenever she needed to be seated, but also his constant politeness and attention when she was speaking to him and to others. Well, she could do a lot worse he found himself thinking.

On Saturday they elected to go and see Norwich City's opening game at Carrow Road. To David's surprise and pleasure he found he was seated immediately behind Reggie and Pamela Sherborne, who he and Charlie had met back in March when he bumped into Reuben at the Castle. After David had made the introductions the Earl said to Reggie "We're neighbours I believe at one spot over near Fakenham, not that I'm often there, I spend most of my time in Worcester."

"That's right my Lord," replied Reggie, "incidentally there's a piece of land there that might interest you coming up at Michaelmas. It's been kept really quiet until now – I'll have a word with you later."

"Thank you Mr Sherborne, that's kind of you."

Charlie butted in. "Now come on Grandfather, no wheeling and dealing allowed at football matches, a football ground is far too serious a place for trivial things like land sales!"

In the meantime Pamela, who when they first shook hands hung on to David's hand for rather longer than would normally be the case, asked him, "Where have you been? I've bumped into Charlie and Reuben a few times during the summer and they weren't able to tell me anything at all, which seemed a bit odd to me."

"Well, I've been away. Perhaps I could talk to you further later on?"

They settled down to the game. David was seated next to Rose who at a convenient break in the proceedings – a player being treated for injuries – whispered, "Who's the girl friend?"

"Someone I met with Reuben earlier in the year."

"She's quite struck on you, you know."

"Oh rubbish, she's probably got half the gentry of East Anglia at her fingertips."

"I don't care if Clark Gable is after her; she's certainly struck on you."

"You mean like the galloping major's struck on you?" he quipped. She thumped him in the ribs and they both resumed watching the game.

After the match they strolled back over the river and up Prince of Wales Road to the hotel. Before leaving the ground Mark had asked Pamela and Reggie if they would care to join the party for dinner that evening, which he had arranged at the hotel. They gladly agreed, on the understanding that they be allowed to pay the wine bill, and that the party accepted their appearing in the tweeds they were already wearing. It proved to be a super evening. The Duke was doubly pleased in that Charlie was more than able to keep his end up in the conversation stakes, and in particular that Rose, to whom he had become very attached, secretly thinking 'she would be just right for Charlie, God Bless him', looking serene and most attractive. It was obvious that the major was captivated by her. Oh well, he reasoned, things will take their course.

David and Pamela sat next to each other at the dinner table. Pamela again broached the subject of, "Where have you been?" to which David had to tell her that he had been on a posting but was not permitted to say where. She looked straight into his eyes and put her hand on his on the table – noted immediately by hawk-eyed Rose as he later named her – "I shouldn't have asked, I'm sorry," she said, "and will you be returning here or going on another posting?"

"I shall not be returning here. But I would like to keep in touch if I may so that I can see you again on one of my leaves."

"We can swap addresses etc later," she replied and then cryptically "I thought I had lost you."

After dinner they retired to the lounge and sat talking until long after the bar closed. At the stroke of midnight Reggie stood up declaring he and Pamela must be away and then asked if they could all join them for lunch at The Priory, "today, as it is already Sunday." He then would arrange to return the soldiers to Highmere, the Earl back to the hotel and David and Rose to the station at 'any time to suit their convenience'.

The Earl replied, having received nods of approval from Mark and David, that this would be most agreeable, Reggie adding that so that they didn't get lost finding the place he would arrange for a local hire car to come to the hotel at say ten o'clock? All agreed.

The Priory was a beautiful house, partially moated, set way back off the main highway about ten miles from Norwich on the road to Aylsham. It was obviously very old, Reggie telling them later that parts of it could be traced back to before 1200. It had been in their family since 1710, he and Pamela having inherited it from their mother in 1936, their father having been killed serving with the Royal Norfolks in France in 1917. After their arrival, and having been served coffee, Reggie suggested they took a couple of guns and have a walk across the stubble. Most of the harvesting was done and they might well bag a couple of rabbits. Charlie and the Earl elected to join Reggie with the guns; Mark and Rose with David and Pamela keeping station a few paces behind. An older man, referred to by Reggie as Harry, made up the party, being in charge of two retrievers who slobbered over Rose when she made a fuss of them, beating David's leg with tattoos from their tails in the process.

It was a gloriously sunny morning. Rose took Mark's arm for support on the uneven ground, as did Pamela with David. Gradually they dropped back a little, Pamela taking the opportunity to give David a sheet of paper with the address and telephone number of The Priory, as well as a second address of a flat she and Reggie owned in London, and used when they visited town.

"I'll be going to Manchester on a course towards the end of the month, after which I shall get leave. Perhaps we could meet in town?"

"I would come and see you in Manchester but getting there from here in wartime is like making a trip to Patagonia. If only we could use the car it would all be so easy," replied Pamela. "Anyway, what sort of course is this, or is it fearfully hush-hush?"

"No, nothing hush-hush. It's a parachute jumping course, though I'm so unfit at the moment I don't think I could jump out of a paper bag."

She squeezed his bicep. "You feel deliciously fit to me," she said. He grinned down at her and impulsively bent over and kissed her on the cheek, which action was clearly witnessed by hawk-eye a few yards away.

They appeared to be making half circle round the house, and an hour or so later having bagged half a dozen rabbits in the process, ended up back at the driveway, more than ready for the beautifully prepared lunch awaiting them. At three o'clock David and Rose had to leave for Thorpe St Andrews, the others seeing them off from the front steps. The train to London was not too full and as they waited for it to leave David asked, "And where did you disappear to after lunch?"

"I went with Mark to the library and told him that I liked him very much, but that I couldn't consider a serious attachment at this time. He was very nice and very considerate. He said there was no problem, we would stay good friends and meet each other whenever we could, as good friends should. I fully agreed with that. The trouble is David." she clung to his arm and in a barely audible whisper said. "I believe I am falling in love with him, he's everything a girl would want, and I don't want to fall in love with him or anyone else."

David put his arm round her. "Don't fret my love; it will work out in time. I'm in the same boat remember, or could be." There was a silence for a while before he continued. "But as Jack said to me the other day, 'life is very short'. I think he meant that you should take happiness if it is offered to you, as long, of course, that you harm no one else."

Chapter Thirty

On Monday afternoon David journeyed to Marble Arch to meet Maria from work. They had originally decided she would travel to Sandbury on her own and that David would meet her there. On second thoughts he changed his mind, thinking that if she was nervous about meeting his people she would probably stew all the way from Victoria. Not wanting that to happen he arranged to meet her direct from work and to travel down with her. To his surprise his father was waiting for them at Sandbury with the Rover.

"Guessed you would be on this one. Welcome to Sandbury Maria – hub of the universe, only that information is not generally known in London and some other parts."

David was very grateful to his father for this warm welcome. Maria was trembling slightly as he handed her down on to the platform, the genial remarks from Fred almost eliminating her anxiety, approaching dread, at meeting the family and in particular, for some reason, Mr Hooper.

The evening went off swimmingly. Jack came to join them for dinner and without making it obvious was very friendly with Maria. Rose, joined by Ruth, took her to see the baby who gurgled away merrily at her when she asked to hold him. Although a little overawed at first, she soon joined in the conversation showing that beneath her tranquil appearance she had a lively mind and a keen sense of fun. They all quickly took to her.

The next morning David walked her to the station to get the 8.30, Mr Stratton having given her leave to get in at 10.30. As they kissed goodbye David said he would telephone her that evening to make sure she had got back alright. Having boarded the train she wound down the window and pulled a small cloth golliwog from her pocket. "I would never be parted from this when I was a little girl," she told him. "Take it on your parachute course for good luck."

He smiled, gave it a little kiss, and said, "I'll never jump without it."

He spent the rest of the day getting his kit together, his mother having insisted upon washing everything that was washable, pressing everything that was pressable and darning anything that looked vaguely in need of darning. "Can't have Paddy thinking you come from an untidy family," she had said.

David replied, "What with you and Paddy I must have the best kept kit in the British Army."

He woke early the next morning. It was Wednesday 3rd September 1941. The war had started exactly two years ago today. His thoughts led his trying to visualise what the next two years would bring. According to Brigadier Lord Ramsford's guess, which in fact proved to be optimistic, it would be at least two more years before he would be back in the field leading his men into action. And what about the rest of the family? In his wildest dreams he could not have envisaged Moira's agony of mind witnessing the dreadful power of the atom bomb during its development in Arizona, all the time horrified at the thought of the tens, possibly hundreds of thousands of Europeans who would be killed by it, and even more horrified at the thought that Hitler's scientists might, at this very moment, be months ahead of the Anglo-American team. The thought that England might be the recipient of the first of these apocalyptic devices with her own family near London being well within distance of the appalling effects of such of catastrophe, was the stuff of nightmares.

Neither could he conceive the appalling brutality and hardships his brother Harry would have to endure at the hands of his Japanese conquerors and their evil Korean lackeys – Japan was not even in the war yet!! Following from that, nor could he have dreamt of the terrible revenge Harry would wreak upon those depraved fiends whose barbarity had caused the death of so many good and loyal comrades.

He was continually concerned about his parents, his sister, the children and the rest of the family living adjacent to a prominent military objective. Sandbury airfield had been bombed on twelve occasions already but this was nothing compared to the coming hazard of the flying bombs. These were totally unknown to him. Thousands would land in Kent and Greater London, despatched from just across the water in Northern France, which would bring far greater dangers to the Chandlers than the air attacks and bombing so far had done.

And what about David Chandler? How would he fare when he was seven hundred feet up and told to jump into thin air? He would need no Ex-lax for a week that was certain. Dropping into Germany, or wherever, sounded exciting, but one slip would mean a firing squad, most likely preceded by the barbarous ministrations of the most evil organisation since Ghengis Khan. He was beginning to wonder whether he should even bother to look two years ahead – if he got through the next eight or nine months he wouldn't complain.

Let's compromise, he decided to himself. Today it is the third of September 1941 – I wonder where we all shall be on September 3rd 1942 – and with that he hauled himself out of bed!!